FALSE PERSPECTIVE

MURDER IN THE ART DEPARTMENT

Colin Barker

FALSE PERSPECTIVE - MURDER IN THE ART DEPARTMENT
Copyright © 2013 by Colin Barker

Book Design by Molly Bradbury

First Printing: November 2013
First Edition: November 2013

ISBN-13: 978-1493618514
ISBN-10: 1493618512

Acknowledgements

No book is written in isolation and I have benefited from the comments and help of many people. Early motivation came from Teresa Miller, Chris Liner, Gill Bockmeulen, Lynn Stegner and the late James G. Watson. I especially appreciated the help and encouragement of my local writing group that included Marigay Grana, Bruce Moss, Charlie Romney Brown, Tori Shepard, Joan Baker, June Ferrill and Margaret Mooney. Critical comments by Noemi DeBodisco and Carla Hall helped improve the manuscript. I thank all of them.

My wife Yvonne patiently put up with my hours at the computer. And the book was written under the watchful eyes of our two dogs—Chile and Glimmer.

Chapter I

"Sign here."

Markham Smyth took the electronic pad from the driver of the UPS van and scrawled his signature across the plastic window. It looked even more illegible than usual. The delivery man stood propped against the wall of the adobe doorway, wrinkling his nose at a slight odor coming from the large cardboard box resting on his hip. He watched Markham sign and was glad to trade the heavy carton for the signature pad and leave. The cardboard box, all forty-five pounds of it, was addressed to Markham's wife. Gwen hadn't told him she was expecting forty-five pounds of anything, but that was no surprise. He didn't recognize the sender's name and the mailing address was in Española, a town only thirty minutes north.

With some difficulty he carried the box back along the curving flagstone path to the side entrance. Although sunny with a clear, denim blue sky, the day was very cold: a typical early March morning in Santa Fe. The walled patio at the side of the house, shadowed from the low winter sun, had patches of snow still dusting the ground among the silvery chamisa bushes. To his left, the carved stone fountain in the flower bed had been shut off all winter and ice filled the pool at the base.

The boxes *he* was expecting—packing crates really—were not scheduled to arrive from Miami until the next day. They'd certainly be a lot sturdier than the cardboard carton he was carrying and they'd all be considerably larger. Probably take most of an eighteen-wheeler. Even the smaller items were supposed to be sent as part of the single shipment—unless they'd missed one or two and needed to ship them separately. He doubted that. The company was far too professional to make mistakes. Anyway, the parcel he was struggling with was addressed to Gwen, not to him. And it had come from Española, not Miami.

He hauled the box into the house through the side door and let the warmth seep back into him. Even with fourteen-foot high ceilings and a wall of plate-glass, the under-floor heating kept the house comfortable. Built with its back to the Sangre de Cristo mountains, the Santa Fe-style house provided spectacular views down across the city and over to the pine-covered hillsides of the western horizon.

Kicking off his damp shoes, Markham shouted to his wife. "Gwen, there's a UPS package for you. It's kind of heavy. I can drag it through to your study if you want."

"If it's so damned heavy, why don't you use the hand truck? No, not you. You'd rather throw your back out and then I'd have to put up with you bitching and expecting sympathy. Stupidity."

He didn't reply, just carried the box into her office. Their relationship was bad enough at the best of times. And this was not the best of times. Since their dog—her dog—went missing four days ago, life had been hell. It was his fault, of course, though why he was to blame was never made clear.

Coffee. He needed coffee. Actually what he needed was a large gin, but mid-morning seemed a bit early. He compromised by brewing the coffee strong. Filling his mug, he took it into the breakfast area and sat looking out the floor-to-ceiling window at the few low clouds building over the distant mountains. The *New York Times* was still on the table folded open to the article he'd been reading when the UPS man interrupted him. He picked it up—and was immediately interrupted again.

A piercing scream reverberated through the house.

Markham rushed across the living room, detoured around the grand piano, and strode down the short passage to Gwen's office. She was standing with her back to him, but he could see her shoulders heaving. The tears would come later.

Gwen was staring down at the floor. She'd dropped the UPS package and the impact had tipped it on its side, disgorging wadded newspaper packing. A plastic bag that had split open was clearly the source of the foul odor now permeating the room. And splattered across the tiled floor were the bloody remains of a severed head and a decapitated dog. Her dog.

Chapter 2

"Should we bury him on the hillside? He was always happy poking around up by the old junipers."

Gwen glared at her husband with pursed lips. "You're so damned practical. And complacent. You ever stop to think who did this? How could anyone be so callous as to kill a sweet dog?" She brushed away the tears. "You know, he never roamed much, didn't even leave the yard—sort of suggests it's somebody nearby, doesn't it. A neighbor maybe?" She thought about that for a minute. "I didn't think we had enemies. I suppose there's always jealous people when you're well-off."

Gwen reconsidered Markham's suggested burial site with thinly-disguised disgust. "You'd like to banish that poor dog as far away as possible. You just can't wait to get rid of him, can you? No, he's going to be buried close to the house, right beside the big aspen. There's not much daylight left. I'll do it first thing in the morning and I'll get Zona to help. I don't need you."

But she did. The frozen, stony soil was hard to dig and it took Markham a good thirty minutes to produce a large enough hole.

And it still wasn't deep enough. "You want some passing coyote to dig him up?" she chided.

He treated that as a rhetorical question, turned away and strode back to the house without answering.

By the next morning, Zona had found a suitable wooden box, carefully padded the bottom and lined the sides with fabric. The remains of the much-loved dog were nestled in and surrounded with flowers.

Zona Pharn was the Smyths' live-in maid. When the aging Liesl Sorenson grew increasingly unreliable and couldn't cope with even the day-to-day jobs, they had hired Zona, but out of compassion for the old woman, let her stay in part of the adobe guest house that served as staff quarters. Zona lived next to Liesl in the other half of the adobe, but spent most of the day at the main house, although technically her position was just half time. She liked not having to work full time. It gave her time to think, to contemplate the larger questions of life. Zona was born at the end of the Sixties to hippie parents—at least a hippie mother, no one knew who the father was. Now in her mid-forties, she still retained much of the flower child approach to life, the universe and everything in it.

Zona knew the power of minerals and had taken two quartz crystals from her collection, putting one above the dog's head and one near his tail. They pointed at each other, lining up to make the energy field for his next life as intense as possible. The doubly-terminated quartz, with pointed crystal faces at both ends, had among her favorites and this was the one she'd carefully positioned between the ears. "You like the way I've arranged everything?" Zona asked. She'd envied the life of that spoilt, carefree dog.

"Yes, you've done a wonderful job. Thanks." Gwen nodded. "I like the flowers you chose."

"I really didn't have much choice this time of year. They're all the florist had. And they only sell cut flowers." She gave a disapproving shrug. "If you ask me, it's just as important to have the roots and bulbs. Then you'll have that connection from a dark underground up into bright sky and sunlight. I put in some grasses and a few juniper shoots that still have roots."

Gwen seemed pleased with her thoughtfulness, but wasn't sure about the tangerines.

Zona was eager to explain. "I wanted to put in something with seeds. I always think a seed is a real promise for the future, don't you? A sort of faith in things to come. And with the roots and all, the seeds complete the cycle of being. So the tangerines and the piñon nuts will, like, help on his journey through the cosmos."

Zona snapped the lid onto the box, fished around in the deep pockets of her padded jacket and extracted a coil of shiny copper wire and a small pair of wire cutters. In answer to Gwen's obvious surprise, she said, "There are dozens of different metals and they're all silvery, except just two—copper and gold. I wanted to use something special, and I couldn't afford gold." She looped the copper wire around the box, first from the sides and then over the ends, cut the wire to length and twisted the ends tightly. Together they lowered the sealed box with its precious cargo into the hole and shoveled earth on top. A few pretty stones and flowers on the low mound completed the ritual.

Even though they were both chilled by the crisp, early morning air, they walked to the house slowly, Gwen dabbing at her eyes with a tissue.

Just before they reached the back door the silence was shattered by the insistent squeal of truck air brakes and a tractor-trailer rig pulled to a stop outside the house.

Markham Smyth met the driver at the front door and peered at the stack of delivery forms he'd been handed. Each item was identified individually and cross referenced to the shipping code. Dimensions and weight were shown separately for all the crates.

"I'll need to check these against the list from the Miami

attorneys. You can go ahead and start unloading." He glanced back at the top page before turning to the driver. "I'll show you where I want them."

Markham walked the driver round the side of the house and they followed the brick driveway that led up through the big iron gates to the four-car garage. The silver Range Rover, and the black Porsche which he seldom drove, were at the far end. He told the trucker to stack the smaller wooden crates along the wall.

"Those eight big crates need to go directly into the house. We'll put them in the entrance hall." He took the driver in through a side entrance and showed him where that was.

Ronnie Garcia had been doing small jobs at the Smyths' house for several years and was always paid generously, promptly and in cash. He liked that and did his best to keep the Smyths happy. When he got the call from Markham on his cell phone, he came as soon as he could. But it took nearly an hour before he could finish the job in Tesuque, drive up towards the ski basin and turn off on the gravel road leading to the Smyths' home. When he got there, the trailer-tractor parked outside was almost completely unloaded and two men were struggling with a wheeled cart to get one of the last large wooden crates down the ramp.

"You guys need help?"

"No, we're doin' okay. One more load, then we're outta here."

Markham ushered Ronnie into the house and together they checked out the larger crates stacked vertically against the far wall of the main entrance hall. The two biggest ones, roughly six feet by eight and a foot wide, were put together with carriage bolts. Screws held the six smaller ones.

"Not going to take the rocket science." Ronnie rummaged around for a power screwdriver in his tool box. Only a little over five feet tall, he was compact, solid and fit. Self-confident and tough with an attitude, he had a shaved head and looked younger than his thirty-five years. He still struggled with English and spoke with a thick Hispanic accent.

Markham could have left him to get on with the job, but he was a hands-on sort of guy and liked to be involved. And anyway, he was eager to see whether the contents would live up to his expectations. They set about removing the bolts and were soon able to pull the front side off the crate. Markham snipped the bindings inside and let the protective materials fall. Fantastic. Even better than he remembered.

He stood gazing at the painting in its simple gold frame.

This brooding, evocative landscape had always hung in the Connecticut house when he was growing up. It showed a muted sun and stratified clouds seen through a small grove of tall trees. As a young boy, he'd always wondered whether it was a dawn or a sunset. In his young mind that made all the difference—were things just starting or just ending? He didn't really appreciate most of Egon Schiele's paintings until he was in his late teens and just about to move away to college. He'd always preferred the brighter colors and obvious geometric designs of more lyrical artists, especially the Klimt portraits. Anyway, paintings of women with exposed breasts would always appeal more to adolescent males. He wondered which crates held those fondly-remembered images. Ronnie had already loosened the screws on five smaller crates and they carefully unpacked the contents. Three were Schiele oils. The other two contained a Gustav Klimt and an Emil Nolde.

Ronnie stood beside him frowning at the paintings. "They foreign?"

"Certainly are. European."

"And old?"

"Yeah. Pre-war."

Ronnie glanced along the row. He nodded towards the Klimt. "Sort of look like the one they show on TV. Sold for a million."

"I'm surprised you knew that," Markham said, grinning. "Actually, it went for over a hundred million."

"Holy Jesus. What guy'd pay all that for some old picture? A hundred million?" He shook his head in disbelief. "They all worth so many dollars? And people like to buy them pictures?"

"Sure. There's lots of collectors who'd love to have one of these."

Ronnie peered at the paintings with undisguised interest.

Markham had a mental image of him walking into a gallery on Canyon Road with a Schiele under his arm, trying to sell it. He smiled to himself.

The art works had been in storage for more than ten years, ever since Markham's father went to live in the Miami house. Without his wife, the cold winters of New England were too depressing, prompting his move to the warmth of Florida. Oddly, he had never hung any of the paintings in his new home. Certainly it was smaller with less wall space, but for him the art work seemed to represent a time in his past that was long gone—a time he didn't want to remember, one he now felt was best forgotten.

Markham hadn't known what his father planned to do with the collection, and it wasn't until his father died, that he found it had been bequeathed to him. This decision embarrassed him and his initial reaction was that it should have been shared with his older brother, Leland. However, he was glad the collection would remain intact, not be dispersed. There was a sense of continuity in knowing it would stay the same as when he was growing up. He'd not heard of any recent additions. Well, apart from the pieces of primitive art, but that was different.

Even though Markham's house was spacious—close to twelve thousand square feet—the wall space was still finite and much of it already displayed his own contemporary collection, though most of those paintings were not near the caliber of his father's, or as valuable. Prices had increased dramatically since his father acquired the art work in Austria at the start of World War II. Clearly, choices and decisions would have to be made.

After paying Ronnie Garcia, tidying up a bit and showering, Markham came back and stood in the hall looking at the paintings of his youth.

Gwen sauntered over and stood beside him. "Not my taste, but nice enough. I could live with some of these."

He nodded his head slowly. "Good."

They stood in silence for a few minutes, then Markham reminded her, "We need to leave in half an hour if we're going to make it to the show on time." He was referring to the art department's annual joint alumni/student opening at the University of Northern New Mexico, UNNM.

"I'm hardly in the mood to drive for hours and stand around looking at third-rate work." Without waiting for a reply, she added, "I know, I know. We've got to foster young talent and encourage it in any way we can. For God's sake, just let the professors do it. That's what they're paid for."

"It's not so simple. You and I sponsor the show. We ought to be there, dammit." Markham glared at her. "Look, I know how you're feeling, but we've got to go. We've got an obligation."

"I don't see why. Isn't donating the money going to satisfy those academic leeches?"

"I put up enough money for your damn music events. If I can sit through all that experimental noise they call music, then you can put on a brave face for one night and go to the student show."

"Noise? *Noise.* You can't be serious. Your trouble is you need to drag your butt into the twenty-first century. Surely you don't think they stopped composing good music a hundred years ago?"

He ignored the rant. "Go get yourself a drink—one—and let's get on the road."

"At least my events are in Santa Fe. Why do we have to drive all the way out to the goddamned frontier?" She glared at him. "Oh, what the hell, I might as well go. I need the distraction. With a bit of luck, I could actually get to talk to somebody interesting. It sure as hell beats sitting alone in this warehouse."

The university campus was an hour and a half north of Santa Fe. They drove the whole way in silence.

When Zona knocked on old Liesl Sorenson's door in the early evening, she got no answer. It was unlocked, as usual, and she let herself in. Liesl was dozing in the big arm chair, her silver hair disheveled, her mouth open. She woke with a start and took a moment to focus on Zona. "Oh, it's you."

"How you feeling tonight?"

"Not bad." She blinked and rubbed her eyes. "Make me a cup of tea, would you?"

While Zona was in the small kitchen boiling water for the herbal tea they often drank, Liesl struggled out of the chair. This was always difficult and she had to lever herself with her arms, but when she finally made it up she moved steadily and surprisingly quickly. "I've still got some of that cake you like from the health food store." She reached into the pantry. Quietly they drank tea and ate the cake.

Zona and Liesl lived in separate parts of the quarters across the brick patio from the main house, but spent many evenings together talking. Liesl shared her views on life, acting like a mother, and dispensed advice whether or not it was asked for. Liesl Sorenson had strong views on most topics and Zona was usually deferential. She had respect for age and in her own life tried to follow the elderly woman's suggestions, although she didn't always succeed.

"So tell me, what's Gwen Smyth had you doing today?"

Zona recounted the dog's burial, then told her about delivery and unpacking of the paintings. "They brought them in a great big *Freightliner* truck. Took them hours to unload everything. And when Ronnie came he helped unscrew all the wood boxes. He's not very big, but he sure is strong. I think the pictures must be very valuable because Mr. Smyth told me at least three different times to make sure the alarm system was on tonight."

Liesl was silent, pensive. "What are they like?"

Zona described the paintings as best she could, although with no fine art experience and only a brief look at them it was necessarily superficial.

Liesl listened carefully and nodded. "That's his father's collection." Very quietly she mumbled to herself, "The Austrian Klimts and Schieles. And all the rest."

"What?'

"Nothing."

Liesl poured more tea, sipped hers, staring into space. "I got to see the whole collection once, maybe ten or twelve years ago. Mr. Smyth took me with him to help sort out his father's house when his stepmother died. Before he moved to Miami. I especially liked the Austrian paintings, the Klimts and the Noldes. But not the Schiele portraits." Her eyes glazed over as her thoughts drifted back. "I didn't know much about them then, but I've been reading. Learned quite a bit."

There was another long silence.

Zona switched back to more familiar ground. "I think Mrs. Smyth's devastated about her dog being killed. And in such an ugly way. It's only natural. She's been depressed and in a totally black mood all day." Zona sat quietly, thinking of the morning ceremony that had sent the dog on its journey to eternity. "We buried the dog in silence. Now I think about that, there should have been, like, some music. I'm surprised Mrs. Smyth didn't suggest it, what with her being so musical and all."

Chapter 3

Dr. Candrew Nor, Professor of Geology, liked to teach and he was good at it. What he didn't like to do was grade exams. For the past two hours, he'd sat grumbling to himself as he struggled to decipher the barely legible essays. He couldn't remember who'd said *to be legible is to be found out*, but it seemed to be the philosophy of at least half his students.

The phone rang. He grabbed it, delighted to get a respite.

The caller was Renata, a close friend and a professor in the archaeology department. "Hi. Hope I'm not interrupting anything." She didn't wait for a denial. "We had to reschedule our graduate student meeting, so I'm going to be delayed half an hour. Can you pick me up at six-thirty instead of six?"

"Sure. No problem."

"Half an hour, we won't miss much. I'm really looking forward to this evening."

"Me too. See you at six-thirty, then."

Reluctantly, he returned to grading. It depressed him to see how little of what he'd said in class the students actually remembered and understood. But he thought back to the time when he'd been in college and it made him more sympathetic to the demands heaped on his students. His course was probably only one of four or five they were taking and he knew that surging hormones had more to do with their life style, and performance in class, than the demands of any professor.

Thirty minutes later grading was done and his mood lightened. He pushed back his chair and for a few minutes stared out the big window across the northeastern foothills to the mountain tops. From his second floor office in Kinblade Hall, the geology building, he had an uninterrupted view of the highest peaks where bare rock exposed above tree line had no pines, only a dusting of snow.

Candrew had an hour and a half before he was scheduled to pick up Renata, and drove out to his home in the foothills. He'd almost got used to arriving at an empty house—no loving kiss, no aroma of cooking to welcome him. It had been six years since Penny died and now life was poorer in so many ways.

The cat and dog greeted him: he was always glad to see them. Technically, Chile was a mid-sized dog, although a bit overweight. A smart animal, he knew where the treats came from and greeted Candrew with enthusiasm, his tail wagging frantically. Pixel, an elderly, long-haired cat, sat serenely on the counter and watched this unseemly display before reluctantly relenting and allowing herself to be stroked under the chin. He put food down for both pets and headed for the shower. As he dried himself, he wondered what to wear. Most of his decent shirts seemed to be in the pile on the closet floor, since he hadn't got round to taking them to the cleaners. Penny would have known what was appropriate, she always did, but he only had a limited selection of clean shirts to choose from and settled for a casual, broad-striped one and wore it with a navy blazer.

Candrew was late arriving at Renata's house, but still had to wait nearly fifteen minutes before she was ready. They drove to the university. Candrew and Renata Alcantara had been friends—just friends—for several years, and Candrew was happy to keep it that way. As an archaeology professor working on Mayan artifacts, Renata had a good mix of art and science and that appealed to Candrew. But Renata was usually the instigator when they went to social events together.

This evening they were attending the opening of UNNM's annual art show for current students and recent alumni. Together with several other late arrivals, they hurried up the flight of broad, stone steps that led through a wall of plate glass to the art department foyer. The exhibition gallery was inside to the right and they were faced with a large canvas executed in the exuberant style of the graffiti that adorns derelict downtown walls. In large letters, spray painted in garish colors, the painting greeted art openers with the simple message: *PAY HERE — PAY WHAT? — PAY ATTENTION!*

The Alumni/Student Show, fondly known as *ASS*, was open to the university community. It looked as though a fair number had shown up and the faculty was well represented in the crowded gallery. Even a few administrators had come. And then there were the art students, many showing their creativity with multicolored hair—or none at all—and clothing that ran the gamut from an orange suit to a tie-dyed tee shirt with an elaborate pattern of holes. In contrast, the wealthy alums and department sponsors wore suits and designer dresses. Markham Smyth was shaking hands, circulating and talking knowledgably to the student artists. He had a knack for remembering names and many of the painters were impressed that he'd not forgotten them from last year's show. Gwen had assumed her outgoing social persona and after briefly surveying the paintings and sculpture chatted amiably to students and faculty.

Markham greeted Renata as an old friend and was introduced to Candrew.

"It's so good to see you again. Gwen and I were in Belize last summer. I wanted to come over to Guatemala and catch up with all that's going on at your new excavation. Unfortunately, we couldn't make it this time."

"Pity. We're finding lots of exciting stuff. One of the burial chambers turned up a couple of skeletons with impressive gold ornamentation. Maybe this summer."

"Hope so." Markham paused, glancing around the crowded room and lowered his voice. "I'm sure you've heard that I inherited my father's collection. It's just been shipped to the house. As well as the paintings, there's a couple dozen pre-Columbian pieces. We haven't unpacked any of them yet, but I know from the documentation there are several large figures and a range of pots." He could see the excitement in Renata's eyes. "Would you have time to come down to Santa Fe and take a look at them?"

"Well, certainly. I'd love to. But I thought Helen Kontorovich was evaluating the collection for you."

"You're right. But she doesn't know a lot about primitive art. Her expertise is with early twentieth century paintings and that's where she really is an authority. Studied at Yale. In fact, it was one of her old professors, he's emeritus now, who told me she was here in New Mexico.

"I'm no art historian," Renata said, "but I can probably give you a good idea of where the pre-Columbian pieces came from and what cultures. And give you some idea of whether they're genuine or not. I'm sure you know there's an awful lot of fakes on the market."

"My father bought his pieces in the early fifties, some in the forties. I'm told there were fewer fakes then."

"Yeah, that's probably right." She thought for a moment and grinned. " 'fewer fakes', but not zero fakes. Anyway, I'll be glad to take a look at them for you."

"There's no great hurry." He glanced across the room. "Though it might be tactful to wait 'til Dr. Kontorovich has finished with the paintings. She can be pretty touchy about her academic turf—and not shy letting you know." He smiled and nodded at the group in the corner where she was holding court.

Candrew left Renata to work out the details with Markham and jostled his way through the crowd towards Helen Kontorovich. As he got closer, he could hear her rasping voice. "Look at this. What a bunch of crap most of it is." She shook her head to stress her disbelief that anything could be quite so bad and pointed towards a large mirror in an ornate gilded frame. Pulsing neon lights presented the message across the face of the mirror: *Art Reflects Life*. "The trouble with you students today is that you're just too damn lazy to put in the time it takes to learn your craft. I despair for the future of the graphic arts."

Exceptionally tall for a woman, her medium frame was capped with a shock of auburn hair. She was dressed conservatively in a navy-blue linen suit with a cream scarf and radiated an intense presence. Her specialty focused on the art of the nineteen hundreds—none of this "pretentious modern muck". The group around her was made up almost entirely of art students and they took her rant with good humor. They'd heard it all before. And they knew her reputation: she never liked any piece of art made in the last fifty years.

Helen noticed Candrew at the edge of the group and waved her hand in a big looping gesture. "Dr. Nor, it's so nice to have a scientist come to our little soiree."

Candrew acknowledged her greeting. "Even scientists can use a shot of culture now and then."

"I wish it were culture. We could certainly use a little more quality." Helen hustled over to Candrew, brushing aside a couple of students, and shook his hand in both of hers. "I'm afraid this year's show is pretty much business as usual."

"You're awfully hard on the artists." He glanced around. "There's one or two imaginative works here, and well-resolved too."

As Candrew turned to leave the group, he bumped into a

17

large, heavy-set man: "Red" Mulholland, the sculpture professor. There was no doubt about the reason for the nickname—he sported a full russet beard and untrimmed hair, most of it tied with a leather thong that produced a foot of free-swinging pony tail. In contrast to the well-dressed, milling around the paintings or grazing at the buffet, Red was wearing plaster-splashed jeans and a black Harley-Davidson tee shirt. He was tall, heavily-built, with a huge bunch of keys hanging from his wide leather belt. The overall impression was of a jovial jailer. He peered at Candrew through circular, wire rimmed glasses. "How you doin'? You and all the rock jocks over in geology. Still getting stoned?"

"Just rocking along."

"You've got an inferiority complex because we've got bigger hammers." He slapped Candrew on the shoulder and threw back his ample mane and laughed. "Why don't you come and see what the other rock chippers have been up to? I'm having a show at the Branderson Gallery, down in Santa Fe. The opening's in a couple of weeks. Bring your checkbook, there'll be a lot of stuff you and Renata won't be able to resist." With calloused fingers, he raked back his unruly hair and laughed again.

Although Red himself could be overbearing, Candrew liked much of the sculpture he produced. "Sure, we'll come. That's if you're going to give me a hefty academic discount." He grinned.

"Tell you what, I'll send you an e-mail," Red said. He knew Candrew's reputation for forgetfulness and if he told him now he almost certainly wouldn't remember.

As if to underline that probability, Candrew took another glass of wine from the passing steward and ambled over to join Renata.

On the opposite side of the room the Director of the School of Art, looking appropriately intellectual in a tweed jacket and bow tie, was leaning forward to catch the quiet information he was getting from one of the members of the Art School's board, a tall, reed thin, older woman with white hair scraped back into a tight bun.

In a quiet, conspiratorial voice she said, "I think you know Markham Smyth inherited his father's art collection. Superb. Most of it acquired in Europe before the war and very few, if any, of the paintings have ever been exhibited. Some of them are rumored to be exceptional." She paused. "I hear his brother's furious. As the eldest son, he probably felt that the father's collection should have gone to him. Or, at least, been shared equally."

"Do you know the brother at all? Would he appreciate the paintings?"

"I get the impression he'd be more interested in how the paintings have appreciated. No, I haven't met him. He's an attorney in Philadelphia and financially isn't hurting, although he's not done anywhere near as well as his younger brother. Has a reputation for being a bit crass and impulsive. And I've heard he has much less interest in art."

"Well, you know lawyers, he'll probably sue." The director casually glanced around the gallery, apparently making a mental note of those present. "Any chance that some of the paintings could be donated to the university?"

She smiled as though she thought it might be good idea. "That I don't know. But it's certainly a suggestion worth pursuing. What a coup if the art school could exhibit them." After a moment's hesitation, she said, "Always a possibility, I suppose. Why don't you have a little chat with Dr. Kontorovich? She's going to be working on the paintings. Could give you an inside track."

Gwen had made the rounds, shaking hands, chatting, complimenting the artists with all the sincerity of a game show host. Her social chores completed, she joined her close friend Anna Meagher. Anna was horrified when told about the sinister incident with Gwen's dog. "Did you call the police?"

"I don't think it's illegal to mail decapitated animals."

"But it's sinister, evil. Surely, killing someone's dog must be against the law?"

"Around here the police only get interested when you kill a human being."

For several minutes they stood gossiping about the other people at the opening, then casually perused the paintings and sculptures.

"You like that?" Anna pointed to a large canvas with a wide red line outlining a simple square on a midnight-blue background.

Gwen lowered her voice. "It's a fucking square, for Christ's sake!"

"Ah, yes, but it's the ten degrees off vertical that gives it deep significance."

Gwen was uncertain whether she was serious or just kidding, but then Anna winked and laughed.

Peter, her husband, sauntered up, glass in hand, and didn't miss the sense of conspiracy. Anna told him she was thinking of buying *Red Square #2*.

"What's that? A painting of the Kremlin?" He glanced in the direction of her pointing finger. "Maybe in twenty years he'll be famous and we'll make a bundle," he said, without enthusiasm.

"But, dahling, by then you'll have grown to love it and won't want to sell."

Peter was no art connoisseur. Only landscapes were tolerable, and then only if they were of areas he knew well. Since he'd spent many summers as a student climbing the Grand Tetons, any painting of those mountains was, by definition, good. Similarly, any picture of the Maine coast was also acceptable. But abstract art? Incomprehensible. He turned to Anna. "How the hell can you tell whether a painting is good or not?"

Patiently, Anna explained. "Good art is expensive art."

The students were devouring the last of the food and only a few determined art aficionados were still in the gallery when

Candrew and Renata left to drive back across campus. On the way they talked about the art, but more about the people.

"You want to come in for a nightcap before you drive home?" Renata asked as they approached her house.

"Sorry to be unsocial, but I'll have to pass on that. Got an early morning meeting tomorrow."

"How's your social calendar?" Renata asked as they pulled into her driveway. "Anna Meagher's invited us to a cocktail party at her home on Wednesday."

"What did we do to merit this move up in the social world?"

"We?" She put her hand on Candrew's shoulder and laughed. "You owe it all to me. This is just one of the perks, now that I'll be part of Markham's 'team.'"

Chapter 4

Candrew pulled his chair up next to Charlie Lister. Charlie, a long-time faculty member in the art department, was a colleague of both Red Mulholland and Helen Kontorovich. A successful landscape painter, his western vistas sold well in Santa Fe and Scottsdale. Charlie put down his fork, wiped his mouth with his napkin and turned to Candrew. "I hear you were at the art opening last night. How did it go?"

"News certainly travels fast around here." Candrew laughed. "There were one or two strong painters, but mostly typical student work."

"Yeah, I agree. I couldn't make it to the show, but I helped hang it, so I've seen it all. At least it's encouraging that our alumni are submitting work and I'm impressed by the way a few of them are maturing." He dumped two packets of sugar into his coffee. "I guess an opening like this is free advertising. And the show usually pulls in a good number of well-heeled people who actually buy art."

Located on the fifth floor of the student union, the faculty dining area had a spectacular view across campus to the mountains and a group of regulars took advantage of it by commandeering the corner table in front of the floor-to-ceiling window. Candrew was half listening to another of the heated discussions that made lunch with his colleagues so fascinating. As usual, the arguments rolled on with several people talking at once.

"You've got to be kidding. We'd have crosses lining every damn road in the county, the rate those drunk drivers kill each other." Although unsaid, everyone knew Ted Devereaux was on another tirade against the local Hispanics, their religious customs and their tendency to drink and drive.

The roadside memorials, locally known as *descansos*, were often quite elaborate with plastic flowers and photographs. Originally marking the resting places of pallbearers along the route from church to cemetery, they were common in northern New Mexico. But descansos had become a political issue.

"Be charitable, Ted. It gives the families something tangible."

"Yeah, but the rate they're putting up new ones, the highways will be lined with them."

"Highway to heaven."

"And I'm just waiting for some enterprising relative to add solar panels and then they'll be lit up all night."

"You're all missing the point."

"Oh. What is the point?"

"They're clearly violating separation of church and state."

"Not in New Mexico. They're protected as *traditional cultural properties*." This information was volunteered by a large, balding man with a generous beard. A professor in the history department, Dr. Lubinsky—affectionately and universally known as Lubie—spoke with a booming, theatrical voice tinged with a slight eastern European accent. And he spoke with authority. This time they didn't all agree with him.

"Now come on, roadside memorials are using public property to endorse religion. That's a violation of the U.S. Constitution, not to mention being a distraction to drivers."

Candrew sipped his coffee and glanced around at the vocal group. But Charlie was still talking about the art show. "We're lucky to have someone as wealthy as Markham Smyth with enough interest in art to underwrite the annual show, and provide some prize money."

"Yeah. He and his wife were there with friends from Santa Fe."

"The Meaghers?"

"How'd you know?"

"They always come. She's an alum from the department, a genuine *yellowlander*."

"Was she any good?" Candrew asked.

"No!" He paused as if reconsidering his blunt judgment. "I should be more charitable, but the unkind said she was a better artist's model than an artist. It hasn't really mattered since she married Peter Meagher. That was quite a few years ago." He paused to top up his coffee. "The rumor mill's running flat out about the collection Markham Smyth inherited from his father. Our director would like to see a few pieces end up at the university. Frankly, I think he's way too optimistic. But you never know. Got to give him credit for trying." Charlie smiled. "And I hear Kontorovich was at the opening, holding forth as usual."

"Those that can, do. Those that can't, criticize," Candrew quipped.

Although she would not have admitted it, Helen Kontorovich was excited by the prospect of working with world class paintings. On the drive down to the Smyths' house she thought about the wealthy—how they got their money and what they chose to do with it. If she ever got wealthy, seriously wealthy, she wasn't sure what she'd do. Almost certainly relocate back east to New York. Northern New Mexico had always seemed somewhat of a backwater after Yale, even with the substantial and growing art market in Santa Fe. But what would she do if she moved to New York? Prowl the galleries looking for outstanding works?

It was precisely three o'clock when she pulled through the gates and parked in the neatly-landscaped courtyard. Zona let her into the house, took her coat and showed her through to the living room. "Would you like something to drink? Coke? Or how about coffee?"

Feeling a little self-conscious in the impressive environment, she hesitated. "Maybe later." This was the first time Helen had been in the Smyths' house and she was overawed by the enormous expanse.

She followed Zona down the passage to Markham's office where he was seated behind a large mahogany desk scanning a catalogue raisonné of Egon Schiele's works. He rose to greet her. After a few pleasantries, he waved his hand towards the stacks of papers. "I've organized the documents from the Miami attorneys into three groups. One's got all the information for the oils, there's one for the watercolors and drawings, and a small group lists the pre-Columbian, primitive art. I thought we'd start doing the boring stuff, get it over with."

Together they worked through the pile of papers. Helen was very familiar with this sort of documentation, but expected information on provenance. That was completely lacking.

When Markham left, her first task was to compare the description of each painting with the manifest, since the papers in the folders only catalogued purely mechanical details. Helen worked methodically down the row of paintings propped against the hallway wall, examining canvas size, frame size, frame description, and the presence and location of the signature.

She was nearly halfway through when Markham came back to check on her progress. "How you doing? Need anything?"

"No. Pretty routine so far. Moving along nicely." She laid her pencil on the spiral-bound pad where she'd been making notes.

"This is an amazing collection."

Markham smiled.

They strolled along the hallway, stopping to examine some of the newly-acquired treasures. Helen was delighted to see two Klimts, an impressive 'mad Max' Beckmann, a couple of Noldes and at least four Schieles, two of which she'd never seen in any monograph. There were half a dozen works by less well-known artists, but all from the early nineteen-hundreds.

Markham stopped in front of a painting of a man, just head and shoulders. "I was surprised when I found this in father's collection. It's a Schöenberg self-portrait. I always thought of him as a composer, you know, that twelve tone, modern stuff." He shook his head. "But I've been told he was a painter of considerable ability. The collection's got two of his self-portraits."

"On that subject, I'm stunned by this Klimt portrait of himself." She tipped it forward and examined the back: signed and dated. "Everything I've ever read about him, and that's a lot, claims he never produced a self-portrait. This piece is amazing. Unique." She stood back, staring at it, engrossed. Leaning beside the painting was a more typical Klimt portrait of a Viennese society matron. "Your father was very partial to Austrian artists."

"True, but he did broaden his collection with a few German and Dutch works." Markham strode down the hallway and pulled a painting out of a stack of half a dozen leaning against the far wall. "Here's a fantastic Grosz. It's amazing he could paint a figure to look so sinister."

They stared at it without speaking, then strolled along the row of canvasses and stopped, captivated, by yet another Klimt. "What a contrast," Helen said, examining the face and the line of the body that showed a vulnerability, an intimacy of sensuous color.

"And it moves you from the individual to universal truth," Markham observed.

After another fifteen minutes spent savoring other Klimts

and the Schieles, Kokoshkas, and a lone Gerstl—the core of Austrian Expressionism—Markham said, "I need to go." He glanced at his watch. "I've got a five o'clock meeting at St. Johns College. Just ask Zona if you want anything. And if you need to move anything heavy she can call Ronnie Garcia."

Left alone, Helen finished examining the documentation for the remaining paintings before moving on to check for damage. The shippers were experienced and obvious places, like the corners of the frames, had been well protected. The paintings had all survived the journey with no obvious ill effects. Except one.

The frame on a large Kokoshka landscape had been loosened a little by the rigors of transit. She was examining the twisted corner, trying to decide how best to tighten it, when she noticed what seemed to be a piece of folded paper tucked between the canvas and the ornate, gilded frame. Helen tried to pry it loose with her fingernail, but there wasn't enough sticking out for her to get a good grip. She always had an old leather satchel with her and it held a notebook, pens and camera. It also contained small tools, including a tape measure, hand lens and pliers. Now, she fished around in it and finally located an Exacto knife. Sticking the tip of the blade into the small amount of exposed card, she was able to carefully coax it out. The brittle paper was a receipt from an auction sale in Vienna, dated 1937. The dealer had described the painting briefly, but accurately, and the price was given in deutschmarks. The seller's name was clearly Jewish and the buyer was listed as *O. v. Lauerfeld.* She went to the manifest and checked the entry. The acquisition date given was August 1937—that matched—but it showed the purchaser was Alexander Smyth, Markham's father. Since both dates were the same, Helen wondered how Markham's father acquired the painting. Had someone else bought it for him? Had there been a subsequent, and almost instant, resale? Or was the name changed when the painting was brought to the States? As Helen stared at the receipt, she was struck by the low price, a ridiculous bargain for a work of this quality, even by the standards of pre-war Austria.

She tucked the receipt into the bottom of her leather satchel.

Candrew stopped the car at the entrance to the gravel driveway and gave the keys to the young Hispanic man in charge of valet parking. As he and Renata picked their way through the patches of snow on the lighted path to the front door of the Meaghers' home, they could see a large throng of partygoers through the expansive windows under the portál.

Anna Meagher greeted them at the front door and remembered Renata from the Alumni/Student art opening. "So pleased you could make it. I know it's a long drive down to Santa Fe." She shepherded them in. "I'm a yellowlander myself." She used the common nickname for students and alumni from the University of Northern New Mexico. It derived from the school's location just south of the town of Tierra Amarilla—a name that translated from the Spanish as *yellow land*.

Searching for some topic of mutual interest, Renata asked, "What was your major."

"Art. I graduated back in . . ." She paused, smiled, and said, "Well, longer ago than I care to admit." Anna took them over to Helen Kontorovich. "Here's someone you probably know from campus."

The Smyths had suggested Helen come to the cocktail party with them, but she knew few of the other guests. Unsociable, even with people she knew well, Helen wandered alone through the house, looking at the prints, paintings and small sculptures, and was unimpressed. When Candrew sauntered up to her and tried to make small talk, asking what she thought of the art collection, she snapped back, "It's like a pizza supreme. They've got a bit of everything." She shook her head. "And none of it of any real merit. The drawings are second rate. That field painting in the hallway looks as if it should be on a motel wall—a cheap motel."

Candrew was not sure how to reply. For a moment he stood in silence. "I hear you started working with the paintings Markham Smyth's just inherited."

"Now there's major art." She sipped her drink and stared into the distance, as if seeing the paintings in her mind's eye. "And Mr. Smyth's own collection has some excellent pieces." She leaned towards him and said in a quiet voice, as though sharing a confidence, "Although I can't say I'm overly fond of the contemporary abstracts." She went on to describe her favorites in more detail than Candrew needed. Eventually he broke away, got himself a drink and joined the main cluster of guests.

Candrew recognized hardly anyone at the cocktail party, but did see Gwen talking in an animated way to a small group over by the fireplace. Gwen, a trophy wife before the term had been coined, was now in her late fifties and still very striking. She had high cheek bones and a somewhat squarish jaw. Her chestnut hair was smoothly swept back and held by a discrete bow. This evening she wore a white silk blouse and a full-length skirt with a pattern of geometric shapes in muted browns and ochres. Gwen reminded Candrew of a sea shell: a perfect, well-polished surface with a wonderful pattern. But something out of its element, stranded, nothing living inside. He knew what *troph* meant to geologists—anything to do with food and feeding—and this trophy wife had found herself a meal ticket. He watched her peer through the throng to Markham and smile. *Don't bite the hand that feeds you.*

As Candrew threaded his way across the crowded room, he was intercepted by the host. "Hi, I'm Peter Meagher."

"Thanks for inviting me, at least indirectly as Renata's escort. I'm Candrew Nor."

"Candrew? Unusual name, never heard that before."

"My father picked it. He was sick of all the kids with Hollywood names and he especially disliked being defined by numbers: IDs, draft number, Social Security number, on and on. He wanted me to start out different. So, he picked a name he'd never heard of—Candrew."

"And are you different?"

Candrew had never been asked that before and didn't have a ready answer. "I hadn't thought about it, guess we're all different in our own ways."

Zona Pharn was busy fetching drinks and picking up empty glasses when Anna Meagher pulled her aside. "Zona, I'm so pleased to have you here to help. I didn't get a chance to talk earlier. I hope you don't mind Mrs. Smyth volunteering your time."

"No, that's fine." Her reply lacked any obvious enthusiasm.

"Would you put those two trays over there?" Anna pointed toward the far end of the room. "The caterers laid them out in the wrong place."

Anna chatted with friends, made sure the buffet was replenished and that everyone's glass was full, in short, acting the attentive hostess. She ended up back with Gwen. "So, Paolo's coming into town?" A furtive smile flashed across her face and she nodded knowingly, setting her long silver earrings swinging.

"Yes. Friday. The Reinhardts are going to fly him in from L.A."

"With Carla?" Anna asked.

"Of course. That dutiful little wife follows him everywhere."

Anna was more interested in the husband. "He's so good looking, and so . . . Italian!"

That was only half true. Paolo's mother was Danish, but hair like burnished pewter, a swarthy complexion, and an ability to charm women were inherited straight from his Italian father. A rising star on the concert circuit, he played the piano with Latin flair and was rapidly becoming a favorite of the cognoscenti. It was well known that he preferred extremely modern composers, in particular Troetschel and Eisler, but the big bucks came from performing the old favorites and he was forced to compromise. Gwen had invited Paolo for a return performance in Santa Fe and organized a concert scheduled at the Lensic Theater.

Like his wife, Peter Meagher was also a practiced host. Now he was chatting with a rotund, balding man in a checked jacket. Struggling at the buffet with his drink, napkin, fork and an over-filled plate, he grinned. "Another million years of evolution and the cocktail party set will have evolved to look like octopuses—we'll have enough arms to cope with all this stuff." Somehow he managed to find a spare tentacle to grab another slice of smoked salmon. When Markham joined them, he stopped eating long enough to ask, "How's the venerable Liesl Sorenson doing?"

"The new girl," Markham nodded toward Zona, "is okay, but she doesn't have Liesl's supercilious, 'down-the-nose' look. Liesl always seemed to be saying *You might be the boss and I might be the hired-help, but I'm my own woman.* I liked that." He grinned and ate the hors d'oeuvre he'd taken from the tray.

The Meaghers lived beside the golf course at Las Campanas, west of town, and when their party broke up Helen rode back to the Smyths' eastside house with Gwen and Markham. Conscientious and thorough, Helen's work documenting the paintings and drawings was going to take several more days and the Smyths had suggested she stay in the guest wing.

"Think you'll be able to wrap up everything by Friday?" Markham asked.

"I should be able to, but things never go as fast as you'd like." Helen didn't mention the old Vienna auction receipt, even though it had dominated her thoughts all evening. On one hand, she knew she was prying. But on the other hand, she was intrigued by the implications. Tomorrow should provide a chance to see if there were any other auction receipts concealed in the paintings.

31

Chapter 5

The following day dawned bright with scattered snow showers. But Candrew saw none of this since he'd forgotten to set his alarm clock and slept until nine. The wind had drifted the light snow into smooth mounds against the chamisa, creating a landscape drained of color: just whites and grays—except for the gaudy yellow plastic wrapping of the half-buried newspaper. Candrew retrieved it, shook off the snow and trudged back to the warmth of the house. Chile and Pixel got their breakfast first, then he sat at the kitchen table eating granola and reading the comics. The serious news on page one would have to wait until he was fortified by at least one cup of coffee. But it would have to wait longer than that—the phone was ringing.

The call was from Maria, the department secretary. "You going to be in this morning? Dr. Rosenberg wants to see you in his office." She paused. "He gave me the distinct impression it's important."

"I'll be in right after lunch. That soon enough?"

"I guess so. He's free most of the early afternoon."

They agreed on a one-thirty meeting and Candrew went back

to his remaining granola, wondering why his department chairman needed to see him so urgently. He flipped to the newspaper's sports page which Earl Warren, the late Chief Justice, had said, "records people's accomplishments; the front page has nothing but man's failures."

Breakfast over, he sprawled on the sofa and read several articles in the *Journal of Sedimentary Geology* and one in *Chemical Geology*. It took nearly two hours to work through the technical minutia and make detailed notes. But the time was well spent and he was excited to realize that the techniques described could be used in his own research.

By late morning a light dusting of snow had accumulated, though not enough to make driving a challenge, and Candrew could think over ideas from the technical articles he'd read and still drive safely. He followed his usual route across campus and over the arroyo to the parking lot behind Kinblade Hall.

While he appreciated the importance of teaching the next generation of geologists, Candrew was also a first-class researcher. At heart, he was a puzzle solver. He enjoyed the intellectual challenge of taking what limited data he could coax from rocks and then try to figure out what happened all those millions of years ago. As he made his way through the department to his office, Candrew detoured to the research laboratory down in the basement. Large and well-equipped, it was where Dr. Judy Westerlund, his research associate, spent most of her time. She was sitting at one of the polarizing microscopes when he hurried in, eager to explain his new insights. "What we have to do is characterize the minor minerals in more detail. Find out what they are."

"How you going to do that?" she asked.

They spent the next half hour discussing possible approaches to the problem of trying to establish a source for the materials that made up the sandstone rocks they were studying, their *provenance*. Sandstones are the eroded debris of preexisting rocks, and while consisting mainly of quartz grains they often have small amounts of other minerals. Candrew was suggesting a much more detailed study of these less common mineral grains.

"We ought to start with microscopy, see what's there," Candrew said. "Then, with that frame of reference, we can do a detailed chemical analysis of the grains. I was thinking electron microprobe."

"Dr. Kernfeld's machine?"

"Right. I'm sure you can sweet talk him into running a half-a-dozen samples on that fancy, million-dollar instrument of his. That'll give us some idea how things might work out. Just don't let him charge you the going rate." Candrew grinned. He sat for a moment tapping his front teeth with his index finger, an idiosyncrasy that was a sure sign he was perplexed. "You'll need to find out how he wants the samples: polished sections, or heavy mineral separates."

"What elements should we get him to analyze for?"

"Let's start with the obvious—iron, titanium, manganese."

Candrew was a couple of minutes late getting to Rosenberg's office. When he was ushered in, Rosenberg was scrawling his signature on yet another of his frequent memos. He glanced up, said, "Have a seat," and continued signing his way quickly down through the stack of memos.

In the three years he'd been department chair, Nicholas Rosenberg had earned the faculty's respect for the research he did on volcanic rocks, but only a grudging acceptance of his role as head of department. He'd found it difficult to adjust to the casual lifestyle of the West after his Ivy League education and east coast administrative positions. Candrew surveyed the room. Mostly well-organized with neat piles of papers, the impression was of someone in control, someone who did not let things get out of hand. Beside a row of precisely aligned books perched a group of mineral specimens, obviously acquired more for their aesthetics than geologic significance. Framed diplomas and photos decorated the wall above.

Rosenberg capped his ink pen and pushed away from the desk in a high-backed chair. "I had a call from the president's administrative assistant this morning." He paused, peering down at his memos. "The president wants a meeting with you, in his office, and he wants me to be present."

J. Creighton Burke had been the university president for ten years. His administrative style was "hands-off" and he dealt mainly with the deans, infrequently with department chairs and almost never with faculty. "Any idea what the meeting's about?" Candrew wondered why he was being summoned.

"We'll have to wait to get the complete answer on that question," Rosenberg replied.

They compared time commitments, blocked out some periods that were mutually acceptable. Both knew that the actual time of the meeting would be set by the president's schedule, not theirs.

The overnight snow in Santa Fe muffled outside sounds and the Smyths' guest bedroom had been still and peaceful. Helen Kontorovich slept soundly for five hours, the result of yesterday's hard work and, more significantly, the generous alcohol at the Meaghers' party. Too apprehensive to sleep longer, she'd read for a while, then sat at the window watching the orange fingers of dawn slowly tighten their grip on the western hills. To the east, over her left shoulder, the shadowed bulk of the Sangre de Cristo mountains loomed dark and indistinct. Her mind ran back through the previous day's work. Inventorying Markham's collection had been routine and tedious—until she'd discovered the auction receipt hidden under the canvas on the Kokoshka landscape. That had added a whole new dimension.

As the sun climbed higher, Helen watched the shadows under the piñons and junipers slowly shorten. Eager to get back to the art work, she expected today to be more stimulating and planned to search the remaining paintings for additional receipts. The prospect excited her. But what if Markham caught her doing it? He'd certainly want an explanation for why she didn't tell him about yesterday's find.

Concerned, and unsure just how early she should appear for breakfast, Helen finally strolled into the seating area beside the kitchen a little after eight. Zona was tipping freshly-ground beans into the maw of the coffee percolator. She'd had less sleep than Helen. It had taken nearly an hour to clean up after the Meaghers' party and then she'd had to get up at six-thirty to make breakfast for Markham and Gwen. "Mr. Smyth wanted me to tell you that he had to go down to Albuquerque for some early morning meeting. Mrs. Smyth said she'd go with him. They're not going to be back until late afternoon."

"Really? I guess that's okay. We talked over everything yesterday and I've got plenty to do without him." Helen was relieved to know she could examine the paintings without Markham peering over her shoulder. *Late afternoon*—should be ample time for a thorough search.

Zona offered eggs and bacon, croissants, cereal, or cherry danish—all of which were refused—and said, "You won't get through before lunch, will you?"

"No. I'm sure it's going to take me a lot longer than that." She smiled. "I'll still be here when you get back." With a slight hangover from last night, she wasn't hungry, but thought that maybe something sugary would help her headache. She changed her mind about breakfast and took a danish to go with her coffee.

"I only asked because I've got to be down on Cerrillos Road by nine." Zona looked uncomfortable. In the Smyths' absence, she felt responsible for the house and its precious contents and didn't like leaving Helen alone. "I've made a fresh pot of coffee, there's juice in the fridge. I'll be back in time to make your lunch. And if you get hungry, there's cake and cookies in the cupboard."

While Zona cleared away plates, Helen scanned the *Santa Fe New Mexican* for a few minutes, then folded the sections and left them on the table. Enthusiastic about resuming her work with the art, she bustled down the passage to the groups of canvasses leaning against the wall. Her response was the same as yesterday: pounding heart, awed by the superb quality.

Helen stood in front of the Oshka Kokoshka, the one she'd examined in detail the day before. The Austrian auction receipt from the frame was concealed in the bottom of her equipment bag. She retrieved it, scrutinized the wording minutely and regretted she didn't have any way to make a copy. Although raising lots of questions about the trivial purchase price and the altered names, by itself the document wasn't conclusive. Helen knew what she needed to do, search the remaining paintings for other receipts, hopefully something more definitive. As far as she could tell from the documents, the paintings had all been acquired in Vienna, most of the important ones during a brief period between May and August, 1937.

The big Schiele was her first target. She could see nothing secreted between the canvas and the gilt frame, which wasn't really surprising, considering how little space was there. The canvas itself was attached to the wooden stretcher in the conventional way, with small tacks holding it. None seemed to have been disturbed and there were no obvious bumps that might suggest something hidden underneath.

As she checked the bottom corner, there was a noise at the far end of the house. She froze, guilty. It sounded like a door closing quietly, was someone coming in, or leaving? Glancing at her watch, she saw it was nine-fifteen. Must be Zona running late. She held her breath and listened, but there were no more sounds.

Helen waited a few minutes, then hustled into Markham's study and searched for information in the documents from Miami. They listed a purchase date for most of the art pieces and she made a list of those obtained within a few months of the date on the auction receipt. It didn't include the Schiele painting she'd just examined. That had been acquired three years earlier. As she turned to go back to the paintings, her glance fell on the printer hooked to Markham's desk-top computer. It was an all-in-one unit combining printer, fax, scanner—and copier. After only a moment's hesitation, Helen took the receipt out of her pocket and punched in instructions for three copies.

While she waited for the machine to disgorge its replicas, Helen perused the study. Probably more of a retreat than a serious workplace, she thought. Not enough chaos for someone really working. Glass-fronted bookcases filled with leather-bound volumes were a sure indication of an interior designer's role, although the stereo and the choice of art work were clearly personal, as were the two silver-framed photos. She stepped over to look. The left one showed the Smyths some years ago—a much younger Markham with more hair and less belly, and Gwen sleek and attractive, much as she looked now. The other photo was of a tall, distinguished-looking man with military bearing, the face humorless. Helen presumed it was Markham's father.

She turned back to the office. Among the Miro prints and the Schnabel sketches, the oil painting hanging on the side wall stood out—not because of its high quality, rather because of its lack of quality. Why was this second rate (third rate?) art work here? She glanced at the printer—still working on the last copy—and sauntered over to take a closer look at the painting. A landscape with two almost symmetrical hills, it was poorly resolved and, in her opinion, the colors were inappropriate. In particular, the river and the overhanging trees were amateurish. The simple, gilt frame was nice, though. No painting with this description was on the Miami list, so it was not part of the collection from Markham's father, and judging from the thick layer of dust on top of the frame, it appeared that Markham had owned it for some time. She examined it again. Why did he keep it displayed when he had dozens of superior works to choose from?

The copy machine lapsed into silence. She grabbed the three copies, retrieved the original and hurried back to her satchel where she concealed the duplicates under her equipment and notebooks.

Helen started searching for more auction details with a Nolde. One of the larger paintings in the collection, it had an acquisition date in her target time period. But there was little room between the stretcher and the frame to conceal anything.

The next painting, and the three after that, were all disappointing and she discovered nothing. But the sixth was worth the wait.

Although the portrait was painted on canvas, it was unusual in that it was not on a conventional stretcher, but on a wooden panel. Also, there was a much larger overlap of canvas, in some places as much as four inches. Several cards from art dealers and galleries were taped to the back and she recognized Sternberg, but none of the others. Rummaging around in her work bag, she pulled out her camera and took several shots. That seemed a good idea: she worked her way along the line of paintings photographing the backs of all of them.

Returning to her examination of the portrait, Helen ran her nail along the surface, trying to detect underlying papers. Any auction receipts would probably be quite thin and she wasn't sure they could be detected. She found nothing. That wide canvas edge was so tempting and she couldn't resist prying underneath, but didn't see anything hidden there. Going back to her work bag, she got a small pair of blunt-nosed pliers, used them to grab the head of the outer tack, and slowly twisted it back and forth, working it out. With two more tacks removed she could look under part of the canvas: there was nothing to see. But working her way across the top led to success, this time she had it. There was a piece of folded, pale yellow paper and she used her tweezers to tug firmly on it. It seemed as if the brittle paper would tear, but with a slow, steady pull it finally yielded intact. Her fingers were all thumbs as she unfolded it as quickly as she could. Another auction receipt. A complete one, with the auction house name, seller's name, date, title and price. And again it indicated the buyer was v. Lauerfeld. And once again, the price was absurdly low.

What stood out, however, was the seller's name, *Eisenstat*, with a single handwritten word scrawled across it: *JUDE*. Jew. She was looking at convincing evidence that an Austrian Jew had been forced to sell the painting for an unrealistic price. And sell it in what was almost certainly a sham auction.

The longer Helen stared at the sales receipt the less she understood why anyone would make an effort to hide this damning evidence. The sensible thing would have been to destroy it. She could only guess that the auction house itself may have been Jewish, or at least had Jewish sympathies. Again, the machine in Markham's office provided her with copies of everything and she put them all in her equipment bag.

Helen stepped back looking at the paintings with new understanding. Her gaze came to rest on the portrait that formed a pair with the Kokoshka she'd investigated the day before. She turned it around. Like the first one, it was painted on canvas stretched over wood board and had wide canvas selvedges. Hurriedly, she pried underneath searching for another receipt. She was not disappointed. This time, there was a single J inked across the Eisenstat name.

She started to take the new receipt to the machine in Markham's office, but stopped, returned to get the rest of the copies and her leather address book. After duplicating the newest receipt, she flipped through the pages, found the fax number she needed and punched it in, faxing copies of everything, hoping they'd transmit clearly.

Certain she'd located all the receipts, Helen took the duplicates down the passageway to her satchel and hid them under the bottom stiffener. She slid the last receipt back into its original position behind the canvas on the portrait. Stunned by her discoveries, she wondered what other information might be hidden with the paintings. Was Markham aware of these papers? Had his father known?

An hour later Helen was kneeling in front of the two remaining pictures propped against the wall, making copious notes. Engrossed by her studies, even in the silence of the deserted house, she never heard the footsteps.

"Those looted paintings are worth millions." The unexpected voice startled her. "And I see you found the Smyth family's secret. You going to turn him in? Let the authorities deal with him?"

She stood up, uncertain, turning toward the intruder. "Well, I, . .I, . ."

"Can't let you do that. Not an option. His high-priced lawyers would get him off with just a slap on the wrist. He needs to pay for his father's crimes." The rising intensity of the voice made it echo down the painting-lined passage.

Helen didn't realize the seriousness of the situation. She had grown up in a suburb where accountants, managers and attorneys didn't go hunting. She'd never handled a gun. Now, she saw all too clearly what was clenched in that menacing fist. Horrified, she watched in hypnotized silence as the gun barrel rose slowly. Adrenaline stretched the seconds to minutes. When the sound of the shot reached her, the bullet was already entering above her left eye, shattering the skull and the brain behind. Helen Kontorovich's uncontrolled body slumped to the floor, twisting as it fell. It hit one of the large paintings that toppled and crashed across her already lifeless form.

Chapter 6

Candrew and Renata drove to Santa Fe under a featureless gray sky that gave subdued light, threatened snow, but cast no shadows. Negotiating the twisting dirt road leading to the Smyths' home, Candrew was intrigued by a strange flickering against the overcast sky. It was only when they rounded the final bend that he saw the police cruiser with its rack of flashing lights rhythmically splashing red and blue across adobe walls. Two more police cars, an unmarked unit and an ambulance were parked in the driveway, and a uniformed officer stood guard while plain-clothed staff hustled around.

As Candrew and Renata hurried toward the front door, their progress was halted by a young Hispanic police officer. "Sorry, sir," he said in his best official tone, nodding towards Renata to include her, "I can't let anyone into the house."

"Why not?" Candrew asked, puzzled. "What happened?"

"Homicide."

Candrew was momentarily speechless. "Murder? In the Smyths' home?"

"Oh my God. Who got killed?" Renata wanted to know.

"I'm not at liberty to divulge that information, sir." Staring straight at Candrew he asked, "Are you relatives of the home owners?"

Renata was explaining the reason for their visit, when one of the senior police officers noticed them and strode over.

"Hi, Prof," he greeted Candrew. "What brings you here at a time like this?"

Candrew told him that Renata had come to work on a project for Markham. He introduced the officer. "This is Carlos O'Hara. He's a yellowlander, took one of my geology courses. We met again a few years ago when he wrote me a speeding ticket. Actually, just a warning."

Officer O'Hara produced a wry smile. "Don't forget that for a while you were a prime suspect in that biology prof's death."

Candrew pursed his lips, uncomfortable.

"Now it's your turn to help," O'Hara said. "We can only release the name of the deceased after the next of kin have been notified. Mr. Smyth doesn't know the relatives. Says he didn't know her real well, she was just here doing some work with his pictures. The inspector's planning to call the university."

Candrew stood in stunned silence, his mouth open, realizing immediately who'd been murdered: *Helen Kontorovich*. He took an involuntary deep breath, overcome by the news. "Oh, my God! Why would anyone want to kill her?"

Renata also realized who the victim was and grasped Candrew's arm. Blankly, they stared at the officer.

"I'll take you guys through to the Chief." O'Hara guided them around the yellow crime-scene tape and led the way into the house. Inspector Martinez was standing to the side of the prone body now covered with a white sheet, Markham Smyth beside him. The police crime-scene photographer was repositioning his equipment, while medical technicians with latex gloves were still swabbing blood samples from the floor and wall.

Martinez, medium height, stocky with a shaved head, stood with his arms away from his body as though ready to counterpunch. Irritated by the new arrivals, he was unsmiling and his attitude aggressive, until O'Hara explained they were from the university. His manner softened only slightly. "Need to find the next of kin. Can you help? Would the head of her department know?"

"Possibly. It's more likely to be the personnel office. If it would help, I can call for you. I'll get the number from my secretary, shouldn't take long."

The inspector looked somewhat dubious.

"I assume the victim is Helen Kontorovich?" Candrew asked.

"Right." Martinez dragged the word out, evaluating Candrew with a lengthy stare. "Mr. Smyth has already made the identification."

Candrew searched through his pockets, finally locating the cell phone. But when he tried to pull up his list of numbers there was nothing: dead. He'd forgotten to charge it. "Can I use one of the house phones?" he asked Markham.

So far Markham had said nothing: he looked overwhelmed, absolutely shattered. Slowly he turned to Candrew. "You won't be able to use the phone in my office—the crime-scene technicians are still working in there." Distractedly, he thought for a moment, stroking his chin. "There's one in the guest bedroom, use that." He glanced towards the inspector who nodded confirmation, but said nothing.

Markham led Candrew away from the murder scene and down a side hallway. They both blinked at the bright flash as the photographer continued documenting the crime setting. The guest room was in the rear with two small windows looking out at the hill behind the house while a larger window gave a southern view. The phone stood on an antique oak table that had a contemporary chrome and leather chair beside it. After Markham left, Candrew got the numbers for both the Art School and Personnel from his department secretary. He called the Art School first and the woman who answered told him the director wasn't in his office. "I can try and find him if you'll hold on a minute." Candrew said he'd wait, and the line went silent.

The Smyths' house nestled into a hillside that was a mosaic of piñon pines, junipers, bare stony patches and native grasses, all dusted with snow. A shallow arroyo, that hosted water perhaps once every five years, meandered across it. Markham often walked this land, which he'd come to love. Occasionally he'd stumble across an ancient arrowhead or potshard and excited by these finds he'd used them to line his office window sill. Gwen only saw land as something that separated you from your neighbors, provided breathing space and cut down the noise. Candrew stood patiently waiting, idly looking across the snowy slopes, when a movement among the trees caught his attention.

As he watched, a figure crept hesitantly around the piñons. Candrew was sure it was a woman. When she ducked under a low branch, furtively glancing behind, he caught a glimpse of her profile and blond hair, even though the collar of her down jacket was turned up. His view was partly blocked by a thick juniper growing close to the house and he moved to the other window. The woman carried flowers and a metallic object that looked like a trowel, although he couldn't be certain. Watching intently, he saw her make her way stealthily across the slope, but she soon shifted out of his line of sight. Odd. Candrew sat on the desk tapping his teeth with the nail of his index finger, mulling over her strange behavior, especially with all the frantic activity in the house.

"I'm sorry, I can't find the director anywhere". The voice startled him: he'd forgotten he was holding the phone. "Would you like to leave a message?"

Candrew said he'd call back later. Right now he was more interested in tracking the mysterious woman.

The small guest room had no exterior door. Looking for a way out, he slipped quietly into the hallway. To his left, it dead-ended in a picture window. He tried following the passage in the other direction and just round the corner found a door that opened out to the yard. He slid back the deadbolt. Candrew had to make a lengthy detour beside a low stone wall before he could double back and follow the woman's route. There was no sign of her. However, with only one set of small footprints high up on the slope, tracking in the patchy snow was simple. Closer to the house, he saw several sets of much larger footprints he assumed were made by the police when they'd searched for the assailant—or at least his point of entry. Eventually, Candrew came to a broad earth mound under a huge aspen tree. On it were a wilted bunch of flowers and the fresh ones he'd seen the woman carrying. To one side, the earth had been dug into and the covering of snow showed obvious signs of disturbance. He checked around, no one was out. With few windows on this side of the house, it seemed unlikely anyone else had seen what happened. Even with scattered large footprints, the small ones were easy to distinguish and he followed their trail to a side door in the garage.

Opening the door, he surprised the woman. Short and blonde, she was standing at a small sink washing her muddy hands, the snowy shoes kicked off.

She shot him a guilty look. "You startled me, coming in real sudden, like that."

"I just wondered who was getting a bunch of flowers at a time like this."

"They're for Mrs. Smyth's dog." She hesitated. "We buried him last Friday."

Candrew vaguely recalled hearing something at the Meaghers' party about the Smyths' dog dying, but not the details. "Who are you?"

"I'm Zona Pharn. I live here in the annex and work for the

Smyths."

"So you put flowers out every day?"

"Yes. Mrs. Smyth likes me to."

A plausible explanation, Candrew thought, but not totally convincing. The wilted flowers looked as though they'd been there more than just one day.

Zona finished rinsing her hands and dried them with paper towels. "Did you, like, know the woman who got shot?"

"Sort of. She was a fellow faculty member at UNNM."

For the first time, Zona looked directly at Candrew. She seemed impressed. "So you're a professor?"

"Yeah, that's right."

"What do you teach?" She tossed the damp towels in the trash can. "No. Let me guess." She studied Candrew carefully. "Music. You've got sensitive eyes. You're a music professor."

Candrew laughed. "That's about as far wrong as you could get: geologist."

"Really?" Zona's eyes widened. Her attitude changed. "You, like, know about the earth and stuff?"

"Yeah. That's what they pay me to teach."

"I read in a book once that you rock people are like priests of the earth, bringing crystals from the dark depths, letting the power of sunlight shine into them, make them glow. The sun can set free their hidden power. You know, like when it makes a rainbow."

Candrew had never thought of himself as an earth priest.

"You must know a lot about crystals and things? I've got a bunch of crystals. All colors. Some real big." Before he had a chance to comment, Zona rambled on. "I've tried to read stuff about minerals, but all those names, I get so confused. My birthstone's peridot. You know what that is?"

"Yeah, gem quality olivine. And olivine's a silicate mineral that gets its name from its olive color."

Zona listened attentively, obviously impressed. "I know

turquoise is the state gem, but there are some important peridot places in New Mexico as well."

"You're right. Have you heard about Kilbourne Hole, down south? It's world-famous."

"No." She smiled at Candrew. "You know so much."

Candrew ignored the compliment, glanced at his watch, and edged closer to the door.

"I've got a friend who gets me lots of crystals. Lives down off Agua Fria. She knows all about their vibrations and how to make elixirs. They really help you stay healthy and in tune with the cosmos." She gave Candrew a tentative, probing smile. "I know about most of the crystals I own, but I've got some I don't know. Could you tell me what they are? They're supposed to have healing effects."

"No problem. I'd be happy to take a look at them and see what I can identify." Candrew hesitated and turned toward the door. "However, I'm not sure I can give you any information about medicinal properties."

Zona looked disappointed. "Well, if you could give me their names, I can look them up. I've got books, they tell you all about crystal powers." She hesitated, and looked around for her other pair of shoes. "Can I call you if I have questions about minerals."

Candrew had run into crystal-gazing fanatics in the past. "Sure," he said, but volunteered nothing more.

"Anyway, I need to get back and see what Mrs. Smyth wants me to do to help with the clearing up." Zona slipped on the pair of clean shoes and hurried through the garage into the main part of the house. Candrew followed, looking for Renata, and found her waiting in the breakfast area with a mug of coffee in one hand, admiring a couple of Markham's newly arrived paintings. When Candrew sat beside her, she told him, "The inspector wants us to stay put. Said he'd be back to talk to us shortly."

The medical technicians completed their jobs as the mortal

remains of Helen Kontorovich were wheeled out to the ambulance. Police teams still worked documenting the crime scene, while Inspector Martinez was busy assembling what facts he could. He'd started with Liesl Sorenson, the only person around at the time of the murder. Liesl told him she'd been reading in her room in the annex and had dozed off. The sound of the gunshot startled her. Although now she rarely came over to the main house, she'd made her way across the courtyard, looked in the window and then entered through the side door. The house appeared empty and she'd seen no one. Liesl thought she might have a heard a car, although it was noisy—could have been a truck. But she admitted she didn't hear too well. When she'd discovered the body and all the blood, at first she didn't know what to do, but recovered enough to call 911. Liesl had nothing more to add. When asked what time it was when she heard the gunshot, the best she could do was "late-morning."

Zona Pharn was next in the inspector's interrogation. She described getting coffee for Helen before going to a store down off Cerrillos Road. Under further questioning, she identified this as the office of *Friends of the Planet*. And Zona also admitted a detour into Sanbusco to buy flowers. As far as she could remember, she'd left the house a little before nine o'clock. She'd got back just as the emergency vehicles were arriving, so her return was well documented.

Now Inspector Martinez was questioning Markham. "I understand that you and Mrs. Smyth were in Albuquerque at the time of the shooting."

"Close. Actually in Rio Rancho."

"Were you there overnight?"

"No. We left early in the morning. About seven-thirty."

"A scheduled meeting?"

"I'd had a call late the previous evening asking me to meet with a real estate developer." He paused and thought for a minute. "Actually, the message was waiting on the answering machine when

I got back from a cocktail party."

Martinez asked for the developer's name and made a note in his black book. "As far as you know, was the alarm system on?"

"Unlikely. Not with Dr. Kontorovich working here. And, of course, Liesl Sorenson was in the annex during the day."

"You know that we've worked all round your home and found no evidence of forced entry. But the front door was unlocked and slightly ajar." He paused, looking down at other notes he'd made. "Unfortunately, we didn't see any tire tracks in the snow because of your heated driveway. The snow had all melted. Is it normal to keep the heating on all the time?"

"Yeah. Zona's been told to turn it on whenever we have a snowfall or ice."

The inspector consulted his notebook again. "Where was Ms. Pharn going when she left the house?"

When Markham said he had no idea, the inspector replied, "No problem. She claims she was with some green group." He smirked as he said it. "Know anything about that?"

"No."

"Easy enough to check. But even if it isn't true, it still eliminates her as a suspect. She can definitely prove she wasn't in your home."

He scribbled down a notation. "You want to tell me who had access to the house? Anyone unusual been here recently, say, in the last month?"

"No." Markham pursed his lips, thinking. "Oh, wait a minute, we did have a couple of men with the truck from the shipping company when they were unloading crates into the house. They had almost unlimited access for a couple of hours."

"When was that?"

"Several days ago. Actually, last Friday."

"You know their names?"

"'fraid not. I'm sure the shipping company has records and

could get you that information." Markham thought for a moment. "There's Ronnie Garcia who does small jobs around the house. He was here helping me unpack the crates. And he's often here doing small jobs."

"You say 'often'. That mean he's familiar with the house?"

"Yes, he is."

"And the alarm system?"

"Yeah. He knows how it's set."

The inspector nodded and made a note of this. "What sort of person is he?"

"Hispanic, Mexican I think. Short and stocky. Good worker. Conscientious. Doesn't speak English real well."

"Okay." He scribbled more notes. "Anyone else?"

"There's a cleaning lady. Comes once a week. Zona's always here when she's working." He thought for a moment. "And the usual people—mail man, UPS driver, but they don't come into the house." He watched the inspector carefully note all this.

"Could it have been an attempted robbery?" Markham asked. "Perhaps trying to steal one of the new paintings? And then aborted when they found someone in the house?"

"Always a possibility. We'll keep it in mind. But from what you and Mrs. Smyth told us earlier, nothing's missing."

Gwen was next on the inspector's list, but had little to add. Finally, he got to Candrew and Renata. He sat with them in the breakfast alcove. "What made you come to the house on this particular afternoon?"

Renata explained the purpose of her visit and added, "Mr. Smyth can confirm that."

"How well did you know Dr. Kontorovich?"

"Not a close friend, just an acquaintance, really. We met at occasional university functions."

"And you, sir. When did you last see her?"

"At a party in the Meaghers' home. Friends of the Smyths.

The party was last night."

"Anything unusual with Dr. Kontorovich's behavior?"

"Not that I noticed." Candrew stared into space for a moment, thinking. "Just her usual abrasive self."

Martinez raised his eyebrows. "Abrasive enough to get someone really ticked off?"

"That I wouldn't know."

The inspector handed each of them one of his business cards. "If you think of anything that might be significant, let me know."

The interrogation was over.

As Candrew and Renata were pulling on their jackets, the deputy medical examiner was packing up the last of his arcane supplies. For such a macabre profession, he was a jovial extrovert and smiled at them. "Sad business. I'm always amazed at the tangled webs people make for themselves, complicate their lives. At least this one ended quickly."

"So, it was a simple shooting?" Candrew asked.

"Yep. Looks like a single shot." He nodded his head several times as if confirming to himself his own diagnosis. "Right in the forehead."

"Can you tell much from a preliminary examination?"

"Oh, sure." He assumed a serious, professional air. "The entry wound was a bit above the left eye, pretty clean. There was an exit wound at the top, back skull. As usual, a lot more damage there. So, I could tell the forensic examination technician the bullet wasn't still in the body. They searched around and found it embedded in the wall."

"Will that help?" Renata asked.

"Yeah. Sure will."

Candrew was surprised the medical examiner was giving so much information about an active case, but was happy to learn more of the details.

"They'll ship the slug off to the firearms lab. With just one bullet those forensics guys can get enough info to figure out exactly what type of weapon the perp used."

Candrew was tapping his teeth, wondering what other information could be obtained. "If I'm understanding this right, Dr. Kontorovich was facing the assailant. That would mean she didn't turn away and wasn't trying to run, or even defend herself."

"Correct. No evidence of any conflict."

"So that meant she knew the gunman?"

"You'll have to let the cops figure that one out." He picked up his bag and started towards the door. "You might be interested to know that there weren't any burn marks on the victim. Tells me the gun was at least three feet away when it was fired."

"One last thing," Candrew said. "Did I understand you right when you noted the exit wound at the back was higher up in the skull than the entry?"

"Sure was."

"And that would mean the assailant was firing upwards."

"I guess so. But most people shoot a pistol with a straight arm at shoulder level. That would place the gun lower than the victim's head." The medic stood nodding, thinking about that.

"But not a lot lower. You said the exit hole made by the bullet was high at the back of the skull."

"Yes. Yes I did. I won't have the exact locations until the autopsy, a rough guess would be, maybe, three inches higher."

"You're the expert," Candrew said, "but if I'm seeing this correctly, the killer must have been shorter than Helen."

"Unless the person with the gun was kneeling or bending, though I admit that's not likely." He grinned.

"And judging from the position of the impact hole up on the wall, where they dug out the bullet, the victim must have been standing up when she was shot."

The medic stood in silence for a minute. "You've made some

good points. They'll be worth adding to my report." He laughed. "But I'll take the credit."

Chapter 7

Subdued piano music diffused through the quiet house, sad and introspective. Markham often played in the early morning, and today the somber chords of the Chopin nocturne provided a distraction from the shock of the previous day's murder. He always described his home as a civilized haven in an unruly world. Why this murder, senseless violence? And why Dr. Kontorovich, what made her the killer's target? Her work with his paintings seemed obvious, but what was the exact reason?"

Irritated by the intruding tones of the ringing phone, he stamped across the room and grabbed it. "Yes?"

"Sorry to call you this early. Hope it's not a problem."

Markham mumbled something unintelligible.

The caller, Detective Inspector Martinez, sounded hassled. "Look, I need to get Ronnie Garcia's cell phone number. You got that?"

"I'll see if I can find it." Markham located the address book in his office. "You want his address as well?"

"Yeah. We're trying to track him down. Got some questions we need to ask him. Tell me, what sort of car does he drive?"

"He's got a battered old Chevy pick-up. Sort of dark green. I've no idea what year it is, or what the license number is."

"Thanks." There was silence while Martinez wrote down the information. "Give me a call if you think of anything else that might be helpful."

Markham stared out the window for a few minutes, calming himself after the interruption, obviously pondering why Martinez was interested in Ronnie. He turned back to the piano. Not accomplished enough to play without a score, he hunted for the sheet music of a favorite Mozart sonata. When he was growing up, his step-mother insisted he learn an instrument and he'd struggled briefly with viola lessons before settling for piano. Although it had never been a central interest, he'd played through his teenage years and used music courses to fulfill humanity requirements at college. Markham had graduated in economics and business from the University of Texas in Austin. There, at a student reception for a visiting string quartet, a friend introduced him to Gwen and her fiancé. She was majoring in oboe. They talked the small talk of cocktail parties, superficially discussing their courses, their professors and their plans to change the world after graduation. Five years passed before he met her again at a dinner arranged by mutual friends in Houston. Gwen, now divorced, was working as an administrator for the local school system. The relationship blossomed and they married the following year.

Gwen continued to be involved with music and, after they'd moved to Santa Fe ten years ago, her interests gravitated towards extremely contemporary composers. Markham, however, stayed firmly grounded in the music of the eighteenth and nineteenth centuries. Their diverging musical tastes paralleled the increasing animosity in their marriage and extended to many other aspects of their deteriorating life together.

Liesl Sorenson and Zona could hear the muted sound of the piano across the courtyard, even though doors and windows were closed against the chill of a frigid winter morning.

"You hear that man? Playing his piano as though nothing happened." Liesl was eating breakfast with Zona, and drinking herbal tea as they did most mornings. And as usual, Liesl was complaining. Always irritated by Markham's playing, she constantly made snide remarks. At first, Zona had been puzzled by her antagonistic attitude, but a few months earlier Liesl explained why she reacted like this— deprived of the chance to learn piano as a child, she still resented that lost opportunity.

Liesl stared off into the distance, let conversation lapse, slouched in her chair wrapped in memories.

The foyer of the concert hall is crowded. She is holding her father's hand, proud. He is handsome. And her mother, walking with friends just a few steps behind, is so pretty. The orchestra played Strauss waltzes and she likes that music: it's so melodic. Her father calls Vienna 'cosmopolitan' and says it has many artists, musicians and architects, but she cannot grasp why he thinks Mahler is a great composer. And she does not understand why he praises Schöenberg. Maybe one day she will know. But she's old enough now to have it explained. Next week is her eighth birthday—practically grown up.

The car is taking them home through streets dark and deserted. Then there are flashing lights and a crowd yelling. Something soft splats against their rear window. The car turns abruptly, is speeding down a side street. She is flung against her mother. But a longer and safer route brings them to the house. This is the last concert she attends with her parents.

The blazing fire warms the spacious living room. She feels secure and comfortable with the thick carpets and big sofas. Hanging on the wall beside the fireplace are familiar paintings: some country scenes that she likes, others with splashes of exciting color. Her life would be perfect if she just had her own piano. Why can't she have a piano? Her mother tells her that political turmoil is getting worse. They cannot risk an expensive instrument that will mark their Jewish family as wealthy and intellectual. Her father explains that it's prudent to blend in, not attract attention. This is something she really does not understand. Anyway, her father says the problems are temporary and things will soon be normal again.

Tears well up. She dearly wants to be a famous pianist.

But music is important in her upbringing and she is encouraged to learn the flute. A flute is portable, she can take it with her if she has to move.

Her reverie ended with a start that jerked Liesl back to the present. It took her a moment to focus on Zona. "All those men in uniforms gone?"

"The police? Yeah." Zona emptied Liesl's cup, refilling it with hot tea. "After they took Dr. Kontorovich away in that ghastly, white bag, they did a bit more snooping around and then they all left."

"How did the Smyths take it?"

"Pretty much what you'd expect. Mrs. Smyth is, like, spooked by a murder happening in her home. I think Mr. Smyth is too, though he tries not to show it."

Liesl nibbled the edge of a lightly-toasted bagel spread with banana. Looking thoughtful, she took a sip of the aromatic tea. "What did the police ask you?"

"Where I was this morning. What time I left the house. That sort of thing."

"They believe you?"

"Don't see why not. I told them the truth. I'd only been shopping down on Cerrillos Road."

Liesl nodded and sipped her tea. "That nebishy young cop asked me a lot of questions about what I'd heard. He was trying to pin down the exact time of the shooting, how long I'd waited before calling 911. Wanted to know whether I'd seen a car, or a truck, or any strangers around the house. I just told him what I knew and he went away." She reached for the tea cup with her right hand, but winced and used her left. Pushing back her thin gray hair, she smiled at Zona. "I seem to have hurt my wrist. Not sure how." She declined the cold-pack Zona offered and sat chewing on her bagel, staring off into the distance, listening idly to Zona.

Liesl's living room in the adobe annex was well-proportioned with round vigas overhead, a tiled floor (partly covered with a Two-Gray-Hills Navajo rug) and small, traditional windows, their frames painted turquoise. A wide archway, with no door, led into the adjacent kitchen. Large shelves along one living room wall supported stacks of magazines, a few piles of books and two framed photographs, both of her as a young girl. The morning paper lay on a wicker coffee table. Liesl settled into her worn but accommodating armchair and brought her attention back to Zona, slouched on the sofa.

"I've been packing up the stuff Dr. Kontorovich left in the guest bedroom," she told Liesl. "Not that there was much. She seemed sort of isolated, I think. She'd moved the flowers I put there, set them off to the side. Just left a thick hardback book about paintings on the bedside table."

"I'm not surprised," Liesl said. "Typical academic. Not in touch with the real world." She slowly sipped more tea. "What about the Smyths?"

"Things have stalled a bit. The only thing Mr. Smyth had done before the tragedy was take down the Nieto that was hanging in the dining room and replace it with a couple of nudes. I think Ronnie Garcia said they were by Shale—is that right?"

"Schiele." Liesl pursed her lips, taut. "I hate his nudes. Hate them. Can't abide those emaciated figures." For a moment she sat in silence, alone with her thoughts. "It's as if he had a premonition of the fate awaiting Jews in the death camps."

Zona tried to lighten the mood. "Didn't he paint anything else?"

"Oh, yes," said Liesl. "He painted his mother—and he always showed her either blind or dead."

"His own mother?" Zona digested that. "But I suppose it's not so strange. After all, I never loved my mother. She never cared about me. Too busy with her drugs and men friends." She glanced at Liesl and smiled. "You always listen to my problems. You're such a caring person. You're more like a mother than she ever was."

This topic had never been openly discussed before. Liesl was a mother—a Jewish mother—to Zona, and dispensed advice on coping with all of life's vicissitudes.

Although a bit intimidated, Zona tried to follow her suggestions, even if she didn't always succeed. There was an awkward silence. Liesl broke it by asking, "So, how's Eddy Chavez? You seen him lately? He still working in that flagstone quarry?"

"Yeah. Not a lot of work for a stonemason this time of year, though. He's just finished a landscaping project in Albuquerque, but he's idle now. We're going to the movies tomorrow night."

Eventually Zona got up to leave. "I'm supposed to help Mrs. Smyth get the house straight. I'll come back this afternoon."

"Need your tools?" Liesl nodded toward the electrical pliers she'd left on the side table after rewiring a plug for the old toaster.

Zona dropped them in her pocket and let herself out, hustling across the bright courtyard to the main house.

Although sunny in Santa Fe, further north on the University of Northern New Mexico campus it was partly overcast and ten degrees colder. Light snow flurries blew obliquely across the plaza. Candrew, hands thrust deep into the pockets of his down jacket, the collar pulled up, walked with Rosenberg over to the president's office, talking about the department. Rosenberg appeared more friendly than usual, almost as though he wanted something. "You interested in teaching the freshman class again?" he asked.

Candrew sensed this was a loaded question. He glanced sideways at Rosenberg. "Do I have a choice?"

"Maybe not." He walked in silence for a moment. "This is a tight budget year and the legislature wants value for its dollars. To them, education is teaching."

"Meaning every prof should teach a full load?" Candrew had been through this cycle before.

"Right."

"And no credit for research that builds the university's reputation? Or for the advanced science that attracts high tech companies to New Mexico?"

"Tell that to your state representative." Rosenberg was defensive.

"So, I'll have to teach more and do less research?"

"Not certain at this point, but a definite possibility."

Candrew enjoyed describing volcanoes, mobile tectonic plates and earthquakes to the history, art and philosophy students who were forced to take a science elective and had chosen geology. At least, they could see rivers and mountains—not like the invisible force fields of physics or molecular structures of chemistry. But freshman classes took a lot of preparation and he needed as much time as he could get for his research. The thought of not being able to pioneer cutting-edge geology depressed him.

They rode the elevator to the president's top floor suite in silence.

President Burke welcomed them into his richly furnished office and shook hands. Waving them toward seats at the conference table, he strode around the office and finally stood framed by the expansive window. Ominously, his large mass seemed to dominate the university campus visible behind him.

Many different types of people become university presidents. The classic route is for an outstanding scholar to earn the respect of his peers and work his way up through the ranks to lead the academic community. This was not the track that J. Cranleigh Burke took to become president. Burke came from an affluent family and after flunking out of medieval studies at Brown, he transferred to Princeton where he'd majored in chemical engineering. But he hadn't yet found his true vocation: that discovery came with his Harvard MBA. He had reveled in the world of business and he was good at it—and it was good to him. The transition into academics was made at a small mid-western university before he became the president of UNNM.

"We are fortunate that this university has a large number of outstanding professors," the president said. "Through the teaching and research efforts of these scholars the institution has been able to build an enviable reputation. We like to reward those who have made major contributions."

Where the hell's he going with all this, Candrew wondered. *Why am I getting a lecture about the quality of the institution I've been teaching at for nearly twenty years?* He didn't wait long for an answer.

"You, Dr. Nor, are one of this university's outstanding scholars, and I am extremely pleased to tell you that you will be the recipient of the newly-endowed Waldhaven Chair." Ever the bureaucrat, he added, "This is, of course, subject to confirmation by the Board of Trustees. But they meet next week and I anticipate a routine approval."

Candrew, caught by surprise, stammered his thanks. "I'm honored. I'm . . . pleased to be chosen. Thank you."

The president strode across the thick-piled carpet, said, "Congratulations," and shook Candrew's hand in his large paw. "Dr. Rosenberg will provide all the logistical details."

Another surprise—so Rosenberg already knew about the Chair.

"In addition to a modest increase in salary, you will have significant funds to support legitimate scholarly activities. You'll be free to use this for research equipment, travel to meetings of learned societies and in other ways you choose. Expenditures will need to be approved by Dr. Rosenberg. The only bad news is that the funds will not be available to you until the new financial year, in effect, Fall semester."

The president paced up to his desk and back, then returned to his spot in front of the window. The backlighting silhouetted his large frame. "You should know that the donor, Benny Waldhaven, is an old friend of mine. Same fraternity at Princeton. He made a small fortune—actually a large fortune—in the construction industry. He's been a good supporter of the university and naturally I was delighted when he offered to endow a Chair. After considerable discussion, in which Dr. Rosenberg played a major role, it was decided that the Chair should go to the geology department, and to you."

One more surprise for Candrew. He'd not known that Nicholas Rosenberg was so impressed with his activities.

"There is one other matter that I would like you to respond to as soon as possible. Benny Waldhaven wants to meet the recipient of the Chair he's so generously funding. He lives in Denver. You should arrange to visit him as soon as you can schedule it. My secretary will give you his phone number and all the other details. I suggest sometime next week."

Candrew was well aware that a "suggestion" from the President meant *do it!* "I'll set up a visit as soon as his schedule permits," he replied.

Chapter 8

Unable to keep Helen out of his thoughts, Candrew again mulled over the few facts he knew about her death. It was devastating to hear of a faculty member being murdered. Universities seemed to offer safe havens—even if some profs abused the privilege and were hiding out from the real world. In the few murder cases he knew of, it was usually a disgruntled student having problems with peers, grades or research. The motive in Helen's case was far from obvious and the Santa Fe PD didn't have much to work with. They'd found no fingerprints and little physical evidence, just the bullet recovered from the crime scene: hopefully it would provide a lead on the type of weapon used.

Candrew pulled his attention back to the task at hand and spent the next half hour reworking lecture notes for the afternoon's sedimentary geology class. Buoyed by the previous day's news of his endowed Chair, he was in a heightened mood and the modifications went smoothly—after he'd taken twenty minutes finding last year's notes. Soon satisfied that the salient points were in order, he glanced back over the pages. It was not the details that concerned him, after years of teaching, he already had all that material at his fingertips.

No, his notes were intended as a guideline to keep him on track and on schedule, to prevent him from digressing too far into topics that fascinated him, but were of marginal relevance for his students.

But now he *was* digressing, his thoughts again drifting back to Helen. With lecture notes completed, he shoved his chair back, propping his feet on a half open desk drawer. He recalled his earlier conjecture that whoever shot Helen was much shorter than she was, he guessed she was roughly five-ten. Candrew sat tapping his teeth. And then in a flash of insight knew what to do.

He ferreted around in one of the bottom drawers of his filing cabinet where he was sure there was some graph paper, but couldn't find any. Eventually he located a pad in a pile of avalanching papers on a side table. He tore off the top sheet. On it, he drew a six inch, vertical line: one scale inch for each foot—that was close enough for Helen's height. A foot was about head size, more or less. Since there were no powder burns on Helen's body, the gun wielder must have been at least three feet away. No—the *gun* was at least three feet away. With an outstretched arm, that would move the assailant's position back another couple of feet. He drew two more lines parallel to the first, one located three inches away and the other five, corresponding to the distances of three feet and five feet. With the entrance and exit wounds differing in height by three inches, he could sketch in a line through their positions on the graph paper and extend it backwards until it intersected the line representing the position of the gun, and then measure its distance from the floor. Simple geometry. The height of the shooter logically followed: it would have to be five feet. Rather short, Candrew thought. Very short. He had enough scientific experience to appreciate all the guesses and approximations that had gone into this unsophisticated calculation. With some reasonable tweaking of his efforts, however, he still came out with a surprisingly short murderer, almost certainly less than five feet three. Would Martinez make this calculation? He made a mental note to call him.

Candrew leaned back, hands behind his head, glancing around his office. How serious was Rosenberg about making him teach freshman geology? Were those savants in the legislature serious in their demands that every prof teach a full load? Such a plan ignored other roles, like student advising, research and duties in professional societies. Certainly, he enjoyed teaching and the challenge of explaining the subtleties of earth materials and processes to non-science majors. And his enthusiasm for geology was contagious. But he needed to devote more time to producing high-quality research. There just weren't enough hours in the day to do everything. His rambling thoughts led him to Benny Waldhaven in Denver. Candrew was sure the visit would be yet another drain on his schedule, but then he could always find time for someone donating substantial sums of money, especially when he was the recipient. He anticipated a boring visit, having to explain his research in terms even a layman would understand—just like teaching geology to non-majors.

Judy Westerlund sat in front of the computer screen idly scanning the rows of numbers. Overnight the thermometer had plunged well below freezing, dragging the humidity down into the teens. Now she was applying moisturizer to the backs of her hands to combat her dry skin, when Candrew strolled into the lab. He'd taken the stairs from his office to the basement and used the time to adjust his mindset, making the transition from his role as teacher to a role as research scientist.

Judy pointed to the new mineralogical data on the screen and then brought him up to date with a quick summary of everything she'd achieved. She also explained how she'd selected most of the samples for analysis with the electron microprobe. "I had a long discussion with Dr. Kernfeld but he won't be able to get to our samples for at least a week." She paused and nudged up her glasses. "You still want to analyze just half-dozen major elements?"

"Yeah. That'll be enough to start with."

After thirty minutes working through the information on the remaining rock samples, Candrew peered at his watch, explained he had a meeting with the college dean, and left.

Dean Hunter O'Neil's spacious suite was on the first floor of the building adjacent to Kinblade Hall and incorporated his office, associated rooms for student advising, records and a reception area. Candrew was kept waiting there for ten minutes before the efficient, but humorless, secretary ushered him into the dean's office.

Insincerely, Hunter O'Neil apologized for the delay, gestured imperiously. "Have a seat."

The dean was a marshmallow: soft, white, unmuscled. Just what would be expected from someone who ran his fiefdom from a padded, swivel armchair. Now he swung that chair partway around to face Candrew and tented his flaccid fingers. "Congratulation on your Endowed Professorship. Most deserved. It's always good to see productive faculty recognized and rewarded. I was happy to help, put in my two cents worth."

Candrew expressed his appreciation, thinking that this was not the reason the dean wanted to see him. Surely, this wasn't about an increased teaching load. He glanced at the corpulent blob overflowing the constraints of the chair's padded arms. It reminded him of a mounded stalagmite. He couldn't resist glancing up to see if a matching, pointed stalactite hung from the ceiling.

The dean stared across at the window as if organizing his thoughts. "Rosenberg tells me you're good friends with Markham Smyth down in Santa Fe. As I'm sure you're aware, he and his wife have been generous supporters of the university's art school for many years. The president has decided to approach him and see if perhaps he'd consider donating a few of his newly-acquired paintings to the university. An alternative possibility is that we could display them on permanent loan." He flexed his fingers, probably the only exercise he'd get today.

"Anyway, we're planning a dinner for him and his wife at the president's home. Wondered whether you'd be able to come. The date's not been finalized. With the unfortunate death of our art historian, we've had to move it back, so it'll probably be in a couple of weeks. And of course, we'd be pleased to have you bring a guest."

Candrew was pleasantly surprised. "I know Markham Smyth, but wouldn't claim to be a close friend, certainly not in any position to persuade him to make valuable donations to the university."

"I'm sure our president will tactfully broach that subject himself," the dean said. "No, we're just trying to arrange a pleasant evening, sort of get the ball rolling."

"Then I'd be pleased to come."

The snow-capped mountains and distant pines drifted in and out of view as low, scattered clouds followed the wind eastward. Framed by a large plate glass window, the vista formed a backdrop to the group eating lunch in the faculty lounge and, as usual, engaged in animated discussion. Candrew had been talking to a balding, overweight professor on his right, and in answer to his questions explained the current research project with Judy. He ended by saying, "... and with the comprehensive suite of rock samples we've put together, the data is great."

Lubie overheard and assumed his mock serious expression. " 'The data *is* great'? In your world, 'data' is singular?"

"A slip of the tongue." Candrew felt like a schoolboy caught cheating.

"English plurals. What a can of worms." Lubie had grown up in Poland with English a second language. His favorite sport was teasing English speakers about their language's inconsistencies and idiosyncrasies. "Why *toothbrush* and not *teethbrush*? You don't clean just one tooth. And why is *bra* singular and *panties* plural?"

Someone broke in, "For the same reason *trousers* is plural."

"Ah, but that makes sense. A one-legged man could wear just half a pair."

Arlan Dee was not convinced. "But that doesn't explain why *scissors* is plural. You can't cut anything with half a pair of scissors."

There was no come back. The subject seemed to have run its course.

Ted Devereaux from the Business Office turned to Charlie Lister and asked, "How's the faculty taking the murder of your art historian?"

"What a nasty shock. Helen Kontorovich wasn't popular, but I don't think anyone would have gone as far as killing her." He glanced away, watched the clouds skim the mountains for a moment, reorienting his thoughts. Charlie had been in the Art School for twenty years and had been on the faculty committee that hired Kontorovich. He said he'd never regretted it. As the only one who'd known her well, at least as well as anyone could, he fielded questions from around the table and told the group a bit about her. "She had an international reputation in her field, well respected by her peers. Her specialty was European art prior to World War II. One of those 'niche-fillers' that gives a department character." He elaborated, explaining that she seemed to have been a loner with no close friends, as far as he knew. If there was a boyfriend, she hadn't brought him to any departmental or faculty functions. And she was often back east acting as an expert witness or giving her professional opinion on art works coming up for auction. "That's pretty well paid, and she wasn't short of money. But robbery doesn't seem to have been the reason she was killed."

Candrew's upbeat mood was tempered by the issues surrounding Kontorovich's death. He sat sipping his coffee in silence and finally left. On the walk back to Kinblade Hall he couldn't think of any reason why someone would want to murder her. But then he didn't know her well, and realized he knew nothing of her private life.

When Candrew turned down the hallway to his office, he was surprised to see someone waiting outside the door. She didn't look like a student, and, although vaguely familiar, he couldn't immediately place her. Petite and fit-looking, her long blonde hair was loosely caught up under the band of a wide visor and she wore jeans, a patterned cotton bandana round her neck and a floral overshirt. No makeup. The overall impression was of a sixties hippie.

"Can I talk to you a minute?" She stepped towards Candrew and held out her hand, obviously trying to do everything properly. "I'm Zona Pharn. We talked a little bit when you were visiting Mr. Smyth's house, you remember, after that art woman got . . . murdered?" She paused as if to let Candrew figure out who she was. "You seemed to know a lot about rocks." Unsure of herself, she added, "And nice, really nice."

Now Candrew could put her in context. It was the woman he'd talked to in Markham Smyth's garage. The one he'd seen out in the snow replacing the flowers on the dog's grave, if that was what she'd really been doing.

"I came to ask you some questions. Is that all right?"

Candrew unlocked his office door and ushered her in.

Zona gushed on, conveying the impression that she wanted to get the information from Candrew before he changed his mind. "You said you study rocks and things. I brought some crystals."

People often brought crystals—as well as rocks, fossils and meteorites—to the department for identification. So that was not unusual.

But Zona didn't ask for identification. She held a large quartz crystal pointing the end with a complete set of crystal faces toward him. "Here, take this quartz and . . ."

"Look, I don't know what . . ."

"No, no. Go on. Hold it with two fingers and make an energy

ring." She gripped the middle of the big quartz crystal between her thumb and first finger. "Like this." Zona held it out for Candrew who reluctantly accepted it.

"Now point it at your chest, your heart."

Even more reluctantly, he followed that instruction.

"Wow." She scrutinized him. "Awesome. I've never seen an aura that strong. You just sort of, like, lit up." Staring at him, impressed, she said, "That means you're strongly linked into the power of the cosmos. I hesitated to come bother you. But now I know I can trust you."

Candrew had been unaware of his supersized aura and had no idea he was so well connected to the universe.

Before he had a chance to comment, Zona said, "I'm very friendly with a man called Eddy." She hesitated, glanced around his office as if unsure whether to go on. "He works in a quarry. That's close to the Earth. He's, sort of, using natural materials. What I wanted to ask you is whether digging out all that rock, like, disturbs the world's balance?"

"No, not really. The total weight that gets moved is pretty small compared with the whole Earth. And it's not being moved very far from where it was quarried, just a few miles. No, I don't think it would make any difference at all."

"How about explosives?"

Candrew was taken by surprise. "Sorry?"

"How about when Eddy uses dynamite to blast out the rocks? Does that, like, damage the Earth? Could it change its balance?"

"There's been plenty of blasting over the years, of course, especially if you include all the explosives used in wars. They don't seem to have caused any major, long term harm."

"Not all those monstrous hurricanes?"

Candrew wondered where this conversation was leading and glanced at his watch. There was a long list of things he needed to do, but he answered civilly. "I think you'll find the intensity of big storms is within statistical variations."

Clearly, Zona was uncertain what "statistical variations" were, but said, "Well, I'm glad to hear that." She brushed some straggling hair back under her visor. "Very glad to hear that." After hesitating a moment, she said, "I really like Eddy a lot and I'm sure Liesl's wrong when she tells me he's not the right guy for me."

Candrew hadn't remembered the name, but assumed Liesl was the old woman, the retired housekeeper, who lived across the courtyard in Markham Smyth's annex.

Zona glanced around the office and seemed intimidated by the piles of paper and the ceiling-high bookcases stacked with rows of publications. "I've always tried to do what Liesl tells me. She's such a lot older. And has lots of experience. She can be such a comfort when things are difficult. Sympathetic." For a moment Zona stared out of the window. "It'd be a shame to waste all that wisdom about life."

Candrew wasn't sure why he was being told all this and didn't know what to say. He snuck a peek at his watch. "So you always do what Liesl suggests?"

"Try to. But she's getting forgetful. Often gives me, sort of, conflicting advice about what things to do. Says one thing in the morning, then right the opposite in the afternoon."

"But I thought you worked for the Smyths and Liesl was retired?"

"Yeah. In the house I do what Mrs. Smyth tells me. And that's another thing. Recently Liesl has gotten sort of antagonistic to the Smyths. She used to be so loyal to Mr. Smyth, he couldn't do a thing wrong. Now she hardly has a good word to say about him." Zona rocked her head from side to side as if to imply that this change in attitude was really weird. "But she hasn't changed towards me. She really cares. She's always trying to help me. I can trust her."

Candrew's increasing impatience showed. He got a bit testy. "So, what else do you need from me?"

There was a long pause. "Now that I know you understand, that you're sympathetic, I have to tell you something before I leave." She hesitated, inspecting her shoes. "I told the police that on the morning that woman was murdered I'd gone shopping on Cerrillos. That's not the whole truth. I didn't go to *Friends of the Planet*, I went to the rabbi to get some things for Liesl, and I also went to *Home Depot.*" Another hesitation. "You're so closely involved with the Earth and the cosmos, I couldn't have you believing a lie." She affected a shy smile. "I ought to go."

As she left, Candrew thought "odd woman." And the last person to see Helen Kontorovich alive—apart from the killer, of course. A killer who was not much over five feet tall, if he could believe his calculations. But then, Zona wasn't very tall. He rustled through the papers on his desk, finally found Martinez's card, and phoned him.

"What bullshit is that? You telling me you can draw a couple of lines on a piece of paper and know how tall the perp was?" Martinez was dismissive. He seemed to resent a geology professor doing police work, especially since he hadn't thought of it himself.

"That's the way geometry works." Candrew was defensive. "There weren't any powder burns, so the gunman must have been more than three feet away. And she was shot square on—so no attempt at defense or a struggle."

"Probably got that right." He heard Martinez sigh. "Our crime scene techs did a pretty good job with the blood spatter. Runs straight down the wall. Means the victim wasn't moving, no attempt at flight. Suggests she knew the killer. But figuring out he was roughly five feet tall? Hell, that seems like mumbo-jumbo to me."

Chapter 9

Leonardo da Vinci designed the first helicopter; performed detailed autopsies; painted the *Mona Lisa* and *The Last Supper*. Candrew lacked any artistic talent and regretted he was nowhere near Leonardo's class as a scientist. But he did share one thing with the renaissance genius—both were inveterate list makers. Candrew scribbled his on three-by-five cards and propped them against the end volume in the book shelf, though it wasn't unusual for the card to get lost in one of his disorganized paper piles. Items added to the list normally kept pace with deletions, the list never getting any shorter, but the crossed-out topics gave him a sense of progress. Now heading the list was a reminder to confirm the schedule for his visit to Benny Waldhaven in Denver and make flight reservations. But Candrew didn't do that, he phoned Charlie Lister.

Candrew probed to see if Charlie knew more about Helen Kontorovich, if he could add anything else to the comments made in the faculty lounge. "What about close friends in the department? People she ate lunch with, that sort of thing?"

"No one I know of. As I said, Helen was pretty solitary, a loner."

"How about graduate students? She have a lot?"

"That I don't know, but let me give our secretary, Brenda, a call and check it out. She's always tuned in to what's goings on. Usually the best source of information, especially gossip."

Candrew sat tapping his front teeth, perplexed. A direct approach seemed best. Rather than waiting for the phone call, he grabbed his jacket and walked briskly over to the School of Art, crossing a campus almost deserted on the cold, blustery Friday afternoon.

Brenda was short and stocky with spiked blonde hair, a round face and a silver stud in her nose. She was filing manila folders. Candrew explained that Charlie Lister had suggested he ask her about Dr. Kontorovich.

"Why would anyone want to shoot her? What a shock." She shook her head and stared past Candrew into the distance.

"True. I was a friend—acquaintance really—and wanted to find out a bit more about her." Candrew had already looked up Helen's address in the campus directory and made a mental note to drive by her house. It seemed to be in the nicer part of town. "What sort of car did she drive?"

Brenda smiled. "One that made all the students—male students—envious. Some fancy sports car. Personally, with our winter weather and the roads around here, I'd rather have a four-wheel drive. One of those SUVs. Anyway, I'll find out what type she drove."

"What about graduate students? A lot working with her?"

"Very few. Right now I think Molly Stein is the only one. I can check real easy." She turned away and a few moments searching produced a file with the information. "Yeah. Her other two students graduated last summer. You want their names?"

Candrew said he did, and she wrote them down.

"Nice girl, Molly. Works hard." She glanced at her huge, black-faced watch. "The students usually get together for a beer about this time on Fridays. In the sculpture studio. Not strictly legal, but the director turns a blind eye." She gave a knowing wink. "I'm sure Molly's there."

Candrew followed Brenda's instructions and at the end of the hall cautiously opened the door into an expansive, high-ceilinged work room. The far wall was lined with lathes, band saws and welding equipment and looked more like a machine shop than Candrew expected for a sculpture studio. A variety of peculiar plaster shapes, apparently unfinished student projects, occupied most of the central space. Two battered sofas had been pushed up against the side wall and chairs of many vintages were scattered around, half occupied by students. In front of them, a piece of sculpture with a conveniently flat top supported a tray of dips, chips and brownies—and several empty beer cans. The full cans were in the cooler.

Candrew felt an intruder, out of place. "Your department secretary said I might find Molly Stein here."

A heavy set student with a shaved head and tie-dyed shirt threw up his hands. "She didn't do it, officer. Honestly. The still was there when she rented the apartment."

"Oh, shush." A sandy-haired girl in a thigh-length sweater put her hand over his mouth, laughing. "I'm Molly. What d'you need?"

"Well, first, to let you know I'm not a cop." He glanced around, smiling, trying to reassure them. He turned back to Molly. "I was told you were Helen Kontorovich's student." The mood in the room abruptly chilled. "Can we talk?"

"About what?" She stood rigidly, eyeing him suspiciously. "Who are you, anyway?"

"I'm a faculty member. In geology." Candrew glanced around the silent group of students. "Her death was quite a shock. I knew her, but not well, and I'm just trying to find out a bit more about her as a person. What she was like."

"Well, I guess that's okay." Reluctantly she got up, parked her beer can on the chair and took a couple of chips. "Let's go to the slide library. It's quiet there."

Molly led him through the labyrinthine passageways of the art school, most of the wall space covered with student work, though there were a couple of posters from recent international art shows. All available alcove space was filled with sculptures in every medium from rolled newspaper to stainless steel.

She unlocked the door labeled *Slide Room* and led him in. "Bit of a misnomer, really. The profs don't use slides anymore, they've all gone over to PowerPoint. But Dr. Kontorovich insisted we store the slides so we've got back-ups."

"And she did all this work?" Candrew asked.

"You're kidding?" Molly laughed. "She supervised, but I did everything."

There was a lull and Candrew asked, "What's the topic for your thesis?"

"I'm sure you know Dr. Kontorovich specialized in early twentieth-century art, focused on western Europe. Had a really great reputation. She wanted me to, like, work on the roots of European expressionism." Molly paused for a moment, then continued. "Well, I didn't want to do that. I was more interested in art from this area. Folk art, really. At first, she was totally reluctant to take me on. Later she changed her mind, probably departmental politics, I guess. At least, she got a role in the graduate program—and a slave to run the slide library."

"So, what did you end up researching?"

"Tinwork." She glanced at Candrew as if trying to evaluate his level of interest. "It was a traditional craft in northern New Mexico after the mid-1800s. They salvaged lard and kerosene tin containers. *Tin* is really a soft iron sheet that's been coated with a very thin layer of tin metal." She bubbled with enthusiasm. "Local craftsmen made candle holders and frames for religious prints.

There's still a lot in the churches around here, as well as in traditional homes."

Candrew had seen tin art in the tourist shops. Now it was sold mainly for photo frames and mirrors. He asked Molly about that.

"The original craft died out. Then it got revived after about 1915. It's still going."

"What did Kontorovich think about this?"

"She actually got quite interested in the patterns, the way repeated shapes were stamped into the tin."

Like most graduate students, Molly was engrossed in her thesis project. Candrew knew she would be happy to discuss tinwork in detail for hours. He changed the subject. "Did you see much of Dr. Kontorovich socially?"

"No way." Molly shook her head, smiling. "I don't think she even had a social life."

"What was her office like? Anything unusual?"

"Not really. Lots of books and papers stacked everywhere. Typical art historian. I could have shown you, but the police took my key away. She never minded if I used her books." Molly bit her lower lip and stared into the distance. "She had a signed photo of herself with Andy Warhol. And she framed it in tin from a local craft store." This information was relayed in a tone suggesting that Molly took it as a validation of her thesis topic.

"Did you ever go to her home?"

"No."

"Anything else you can think of?"

"No. Not really." Molly fiddled with a stack of slides for a moment. "She was going to be away next week. Don't know where she was going."

"What about her car? What did she drive?"

"A BMW sports car. Z4. Red."

Not bad on an art professor's salary. He got up and thanked her for taking time away from her friends. "I'll let you get back to preparing for the weekend with the rest of the students." They both grinned.

Candrew returned to Kinblade Hall thinking about the new information on Kontorovich, not that there was much. He mulled over the news that she was going to be out of town. That's something he ought to check up on. More expert witness work? Maybe Brenda would know?

Distracted, he sauntered down the familiar corridor and didn't notice the small package lying on the floor outside his office until he was unlocking the door. He picked up the thick, white, mailing-envelope with its bulky contents. It was folded in half, scotch-taped and addressed to *Professor Candrew Nor* in expert calligraphy. He stepped into his office but couldn't find his metal letter opener and used a pair of scissors to slit open the package. Inside there was no letter, just a bulky black, plastic box roughly five by seven, half an inch thick. Curious, he turned it over—an eight-track tape. He hadn't seen one of those old Stereo-8 formats for years. Why would anyone leave him an outmoded tape—and, more important, what was on it? Probably some grad student trying to convince him he should listen to the current fad rock group. But that didn't make sense, they always had sophisticated electronic gear, not something thirty years out of date.

It slowly dawned on Candrew that he had no way of actually playing it. Like almost everyone else, he listened to CDs not tapes and although his Jeep Cherokee had a tape-unit it wouldn't handle this ancient format. There must be someone in the department with an old tape player. He dropped the cassette into his jacket pocket and took the elevator down to the basement lab.

Judy was in her office, a glassed alcove off to the side of the main work room. She took one look at the tape and laughed. "What you need is an antique store. Nobody's used those things for years."

She flipped it over and looked at the back. It was blank. "What's so important about this one?"

"I have no idea. Someone left it outside my office door."

"Sort of like an abandoned orphan on your doorstep? Well, I'll bet you a dollar it's not one of the grad students. None of them would be seen dead with this Neanderthal technology." She ran her hand back through her hair, paused, thinking. "Try Dr. Kernfeld. He's a packrat. I don't think they ever throw anything away in his lab. Maybe he's still got one of the old decks lying around."

"Worth a try." Candrew picked up the phone and dialed Mark Kernfeld. The research associate who answered vaguely remembered that people had used tapes like that years ago. "But I've never seen one around here. Maybe we've got one in storage. Could've been used for data backup. I'll check." Candrew thanked him, put down the phone, and then on impulse called Renata. There was no answer, he left a message.

A hundred miles south of the university, and southwest of Santa Fe, the quiet of the late winter afternoon was shattered by the roar of twin jet engines as the Citation Sovereign descended through the scattered clouds, rolled along the runway and parked in general aviation. The plane had been chartered by Max Reinhardt. In the lushly appointed cabin, he and his wife Lucinda were donning coats and helping their two guests, Paolo and Carla. The Reinhardts' daughter, Betina, was also on the flight. Max leaned into the cockpit, telling the pilot to contact ground control and have his car sent out.

As they made their way down the steps to the tarmac, Carla quietly said to Max, "You've got a charming daughter."

"Yeah. And bright too." Betina worked for a Los Angeles law firm, but Max admitted that he felt vaguely insulted by this. He was rich enough that any daughter of his should not have to work, just get married to some good-looking, wealthy guy and produce grandkids. She'd wasted her time at Berkeley. While she did get a biochemistry degree with straight A's and finished near the top of her class in law school, Max was disappointed that there was no sign of a likely husband, and she was now nearly thirty-five.

Betina was in Santa Fe for a week's skiing, but Max and Lucinda only planned to stay long enough to attend Paolo's concert. The Hummer arrived promptly and Max opened the back doors, showing the helpers where to stack the travel bags. Dressed in a full-length, dark vicuna coat, leather gloves and short scarf, he looked too corporate for Santa Fe. But then, this was just a flying visit—literally.

Max tipped the young man loading their luggage and hustled "the girls" into the car. Paolo closed the car doors with a flourish and was about to get in himself when he said, feigning surprise, "Look, my friend, you have a UFO nesting on your roof." He spoke with a pronounced Italian accent. With his forefinger out, like a pistol, he pointed at the circular disk mounted on Max's silver Hummer.

"Satellite TV. Can get 140 channels with that baby."

"That's just fine if you've got 140 pairs of eyes—or 141. You'll need to keep a couple on the road."

"It's there for safety."

"You're kidding me, my friend."

"All the passengers watch TV and don't talk to me. I just concentrate on driving."

Max and Lucie, as she was always known, owned a second home at Las Campanas, the gated community west of Santa Fe, and used it whenever they came to ski in the winter, attend the opera in the summer, or to play golf. Empty most of the time, they arranged with a local service to have it ready for their infrequent visits. The sun had just dropped below the western hills, leaving a bright orange band that shaded across the sky to a deep purple-blue as they pulled into a flagstone courtyard ringed with piñons. With all the lights on, the house looked warm and welcoming. They had only forty-five minutes for a quick cocktail before heading back into town for dinner.

Sena Plaza was bitterly cold and deserted, but managed to appear cheerful with lights strung among the trees. The visitors to Santa Fe were glad to get to the warmth of the piñon fire in the restaurant and join Peter and Anna Meagher at their corner table.

Peter shook Paolo's hand. "So, itinerant maestro, what have you been up to?"

"Practice, my friend, practice." He held out his hands and rippled his fingers. "One day without practicing and I can tell the difference. Two days and the critics can tell. And after three days the audience knows too." He pulled a somber face that implied *disaster*. "Rubinstein said that, and I wholeheartedly concur."

"Did Rubinstein say you could have a drink the night before your performance?"

"Of course." He grinned and pushed back his lush hair. "Like so many of my fellow Italians, we were prisoners of the Catholic church for two thousand years. But I escaped." He flashed his grin again. "No more need to go to confession." Even a simple statement like that couldn't be uttered without copious hand gestures. "I was reading about Santa Fe and your patron saint, Saint Francis of Assisi. His life as a young man was all wine and women. I admire that. Just like me."

Paolo laughed and Peter called the waiter.

The Meaghers and Reinhardts were old friends and the dinner was convivial. The casual banter avoided serious topics and they skirted politics and business. When the men finished dessert, which the women had declined, Max suggested everyone go back for a nightcap.

After the long drive, Max ushered them all into the house and guided Peter and Paolo through to the media room. There he turned on the oversized television, changed the channel to the basketball game and headed for the conveniently located bar. Paolo, although not a basketball fan, he'd rather support soccer, was content to watch other people exerting themselves, sip his drink and savor the excellent dinner.

Betina retired to her bedroom to check e-mails in peace, leaving Lucie, Carla and Anna to settle into the living room. A large space with tiled floor, adobe walls and square vigas, the southwestern architecture nicely complemented the ultramodern furnishings. Anna slumped into the white contemporary sofa, putting her drink on an adjacent circular glass table, while Carla and Lucie lounged in black leather Corbusier cube chairs. It was not long before their gossip got round to the Smyths.

"I heard the terrible news about that art expert being murdered in Gwen's home," Lucie said. "I'd find it spooky to keep living in a house where someone died. And died violently."

"She's upset for sure, but seems to be coping. Puts a brave face on it."

"Do they have any idea who'd do a thing like that? Or why she was killed?" Lucie asked.

"No. The police don't seem to have any suspects and, as far as I know, haven't established a motive. At least, they're not saying anything. Quite a mystery."

Carla was an outsider and hadn't heard about the murder. "What was the woman doing in their house?"

Anna outlined what she'd learnt about Markham's inherited collection. "My understanding is that the paintings are mostly pre-war European. Apparently there are some really great pieces. The ones I saw included at least two Klimts. At least that's what I think they were." She laughed. "Should have paid more attention in my art history classes."

"A collection like that must be worth a fortune," Carla said.

"Right. And the rumors are that Markham's brother thinks he should get part of it. He's an attorney in Philadelphia." Anna smiled. "The city of brotherly love."

Lucie was curious. "Have you ever met his brother?"

"No. I've heard he can be unpleasant, quite irritating. Gwen's only met him a couple of times, but that was enough. She can't stand him."

"Well she's certainly had her troubles in the last few weeks, what with the dog and all."

"What happened to the dog?" Carla wanted to know. When Anna filled in the details, Carla was horrified. "I can't believe anyone would kill a dog—and then mail it to the owners? That's weird."

"Another mystery. Another crime without an obvious motive."

"Where's the powder room?" Carla asked.

Anna gave directions and Carla disappeared down the passage. With her exquisitely-manicured fingers caressing the long stem of the wine glass, Anna swirled the pale blonde liquid and leered at the men watching March Madness basketball in the media alcove off to the side. "I could go for him."

It was obvious to Lucie who she was talking about. "Too late, honey. Gwen's got Paolo all tied up." She winked.

"Literally?" Anna asked, keeping a straight face.

"You've got a kinky mind!"

They both laughed.

Chapter 10

Liesl Sorenson, exhausted, slumped into the armchair, flopped her head back on the cushion, sighing loudly.

"You okay?" Zona asked.

"I'm fine, just worn out. Getting too old for this sort of thing."

Liesl had insisted Zona take her to one of the electrical suppliers and afterwards they had spent the afternoon meandering through a couple of department stores and the adjacent mall. There, on the wintry Saturday afternoon, teenagers had been hanging out in raucous groups, while younger kids were being dragged around by their parents.

Now Liesl, sprawling in her well-used chair, glanced around the familiar surroundings. "American kids . . . they have so much— and don't appreciate what they've got."

A scared eight year old, she is clinging to her mother, crying. The train makes a noise that frightens her. Mother holds her close, crying herself, while father is trying to reassure them both. A consoling, older man offers his hand and leads her to a small group of waiting children and together they board the train. They are leaving Vienna; leaving Austria. She does not understand why her parents aren't coming. They say it's best for her. How can that be? All she has is one small suitcase that she can hardly lift. In it is the black leather valise from her father—special, he says. And she clutches a passport stamped with a bold 'J', blood red, virulent.

She sees little of the countryside as the train wends its halting journey to Switzerland and what she does see is through tear-filled eyes. At the railway station, a caring Jewish rabbi meets the children and guides them safely onto the train for Portugal. There, in Lisbon harbor, she has to give half her money to the Catholic priest who takes her to board the ship for Toronto.

A lonely, miserable, seasick week is over. She stands alone in the dank room at the docks, the marine odors of rope and seaweed so different from those of landlocked Austria. She thinks of the sachertorte she adored and the aroma of her father's schlagobers, the strong black coffee topped with whipped cream. Unable to stifle sobs, she greets Hella and her husband: strangers.

Hella, kindly but aloof, is a distant relative and the young girl endures life in the couple's small, wood-framed house, so very different from her expansive Vienna home permeated with music and hung with modern paintings. She lives for news from her parents. The first letters are optimistic, her father explaining away the dire Austrian situation as politicking that will soon end. She waits impatiently for each piece of mail, but correspondence becomes less frequent, often arriving through her father's friends. Then it stops abruptly. She never again hears from her parents.

Zona watched Liesl doze, raised herself quietly from the chair and noiselessly made her way to the door.

But Liesl wasn't sleeping. "Make some tea before you go, will you? It won't take a minute." She sucked in a slow, labored breath and with the back of her hand brushed away a tear. "I know you're supposed to help Mrs. Smyth with the concert reception, but there's plenty of time."

"Yeah. I'll make us tea." Zona flicked the switch on the kettle, happy to help with Liesl's perceived tiredness, not realizing the intensity of her pervading sadness.

They sipped tea and talked until Zona ran out of time and had to leave. Liesl settled back into her armchair.

The art teacher is standing beside her at the easel when the message comes: school is dismissed, the war in Europe has ended. Her first thought is that she will see her parents again. She lives in hope. A month later, Aunt Hella dies unexpectedly, her uncle isn't able to cope and she will be going to other distant relatives, the Sorensons, who live in the garment district of New York City. America. She is fifteen and losing identity, like an ice sculpture melting; she becomes Liesl Sorenson.

Teenage independence grows. With others her age, she ventures out of the neighborhood. It is summer, and a frequent destination is Coney Island where other children, just like her, play on the sand. Then she goes to a private beach—but the freshly-painted sign is adamant: "No dogs. No Jews." She is overwhelmed by the full implications of being a Jew. There is no thought of disobeying and none of her friends suggest it. She knows well the sense of community, of belonging, surrounded by other Jews and protected. Now, the encumbrance of

Jewishness is clear. "No dogs. No Jews."

The double chimes echoed through Renata's house and Candrew stood at the front door, waiting. He was only five minutes late. By Renata's expectations, that's unprecedented. She'd inherited her Guatemalan mother's laid-back social standards and arriving within the hour was generally good enough. But it was cold outside and Candrew wished she'd answer the door. Impatiently, he rang again and this time Renata hurried to let him in. "I'll only be a couple of minutes. Make yourself at home." She left him in the living room. With an oriental rug, European furniture and modern central-American paintings, there was no pretense at "Santa Fe style".

He sank into the overstuffed lounge chair, thinking about the concert they were going to. Paolo Magnelli, a rising star, was well-known for his interpretations of atonal, contemporary piano music. A bit avant-garde for Candrew's taste, although he was open-minded. He certainly looked forward to meeting Magnelli at the reception afterwards. Performing artists, as well as visual artists, were stimulating and he found that generally their behavior, as well as their perspective on life, was quite different from his. Candrew had developed a familiarity with scientists as a subspecies: he knew them too well, even their eccentricities were predictable. Businessmen, like the Smyths and the Meaghers, were a contrasting group, rich enough they no longer had to work and with enough money to do anything they wanted. How would he spend his time if he didn't have to make a living? That was an academic question, since he enjoyed his research—and his teaching—not really considering either of them work. But he would sure like to get out of all those committee meetings. His inner groans at the thought of starting next Monday with an early morning faculty meeting were interrupted by Renata. She sauntered in with her hands behind her back.

"Sorry to make you wait."

"Not a problem."

"I've brought you a surprise." She held out a black box about eight inches long. At first, Candrew didn't recognize it, then realized it was an old 8-track tape player. "You got the tape with you?"

"It's out in the car." Candrew helped her with her coat and they set out on the drive down to the concert in Santa Fe.

Renata had replaced the dead batteries in the ancient unit and now it seemed to be working just fine. But there was only a hiss on the tape. While Candrew negotiated the evening traffic, Renata rewound the tape to the beginning and tried again.

"A message . . . from the City of Holy Faith". The tape hissed quietly for a moment. *"And from St. Francis. He won't let you forget man's best friend. Man's best friend."* The second repetition of the word *man's* was heavily inflected making it into a question: *"man's? best friend."*

A lengthy silence followed with a few, almost inaudible, background sounds. Then the voice was back. *"Frame your point of view and search for knowledge. Know that a little knowledge is a dangerous thing. But so is too much, and then not even a thousand ships can save you."*

Neither Candrew nor Renata recognized the male voice. They played the tape again. Certain lilting inflections made Candrew think it was probably Hispanic, though he couldn't be sure.

"Odd message. And not very long. What do you think it means?" Renata asked.

"It's clearly from Santa Fe, since that's the City of Holy Faith. And St. Francis fits in: he's the city's patron saint."

"Yeah. And it's Saint Francis of Assisi, which links to *man's best friend.*"

"Except that it's been made into a question, almost as if it should be 'woman's best friend'—a woman's dog." As Candrew said the words he immediately recognized their significance. "Could it be Gwen Smyth's dog?"

Renata was nodding. "That's exactly what occurred to me. But what's all that about a thousand ships?" She tapped her fingers on the shell of the tape recorder, her lips pursed. "Remind me, who was the face that launched a thousand ships?"

"Helen of Troy," Candrew said. "Helen!" The car swerved slightly as his attention to driving lapsed for a moment. "This is about Helen Kontorovich."

"Yeah. And the comment on *'framing* your point of view' would seem to confirm that."

"So, whoever sent the tape is commenting on a murder. That gives it a whole new significance."

Candrew tried to remain focused on Paolo's playing, but found it difficult to concentrate on the unfamiliar, atonal works. Somehow, the Lensic Theater seemed inappropriate as a venue for such an ultramodern performance. The muted colors and psuedo-Moorish designs were not contemporary enough. The audience in the Lensic, however, was enthusiastic, standing to give Paolo Magnelli sustained applause. Unlike the famed Canadian pianist, Glenn Gould, who gave no public recitals for the last eighteen years of his short life, Paolo thrived on audience acclaim. He found Gould's remark that "the ideal artist-to-audience relationship was one-to-zero," incomprehensible. Paolo lived for applause. Gould had also claimed that onstage he felt like a vaudevillian—but that's exactly what Paolo was. He bowed several times to the appreciative throng, then acquiesced to their obligatory demands by playing a short encore. Both the audience and Paolo considered the concert a success.

Paolo was high on acclaim and the reception at the

Meagher's house was just another chance to continue performing, merely another audience to entertain. Gwen piloted him around and stood basking in reflected glory.

Slightly above medium height, Paolo had coarse, silver-gray hair that was shaggy over his ears and brushed the collar of his jacket. There was a hint of stubble around his large mobile mouth, a somewhat coarse feature that with constant motion didn't show. "It would have been fun to play Sorabji's *Opus Clavicembalisticum*. It only takes four hours." He gave a mischievous grin. "What I really wanted to play was his *Symphonic Variations* which takes six hours." He glanced at Gwen. "Maybe next time you invite me to perform in Santa Fe?"

She smiled as if to imply, *anything you want Paolo*.

"That piece takes the soul of an artist and the body of an athlete—and musical skill *par excellence*." He was clearly implying that he possessed all these characteristics. "But even I have to admit, my friends, that I am not up to playing Jarvinen's *Serious Immobilities*." He surveyed the group, none of them showing a flicker of recognition. "The 840 variations on Erik Satie's *Vexations* takes 24 hours to complete." Laughing, he raked his fingers through his unruly, pewter hair.

The enthralled, and entirely female, group broke up and Gwen went to check on Zona. She'd volunteered her help with the reception at the Meaghers. Everything seemed to be under control.

As Zona was putting a tray on the side table, an arm reached around and deftly removed one of the small pastries. She wheeled, not knowing this was Paolo Magnelli, the main attraction of the night's social gathering. Paolo moved the tip of his tongue across his upper lip and ran his eyes over her, as if comparing her to some personal standard of female adequacy. Zona seemed to meet his criteria. "Ah! If only I was young and single," he said, leering. Then, brushing back his shaggy hair, he turned his charming smile up to full volume. "At least, I'm young at heart."

There was a flicker of recognition as Zona realized who he was. She had heard the rumors and knew his reputation. "And are you single at heart?"

"Woman is monogamous, man is polygamous." Again, the disarming smile and the gesturing hands.

"In your dreams," Zona muttered under her breath before beating a retreat to the kitchen.

Paolo was not left alone for long. Gwen was beckoning from across the room. At ease in this company, her carefully-chosen designer dress complemented stunning good looks and elegantly-styled chestnut-brown hair. "Don't hide away, you're the star of the party, dahling. Come meet these nice people."

Paolo, clearly happy to be back in the center of a group, especially one made up mostly of women, greeted each with a Latin kiss on the hand.

"Doesn't he play the most amazing music? Tell them about Gravini's new piece." Gwen smiled at him, but left no time for a reply before continuing. "Gravini wrote it especially for Paolo. And he's going to play it in Cleveland next Sunday." She beamed at the group. "I'm always delighted when I can bring top quality, contemporary music to the Lensic." She made it sound as though she was solely responsible for much of the new performing arts in Santa Fe.

Candrew swirled the chilled white wine in his glass, sniffed the bouquet and surveyed the gossiping groups of guests. Markham Smyth and Max Reinhardt were bulky, conservatively-dressed men, almost caricatures of top executives. Both had built huge conglomerates that dominated their respective markets, but responded to changes in the market place with inertia and glacial slowness. If they had been the dinosaurs of the business world, Peter Meagher was one of the mammals who moved in when dinosaurs went extinct. Athletic, lithe and quick, he moved with the speed of electrons and had harnessed the Internet to build his wealth. He thrived on information transfer. He'd embraced the NASA mantra: *better, faster, cheaper*—although, if you'd asked Peter himself, he'd quote a very different NASA slogan: *failure is not an option.*

Max, broad-shouldered and tall, strolled over to Candrew with a rolling gait. He looked as though he'd grown up on a ranch, which he had. Home was the *Bar Seven* west of San Antonio—or as he called it "San Antone". Max's hair was piled high in front, parted down the middle and long at the nape. The blonde color had been enhanced by winter sun on the ski slopes, summer sun on the beaches and the cosmetics industry all year long. He stood with arms folded, strong and silent. Still fit, but with age showing, he sported the first hint of a double chin. Max made direct eye contact with Candrew. "So, you're a professor of geology?" He pronounced it gee-ology.

"That's right."

"The closest I get to minerals is the gem stones in my wife's jewelry." He smiled ruefully. "A scientist." He looked Candrew up and down as though he was from an alien race. "The universe all you guys describe is way too bizarre for me—Big Bang – global warming – DNA. Too complicated. Easier to ignore it all and flip to the sports channel."

"You wouldn't have a sports channel without all the 'weird science'."

"Yeah, true, but I can leave that technical stuff to you egg-heads." He laughed, turned and made his way to the hors d'oeuvre table, walking with the slow purposeful tread of a tiger. When you're a top predator, there's not much to worry about.

Carla was quiet and reserved in marked contrast to her husband, Paolo. As Candrew headed back toward the bar, she was standing with a group of people he didn't recognize. He was pushing his way through the crowd when he heard the plump man in a polo-neck shirt finish his joke. " . . . and the vulture said to the air hostess "carry on?", I thought you said "carrion!"." There were howls of alcohol-enhanced laughter, but Carla only smiled tolerantly.

When Candrew finally made it to the bar, he waited patiently for the barman to top up his glass and listened to Lucie talking about Max. "He's bought so much acreage out here in New Mexico, it's like he rules a third-world country." She beamed around the group giving them time to realize it was her land as well. "And I have to add, it's a democracy—"One person, one vote." She glanced around the group again. "And Max is the one person with the one vote!"

There was knowing laughter all round.

"After living in LA, being out here in the desert he must feel like a dinosaur out of water," Anna said.

Candrew noticed Markham grimace at the mangled cliché and went over to chat. "How's the murder investigation going?"

"Slowly." Markham shook his head from side to side. "Although I've got to give the police credit. They seem to be doing a very thorough job." He sipped his scotch and water, pensively swirling the ice cubes. "They still don't have the murder weapon and they never found the cartridge case. But they did retrieve the bullet. Apparently, it's pretty unusual, they think it's some sort of antique. So far, they haven't been able to pin down the type of gun that fired it."

Candrew told Markham about his rough calculations that suggested the assailant wasn't very tall.

"That's an ingenious way to come at it. You told the police inspector?"

"Yeah. But he didn't seem too impressed."

Renata joined them, glass in hand.

Markham turned to her. "Sorry we had to put off your visit to look at the pre-Columbian pots. And for such a sad reason." He looked away for a moment, saying nothing. "Are you sure Sunday's okay?"

"It's really the best day for me," Renata said. "Doesn't

conflict with any classes."

"When you don't work anymore, almost all days are the same." Markham sounded as though he wasn't happy with that and took a generous swig of his scotch.

Gwen was by herself in the passageway when Paolo came up. He glanced over his shoulder, saw they were alone and pinched her on the bottom. "Now Paolo, don't be naughty." She was smiling, her tone clearly implying she much preferred him when he was mischievous.

His response was to pat her on the butt. "Lunch on Tuesday?"

Gwen nodded. He kissed the back of her neck, said, "Ciao" and headed for the next group of admirers.

Paolo and Carla were the Smyths' house guests for the rest of the week. Now that the Meaghers' party had ended, they drove with the Smyths down past Bishop's Lodge, into town, and through deserted late-night streets to their home in the foothills. Carla and Gwen relaxed in the back seat, chatting. Drained, Paolo sat in silence as Markham negotiated the road towards the ski basin.

When they made the final turn onto their dirt road, the darkness was broken by intermittent, distorted shadows of piñon pines flickering across the adobe walls. A police cruiser, with its rack of lights flashing, was parked in the driveway.

Chapter 11

They'd promised to be there "first thing in the morning", but it was now nine-twenty and there was still no sign of them. After downing two mugs of coffee, Markham flipped through the morning paper, but only cast a casual glance over its contents. Impatiently, he sat waiting for the police.

Markham had spent the early morning thoroughly checking the house. He was sure that the only thing missing was a small oil painting from his office: a traditional landscape he'd had since he was a boy. Gwen was in no doubt that none of her jewelry, gowns or furs had been taken.

Filling his coffee mug for the third time, Markham paced through to his office and set the mug down beside the stack of papers listing information for the artworks from Miami. He'd already checked to be certain that none of the paintings from his father's collection had been stolen and the paintings from his own collection were still on the walls, none missing. The little landscape seemed to be the sole casualty.

Alone in the house now that Gwen had left with Paolo and Carla, Markham lounged in his leather chair, staring across the desk at the plaster chips on the floor and the cracked area where the painting had hung, now just a blank space on his study wall. Well, not completely blank. In the middle was a flat metal door about twelve inches square with the recessed dial of a combination lock that secured the wall safe. The safe was still locked. And it didn't look as though anyone had tampered with it.

The doorbell rang. Markham heard Zona usher in visitors and a few minutes later she came to the study with two police officers in tow. "Inspector Martinez and Officer Handly."

Markham shook hands. "What can I do to help?"

The inspector took out his large, spiral-bound, black notebook, an action that reminded Markham of Helen Kontorovich's murder investigation.

"How's the Kontorovich inquiry going?" Markham asked.

"Okay. We're making progress, but nothing I haven't told you already. Only the information about the bullet." No more information was volunteered. Although medium height, Inspector Martinez commanded attention and was direct, systematic and efficient. He promptly returned to the current crime. "Last night's robbery . . . let's start with house security."

"There's an alarm system for the whole house, of course. That's what alerted the security service when the window was smashed." Martinez said nothing, content to jot comments in his black book and let Markham keep talking. "My understanding is that Liesl Sorenson also called 911 as soon as she heard the intruder."

"And this Mrs. Sorenson, she the employee I talked to last time we were here? Investigating the homicide."

"*Miss* Sorenson," Markham corrected. "Actually she's retired, but lives in the staff quarters."

"And she lives there alone?"

"Zona Pharn, the woman who answered the door a moment ago, has her rooms in the same building."

"And Ms. Pharn, was she here last night?"

"No. She was working at a reception we attended for a visiting pianist. She was still there helping to clear up when we left to drive home, so wouldn't have got back here until after we arrived."

There was silence while Martinez looked around the study with its oversized mahogany desk, antique Navajo carpets, high-end stereo system and crowded bookshelves. "I take it this is your office?" He didn't wait for confirmation. "Who's been in here since the theft?"

"Only me," Markham said. "Apart from getting some papers out of the file, I tried not to disturb anything."

"And you're still sure that the painting in here was the only item stolen?"

"Yeah. Quite sure."

"Who's had access to the house recently? Say, in the last couple of weeks."

Markham pursed his lips, searching his memory. "Well, the ones I told you about when you were investigating Dr. Kontorovich's murder. That would be the two guys who delivered the packing crates with the paintings." He paused, thinking. "One of the landscapers was here looking at some dying piñons. But he didn't come in the house. And then there's Ronnie Garcia. As I said, he's often here. He helped uncrate the paintings and came back a day later to clear up the packing materials and disassemble the crates."

"Oh, yes, Ronnie Garcia." Martinez nodded knowingly. "The shippers, were they short or tall?"

"Both above average height, as far as I remember. Pretty well muscled."

"And what about Garcia?"

"He's not very tall. Short and sort of compact. Can't be much over five feet."

"Really?" Inspector Martinez stared into space for a moment, then flipped the page in his black book and made some notes. "And as I recall, he knows his way around the house and the security system."

"Yes, he does."

The Inspector changed tack. "Tell me about the missing painting."

"The details are all here." Markham handed him a manila folder. "It was catalogued when I insured my own collection."

Martinez took the envelope, slid out two eight-by-eleven colored photographs and a short, typed description:

Landscape: oil-on-canvas. Framed: 34 ins. by 27 ins. Artist: Friedlandt (no initial); Date: 1901; Provenance: Unknown; Subject: Two symmetrical hills with stylized river and idealized trees; . . . . many more details followed. At the bottom someone had penciled in, *not a high quality work.*

While Inspector Martinez scanned the information, Markham stood mesmerized by the bald spot on the wall. The missing picture had been part of his life—an important part—and all through childhood, it hung in his bedroom. The unreal character of the mountains and the river had been magical to Markham as a young boy and they played important roles in many adventure fantasies. Although the painting was of little artistic merit, his father had stressed to the youngster that it was important—that he should always keep it. But it would be many years later before Markham found out why.

The inspector snapped him out of his reverie. "Can I keep this description?"

"You're welcome to it, it's just a copy. But I'd like to get the photos back when you're through with them."

The inspector tucked the file under his arm. "With your permission, I want Officer Handly to dust the frame around the broken window and the wall area for finger-prints. And we need to walk the perimeter."

"Oh, sure. Do whatever you have to," Markham said.

He left the police to take their photographs and search for fingerprints.

It was shortly after lunch when Candrew and Renata pulled into the Smyths' paved driveway, parking on the adjacent bricked area. Renata had come to inventory Markham's pre-Columbian ceramics, and she walked with Candrew toward the imposing double front doors. But before they got there, the right-hand door opened and Markham emerged with the two police officers. Inspector Martinez recognized Candrew. He offered a half smile. "Is it just coincidence that every time there's a crime in Mr. Smyth's house you arrive soon after? I assume, sir, there's a good reason?"

Candrew wasn't sure whether the inspector was joking, although that seemed unlikely. "It's difficult to give a convincing alibi when I don't even know what crime's been committed."

"Well, it's not murder this time," Martinez replied. Disinclined to provide further information about the ongoing investigation, he nodded toward Markham.

"One of my oil paintings has been stolen," Markham said very quietly, frowning.

Shocked, Renata involuntarily put her hand over her mouth. "Not one of your father's paintings?"

"No, fortunately. But it's a landscape I've had since I was a boy. Strong sentimental value."

Martinez interrupted to say he'd be back in contact later and that Handly had lifted all the prints he could find. The two officers headed towards the police car. Before the inspector had gone a dozen yards, however, he turned abruptly and beckoned Candrew over. "I want to thank you for your phone call, the one suggesting that the perp in the Kontorovich homicide wasn't very tall."

"I hope the information was helpful." Candrew smiled, realizing that the inspector had changed his mind about the value of the simple height calculation. "But you should understand, I had to make a lot of assumptions to work out the killer's height. It's only a rough estimate."

"But a good start. And as you said when you phoned, the way the entrance and exit wounds kinda line up shows she was shot square on. There isn't any evidence of conflict."

"So you agree, there was no attempt to turn and run? Wouldn't that suggest she knew her killer?"

"It could." Martinez glanced around at the police officer waiting by the car. "Like I said, the blood spatter on the wall showed she wasn't moving, not trying to get away." He smiled, a rarity, and strolled over to the police cruiser. "If you have any other bright ideas, let me know."

Markham accompanied Renata and Candrew into the house.

"Looks as though we've come at a bad time," Renata said. "I can come back later if that's easier."

"No need. There's nothing for me to do now." Markham sounded as though that thought depressed him. "Let's get on and look at the ceramics." He led Renata down a passageway to a small exercise room at the back of the house. Candrew tagged along.

The space was set up with a Nordic track and a bench for exercising with free weights. The left-hand wall was completely mirrored and in front of it were a dozen substantial wooden boxes. One of the sturdy tops had been removed showing foam packing materials that protected the fragile contents.

"I only got Ronnie to remove the screws from one lid," Markham said.

Renata knelt beside the opened box, rummaged through the plastic peanuts and exposed the top part of a stylized female form wrapped in plastic sheeting. Judging from the height of the box, the ceramic figure was about three feet tall. "This'll be too heavy to lift without risking damage. We're going to have to disassemble the crates," Renata said. "Take the sides off."

"You want me to get Ronnie back?"

"Yeah. He'd be a great help. How long before he'd get here?"

"If we're lucky, and he's close, maybe twenty minutes."
Markham got his cell phone and called.

A woman answered. "He no here." There was a pause. "He gone *rico gringo*."

Markham was certainly a *rico gringo*—a rich anglo. And clearly Ronnie wasn't at the house. "What time did he leave?"

"*Qué?*" The woman struggled with English.

Markham rephrased. "Did he leave early?"

"*Si*. Much early. He gone."

"Okay. Thank you," Markham said. "*Gracias*." He turned to Renata. "Looks like we'll have to unscrew the boxes ourselves." He paused, obviously puzzled. "Ronnie never goes anywhere without his cell phone. If that woman answered it, he must have left it with her—which is very odd." For a moment he stood in silence, then switched back to their immediate problem. "There's a rack of screwdrivers in the garage workshop. I'll see if the power driver's charged."

Renata peered into the only open crate. "We probably should get some plastic bags otherwise these packing peanuts are going to get everywhere."

"Zona'll have stuff like that," Markham said, making his way out to the garage.

Candrew was left to hunt for Zona, which turned out to be easy: he found her in Markham's office cleaning up after the police. She smiled and seemed pleased to see him. But before he had a chance to ask about trash bags, her demeanor changed. "It's so sad. The Smyths have suffered such a lot of trouble in the last few weeks." Frowning, she stood holding the dustpan and brush she'd being using to sweep the debris off the floor. "I haven't said anything to Mr. Smyth, it's not my job to do that, but I know his life would, like, run smoother if he'd just move his desk to the other side of the study. Better feng shui. Now he's blocking all the energy flow."

Zona smiled at Candrew's obvious skepticism. "Feng shui really works. It does. I told Eddy—he's my man friend, the one who's a stone mason—he'd have more success in life if he moved his sofa to the other side of the trailer. He said it was fine where it was: close to the refrigerator—and the beer. Anyway, I finally persuaded him to move it and the energy flow got a lot stronger. It was only two days before he had a job offer. He even had to go back to the quarry and help them blast a new face so as to get all the flagstone he needed. Really big project."

Curious, Candrew peered at the fragments of flaked paint in Zona's dustpan.

She eyed him suspiciously. "They must have damaged the painting when they pulled it off the wall. You can see where they dragged the hook right out and broke the plaster."

On a whim, he picked half a dozen larger flakes out of the dustpan, took an envelope from the desk and dropped them in. The intense colors of the pigments reminded him of particular minerals in the department's teaching collection and he was curious to know what compounds artists used to achieve those same colors. He slid the envelope into his pocket.

Zona, obviously puzzled by his action, didn't say anything. When Candrew asked for some trash bags, she bent over and pulled a handful from her cleaning bucket, giving them to him without comment.

Back in the exercise room, Markham was busy loosening screws that held the side panels of the wooden boxes and Candrew knelt to help. Renata carefully detached the side of the first box and tried to corral the Styrofoam packing into one of the plastic bags, but with only marginal success. Zona was going to have her hands full clearing up this mess. The crate contained a seated nude female figure. Abstracted, and about three feet tall, it was a powerful example of the ceramic sculpture produced in western Mexico around 100 AD. With a small digital camera Renata shot reference photos, using her tape measure for scale.

Candrew and Markham helped uncrate the next half-dozen boxes. They also contained figures, male and female, although one had a charming dog with a corn cob in its mouth. Candrew got the distinct impression that Markham was only mildly interested in the pre-Columbian figures, and there was no question that his real passion was for paintings. With the unpacking well under way, Markham suggested they leave Renata to her task and go get a drink.

In the lounge, Markham lowered himself into the accommodating arm chair. "This is the second time in a week we've had police here investigating a serious crime. I never expected a cold-blooded murder in my house. Poor woman." He pushed back what little hair he had and stared, unseeing, across the room. "Then there's that peculiar incident with Gwen's dog. I'm not the paranoid type," he sighed, "but it's starting to look as though we're being targeted by somebody." For several minutes he sat watching the flames lick up around the piñon logs in the fireplace.

Abruptly, he remembered Candrew in the other chair. "Would you like a drink? I certainly need one." When Candrew accepted, Markham walked over to the bar at the side of the lounge and poured scotch into two glasses, each getting a generous measure over ice.

Candrew watched while he stood bottle in hand. Markham, now in his mid-sixties, was unfit and overweight—Candrew knew he got no exercise, not even golf. The mirrored exercise room where Renata was unpacking crates was not going to be worn out anytime soon.

Markham returned with the drinks, took a liberal sip, half emptying his glass. As he swirled the ice cubes in the remaining amber liquid, Candrew asked him if there were any progress investigating Helen Kontorovich's murder.

"Not much, as far as I know," Markham said. "Although the police inspector did tell me the FBI identified the type of gun used. Apparently it was a Walther pistol. Pre-World War II. I don't know much about guns, but he said it's a type they don't make anymore. I think the inspector said it was a Model 7, if I'm remembering correctly." He paused, gulping his scotch. "Makes you wonder where someone in Santa Fe would get an obsolete weapon like that."

"And where they'd get ammunition for it," Candrew added.

Markham hauled himself out of his chair, raised his empty glass and cocked his head to one side in a mute question.

"Sure. If you insist," Candrew said.

While they were consuming their second large scotches, Renata came in and told them she'd finished her preliminary documentation. "But I'll still need to consult some of the references in our library. And maybe go down to the university in Albuquerque." She turned to Markham. "You've got some incredible Mexican west coast examples, Colima and Nyarit. And there's also a pair of exceptional Panucho River figures. They're the ones with black tar outlining the mouth and eyes. As far as I can tell, they're all authentic."

"Well, that's good to hear. Best news I've had all day." Markham levered himself out of the chair. "How about a drink to celebrate?"

Candrew had already drained his glass, and even though in a somber mood over the multiple crimes, he declined a third drink. He glanced across at Renata. "I think you'd better drive back."

"Not a problem. A Perrier'll be fine for me. I'm all psyched up after looking at those superb pre-Columbian pieces."

Low clouds, hovering over the silhouette of the Jemez mountains to the west, were splashed with orange by the setting sun as Renata and Candrew drove back to the university. Renata negotiated traffic merging onto the Taos highway, conversation lapsed and Candrew dozed. He woke with a start shortly before they turned across the Rio Grande at Española.

"Sorry to leave you with the driving."

"*No problema.* Anyway, it's pretty quiet on a Sunday evening."

Renata drove in silence for a while, then enthused about the impressive quality of Markham's primitive art. "His father must have had excellent taste, a real connoisseur."

Candrew told her about the gun. "Markham said the FBI had identified the weapon used to murder Helen Kontorovich. Apparently it's an old type of pistol that isn't made anymore. I got the impression it's rather rare."

"Why would the killer use such an odd gun?"

"I've no idea." He looked out at the disappearing sun and darkening clouds. "The Smyth's have certainly had their troubles in the last couple of weeks."

They talked about Helen's murder, the art theft and the strange dog death, searching for a pattern. Inevitably, the conversation drifted back to the stolen painting.

"The inspector told Markham the front door was open when they arrived, but, of course, the intruder was gone. There wasn't any snow on the ground, so no tracks." Candrew paused, mulling over what Markham had told him. "Everything sort of points to someone who knew what they wanted and went straight for it."

"Which means they were familiar with the security system. You think it's possible the thief—or thieves—had inside information? After all, they broke in when no one was home and knew exactly how long they'd have with the security system after they smashed the window."

Candrew thought about that. "Yeah. They knew their way around the house well enough to plan what they were going to take and where it was."

"But I still don't see why anyone would steal a second rate painting from the Smyths' home. It's like going to a sumptuous buffet and only taking iceberg lettuce."

"But remember, the painting was over the safe. Could be the thief didn't have enough time to force the lock."

"Possible, I suppose." Renata braked, saying nothing as she concentrated on passing a slow moving pickup truck with huge wheels and jacked-up suspension.

"And of course, any painting hiding a safe would be jostled every time the safe was used," Candrew said. "You wouldn't want to hang a major piece of art there."

"But that brings us right back to the critical question—why steal a poorly-painted piece of art? What's so special about it?"

"Perhaps nothing." Candrew grinned. "Absolutely nothing."

"How'd you figure that?"

Candrew was stabbing the air with his forefinger. "I've thought of another possibility we haven't considered. We've ignored one crucial piece of information."

"We have? What's that?"

"The coincidence."

"Sorry?" Renata obviously didn't understand.

"The theft occurred just three days after Helen Kontorovich was shot. What's the chance of these two crimes happening in the Smyths' home only a few days apart, being unrelated?"

"You mean the crimes could be connected?"

"Exactly. What if Helen's murderer realized he'd left behind some key piece of evidence that would incriminate him. Something that would tie him to the killing. So, he came back to get it. Stealing the painting made it look like a burglary, but was just a red herring."

"It would certainly explain why nothing else was disturbed. But what did he come back to get?"

Chapter 12

Candrew stood evaluating his reflection. *Not bad. Hair starting to thin a bit. And a tad overweight. But generally in good shape.* It was a little after eight-thirty in the morning and the overcast March sky, scattered with snow flurries, produced a dreary light that made the window of his office act like a mirror. He was standing staring at it, phone to ear, listening.

" . . . so the meeting would have to be sometime in the next ten days."

"Yeah. I understand that, Peterson, but it's pretty short notice. And I do have a full time job here at the university."

Gary Petersen was exploration manager for McCullum Oil Company. The main office in Carrizozo was about four hours south of the university and Candrew often worked there as a consultant with their petroleum exploration team.

"Granted, but it'll only take a couple of hours," Petersen said.

"Plus the time to get there, not to mention preparation." Candrew paused, scheming. Irritated, he asked, "Why can't Allan do it? Philadelphia's a hell of a lot closer to New York than to New

Mexico. He's a geologist. He knows as much about McCullum's proposed drilling project as I do."

"I already called him. His secretary said he'd gone to a conference in Kuwait and won't be back for a couple of weeks."

Candrew stood tapping his teeth, considering the options. Then he turned around to his desk, removed the sheaf of papers that had shingled the weekly planner and said, reluctantly, "Okay. I guess I can squeeze it in." He hesitated, running his pencil over the calendar. "How about a week from Tuesday?"

Petersen was asking Candrew to fly to Philadelphia and make a presentation for a group of investors. The aim was to persuade them to put up the money for a cluster of petroleum wildcat wells in Lea County, down in the southeast corner of New Mexico.

Philly was hardly the center of the oil business, but it was in the state where the U.S. oil industry began when the self-styled 'Colonel' Drake drilled the first well deliberately looking for oil. And at sixty-nine feet, he'd found it. Pennsylvania now plays a minor part in U.S. petroleum production and long ago relinquished any major role to Texas, Alaska, Louisiana and even New Mexico. What Philly does have is investment money. Candrew had agreed to present the plans for McCullum Oil's latest exploration project to financially savvy money-men in hopes of getting them to fund five wells. The trick was to explain complex geology to a group of investors with no technical background. But that's exactly what he'd done in freshman geology classes for non-majors. And he'd become good at it.

It was still early on the dismal Monday morning, and Candrew's thoughts had not yet focused on departmental matters. He was mulling over yesterday's events at Markham Smyth's home. Out of curiosity, he pulled his chair up to the computer and Googled *Walter*. He knew little about firearms and was interested to see what sort of gun the FBI had identified. And he was forced to admit to himself he felt a morbid curiosity about the type of weapon that had been used to kill Helen Kontorovich. Before anything came up on the computer screen, he was interrupted by a tentative knock on his open door.

"Can I come in?"

Candrew recognized the student who was wearing a down vest with a green John Deere baseball cap, but couldn't recall his name. Beckoning him in, he waved to an empty chair. "What can I do for you?"

The student seemed unsure of himself. He parked his gray backpack beside the chair. "I .. uh .. my name's Joe Bennington. I'm a junior in the department. I'm sure you know, I've got to take field geology this summer."

Candrew certainly did know. Six credit hours of field camp were required for all majors. It was the course that got them out into the "field"—the real world—where they'd spend six weeks putting together everything they should have learned in the classroom. Students could take the course at any university and transfer the credits back. "Well, Joe, which field camp are you planning to go to?" Candrew asked.

"That's why I came. I'm, like, not sure. Chairman Rosenberg said you knew a lot about courses at other schools."

"What's your main interest?"

"Hard rocks." He used the slang term for crystalline rocks like granite and basalt, not the "soft rock" sandstones and carbonates that dominated Candrew's research.

Raking his fingers through his hair, thinking, Candrew mused, "University of Montana might be a good choice." He ambled over to the file cabinet and from the third drawer down pulled out a bulging folder. "Here's a stack of field camp brochures I've collected. Take a look, then check them out on the web." He handed the file to Joe. "And make sure I get it back."

The student promised to return the information promptly,

but he didn't leave and stood by the door, hesitant. "I'm real short of money." He appeared embarrassed. "I'm looking for a part-time job. You know any of the profs who, like, need someone to work for them? In their lab, or grading, or something."

Candrew wasn't surprised: students always needed more money. "You could try Dr. Mann, especially since you're interested in hard rocks. And ask Dr. Rosenberg if he knows any other possibilities in the department."

Joe looked relieved that he might have some options, thanked Candrew and set off down the hall.

When Candrew turned back to the computer, the screen had a list of sites, but none of them involved handguns. He tried a few modifications to the search without success. Frustrated, he typed in *antique firearms* and that solved the problem: the name was *Walther*, not *Walter*. A new search and a thorough review of half a dozen locations got him the information he needed. The web provided a quick education and he learned that the Walther Model 7—the pistol the FBI had identified—was made in Germany for only one year: 1917-1918. Apparently it was a smaller version of an earlier weapon, the Model 6. The design involved a blowback single action (*whatever that was*) and had a concealed hammer. Caliber was 6.35 millimeters and spent cartridges were ejected to the right. Like most visits to the internet, he discovered a lot of information that was interesting, but irrelevant. Anyway, he could impress people at the next cocktail party by talking about the Walther Model PPK that James Bond carried.

Candrew pushed the print icon and as his DeskJet spewed out the first page there was another knock at the door and Judy bustled in.

"Know anything about guns?" he asked her.

"No. Why? You planning to shoot your failing students?"

Candrew smiled. "I'm tempted sometimes." He told her about the Walther pistol the FBI had identified.

"So, they found the murder weapon?"

"No. Only figured out what type of gun fired the bullet that killed her."

"Talking about smoking guns, I think I've got a pretty good handle on our sandstone environment." She was obviously eager to change the subject back to geology. "It's a deep-water turbidite." She unfolded her sketch of a profile covering nearly four hundred feet down one of the gas wells they were studying

Turbidites form when fast-moving, turbid, submarine currents slow down and drop the heavier sand grains first with the finer-grained, mud particles settling on top. This creates a vertical profile that gets finer-grained upwards—which was exactly what Judy had documented. Candrew found her detailed vertical profile convincing.

"For years and years nothing much happened, just fine-grained mud slowly accumulating," Judy said. "Then, *Pow!* the turbidite suddenly came roaring down and got dumped on top."

As Candrew studied her computer printouts, he realized turbidites were a metaphor for life—a short burst of action with lots of excitement, followed by the slow passage of featureless days. Except that it seemed to be a long time since he'd had a "featureless day"—after Kontorovich's murder, so much had happened in a short period.

"You're made a lot of progress," Candrew said, impressed by all the data Judy had assembled. He pushed his chair back from the desk and took a less serious attitude, laughing. "And as a reward for all this hard work, I'm going to let you teach my class—twice!"

"How come?" She looked puzzled.

"I've got to go to Denver next Thursday and I'll miss my lecture. The donor of my new endowed Chair wants to see if I meet his expectations. Though as far as I know, he's committed and can't withdraw the money, even if I don't impress him."

"I'm sure you will." Judy was being polite, but honest. "What do you want me to cover?"

"I'll let you explain the mysteries of turbidites to my class."
He grinned, and she said, "No problem."

"And I also have to be at a meeting in Philadelphia on the
following Tuesday."

She smiled, tolerantly. "I can handle that too."

Judy was leaving, pulling the office door behind her, when
Candrew called her back. "Before you go, I've got one more favor
to ask." He bent over and rummaged through the jumbled contents
of his briefcase, finally locating a white, business-size envelope.
"Would you take these flakes of paint to Mark Kernfeld and ask
him to run a microprobe analysis." He tipped the envelope so that
she could see the pieces he'd picked up in Markham's office. There
were four large, brightly-colored fragments and half a dozen smaller
ones.

"What are you looking for?"

"Nothing specific," Candrew said. "Just get me an element
scan. Talk to Kernfeld and see what their schedules are like."

"Anyway, why are you so interested in the composition of
paint? Does it make any difference what materials the artist used?"

Candrew told her about the theft of the oil painting from
Markham Smyth's study and the paint flakes that had been knocked
off when it was snatched from the wall.

"Just curious. Lots of pigments have been made from
minerals. And different pigments have been used at different
times and by different artists. I wondered what these were like."
Puzzled, he stood tapping his teeth with his forefinger. "I still don't
understand why that particular painting was stolen."

"Could it have anything to do with Kontorovich's murder?"

"I'm beginning to think so. Both crimes happened in the
Smyths' home and just a few days apart. Both involve art, although
apart from that I don't see much of a connection." Candrew shook
the bits of paint back into the envelope, snapped an elastic band

around it and handed it to Judy. "It'd be damn difficult to sell one of the well-known pieces of art. An unknown work could be a lot simpler to fence."

"That doesn't make any sense," Judy said. "If the thief wanted money he'd have taken the stereo, or cameras, or something easy to sell."

"True." He pursed his lips, shaking his head. "Nothing seems to add up."

By seven thirty that evening, Judy was dripping with sweat and exhausted. She'd just won the racket ball game with Mindi Allison, her regular opponent. Both excellent players, their Monday evening games were always tightly contested.

As they staggered back to the changing room, Mindi said, "Fritz Rand invited me over for a beer. You want to come?"

"Sure. I need rehydrating."

They showered, changed and drove to the edge of campus where Fritz rented a small house. A line of cars was parked outside the one-story, wood-frame building and several bikes leaned against the portál. They could hear music, even out on the street.

Inside, a dozen young profs and staff members were eating pizza and drinking. Happy to welcome a couple more women, they greeted Judy and Mindi enthusiastically: "Hey there. Nice to have you girls here." Cans of chilled beer were pressed into their hands.

Fritz was in his fifth year on the chemistry faculty and the prospect of tenure loomed. With his review scheduled for the Fall, the beer-swilling throng was overwhelming him with advice, often with several people talking at once and frequently making conflicting suggestions.

"Remember, there are just three things you really have to do—publish, publish, publish."

"And get a few big budget proposals funded. Money talks."

"Talks? It yells: *'Give me tenure. Give me tenure'.*"

"Give me tenure or give me death."

"That's only at the University of New Hampshire."

"So, the bottom line is: don't waste your time drinking beer and eating pizza with friends. Start writing."

"Then you'll get to spend the rest of your life in an ivory tower."

"Hey, don't forget it's illegal to import ivory—towers are going to get more difficult to come by." There was a pop of a beer can being opened.

"Even God himself wouldn't get tenure here."

"How'd you figure that?"

"Well, He's only got one publication—and that wasn't in a peer-reviewed journal."

"And nobody's been able to duplicate His results."

Mindi put down her slice of pepperoni pizza and broke into the verbal melee. "You're lucky to be in a tenure track position, don't screw it up."

A voice from the back said, "Just think of it like a Roman Forum. Dean O'Neil sits up on high giving the thumbs up or thumbs down and your future's sealed."

"Odd when you think about it—give someone a job for life, or fire 'em. No middle ground."

"And another thing, don't antagonize the senior faculty. They're the ones who're going to vote on your tenure."

"Speaking of senior faculty, Mark Kernfeld wandered into my office today. Wanted me to run paint samples on the microprobe." Paul, sandy-haired, lanky and with pebble-thick glasses, worked for Kernfeld as a post-doc supervising the day-to-day operation of the micro-analytical lab. He turned to Judy. "You probably know more about the samples, they came from Candrew Nor."

"Can't tell you much, I'm only the messenger" Judy said. "I do know they flaked off a painting that was stolen from a collector in Santa Fe."

"So why the interest in having them analyzed?"

"I've no idea. You'd have to ask Professor Nor."

"Analyze paint? And did you?" a beery voice asked.

"Well, of course. Kernfeld pays my salary—and he's the one who's going to write all my glowing letters of reference." Glancing around the group, Paul smiled. "I've only had time for a preliminary run on one sample and that showed nothing very exciting—not that I've ever analyzed a paint sample before."

"Well, look on the bright side," said a graduate student throwing a piñon log on the fire. "If you help Paul get some experience and he doesn't make tenure, he can always go and work for Sherwin Williams."

Candrew was still pondering the mystery of the theft later that evening while he fed Chile and Pixel and prepared his own meal. After dinner as he washed dishes, including those left from breakfast, he remembered the way Renata described the painting as a rather amateurish northern European work. And that struck Candrew as odd for a couple of reasons. First, the quality was not up to the standards of everything else in Markham's collection. And, second, the style was not typical of his extremely contemporary tastes.

Pixel, Candrew's long-haired cat, had strolled away from her half eaten food, while Chile sat, tongue out, in front of an empty bowl, licked thoroughly clean.

"You need exercise, not food." Candrew often found himself talking to his dog. "Come on. Time for a walk." The leash wasn't on its usual hook at the back of the door and he hunted for several minutes before finally locating it under a pile of unread newspapers.

They followed the usual route through the sage and chamisa, the aroma of piñon hanging in the air. It was bitterly cold with only a thin sliver of moon in the clear, cloudless sky giving virtually no light. With the moisture frozen out of the air, humidity was low and the stars shone brilliantly in the crystalline sky—millions of them, or so it appeared. But Candrew knew that the naked eye can only see about three thousand—and that's when there are no bright city lights.

Candrew could recognize many of the constellations and tonight the Pleiades were especially prominent. The light he was seeing had left those stars seventy million years ago. If aliens were up there looking down at us they'd be seeing the earth as it was when dinosaurs were roaming and roaring. They'd have to wait patiently for another seventy million years before they could intercept our television signals, see our reality shows and hear Howard Stern. Sobering thought.

Thinking of the media reminded Candrew of the puzzling 8-track tape. Such a strange message. And no indication of who sent it. He hadn't given any thought about forwarding it to the police inspector, but maybe he should, since it seemed to be commenting on the Kontorovich homicide. Again, he pondered the reference to a little knowledge being a dangerous thing. What was the insufficient knowledge that led to her murder?

Candrew pushed his hands deeper into his pockets, waiting while Chile nosed around a clump of low sage brush, thoroughly checking the myriad smells. Watching the dog with affection, he sadly recalled Gwen's loss, also alluded to on the enigmatic tape. He couldn't conceive of anything that would prompt someone to kill an innocent dog just to spite its owner. What were they getting at her for? Nothing he'd heard had answered that question.

Chile was unenthusiastic about walking in the cold and when the dog had done what a dog has to do, he was ready to head for home. Candrew didn't need much persuading to escort him back to the warmth of the house. As he hustled up the track, trailing behind Chile, he again mulled over the possibility that the murder and the theft were linked. What was the common element? Could it be Ronnie Garcia? He was very familiar with the house and its alarm system and was not very tall—close to Candrew's estimated height for the assailant. But what possible motive could he have?

Candrew recalled Markham's phone call when Renata was unpacking the pre-Columbian pieces. The woman who answered had said Ronnie wasn't there. Either he'd left without taking his cell phone, which was uncharacteristic, or he was avoiding talking to Markham. Either way it was strange behavior—suspicious behavior?

Chapter 13

Max and Lucie Reinhardt had flown back to Los Angeles on their chartered jet leaving Paolo and Carla in Santa Fe where Gwen had arranged for them to stay as her house guests for the rest of the week. Then, Paolo would have to leave for his next concert in Cleveland.

After the ongoing investigation of Helen's murder, the theft of the painting, and uncrating the pre-Columbian ceramics, Monday had been a mercifully quiet day. In the evening, they had a leisurely dinner and more than a few drinks, and then Gwen insisted Paolo play. Paolo never needed much persuading, and Markham, always the polite host, had patiently endured several hours of experimental contemporary music.

Early next morning, long before any of the others had appeared for breakfast, Markham himself sat at the grand piano playing quietly. With all the ultra-contemporary, atonal piano "music" he'd been obliged to listen to over the last few days, he needed to reassure himself that there were still tonal, melodic pieces. And he needed to ease into the day of Helen's funeral.

Low-angled, early morning sunlight splashed across the

antique Navajo rug as Markham immersed himself in the music of the nineteenth century. Now it was Paolo's turn to be the judge. Sprawling in the overstuffed armchair, bedroom door ajar, he listened. Carla sat on the bed, still in pajamas.

Paolo was charitable. "Obviously he isn't a professional, but overall, not bad. He handled the phrasing in that last movement beautifully."

They listened in silence for several minutes.

When the piano music paused, Carla got up and sauntered over to the walk-in closet, trying to decide which outfit to wear. "Gwen and Markham have such a wonderful house." She turned and gazed out the window at the Ortiz Mountains, purple shadows on the lower slopes etched dark against the sun-tipped crests. "I wish we had a real home."

"What do you call that expensive Thing in New York City?"

"Oh, I'm not being critical. It's a beautiful apartment. But it's not ours. We only rent it. It's about time we had a place of our own. I'd like a garden, maybe a pool."

Paolo was in no mood to rehash their lifestyle yet again. He sat unmoving, gazing out of the window.

"I want to travel less." Carla held a pale blue dress up in front of herself and studied the reflection in the full-length mirror. "You don't really need me on your concert tours. You seem to manage quite well by yourself. I'm not sure you need me at all." She turned and fixed him with a penetrating stare.

Paolo was drawn in. "You'd enjoy travel on the circuit a lot more if you'd be a bit more outgoing. Get involved, talk to people, don't just hover in the background. Anyway, you'll get your wish this morning. You can stay in the house." He paused, as if unsure how to explain his absence. "I need to meet with some of the Arts Board members and I'll have to be gone part of the day." He eased himself out of the chair. "Markham's lent me a car, so I won't need a ride."

For a moment he stood silently, his head nodding slightly, marking time as the piano music filtered through the quiet house.

Across the courtyard, Liesl Sorenson was also listening to the sound of the piano. But not enjoying it. The deep emotional scars from childhood, left from being denied the opportunity to learn the piano, had simmered her whole life. Now they often welled up into an intense hatred and Markham's frequent early morning playing always left her seething. Zona knew the symptoms.

Liesl usually slept fitfully and rose early. Most days Zona shared an early breakfast with her before going to the main house to cook for the Smyths. Now Liesl sipped her herbal tea, frowned and watched the young woman fussing over the breakfast plates. "How're you coping with a couple of extra people in the house?"

"Oh, they're not too bad. Paolo, Mr. Magnelli, is gone a lot of the time and, when she's here, his wife is quiet as a mouse. She either reads or stays in her room." Zona topped up Liesl's cup. "They eat out most of the time, so I really don't have a lot of extra work to do."

Liesl drank half her tea and put the cup on the side table next to the novel she was reading. She liked historical fiction: there was always a chance that the ending would be better than reality. "You reading any novels?" she asked Zona.

"No. Not all that make-believe stuff. I try to, like, stay in the real world, stay with what's true."

There was an extended but sociable silence for a few minutes as Liesl ate the remaining half of her toasted bagel. "What about the painting that was taken from the office?"

"Like I told you, the police were here on Sunday. Asked lots of questions. Said they'd be back, but so far they haven't come." Zona picked up the empty plate and was headed for the kitchen when she suddenly jumped back. A large mouse had staggered out from under the sink. It stopped, head up, nose twitching, disoriented.

Liesl didn't hesitate. "Kill it."

Unsure, Zona furtively picked up the newspaper and rolled it into a loose club. Stealthily, she sidled toward the unsuspecting creature and with a determined swipe, hit it. The mouse was stunned, jerking, but not dead. Zona glanced at Liesl who, unblinking, nodded her head slightly. "End its misery." Zona swung at the injured mouse a second time and stopped its struggle. She could never deny any request of Liesl's.

Neither of them spoke for several minutes.

"That had to be done, my child."

Zona both hated being talked down to and loved the feeling of warmth that came with being enclosed, associated. She felt vaguely nauseous, confused. She didn't know whether it was ever right to kill another living thing and wasn't sure if she had changed the balance of nature. Zona knew she was connected to—was part of—the cosmos. Her voice quavering, she asked Liesl, "Do I have the right to destroy another life like that?"

But Liesl, an older and wiser mentor, reassured her that she'd done what had to be done. "We must kill to survive. We must kill pests and germs so that they don't kill us. And, of course, we have to kill for food, to eat." They'd had similar discussions before and Liesl always stressed that humans were obliged to slaughter cows, chickens, fish. "And we must kill our enemies before they destroy us." She downed the last of her tea and continued the justification. "It's part of the balance of nature. We're carnivores. We eat meat. And we have to kill it first."

"Vegetarians don't eat meat. They don't kill animals."

"But they kill plants. And plants are living organisms. Do we have the right to select what level we kill at?" Not expecting an answer, she smiled reassuringly at Zona. "You kill or you perish."

This Tuesday morning was still, quiet and overcast, somber—a grey day entirely appropriate for a funeral. The service for Helen Kontorovich was planned for ten that morning and was scheduled on campus in the university chapel. The heavy pine doors of the Chapel of Saint Cecelia were open, but still in shadow from the huge adobe buttresses. Groups of two or three, and a few lone mourners, drifted into the cool interior. Candrew and Renata had arrived early and stood inside the entrance chatting to the people they knew. As well as university colleagues and friends, a surprising number of students from the art department were there. Markham and Gwen had arrived and brought Anna Meagher, the *yellowlander*, with them. Zona had also driven up.

After hymns and Bible readings the university chaplain took the podium. He'd not known Helen very well, but had patched together a credible eulogy, although it was delivered in a flat, monotonous voice. Candrew's thoughts wandered. He knew most of the mourners, but didn't recognized the lean, rather ascetic-looking man in an expensive suit who sat by himself at the end of a pew with his hat beside him.

Candrew couldn't help wondering if the murderer would come to the ceremony. Not if he was Ronnie Garcia, Candrew mused. Inspector Martinez was sure his motive was drug payments, but then that was always his first suspicion. It could just have been a simple burglary gone wrong. Martinez had grudgingly conceded that Candrew's calculation suggesting the gunman was roughly five-feet tall fitted his prime suspect. And since Ronnie had disappeared, that seemed to confirm his guilt.

At the reception, Candrew stood talking to Markham and Gwen. Anna was deep in conversation with the Art School's director.

Gwen was bitching that Paolo should have been asked to play at the funeral service. "Something contemporary would have been a lot more interesting than that dreary organ music."

"But Gwen, Dr. Kontorovich was pretty conservative. The music they chose was right for her," Markham shot back.

Candrew agreed with Markham, but didn't want to get

drawn into this argument. He glanced away and noticed the tall, elegant stranger hovering close by, holding his hat. Being sociable, Candrew strolled over. "I don't think we've met. I'm Candrew Nor."

Candrew's proffered hand was shaken. "I'm Phillipe LaBarre."

"So, were you a friend of Helen's?"

"Yes, in a way. Many years ago, I was one of her professors at Yale." He spoke with a clipped academic tone of voice. "I am so sorry. So sorry to hear of her untimely demise." There was a long pause and then, as if searching for happier memories, he said, "I remember her as an outstanding student: enthusiastic, hard-working, perceptive. I wish more of them had been like that."

"She did her art history degree with you?"

"Yes. Eastern European art before the Great War. One of my overriding passions." Another pause suggested he was searching his memory. "Helen was quite serious. Even worked part time in a New York gallery that dealt in Eastern European art to gain experience. Made many useful contacts." LaBarre returned to academics. "Helen only did her doctorate with me. Her masters was in painting. And she was an exceptionally talented artist."

Candrew knew Yale's reputation tended towards contemporary art. "What sort of works did she paint?"

"Well, they leaned more to the traditional. I think this is why she switched to art history. Still, she put it to good use. Her painting knowledge gave her a way to probe the techniques of the artists she was studying. Did some pioneering work with this approach."

"So, she'd try and duplicate the original painting as closely as possible, hoping to understand the artist's procedures and techniques?"

"Exactly."

Candrew realized he was asking a lot of questions, but LaBarre seemed happy to talk. "Did you stay in contact with her over the years?"

"On and off." There was a long pause. "We weren't close. I saw her at an occasional academic meeting. And we ran into each other once in a while at some legal wranglings over restitution of looted artworks. By then she'd become an authority in the field."

"You're saying, she was involved in litigation as an expert witness?

"Yes indeed. As far as I recall, she assisted several attorneys at different law firms."

Candrew listened to more reminiscences, before suggesting Phillipe come and meet Markham.

Phillipe transferred his hat to his left hand and shook hands with Markham and Gwen. Candrew explained Professor LaBarre's relationship to Helen, and Markham broke in to say he'd clearly done a good job since she was so knowledgeable.

Evidently pleased, LaBarre smiled and gave an appreciative nod, almost a bow. "I'd heard about the spectacular collection you inherited. I gather she was working on that for you when she was shot?"

"Yes. Yes, that's right. Very sad," Markham said.

"Would it be too much of an impertinence if I asked to view the art works she was curating before I return home?"

"Not at all. I'd be delighted to show you."

Candrew and Renata spent half an hour circulating among Helen's friends and fellow faculty members and were on their way out, and gossiping to Red Mulholland, when Candrew saw Zona chatting to Phillipe LaBarre. He was probably a little over six feet, though his slim build made him look taller. Zona barely came up to his shoulder. Candrew stared. In a flash he knew: she was short—only a little over five feet; she had unlimited access to the Smyths' house; and she had been alone with Helen. He found he was breathing fast. Could she really have shot her? What about motive?

And timing? Was Liesl protecting her?

"What are you staring at?" Renata asked.

Candrew took her by the arm, guided her out to the car and said, "I'll tell you on the way."

Renata had taken her notes, together with the photographs and sketches of Markham's pre-Columbian pieces, to the university library. An exhaustive search had produced almost all she needed, but not quite everything. She would have to check some of the more obscure references in the Zimmerman Library's holdings on the University of New Mexico campus down in Albuquerque. And now, that's where she was driving.

Candrew was also on his way to Albuquerque, the first stage of his trip to Denver and the social visit to Benny Waldhaven. They had combined their travel plans.

"I guess going to Colorado's a small price to pay," he said. Since Waldhaven was providing the money that would fund the endowed Chair in geology, and Candrew was the first recipient, Waldhaven wanted to meet him in person. While Candrew understood the social and political necessity of visiting a wealthy donor, especially one who was a close friend of the university president, he was irritated at having to spend a whole day on what he considered to be a waste of time: *shake hands; tell him about the department; explain the research he was doing in layman's terms; thank him; head home.* "Look on the bright side, it's giving us an excuse to have a first-rate lunch together."

"I'm not complaining about that." Renata drove in silence for a few minutes, threading her way through traffic. "Just why did you pick Chimayó?"

The Hispanic village of Chimayó was a few miles north and east of Española and a thirty minute detour. Famous for its weaving and its Santuario, it was also the location of the *Rancho de Chimayó Restaraunte.* With a well-deserved reputation for excellent New

Mexican food served in an historic setting, it was always crowded. But since it was out of tourist season and midweek, they were able to get a table in the enclosed patio area after only a five minute wait. A friendly, dark-haired waitress wearing a white Mexican peasant blouse, black skirt and a wide red sash, delivered menus and took their drink orders. Candrew had a Negro Modelo and Renata, as the driver, reluctantly ordered Diet Coke.

"You didn't answer my question. Why here?"

"Good food, and I wanted to bring you somewhere with geologic significance."

Renata glanced out the windows, but couldn't see any spectacular rock formations or anything obvious.

"*Chimayó* means *superior flaking stone* in the Tewa Indian language," Candrew explained.

"You're a mine of information. So what makes a good flaking stone?"

"In this case, obsidian. Great for scrapers and arrowheads. Weapons grade!"

Renata was impressed. "How do you know all this?"

Candrew assumed a serious air. "Years of historical study and research into obscure sources." His face broke into a broad grin, "And it says so on the back of the menu."

She slapped him playfully on the arm and laughed.

For a few minutes they sat in companionable silence, perusing their culinary options.

When Renata closed her menu and laid it on the yellow tablecloth, Candrew said, "This invitation to lunch is not entirely innocent."

"Do tell." Renata raised her eyebrows quizzically.

Candrew was grinning. "I figured that if I ply you with good food, I could ask for another favor." He told her about the planned visit to Philadelphia. "I've become a traveling salesman. My job is to persuade the guys with the big bucks to invest in McCullum

Oil's latest petroleum exploration venture. Fortunately, I believe the project is soundly based, so I don't have to perjure myself." He pulled the corner off one of the still-hot sopapillas, poured in honey and relished the aroma.

Renata said she'd be happy to feed the dog and cat while he was away, and they continued chatting through lunch in the pleasant, easy-going atmosphere. They declined dessert, but ordered coffee.

While they waited, Candrew headed for the men's room. He hardly noticed the gourds, strings of chiles, flowers, and paintings that decorated the walls, but the photographs intrigued him. The restaurant had been owned by the same family for more than forty years and the fading photos presented an informal family history. He made his way past them, through the bar area with the huge fireplace and massive wood mantle, and down the short passage.

As he returned, he felt the warmth from the remnants of the logs burning in the fireplace and casually glanced into the small room off to the opposite side—and stopped in mid-stride. Sitting in the corner was Paolo Magnelli and facing him, with her back to Candrew, was Gwen.

Candrew's instinct was to raise a hand in greeting and say *Hi*. But he quickly squashed that idea and kept walking. A few yards down the passageway, he stopped in front of one of the old photographs, pretending to examine it in detail. From this vantage point he could see into the side room. Both Gwen and Paolo were leaning forward, their foreheads not more than a few inches apart. Paolo's right hand was resting on Gwen's and with his left hand he stroked her shoulder. This was not a casual business lunch. After watching their close intimacy for a few minutes, Candrew threaded his way through the tables back to Renata.

"We have friends in the next room."

"We do? Who?"

Candrew told her about the cozy tête-à-tête. "Clearly

they're not here to arrange another of Paolo's concerts."

Renata took a long, thoughtful drink of coffee. "So, if Gwen is playing around behind Markham's back, what else is she up to? There's certainly no love lost between those two."

"True." Candrew absentmindedly stirred his coffee. "Think she could have had a role in the theft of his painting? Perhaps as a way of getting at Markham, taking something of sentimental value."

Renata pursed her lips and tilted her head to one side as if to imply, *interesting idea*. She let the waitress replenish her coffee and without paying much attention poured milk and dumped in a packet of sweetener. She was staring into the distance, speculating. "There's a more sinister possibility. What if she was the one involved in Helen Kontorovich's death?"

"Possible, I suppose." Candrew sipped his coffee and smiled. "But I've got an alternative suspect: Zona."

"Zona? You can't be serious."

"Why not? She knows the house well, and has unlimited access. And she's short so she fits my calculation for the height of the gun wielder." He paused, frowning. "And remember, she was burying something out on the hillside the day of the murder."

Renata was shaking her head.

"Although the police know exactly when she returned to the Smyths after the murder, they have no idea what time she left. I'm not sure of a motive, but she had ample opportunity."

Chapter 14

The immaculate black Mercedes limousine glided through the early morning traffic. Candrew could have settled into the back seat and traveled like royalty; he could have closed the sliding glass panel for privacy. But he was too egalitarian for that, and chose to ride in the front and talk to the driver. The car made its way out of the congestion around Denver airport and headed for Waldhaven's home. "We have far to go?" he asked.

"No. Forty-five minutes should do it."

They were driving towards the mountains, climbing, the road at first straight, but becoming more sinuous.

"What's Mr. Waldhaven like?"

"As an employer, fine." The driver hesitated. "As an individual, I wouldn't know. I don't get to socialize much."

"Is he married?"

"Not any more. Wife number three just moved out."

The chauffer was pleasant enough and responded to Candrew's questions politely. But no extra information was volunteered. Clearly, he was not the gossiping type. *Just the sort of employee the wealthy chose,* Candrew thought. *Like to protect their privacy.*

The driver's estimate was close and in less than an hour he pulled into a gravel driveway barred by a heavy metal gate. When he poked a plastic card into the slot on the post, the gate retracted smoothly and silently. The car powered through, following the driveway as it curved among huge granite boulders overhung with pines, eventually pulling to a stop in front of a lavish house. A pair of broad steps led up to wide, double doors protected under an ample portico with impressive pillars. As the driver retrieved Candrew's briefcase from the trunk, the house door opened and a young woman greeted Candrew stiffly. She ushered him through the entrance, informing him that Mr. Waldhaven would be with him shortly.

Candrew marveled at the cavernous, double-storied entrance atrium and the half dozen contemporary paintings. A broad staircase climbed the far wall and there was a balcony that ran the full length. Clearly the home of someone mega-wealthy, this was like the lobby of an expensive, and exclusive, private club. Feeling awkward, he was not sure whether to sit on the formal sofa, or remain standing. Before he had a chance to make a decision, Benny Waldhaven came striding in.

He was not what Candrew expected.

Tall and lean, almost gaunt, Benny bounded up. For a second, Candrew wondered if he was ill, but this thought was quickly dispelled by Benny's athleticism and the quick, lively eyes that swept over him, summing him up. He was wearing a violet polo shirt tucked into faded jeans with a wide leather belt. He had on well-worn sneakers, but no socks. A loose, heavy gold chain circled his right wrist and on the other he wore a watch with a turquoise-studded silver band. Benny grabbed Candrew's hand in both of his. "Good of you to come all this way. Hope I'm not taking too much time away from your students." He pushed unruly white hair back from his forehead. "Let's go into the other room. More comfortable."

He led Candrew down a side hallway, but stopped in front of a painting of a rock: black, almost like a lump of coal. Not large, it was roughly two feet by three. "Art and minerals." He smiled. "Combines my two interests." He tapped the painting on the frame. "This one's a Daniel Lefcourt. Calls it *Eternity's End*. No idea why, but I like that title." He paused to savor the painting. "You know Ed Mell?"

"Not personally. I've seen quite a few of his works in magazines," Candrew replied.

"Wish he'd paint some minerals. You seen those light, luminescent cactuses of his? They're pretty angular, almost have the feel of crystals." Benny turned to Candrew. "Art and geology. Been together since the beginning. Like Çatal Hüyük."

"You mean the ancient village in Turkey?"

"You got that right. Oldest mural in the world—well, oldest landscape. And know what it is? An erupting volcano: lava, ash, the whole bit. Nine thousand years ago. Hagan Daz."

Candrew was surprised, then realized he meant the name of the volcano. "Hasan Dag."

"Yeah, right." Benny grinned.

They continued down the passageway into a dramatic, sunlit room. Spacious, with a high-beamed ceiling, it had full length, plate glass windows that gave a spectacular view across a small lake and up to the snow-capped peaks. Stylistically it appeared to be in marked contrast to the rest of the more traditional house. "Added this on," Benny said, waving his hand with an inclusive gesture. "What's the point of living in the foothills if you can't see the damn mountains?"

But Candrew wasn't looking at the view. He was standing in silence, his mouth open, overwhelmed by one of the most impressive collections of minerals he had ever seen. Glass shelves across the lower half of the far wall were loaded with magnificent crystal clusters, all beautifully displayed. Huge, interlocking cubes of intense blue fluorite and a slab of Brazilian quartz stood off to the side. Facing them on the opposite wall, a superb group of tourmalines that graded along the crystals from pink to watermelon green and a rich red rhodochrosite glowed in the sunlight. It was not just the quality, but the sheer size of the specimens that impressed him.

Benny Waldhaven was obviously pleased with Candrew's reaction. He waved him to the sofa and unceremoniously slumped into an old, well-worn leather arm chair.

"I'm a field geologist myself," he volunteered and seemed amused by Candrew's surprise. "I've moved more rock than all you illustrious professors put together." He went on to explain that for years he'd been in the construction business. "That's right. Built forty miles of Interstate 25. You drive up to Wyoming?" He didn't wait for an answer. "Then you've motored over some of my handiwork." Benny seemed satisfied with what he'd achieved. "Lucrative business construction, but collecting more and more dollars gets to be a bore—what's the fun in looking at a few more zeros on the numbers in your bank account?" He laughed at the thought. "Of course I had a wife—ex-wife, ex-wives, actually—who were only too happy to help reduce the total. Never did understand why those flimsy gowns cost so much." He smiled at his own incomprehension of the world of fashion. "Enough about me. Tell me about yourself."

As Candrew described the department, outlined the courses he taught and explained his research interests, Benny went over to the side table and pushed a small buzzer. A few minutes later, a maid brought a Thermos emanating a strong aroma of freshly-brewed coffee, and a large tray with cups, saucers, and a plate of cookies. Benny asked several pointed questions about Candrew's research and was particularly interested in how the work was financed.

"When I mentioned to Cranny that I'd like to endow a Chair at his university, he suggested geology. Naturally I was delighted. I'd seen plenty of it in our excavations over the years—and most of it problematic." He threw back his head and laughed.

Candrew also smiled to himself. He'd never heard anyone call J. Cranleigh Burke, the pompous university president, "Cranny."

"When I first thought about giving the university some money," Benny said, "I was really thinking about the art department. I've always collected, ever since I was a kid. Of course, then it was mostly posters." He set down his coffee cup and bounced out of his chair. "Okay, time for the tour."

Slowly they made their way around the room while Benny enthused about each painting, why it was so important and where he'd bought it. Candrew was not familiar with many of the artists, especially the eastern Europeans, but recognized the more famous ones. He knew the female portrait was an Egon Schiele and thought another was a Kokoshka. But the "mad Max" Beckmann had to be identified by Benny.

They stopped in front of a second Schiele painting. An erotic depiction of two intertwined, nude women, Benny admitted it was one of his favorites. "I hope I get to keep it," he said pensively.

"Why? You planning to sell it?"

"No. It's more a case of giving it away."

"Oh, I see. Some lucky museum getting a donation?"

Benny laughed. "Nothing so charitable."

Now Candrew was confused, and wondered whether one of the ex-wives had a claim on it.

"There's a question of ultimate ownership." Benny became serious and his smile faded. "A certain Herr Grunau in Vienna says that the painting was part of a collection his father, a wealthy Jewish doctor, accumulated in the twenties and thirties. His lawyers are demanding its return."

Candrew immediately realized the implications. "You mean they're claiming the painting was commandeered by the Nazis?"

"Exactly." He let his eyes wander over the familiar art work. "Sadly, Grunau's father and mother did not survive Dachau. The issue is far from simple. I bought it from a reputable New York dealer who assured me that it came from a Swiss gallery and had impeccable provenance. But then, when very large sums of money are involved, peoples' interpretation of *impeccable* develops a certain . . ," he waved his hand, searching for the right word, ". . flexibility."

Benny's eyes swept across the rest of the paintings and drawings hung around the room and Candrew wondered whether other pieces in his collection were under scrutiny by dispossessed heirs.

"Apparently, the Swiss dealer claims he bought the collection from the doctor's cousin many years ago. In any case, under Swiss law, the gallery would have legitimate title because it acted in good faith and because it acquired the art work more than five years earlier. And as Clem points out, if the cousin had possession of the collection, then, of course, it never fell into Nazi hands."

"And who's Clem?"

"Clem Forleigh, my attorney. First rate. Practices as a partner with the law firm of Starber, Whitney and Ray in Philadelphia. They're pretty well-connected, handle lots of international litigation." Benny sauntered back to his chair. "Of course, he costs the earth. Probably end up paying him more than the damn painting's worth." He grinned as though mere money was a secondary consideration.

As Candrew settled back into the sofa, he noticed the large piece of amber on the end table. One face had been polished and it was lit from underneath, looking like a lump of solidified sunlight. The careful mounting showed several bees superbly preserved.

"Can't remember where that's from. Probably Dominican Republic. Give me a minute and I'll check for you." Benny leapt out of his chair and headed into an adjacent room that served as an office.

While Candrew sipped his coffee, ate a cookie and waited, he couldn't help comparing this art collection with Markham

Smyth's. Markham's own collection was mostly late twentieth century, whereas his father's and Benny Waldhaven's both seemed to be concentrated more on the first half of the century. He wondered whether any of Markham's newly acquired pieces were likely to be claimed by heirs. Interesting thought, particularly in the light of Helen Kontorovich's murder.

Benny came bouncing back into the room. "I was right. Dominican Republic. That particular chunk's the mausoleum for 20 million year old stingless bees." He gave it an appreciative glance. "The resin oozing out of the Algarrobo trees trapped all sorts of bugs before it hardened into amber."

Candrew was impressed. The fossils he dealt with were mere bones or shells, no fleshed out bodies.

"And look at this." Benny had brought another piece of amber with him. It enclosed a well-preserved scorpion. "See, perfect 3-D preservation. You can even see the color patterns. Cost me north of ten grand. Haven't had time to get it mounted."

Together they examined it for a moment and then Candrew said, "Before we get off the topic of your art collection, would you mind if I went to see Clem Forleigh? I'll be in Philadelphia for a meeting next week. I could drop by his office."

"No problem. Good heavens, he needs all the work he can get." Benny laughed at the blatant lie.

"Well, I can't afford his fees. I wonder if I could ask a favor and get you to give him a call, see if he'd meet with me for a few minutes, *pro bono*?"

"Consider it done."

An hour later, as Candrew got into the limousine for his return trip to the airport, he thanked Benny Waldhaven once again for funding the endowed Chair.

"Hey, no problem. Just make sure you teach those kids to appreciate the beauty of the natural world. And if they can make a buck while they're doing it, so much the better."

Candrew's flight back to Albuquerque was uneventful—if you discounted the forty-five minute delay for a thunderstorm and the grossly overweight man in the adjacent seat who kept encroaching on Candrew's space. Renata met him at the Albuquerque Sunport and they hurried through the bitterly cold parking garage to the car, which, fortunately, was still warm.

Enthusiastically Candrew told her about Waldhaven and his superb collections. "He's got some of the most gorgeous minerals I've ever seen. Most of them, huge. But that's only half of it. He's also an avid art collector with an impressive group of paintings, mostly turn-of-the-century through the fifties. Seems to prefer central European works, although he does have a few American pieces, even one or two from South America. His collection certainly rivals Markham's."

"Interesting you should mention that. I've got some news for you." Renata paused as she drove up to the booths at the parking lot exit, futilely trying to guess which one would be the quickest. "Remember that after the murder in Markham's home, the police were trying to track down Helen Kontorovich's next of kin. Well, they finally found a cousin in Boston. Inspector Martinez talked to her on the phone last night and called me to ask if I'd host her when she visits."

"So, we'll get to meet her?"

"Yeah. She'll be here next week." For a moment Renata drove in silence, but the car tires squealed as she took the tight bend onto the I-25 ramp a little too fast. "Apparently Helen's cousin works as a beautician and hasn't any interest in graphic arts. She was sorry she missed the funeral, but plans to come back when she has more time. Then she'll sort out Helen's house and put it on the market."

Renata slowed, looking over her shoulder, and merged into the stream of headlights heading northbound on the interstate. For a few minutes they drove in silence.

"How was your visit to the library?" Candrew asked.

"Great. I got almost everything I needed in a couple of hours. So, I drove back up to Santa Fe to check one of the figures and spent some time talking to Markham."

"Gwen there?"

"No. But I'll tell you who was: Philippe LaBarre."

"Really? What was he doing? Looking over the collection?"

"More than that. Markham had invited him to stay for a few days, so he's a guest of the Smyths."

"With Paolo and Carla, they've got a full house."

"Yeah. And talking of the collection and Helen, Markham told me that the police searched her work bag, decided it didn't have anything important, and said it could be turned over to the art department. When I left, I threw it on the front seat of the car with my other papers. It wasn't until I parked in Albuquerque that I remembered it. With three-quarters of an hour to kill while I waited for United to deliver you, I went through the contents." She slowed to negotiate traffic and adjust her rear-view mirror.

"Anything significant?" Candrew asked.

"Just what you'd expect. Tape, hand lens, pencils, small tool kit, that sort of thing. Her camera and cell phone were there as well. The police had stored her notebook in a separate plastic bag, but put it in the work bag. I flipped through the pages. It had only routine information on the paintings, except that four of the descriptions had asterisks beside them. I was scrabbling around in the bottom of the leather bag when I realized it was the sort that had a stiff fold-down base to keep the bag rigid. It fitted tightly, but when I forced it up I found half a dozen papers hidden underneath. They turned out to be photocopies of old auction house receipts. They're in German and in each case the buyer seems to be someone called Otto von Lauerfeld. All of them are dated in the late thirties. And they give the names of the auction houses and the prices." She paused. "But the most interesting thing is that they have '*Jude*' scrawled across them."

"Wow! Were the receipts for paintings in Markham's collection, the one he inherited from his father?"

"Yes. They were the four marked with an asterisk in Helen's notebook."

"So Helen knew about the paintings' dubious provenance. I wonder who else knows. Markham?"

Candrew told Renata about the Schiele painting in Benny Waldhaven's collection and his legal difficulties with Austrian heirs. "I'm going to see Benny's attorney, a guy called Clem Forleigh, when I'm in Philadelphia next week. He's a partner in a law firm that specializes in international litigation. Benny says they handle cases dealing with repatriation of art looted by the Nazis." He gazed out the window, thinking. "I'll have some interesting questions for him."

They were starting the long haul up La Bajada hill, passing the slow-moving eighteen-wheelers, when Candrew asked, "Where's Helen's bag?"

"I moved it to the back seat to give you more leg room."

Candrew turned, knelt on the seat and reached for the bag.

"What're you looking for?"

"Oh, just a hunch. Might be interesting to check out her cell phone. Ah, here it is." Candrew fussed around with the phone for several minutes, muttering under his breath. "Got it," he said suddenly. "I wanted to see her list of phone numbers." He was silent for a moment, scanning down the list. "Well, well, well. Here's LaBarre's number."

"I thought they didn't have much contact."

"That's what LaBarre said. But maybe there's more to this relationship than we know."

Chapter 15

Tired from the previous day's visit to Denver, Candrew forgot to set his alarm clock and slept late. After a leisurely morning at home, he finally arrived at his office just before noon and his working day started with lunch. This involved clicking on the small coffee maker that perched at the end of his bookshelf and eating a power bar while checking his e-mail.

One message from a professional journal asked him to review a manuscript. He pulled up the attached document and realized it was close to his area of expertise, but in a location he wasn't familiar with, so he'd learn something. Anyway, he thought peer review important and was pleased he could contribute to the system that underpinned contemporary science. Candrew was typing in his acceptance when he was disturbed by a student standing hesitantly in the doorway.

"Yes?" Candrew asked.

"Have you got a minute?" He added "Doctor" as an afterthought and took a tentative step into the office. "It's about the term paper. I couldn't find anything on 'soft sediment defamation.'"

"De*form*ation," Candrew corrected, thinking that's probably why he couldn't find anything. He swiveled in his chair, scanned a row of books, puzzled he couldn't seem to see the one he wanted. After a few minutes searching through a couple of piles on the floor, he pulled out the relevant volume. "Here, try this. And check out the references they give."

Obviously relieved, the student thanked him and backed out of the office.

Candrew got up from his desk, ate the last mouthful of his raison-and-apricot bar and, dropping the wrapper on his desk, glanced at the clock. A couple minutes to one, just enough time to walk down to the first-floor mineralogy lab where Rosenberg had scheduled a short meeting. That's what the e-mail said: *a short meeting*. Candrew knew from experience that the chance of it actually being brief was slim.

A dozen geoscience faculty members had reluctantly gathered in the lab. Rosenberg started promptly, methodically working down his list of topics. "I need to submit a nominee for the college tenure committee." After a short discussion Gustav Mann was reluctantly persuaded to volunteer.

Next came a request from a local middle school wanting someone to visit and talk to the kids about rocks. This was promptly dealt with when the bearded prof at the back suggested one of his graduate students would do it.

The annual award for Outstanding Undergraduate generated considerable argument, mainly about the criteria that should be used. Was a simple GPA enough? How much weight ought to be given to other activities, like serving in undergraduate societies? What about outside activities? Rosenberg suggested he circulate an e-mail list of the likely candidates with their credentials and let the department vote democratically.

Finally, Rosenberg had worked down through his list of topics, each one ticked off, and put his papers back in the folder. "One last item. I want to make a formal announcement that the department is going to get funding for an endowed chair in sedimentology. Candrew Nor will be the recipient. I think some of you already know this, but I wanted to make it official."

There were congratulations all round and the meeting broke up. Although not exactly "short", it hadn't been as protracted as many that Rosenberg chaired.

Relieved that he still had most of the afternoon free to work, Candrew hustled back up the stairs and turned down the hallway to his office. Someone was bending over outside the door, but when he glanced up and saw Candrew, he turned and ran, disappearing round the corner. Odd. All Candrew had was a fleeting glance of someone obviously male and probably a student. It was only when he got to the door and saw the bulky envelope, just like the one that contained the enigmatic audio tape, that he realized he'd almost caught the deliverer red handed. Too late to give chase now.

Candrew sat at his desk with the tape in hand. It was an outmoded 8-track like the previous one. But this time he had a tape player, even if it was down in his car. Intrigued—and impatient—to know what this new message said, he took the cassette with him and hurried down to the parking lot. The tape player was lying on the back seat, waiting to be returned to Renata, and he reached for it, slipped in the tape and pressed the start button. He sat with the car door open, one foot on the ground, listening.

Candrew waited impatiently through the quietly-hissing lead in. Like the previous tape, the voice was male and Hispanic. Again, there were long pauses. "*A visitor from the past, one more practical than prestigious. Looks can be deceiving. Line and form and color: red, yellow, blue—and black. Rainbow gone. Guilt. A message from history triggers memory—now you see it, now you don't. From the dreams of childhood: mountains of memory, river of reverie. A moment that never existed, captured forever. A moment of memory captured, then stolen away to be hidden from prying eyes. Beauty is in the eye of the beholder, but beauty is only skin deep.*"

For several minutes the only sound was the hissing tape. Candrew rewound it and played it again, listening intently. The first tape had referred to events in the Smyths' Santa Fe house. He guessed this one did as well. Could it be about the stolen painting? *'Memory . . . stolen away'* and *'now you see it, now you don't'*. That certainly fitted. And 'guilt'? Did that allude to a remorseful thief, or was it *'gilt'* and about the frame on the art work? Maybe both. Candrew had only the vaguest recollection of the painting from his single visit to Markham's office and remembered a rather formal landscape with no people. *'Mountains of memory; river of reverie'. 'A moment that never existed, captured forever'*. That was all appropriate. But *'beauty is in the eye of the beholder'* and *'beauty is only skin deep'*. What did that mean? And what was the significance of *'Rainbow gone'*? He put his hands behind his head, leaning back in the car seat, hoping for inspiration. None came.

Paolo had practiced the piano daily since he was five years old. Unrelenting practice, practice, practice had developed the supple fingers and delicious control that put him in the top cadre of concert pianists worldwide. Now his agile fingers moved with grace and dexterity. He leaned to his right, letting his fingers ripple along, the left hand chasing the right, in a long simulated arpeggio. With immaculate control he stretched to his right and ended with a flat-handed slap on her bare buttock. Gwen laughed and his fingers continued playing across the smooth skin of her naked back, trolling over the warm flesh, up to her shoulders and down to another playful slap on her butt. She rolled onto her back. "I think I envy your piano if it gets treated this way. Was that a real piece of music—or did you fake it?

"My dear, sweet friend, when it comes to romance, I never fake it. That was a composition called *Fore Play*," he smiled mischievously, "by *Handle*."

Lying together on the bed—he, swarthy with a chest of

thick black hair; she, pale-skinned—they looked like a pair of black and white piano keys. She lay back with her hands behind her head, exposed. He caressed her with his eyes and then his hands, running them over her firm shoulders, soft breasts and hard nipples.

"If you ever need proof there's a God, just look at a woman's body. It would take the Almighty to come up with something that erotic." He leered, fondling the object under discussion. "Especially you. So perfectly formed. So arousing. Almost makes me believe in intelligent design. I'm not sure something this beautiful could have come about by accident."

"I'm flattered you think I'm intelligently designed." She smiled demurely, like a school girl. "But we're in the realm of art, not science."

"Aesthetics."

"I've got to agree with you about the perfection, the sheer eroticism of the female form," Gwen said. "Arousing." The smile had faded and a more serious tone crept in. "It's often hard to resist." She gazed directly at him as if trying to decide whether he understood what she was implying. "I must admit, I've had the occasional affair."

"You mean . . ."

"Yes I do." Gwen was smiling at the recollection. She opened her mouth as if starting to say something, but paused to rephrase. "Why don't I give her a call, invite her over? Isn't it every man's fantasy to have two naked, willing women in bed with him?"

He treated this as a rhetorical question.

"You up for it?" Gwen asked. He obviously was.

Gwen got off the bed and reached for her cell phone, pushing buttons as she walked out into the hall. Paolo could hear the mumbled sounds of conversation. She returned. "Ten minutes."

The door bell rang. Gwen tugged on a silk robe and headed to the door. Paolo watched with approval her thinly-clad bottom wiggle out of sight and caught a hint of her perfume. He was not sure how to behave. How do you greet your mistress' mistress for the first time? Lying naked and uncovered on the bed seemed a bit too much like an exhibitionist. But being completely covered by the sheet would be far too coy, at least for Paolo. He compromised and pulled the sheet halfway up, almost to his waist and smiled at the prominent hump—a macho unicorn.

Gwen, grinning broadly, returned with the other woman in tow. She wordlessly waved an introduction with a flourish. Paolo was stunned; speechless; immobile. "Carla! CARLA!" Vulnerable, he instinctively grabbed the sheet and hauled it up.

His wife stopped abruptly. For a fleeting moment she stood in silence. Then, tears welling up, she took in his lack of clothes and the disheveled bed. "You rat! You snake!" She sucked in a deep breath and stifled tears. Searching for a lower life form, one adequate to characterize her errant husband, she yelled, "You louse!" Paolo saw he was being driven down the evolutionary scale and wondered just how far she'd demote him. "You pond scum!" That was about as low as he hoped he would get. The unicorn had gone extinct.

His heart was pounding, but he felt a strange sense of detachment, a feeling of isolation. "Honey, she's your girlfriend too." There was a dazed silence and an obvious lack of understanding as Carla fixed him with a stare, her eyes glowing like hot lava. "You bastard." She turned, hesitated as if she was looking for something to throw, then strode out of the room. Paolo and Gwen stared at each other in silence as the door slammed and a moment later they heard car tires squealing as Carla pulled out of the driveway far too fast.

Paolo was furious and turned on Gwen. "What the hell did you do that for?"

"Because you're a scheming, two-timing son of a bitch." She said it quietly, slowly and with intensity.

"What?"

"Don't think I don't know what's going on. All the other

women. I know about that cute young redhead on the Lensic staff. I bet she helps your performance."

"Now, my sweet bonbon . . ." But he knew immediately, charm wasn't going to get him out of this mess and for once he was lost for words. Mistress and wife gone in one fell swoop. He'd had problems with the women of his casual liaisons before, but this was the first time Carla had been directly involved, although he always knew she must have had her suspicions.

He was forgetting the reason he'd agreed to a triple tryst. Turning to the gloating Gwen, he demanded, "Is she really your girl friend?"

Gwen was quietly sarcastic, relishing his discomfort, purring, "Oh my. A sweet spouse caught cheating. How could that be?" Her whole bearing hardened. "Go ask her. And get the hell out of here."

Chapter 16

Thursday morning dawned bright and cold with scattered, sunlit clouds low over the distant mountains. Scrub jays argued noisily among the piñons. The cooing doves ignored them.

Markham had risen early, as he often did, and eased into the new day with an hour at the piano. Now, he sat perched on a kitchen bar stool, sections of the morning paper scattered across the granite counter top in front of him, the aroma from his mug of hot coffee permeating the whole kitchen. He was half way through an article on the severity of western drought when Paolo sauntered in.

Not fully dressed, Paolo still wore a robe and slippers. His restrained greeting—a bland "Good Morning"—was uttered without the usual enthusiasm, as though he really didn't consider the morning *good*. Much more subdued than usual, he hoisted himself onto one of the stainless-steel and leather bar stools.

Markham sensed his depressed mood. "How'd you sleep?"

"Well enough. Carla was restless though, awake half the night." He yawned and glanced around the kitchen. "She's decided to sleep in, have a relaxed morning."

"You want Zona to take her some breakfast?"

"Not necessary. She'll come out when she's ready."

"Gwen's idea of relaxation is *Ten Thousand Waves*. She left an hour ago to get a massage and a soak."

Paolo seemed reassured to hear that she was out of the house, sloshed coffee into a glass bistro mug, but declined breakfast. He felt at home in the Smyth's kitchen. The polished granite counters reminded him of the house outside Florence where he'd spent his childhood. Rock-built, it had copious quantities of cut stone on doorsteps, window sills and kitchen surfaces. Paolo's father had played almost no role in his upbringing, and it was his mother's encouragement that led to his first piano tutor and subsequent musical education. He saw little of his father whose political ambitions (of the extreme right-wing variety) led to frequent out-of-town trips. An outspoken critic of communism and the government in office, the father was widely disliked and although he developed a number of close collaborators, he also made many enemies. Temperamentally unsuited to be a parent, he had a cool and unloving relationship with his wife. Paolo had been glad to escape the withdrawn father, ambitious mother and strained atmosphere of the house. Although sorry to leave Italy, he'd looked forward to the excitement of music in America—and was not disappointed. He settled in well, studied with concentrated enthusiasm, and achieved his potential as an outstanding performer, later making a smooth transition to the international concert circuit.

After a few minutes of sporadic small talk with Markham, Paolo drained his coffee and set his mug down. "I'll have to leave pretty soon. The College has been good enough to let me use one of their practice rooms. Need to keep those flying fingers supple." He grinned. Coffee, and the knowledge that Gwen had left, appeared to be reviving his flagging mood.

"You're welcome to use the piano here in the house any time," Markham said. "A Steinway. Excellent instrument—and in tune," he added, smiling.

"Yeah. I know." Paolo looked thoughtful. "It's just that I don't like to inflict the tedium of rehearsing on you, my friend. Perhaps tomorrow morning. I won't have enough time to get over to the College since we'll need to leave by lunchtime."

"No problem. It's there anytime you want it."

For a few minutes Paolo sat in silence, staring out across the hillside, watching a pair of crows ride the wind. "I don't think Carla likes all the traveling, but she always insists on coming." He spoke softly, as if sharing a secret.

"You don't have to explain," Markham said. "When I was building up the company in Houston, I traveled a lot. Gwen was keen to come at first, but quickly got sick of airports, hotels and waiting around for me."

"Travel's one of those things that sounds romantic; the reality is tedious as hell."

Paolo left to get dressed and reappeared ten minutes later, gripping a black leather music case. Together they walked out to the car and Paolo asked Markham to tell Carla he'd be back in a couple of hours and drove away. As the car pulled through the stone pillars at the end of the driveway, Markham strolled over to the black metal mailbox and pulled out the contents.

Buried among the magazines, invitations to gallery openings, and free offers was a formal-looking, long white envelope. He recognized the return address, an affluent suburb west of Philadelphia, and knew it was from his brother, Leland. That was unusual; they rarely corresponded. As he retraced his steps up the driveway, he tore open the envelope and eased out the single, folded sheet.

"*Dear Otto von LauerfeldSOHN.*"

Markham stopped in mid-stride, stared, but read nothing more. Hurriedly refolding the page, he stuffed it back into the envelope and quickly strode over to the side door of the house. Without looking through the glass panel, he flung it open and almost collided with Zona.

"For Christ's sake, Zona, watch what you're doing." It was clearly his fault. He modified his aggressive attitude a little. "I almost knocked you over."

She was startled, as much by his tone as by the encounter. "I was just on my way to fill the bird feeder. They eat the seed real fast when the weather's this cold."

"Well good. Just be more careful next time."

Markham hustled into his study slamming the door behind him, then turned and locked it. For a moment he stood gazing across the hillside quilted with piñons and junipers and down over the city of Santa Fe, spread out like a map on the plain below. Snow capped the distant Jemez Mountains.

As if having decided he was now mentally prepared to handle whatever his brother had to say, he snatched up the letter and slumped into his capacious leather arm chair.

Dear Otto von LauerfeldSOHN:
Now I have your attention . . .

He certainly did. *Son of Otto von Lauerfeld*. Both Markham and Leland were sons of Otto von Lauerfeld. But that was a name from the past. One they never used. One they had been ordered never to use.

With apprehension, he continued reading.

I am well aware, of course, that the collection of paintings assembled by our Father was bequeathed to you. But that could be challenged in court. And given the special circumstances under which many of those paintings were acquired, it would make for interesting litigation. Very interesting.

I have no idea how much you know. How much you

gleaned over the years. You, of course, were only a few years old when we arrived in the U.S. But I was three years your senior, a big difference at that stage of life.

Where's he leading? Surely, he's aware that I know all of this?

While you have been ogling the paintings, I was sorting out the rest of Father's belongings. His collection of books and music I appreciated. And I was also delighted to receive the silver. But with it all came a lot of junk, although some of that turned out to be quite rewarding.

I had to force the lock on one old, battered trunk. Remember how we played with it as kids in the attic, the one we were sure was stuffed with pirate treasure? Well, no pirate horde, just a neatly folded military uniform and under it a leather-bound notebook. Dates and hand-written contents made me think it was a journal or a diary, even though everything was written in German. My language skills in that department are limited, since we were never encouraged to learn our mother—father?—tongue. I took it to a colleague in the firm who's fluent in German and he read it to me. Quite a revelation.

Apparently, our dear Father started his art collecting while working for the Third Reich. He helped implement Aryanization in Germany in the late thirties acting under the direct supervision of the Nazi SS. With his education and artistic sensibilities he became something of a specialist in acquiring Jewish-owned art.

Right after Hitler proclaimed the Anschluss on March 13th, 1938, he moved to Vienna and continued his quest for outstanding art.

On impulse, Markham leaned over and retrieved the envelope he'd thrown in the waste-paper basket, checking the postmark: March 10th. Close. Today was the 11th. The letter could just as easily have taken a couple of days and arrived on March 13th. Coincidence?

Vienna, with its cultured and affluent Jewish community, provided rich pickings. He mined this valuable lode of Nazi loot. It was his role to make selections for Göring. And that put him in competition with those charged with acquiring art for Hitler's planned megamuseum in Linz, the Führer's boyhood town. But there was enough art to go around. The Rothschild family alone "contributed" 3444 paintings. Jews had few options. Some tried to sell their art work before it was confiscated "for safekeeping". But the market was glutted and prices depressed. Many auction houses ran sham sales with absurdly low prices. There was also the question of "degenerate art". Modern art was anathema to Hitler and Göring.

And to Leland. Markham knew he had no appreciation of most graphic art and especially disliked modern works.

Much of it was on the market, cheap and unwanted. Quite an opportunity for Colonel Otto von Lauerfeld. He made the best of it, becoming a connoisseur of contemporary art in general and Austrian art in particular. Snapping up prime works of Klimt, Schiele, Nolde and others, he built an outstanding collection. And he was not averse to acquiring the occasional Renaissance painting. But here I'm probably not telling you anything you don't already know about his collection. You've probably got the best of these works hanging on your walls already.

To his credit, Father was sickened by what he heard from the concentration camps and when our mother died he made the unilateral decision to leave the service of the Third Reich. The journal I'd had translated describes his detailed planning and how he finally crossed into Switzerland at night. The German guards at the border were suspicious. His diary relates the alarm he felt when the small truck he was driving was pulled over. Several paintings were dragged out and unwrapped. Two were Schiele male nudes, quite explicit, and the guards eyed Father with suspicion as some sort of pervert, especially since he was traveling with two young boys. But it was the middle of the night and they had better things to do than stamp around in the snow, so with Father's high rank and all his credentials in order, they let him through. We went with him and so did the stack of paintings. These were all later shipped to the U.S. Immediately after our arrival in the States he changed his name (and ours) and merged into American society. I suspect he intended to sell the paintings for income, but he quickly began earning a decent enough salary as a history professor and later succeeded in business. He kept the art work. You are now the proud owner of his Nazi-looted collection.

Or most of it. I hear you arranged to have a small landscape stolen. Neat ploy—but I'm not fooled. You may think that the 1952 shield from lawsuits protects you. It doesn't.

Christ. How the hell had Leland found out about the theft?

It happened just a week ago. Who could have told him? And why would anyone want to give him that information?

Pity about Dr. Kontorovich. Odd that she should have died in your home. Not a smart move to let her study the collection, was it? She discover too much? And just what was it she discovered? I'll be intrigued to find out who killed her. I'm sure you know, but I'm also sure you won't tell me—yet.

Arrogant bastard, implying I was involved in murder. And how on earth had Leland found out about this? He have a friend at the university? Or maybe in the police department?

Outraged, Markham jumped up and stood staring out the window, the letter still in his hand. A few minutes later he continued reading.

Markham, you're on a tightrope. You're standing at the edge of a precipice—take a deep breath and a step back. Let's talk. Together we can work something out— something to our mutual advantage.

I may not have your aesthetic sensibilities. I may not like all those splashes of color, wavy lines and squares that pass as contemporary art, but I know what Father's collection is worth. I'm not naïve—I know the complications of putting it on the market. And I know an increasing number of Jews are determined to reclaim their family's looted art.

You moved to Santa Fe. There may be some gains, but movement is always accompanied by loss. Think about your losses, both real and potential. Think about our history and give me a call.

The page was signed with Leland's illegible scrawl.

Slowly he put the letter down on the desk beside his chair and for several minutes remained motionless. Leland's tone was no surprise and his profession as a lawyer obvious. While Markham hadn't known all the details, he had long ago figured out his father's past. Seething, he wasn't sure how he'd reply, and needed time to think about that, to plan.

Markham squirmed in his chair and turned to face the Nolde landscape leaning against the side wall. It was the only painting in the office that had come from his father's collection. He'd chosen this piece to replace the stolen landscape, mainly because he liked it, but also because the dimensions were appropriate. But he wasn't thinking about the theft or the Nolde. He was thinking about the wall safe that the stolen painting had covered and what it contained—the Austrian letter.

When he'd been a freshman in college, that time for experimentation, he'd tried to expand his knowledge of classical music. He had borrowed, without asking, several gramophone records from his father's extensive collection, and hidden inside one of the cardboard sleeves had found a letter several pages long and written in German. Like Leland, Markham couldn't read German and a friend majoring in modern languages had translated it for him. He'd been stunned to read of his father's complicity in looting art. This had been his first intimation of the role his father played for the Nazis in confiscating Jewish-owned art. Markham had taken photographs of the letter—this was in the days before copy machines—and kept them with the translation. Carefully, he'd returned the original to its hiding place in the record sleeve. From then on, he had never looked at his father in the same way. Now, he wondered if the letter was still there—and whether Leland would stumble on it.

Markham sat unmoving, gazing out the window at the

overhead ocean of azure with long, hummocky piles of white cumulus building above the western mountains, like waves breaking on a beach. And like waves triggered by distant events, his emotions had been set into turmoil by the news from his far off brother. Was a tsunami imminent?

Chapter 17

Candrew sat alone in the unfamiliar lab feeling like an interloper. Everything seemed to be operating smoothly without help from him, not that he was in a position to provide any. Rows of diminutive lights flickered. Embedded in the center of a tall rack of electronics, a glowing screen silently displayed columns of numbers that updated every few minutes. Without warning, the indistinct, subdued hum of hidden vacuum pumps and cooling fans was interrupted by the clacking of a printer as it abruptly began spewing pages.

He glanced along the racks of equipment, curving in a semi-circle, that were essential components of the million-dollar electron microprobe—the centerpiece of Mark Kernfeld's microanalytical facility. The lab housing it was immaculate, with the clean, sterile ambience of a hospital. *What a contrast with my lab*, Candrew thought, recalling all the dusty rocks, cardboard boxes and field gear scattered around. But he had no urge to trade: field work and rocks in their natural setting was what he thrived on.

As another screenful of arcane numbers scrolled up, the lab door burst open and Mark hustled in. "Sorry to make you wait. I've got one of the manufacturer's technical guys here checking out a new detector."

"That's okay. It's fun to commune with geochemistry at the central shrine."

Mark smiled at the compliment. Tall and lean, with the build of a marathon runner, he had a shock of sandy hair and rich brown eyes. "I've got almost all the data you wanted for those paint samples. Paul's still got one more to analyze, but the others look like they fall into two very different groups."

"Interesting. What did you base that on?"

"Well, five of the eight are mostly silicon with some minor amounts of iron, potassium, aluminum."

"And the others?"

"Much more variable. A couple have high titanium, even some with arsenic. And traces of zinc, cadmium and selenium are pretty common."

Candrew nodded his head as Mark ran through the list. He wasn't sure about the significance of all this. That was the next thing he'd have to work through.

"I've printed out the quantitative info and we should be able to get you the last analysis by tomorrow." Mark stepped over to one of the racks and turned a control knob on the front of a vacuum gauge. For a moment he studied it intensely, then turned back to Candrew. "Don't know anything about paint, so I can't tell you whether these compositions are unusual or not." He ran his hand through his unruly hair and scanned the computer printouts again. "You still haven't told me what you're going to do with the data. Think the dean's going to put up the money to repaint your office?"

"I doubt that." Candrew smiled ruefully.

They chatted for a few minutes and Candrew thanked him again. He gathered up the computer printouts, retrieved his down jacket from the back of a stool and pulled it on as he made his way out of the lab and down the stairs.

It was barely a ten minute walk across campus to the faculty club, but it was bitingly cold and Candrew was glad of the padded coat. Hands thrust deep in his pockets and head down against the wind, he thought about the analytical results from Mark's fancy machine. One set of numbers appeared to show the composition of silicates, typical rock-forming material. But as far as he knew, these were never used as colors by artists. He needed to find an expert on pigments to help him, particularly in unraveling the information from the second group, the one that showed much more variation.

Candrew joined the group of regulars that staked out the large table in the far corner of the faculty dining room. As he scanned the menu, a short, stocky woman with cropped silver-gray hair and rimless glasses pulled up a chair and sat with them: Patricia Stanley—not Pat, not Tricia—Patricia.

She settled in. "That was quite a snow storm. I just crept down the road out of the mountains at five miles an hour. They need to get a snow plow up there."

"A *snow plow*." The words were said slowly and precisely by Lubie, his eyes twinkling mischievously. "As a newcomer to English . . . " (Lubie had moved to the States from Poland nearly fifty years ago) " . . . I thought that if both words were spelled the same, you might reasonably expect that they'd be pronounced the same— *snow ploe* or maybe even *snau plow*." For a moment Lubie gave her a serious direct look, then burst into laughter.

Patricia, not known for her sense of humor, smiled at the irony.

While the discussion continued on the Transportation Department's inadequate number of snow plows (pronounced the traditional way), Charlie Lister turned to Candrew and asked, "You going down to Red's show tonight?"

"You bet. And you?"

"No. Going to miss this one. I get enough of him in the department."

*   *   *

Liesl Sorenson sipped herbal tea and settled into her well-worn, wing-backed chair. "You seeing that boyfriend of yours?"

"Yeah. Eddy and I are going to a film later," Zona said. "I got to choose it this time." The thought made her smile. She checked that there were cookies on the plate beside Liesl.

"Mr. Smyth told me he's going to one of the art openings on Canyon Road. You know what he's like, always supports art department affairs."

"But won't that be a private gallery?" Liesl asked. "It wouldn't have anything to do with the university."

"I suppose you're right. Although I think the sculptor is from UNNM. Anyway, he's going to be there. And he's going to take the pianist and his wife with him." Zona buttoned her coat and picked up her bag. "But Mrs. Smyth isn't going to the art show."

With that news, Liesl sat bolt upright. "So, she's going to be home all night?"

"No. She's going out to dinner with a couple of old friends from college." Zona tucked in her woolen scarf. "Look, I need to leave. I've got to get down to the health food store."

"Everything taken care of?"

"Yes. I got it all together. Should be easy for you."

"And that boyfriend of yours, Eddy?"

"He's so in tune. Helps me with everything."

Left alone, Liesl sat pensively drinking herbal tea for half an hour. Then she began the ritual of the black valise.

A disk of a Haydn string quartet was already in the CD player and she pushed the Start button, listening to the music for a moment before reaching to get the coffee container. She poured a generous pile of ground beans on the counter top and spread it out, bending to savor the aroma. A scent spray bottle, of the type popular in the forties, was stashed away in the corner of the kitchen cabinet. It was half full of a perfume her mother liked. Liesl gave the bulb a hard squeeze, the atomized contents permeating the room. Chamber music, coffee, perfume: aromas that still stirred distant memories she associated with her Vienna home. Those three—and the black valise. She went into the bedroom and retrieved it from the rear of a bottom drawer.

Liesl wondered what a normal life in Austria would have been like and thought of her parents more often. Now they were stragglers in the distance of time. Knowledge of them as real people had eroded over the years, reducing them to shadows.

Unbuttoning the stiff and cracked black-leather carrier, she glanced at the flute she never played and tugged out the cardboard folder that protected the precious photographs. The larger one showed her parents in their pre-war home—one of the last times she had been with them. Though both were smiling, she always knew they were making a brave effort in a desperate situation. She sensed the panic that must have gripped them as Vienna descended into chaos. The smaller photo was of her mother. She was standing in their drawing room before an elaborate mantelpiece with a huge gilt-framed mirror over it and paintings on either side. Liesl had stared at this photo many times during the last week. Again, she studied the two paintings. Both were clearly imaged, even though the photo itself was starting to discolor. One was a portrait of a woman, the other, a landscape she didn't recognize. Both looted by the Nazis, she was sure. She flushed, hate welling up again.

Liesl gripped the arms of her chair tightly, steadying herself. Her breathing slowly calmed, became more regular. She relaxed, sinking back into the armchair.

It is Tuesday morning. November. Six years ago. Mrs. Smyth had left thirty minutes earlier for a ski lesson. Now the phone is ringing and it's the police. They want to talk to Mr. Smyth. A moment later, he dashes past her, phone in hand, shouting, "Mrs. Smyth's car skidded off the road," and runs out to the garage.

She is alone in the house. The study door is open and she goes in to replace the phone. The landscape painting that belongs on the south wall is leaning against the bookshelf and the wall safe it covered is open, its door hanging wide. The safe is empty, although the desk is covered with papers. She picks up a letter from the pile, but can't read the handwriting. It's probably German, a language she no longer remembers. But the letter is clipped to a large, stiff piece of photographic paper and behind that is a page typed in English. Her attention is drawn to the bottom lines:

"I have completed all you requested. / Colonel Otto von Lauerfeld. / Hiel Hitler!"

She glances at the top: a Viennese mailing address for an SS recipient in Berlin named Walter Andrews Hofer. Beside it, a hard-edged swastika: black and angular, harsh with nothing curved, smooth or forgiving. Evil.

The English translation begins: As the primary art agent for Herr Göering, . . . *Quickly scanning the rest, she reads of panicked Jews selling paintings and sculpture at bargain prices; of a market saturated with high quality art and correspondingly depressed prices; she learns of rigged auctions with absurdly low bids; she finds out that the art she loved as a child is "non-Aryan degenerate" and classed as worthless. She gets an insider's view of the systematic looting of Jewish collections.*

Shaking, she puts the document back on the pile. The letter is not about Nazi violence, not about killing Jews, only about stealing their art—her parents' art.

She puts a hand on the desk to steady herself.

Apprehensively, she glances over her shoulder, but the house is quiet, deserted. What else is in the pile? Diligently keeping the papers in their original order, she flips through.

There are mortgages and land deeds she doesn't understand. Her gaze is attracted to an apparent birth certificate. "Apparent" because it's in German and she's not sure. The name however, is clear: Mikel von Lauerfeld. *The certificate is paper-clipped to an American INS Naturalization form. Behind that, there's another United States form, this one an official name change.*

Mikel von Lauerfeld *has now legally become* Markham Smyth.

At the bottom, larger than the other papers, is the photograph. She thinks it's a painting, the frame is evident. But it's a ghostly specter of twin mountains and a meandering river with a pentimento of what looks like names, dozens of them in neat columns. Although somewhat indistinct, the veneer of names is in German. Most have addresses beside them. They look like businesses. The muted grey shades of the photo remind her of a medical X-ray.

After carefully replacing the pile of papers, she leaves the office.

Candrew had arranged to meet Renata at four-thirty. This time, Renata only kept him waiting ten minutes, and the drive to Santa Fe got them to the gallery on Canyon Road a little after six. But Red Mulholland's sculpture opening was one of several that evening. Too late to find a convenient parking space close by, they spent another ten minutes driving up the one-way street to the municipal lot at the top end of the road and walked back to the gallery.

Even out of tourist season, Canyon Road was busy on Friday evening, and Candrew and Renata had to negotiate a small group standing by the roadside before taking the irregular stone steps that led up to the Branderson Gallery. Inside, a large throng crowded into the five connected rooms of the ancient adobe that provided the main display space. There was also an outdoor, gravel sculpture yard, but it was too cold for people to linger there.

Candrew guided Renata toward the small room on the left where white wine was being served, but before they got there, Red Mulholland loomed through the crowd. "So you made it. Hope you've got your pickup truck out back so you can haul away some priceless art."

"If by price-less you mean free, you may have yourself a deal."

Red laughed, setting his pony tail swinging. He wore a tweed jacket and black round-necked shirt for the occasion. But jeans and cowboy boots were non-negotiable, part of his uniform. He always wore them. "Look around. I'm sure a rock star like you is going to find something to pique your interest, something irresistible."

Candrew stayed with the banter. "I'm petrified I'll succumb to one of your bo(u)lder pieces."

Red grimaced at the double pun, resettled his wire-rim glasses and gulped his drink.

Candrew seized the opportunity to try and find out more about Helen. "How well did you know Helen Kontorovich?"

"Not well. Sure, she was a colleague in the department, but I only saw her once in a while at committee meetings—and I slept through most of them." He grinned. "She'd get so hetup about things, she'd yell and bang the table and wake me up. You know what the "vich" in Kontorovich rhymes with?" He didn't answer his own question.

"So, you knew little about her as a person."

"Abrasive. I'll tell you that."

Renata wondered whether she'd been scathing about his sculptures. "She show any interest in the sort of work you do?"

"Hell no. She still believed in a flat Earth—you know, only two dimensions." He stroked his beard. "Never looked at sculpture, only paintings. Flat. Couldn't handle a third dimension." He grinned again. "Not like us."

Candrew was well aware that geology was very much a three-dimensional science—four-dimensional, if you included the way it changed through time.

Red left to hustle more clients; Renata headed for a friend across the room, and Candrew advanced on the table spread with olives, little cubes of cheese and tomatoes. As he tried to make a selection among the yellow, white and blue cheeses, a rotund man on the opposite side of the table speared three lumps of Edam on a tooth pick. What caught Candrew's attention was the large button pinned to his lapel—*WIDE*. Not a bad description of the man himself. Candrew impaled a chunk of cheese and took a couple of crackers before curiosity got the better of him. "What's *WIDE* stand for?" he asked.

"Ah, yes. Glad you asked. When In Doubt, Eat! A pretty good philosophy of life, don't you think?" As if to underline the point, he slid the cheese off the toothpick with his teeth and pronged a few more pieces, and for good measure, grabbed two cherry tomatoes and a handful of crackers.

With food and drink secured, Candrew set off to peruse Red's latest sculptures. Before he'd even made it into the next room, he stumbled into Paolo and a very sullen Carla. Paolo himself was more subdued than usual, lacking his usual female entourage. Carla, now the sole companion, was holding his arm in an overtly possessive manner. He recognized Candrew and was just starting to expound on the significance of modern sculpture when Markham Smyth ambled over to join them. He slapped Paolo on the shoulder, shook hands with Candrew, and kissed the back of Carla's hand with a Gallic flourish. "So, Arts and Science together. NeoRenaissance. The core of creativity."

"And creativity in business?" Candrew asked.

"You mean like the creative accounting à la Enron?' He answered his own question. "The less said about that the better."

"But even in art and in science the creative leap is quite different." This was a subject that fascinated Candrew. "In art it's solitary, but science is a group effort."

Paolo rocked his head to one side and frowned. "How do you mean?"

"Well, take Beethoven. If he'd only written eight symphonies, there would never have been a Beethoven's Ninth. But if Einstein never lived, someone would have eventually hit on the idea of relativity. Of course, lots of people might have contributed, and it may have taken years longer, but eventually we'd have got there, there'd be a Theory of Relativity."

"Same with the Theory of Evolution?" Markham asked.

"Right. Without Darwin it may have taken a while longer with lots of scientists all contributing small bits." Candrew nodded his head as if agreeing with himself. "In science creativity is the starting point, then others develop the ideas. But no one would have taken Beethoven's Fifth, altered a theme here, tinkered with a phrase there, changed the key and ended up with the Sixth."

"This is getting way too heavy for me," Markham said.

"Sorry. Give a professor an audience and he'll just launch into a lecture!"

Although Anna Meagher claimed she was not good at small talk "of any size", she and Peter were chatting to a couple of old friends at the back of the main room. A slim, elegantly-dressed woman said, "I saw Markham, but I don't see Gwen anywhere."

Anna explained. "No she won't be able to make it this evening. Apparently had a conflict—too many axes in the fire. I ran into her at *Home Depot* . . ."

"What was she doing there? It's hardly her normal habitat. And come to that, what were you doing there?"

"Me? I was picking out a handicraft set for my nephew's birthday." She smiled almost apologetically, as if implying, *you can't leave everything to the staff.* "Gwen came hustling up one of the aisles with a lot of wire and electrical stuff in her cart. Said she was going to rewire a bedside lamp. Seemed eager to explain."

"Really? And is she going to start doing all the household chores?"

"Rewiring her lamp could be the thin end of the web," Anna said smiling.

The double doors to the outside patio had been propped open. Candrew could see an amorphous shape formed by a white sheet draped over a large piece of sculpture that stood against the high enclosing wall. The gallery director called for silence, with only limited success, and introduced Red Mulholland for the benefit of those who hadn't yet met him. On cue, Red stepped forward, relishing his moment in the spotlight.

"The role of an artist is to convert the dross of mundane experience into something beautiful. Something as ugly as a drop of oil can splash onto water and make a film of rainbow colors. I take the commonplace, rocks—Mother Earth—and with the human spirit change it into something eloquent, symbolic."

He took the cord from the gallery director and with a flourish, pulled. The white fabric billowed away on the slight breeze exposing two eight-foot high granite blocks strapped with wide, wrought-iron bands. There was a polite ripple of applause. But what caught Candrew's attention was the dark shadow behind the sculpture. The small, intense spotlight cast a profile of Red onto the whitewashed wall, as if his ego was being projected. And fittingly, the ego-shadow was three times the size of the man.

Back in the crowded gallery, Renata introduced Candrew

to a tall, wiry black woman. "Yvette's a sculptress down in Albuquerque."

Yvette stuck out a gnarled hand and Candrew shook it. She introduced her boyfriend, Todd, who was affable and tall, but balding prematurely. He smiled broadly. "I'm also in the arts, but don't actually produce anything." He waited for the surprised looks, smiled again and said, "I'm an art history professor."

After chatting for several minutes, Todd took a more serious tone. "I knew your art historian, Helen Kontorovich, though not well. So sad." He shook his head. "Our fields were a bit different. I'm more interested in what paintings are made of than what they present." He saw Candrew's puzzled look. "I do my research on canvas types, paints, varnishes, that sort of thing."

"So you know about pigments used in making paints?"

"Yeah. Actually quite a lot."

"Would you be able to tell me anything of the history of a paint if I had the composition?"

"Maybe. It'll depend on whether there's anything unusual. Copper wouldn't tell you much, it's been around forever. But titanium, that's different." He sipped his wine and thought for a moment, then handed Candrew one of his business cards. "Why don't you e-mail me the compositions you've got and I'll see what I can figure out."

Candrew promised he would.

Chapter 18

Candrew sat tapping his teeth, mulling over the composition of the pigments. The group with high silica percentages was quite distinct and reminiscent of the sandstone rocks he and Judy worked with. He thought back to that morning in the Smyths' house and the fragments he'd snatched out of Zona's dustpan. It had been the bright red flakes that caught his attention, but most of the chips were slightly off-white, sort of buff. Now as he thought about it again, he realized Zona had swept up a lot of dust particles and chunks, too many to have flaked off the picture, even if it had been roughly handled during the theft. And then he remembered the pock marks on the wall where the painting's mounting bracket had been ripped out. Probably most of what Zona had in her dustpan was simply wall plaster. He studied the analyses in this new light. It would explain the presence of aluminum, potassium and magnesium. So, the group with high silica probably had nothing to do with the theft—and he really wasn't interested in the composition of Markham Smyth's walls. He'd have to wait to see what Todd, the art historian, could tell him about the few pigment samples that really were from the stolen painting.

Candrew strode over to the armchair where he'd draped his jacket the night before and hunted through the pockets for Todd's business card. Eager to send him the information on pigments as soon as possible, he felt frustrated when he couldn't find the card. For a moment he stood with pursed lips, frowning. Then he hurried back to the bedroom and finally found it in his trouser pocket folded in with a couple of cocktail napkins. The pages of analytical data from Mark Kernfeld were still in his briefcase and a few minutes sorting through the jumbled contents of books and papers produced all the relevant numbers. He e-mailed everything to Todd.

That done, Candrew sauntered back into the kitchen, fried eggs and sausages, and dropped a slice of bread into the toaster. He leaned on the butcher-block counter, looking out the kitchen window, watching the birds hunt for seeds in the snow, waiting patiently for his toast to pop up. It seemed to be taking forever, and when he checked he found he hadn't pushed the lever down. After it finally got toasted, he slid the slice onto the edge of the plate beside the eggs and sausages, poured a mug of coffee and ambled into the living room. Chile was already stretched out in front of the fireplace, the piñon logs blazing. During the week, breakfast for Candrew was a rushed affair, typically granola and coffee. But weekends were more relaxed, and today he enjoyed the rich aroma of his coffee while reading the newspaper, his breakfast plate balanced on one knee. Later, he'd reluctantly do the washing, sort clothes destined for the dry cleaners, vacuum and tidy up the house.

The side window of the guest bedroom in the Smyths' home faced east and the early morning sun, just nudging over the Sangre de Cristo mountains, sent sunbeams slanting across the room. Carla was folding sweaters and skirts, trying not to make eye contact with Paolo. Slowly and carefully she laid the clothes in the suitcase, then turned, hands on hips, staring at him. "Life with you has been one long disappointment." She sucked in a deep breath and exhaled slowly. "This is going to be the last time I travel with you. Everyone else is enjoying a relaxed weekend, but no, we're on the road one more time."

"Well, I . . ."

"I can't trust you. This is the end of the line for us." She glanced at the half-packed suitcase. "I don't want to be cloistered in yet another hotel room while you're out feeding your ego. And don't give me your damned excuses." She was on the verge of tears. "I'm going back to New York to get on with my life—and I'm going to live life without you." She emphasized the last two words.

"Look honey, I know you're upset, you're angry. Let's not fight about this."

"Fight. *Fight*. That's such a male perspective."

"Can we talk this over later, sugar? I'm sure together we can work it out." With a hesitant half-smile, he wheedled, "Please honey." He tried appeasement. "Maybe we could have lunch somewhere nice before we get the limo. Talk things through. I can explain." For a moment he stared off into the distance as if trying to think of a suitable restaurant. "Look, I'm sorry, but I need to get in one last practice session on the new piece before we leave. It'll only be an hour and I'll be here in the house. We'll have all the rest of the morning together." He gave Carla a tentative smile, left her to finish packing and closed the door with elaborate quietness before heading into the living room.

The superb mechanism of the Smyths' Steinway grand piano faithfully transcribed Paolo's dexterous touch from keys to strings, all the subtleties of his execution reproduced precisely. As he played a few simple pieces to warm up, the little finger of his left hand struck a B flat, the damper rose, the hammer struck the metal piano wire and the sound resonated through the house. Fractions of seconds later the third, middle and forefingers sent hammers pounding onto the taught wires, propagating notes of the arpeggio to his imagined audience.

As the right hand rippled down across the key board, the index finger struck middle C, the damper rose, the hammer moved towards the wire—but it was not the soft padding that struck, it was metal cladding, copper sheathing, copper that was connected by wire to a small battery. The piano wire itself completed an electrical circuit and sent current flowing to a blasting cap that detonated, driving a shock wave into the main explosive that produced a huge cloud of gas with enormous destructive energy. The rapidly expanding gas powered the explosion, the main force directed through the keyboard. Splintering ivory keys blasted Paolo like shrapnel, flinging his mangled body off the piano stool onto the floor.

He never heard the sound of the tinny middle C, the last note he would ever play.

The grand piano's heavy metal frame and solid wood construction channeled the blast, partly protecting the rest of the room. But the concussion was violent enough to shear the door into the kitchen off its hinges and blow out two large sections of the plate glass windows, sending a hailstorm of shards into the yard.

House finches, doves and a lone canyon towhee pecked at the seeds on the ground, blissfully unaware of the predator. Well camouflaged, the mottled black and ginger cat stealthily picked his way through the underbrush—until the shock wave from the blast knocked him off balance, making him yowl loudly in protest. Fur and erect tail fluffed up. Birds flew into the air in a frantic cloud; a chaotic, squawking flock.

Two houses to the north, the explosion startled the Smyths' neighbor and he sloshed coffee onto the morning paper. "God damn it!" He jumped up to avoid the stream of hot liquid pouring onto the floor. "Who the hell is firing guns at this hour in the morning? I thought shooting in the city limits was illegal. Disturbing everyone."

He made a mental note to write to his city councilman.

The blast rattled the windows in the house to the south, provoking the owner's attention. When he hurried to look out, he could see hundreds of circling birds, a cloud of dust drifting through the trees, shattered windows and several people running into the street. He called 911.

"Fire, Police or Ambulance?"

"Better send all three."

Chapter 19

The emergency services arrived promptly, the paramedics first. Markham met them in the driveway and they ran to the house with the overweight Markham puffing behind. Before he reached the door, a police cruiser with flashing lights and wailing siren swung into the driveway, followed a moment later by a fire truck, its emergency lights also flashing.

The firemen tramped through the house in their heavy boots and elaborate gear, establishing quickly and efficiently that there was no fire risk. None of the gas or power lines had been severed. They returned to their truck, sat for a few minutes filling out paper work, then drove away.

While one policeman leaned into the cruiser radioing for support units and the ATF, others strung tape and began to secure the crime scene. From the start, Paolo's death was treated as homicide.

The explosion had startled Markham and he'd rushed out of his office into the living room. Through the dust and acrid fumes he'd seen Paolo lying in a pool of blood, not moving, seriously injured. It was obvious he'd not survived. Markham felt sick. Oddly, he noticed that the painting on the wall had ben shredded by flying debris and splattered with blood.

Now Carla, sobbing uncontrollably, staggered though the splintered debris, hysterical. Gwen, not thinking clearly, leaned against the wall with a dazed, unemotional face, then stumbled up to Carla and put her arms around her. But Carla pushed her away, averting her face streaked with tears, saying nothing.

The local police made way for the investigators from Alcohol, Tobacco and Firearms, the ATF, who specialized in bombings. They sent everyone out into the cold while they completed a thorough search of the house and cars for any additional bombs. None was found. While the team in the house hunted for fragments that may have been part of the explosive device, swabbed the body for chemical residues and mapped the direction of the blast, another team member interviewed neighbors trying to glean useful information about timing, flash and smoke colors. The team leader, in a dark blue jacket with prominent ATF letters, questioned Markham. "This has all the characteristics of an ammonium nitrate explosion," he said. "You any idea where that stuff might have come from?"

"No, I don't." Markham had nothing more to contribute.

Two hours later ATF and the forensics team had taken their photographs, filled evidence bags with the things they needed and were loading Paolo's remains into the body bag. The medical technician turned to Markham. "First time I've seen a piano key embedded in a human brain."

Inspector Martinez told Markham they would be back later for more detailed interviews. "I'd like to talk to everyone who was in the house at the time of the homicide. I assume Mrs. Carla Magnelli is the next of kin. Any other close relatives in the house?" Markham told him there were none. "Are there others in town who knew Mr. Magnelli well?" He didn't wait for an answer. "I'd like to get a list of names and contact information."

Markham said he'd do what he could.

The inspector glanced around the chaotic room. "Better get those windows boarded up. You'll have a real mess if you let your pipes freeze."

"I tried to get Ronnie Garcia over here, you remember, he's my handyman. But there wasn't any answer when I phoned. Kinda odd — he always has his cell with him." Markham paused, mulling over the situation. "Now I think about it, he never returned my call from yesterday. Not like him, he's usually pretty reliable."

For a moment the inspector stood in silence, then shook his head. "Don't waste your time."

"What?"

"He's dropped out of sight. You ask me, he's already out of the country."

"I don't follow. Why would you think that?"

Martinez pursed his lips, stared off into the distance. "That geology professor up at the university, the one you're friendly with, he figured out the perp who shot the lady professor, Kontorovich, was real short, probably not much over five feet. That fits Garcia real well. He knew his way around the house, had access and became a prime suspect. Seems as soon as he figured out we were on to him, he vanished."

Markham went rigid, shocked. "Ronnie? A murderer? I can't believe that." For a moment he stood saying nothing, struggling to comprehend this news. "He was such a gentle guy. What possible motive could he have?"

"That's something we're trying to figure out," the inspector said. "For this pianist guy as well as Dr. Kontorovich. Who knows, maybe Garcia was supplying them with drugs and they owed him money." He seemed to be thinking about that for a moment. "It's not entirely unknown for musicians to do drugs. And academics too, especially those in the arts."

Inspector Martinez had just left when Gwen came in wearing

a bulky sweater. "For God's sake get that window fixed." Markham told her about Ronnie Garcia. "Doesn't surprise me one bit. I never did trust that little runt." She seemed more interested in warming up the house than solving crimes. "Well, we have to get somebody. Call the Meaghers, they've got a man who does work for them."

When Markham called, Peter Meagher answered. "Sure no problem." He read out the phone number for his workman. "I'll call him for you, if you like."

With a helper in tow, the repair man arrived an hour later looking very efficient with his leather belt crammed with tools. Markham explained the need for some temporary repairs to patch the splintered window and they quickly summed up the situation. By mid-afternoon, all the glass shards had been removed from the window frames and with the help of copious amounts of duct tape, they had sealed the opening with plastic sheeting. Although it flapped a bit in the wind, it was serviceable and the main living area slowly started to warm up.

Candrew swallowed the last of the merlot, draining his glass. And then, everything happened at once. The log in the fireplace collapsed, blasting up a flurry of glowing embers, and the Sibelius symphony came to its crashing conclusion. The need for another piñon log on the fire was obvious. But what CD should he play next, and did he want to open another bottle of wine? This all depended, of course, on what he expected to accomplish during the rest of his Sunday afternoon. While there was still work that really ought to be done, the novel he was reading was nearing its climax and maybe he should finish that, get it out of the way. The need for a decision was taken out of his hands when the phone rang.

"Hi. It's Renata. You hear the news?"

"What news?"

"Paolo Magnelli, the concert pianist who was staying with the Smyths, was playing their piano, there was an explosion and he got killed. It seems to be murder. Grand pianos don't just blow up."

"Murder?" He stood for a moment in stunned silence. "You mean, this is the second one in their house?"

"Looks like it."

Open mouthed, Candrew stared into the fire, not seeing clearly, his vision blurred. He didn't know what to say.

"I thought it best not to call the Smyths, they've got enough on their plate," Renata said. "So I phoned Anna Meagher to see if she'd heard anything. Apparently, Paolo and Carla were packing, planning to leave at lunchtime, and Paolo was getting in one last practice session. That's when the piano blew up and killed him. There was lots of damage—it shattered the big plate glass windows in the main living room—but nobody else was hurt."

"That's a really peculiar accident. Weird. Do the police have suspects?"

"They've only just started investigating. Anna has her suspect, of course. She's convinced Carla did it. She thinks anyone that quiet and reserved has to be sinister. As she put it, with her usual mangled cliché, 'Still waters run steep'."

Quietly under his breath Candrew murmured,

"silence the piano, muffle the drum
bring out the coffin, let the mourners come"

"Sorry?"

"Nothing."

Candrew stood gazing at the piñon log as it crackled and flared. Renata's earlier news had knocked him out of equilibrium and, after sitting around all evening feeding the fire and drinking wine, he needed to do something, something physical. He whistled for Chile and grabbed the dog's lead. Together they headed out into the invigorating cold night air and set off down the road through the chamisa, sauntering at first, but then settling into a more purposeful stride. Few stars were visible as the slow-moving, ragged clouds alternately shaded and exposed the nascent moon. Distant coyotes howled.

Candrew thought that, to an outsider, Markham Smyth seemed to have everything. He'd built an immensely successful business, then sold it for a huge profit, making enough to support a lavish lifestyle. Inheriting his father's collection was icing on the cake. But looking back, that's when Markham's problems started. First Kontorovich's murder, now Paolo's. And in between, the theft of one of his paintings, though not an important one. *Too much of a coincidence*, Candrew thought, even if he couldn't see any strong connections among the crimes. True, Kontorovich and the stolen painting involved art, but Paolo had no connection to the graphic arts. Where did he fit in? And why was he a target for murder?

Chapter 20

The news of Paolo's bizarre death had left Candrew drained and he'd slept only fitfully. He woke early and, still yawning, ambled down the driveway to retrieve the morning paper. Walking slowly back, he scanned the front page where the lead story, under banner headlines, reported the murder in the Smyths' house. He drank two cups of coffee while he read the article with careful attention, but it was mostly speculation and he learned little that Renata hadn't already told him.

Not feeling like eating, Candrew skipped breakfast, something he rarely did, and drove to the university in a daze. His brusque, unsmiling "Good morning" to the few students he passed in the halls bordered on the unsociable.

He let himself into the cluttered office, threw his down jacket into a corner and sat at the desk, staring out the window at the snow-capped mountains and wondering what he was in a mood to accomplish. Before he had an answer to that question, the phone rang. It was the art historian, Todd.

"Thought I'd call rather than e-mail. I read the cover story in this morning's *Journal*, the one about the pianist being blown up by a piano. Very strange. If I remember correctly, wasn't that the house where the painting was stolen?"

"Yeah. It was," Candrew said.

"And it's the one where you got the paint chips and wanted me to check out the pigments?"

"Right."

"Well, I've had a chance to look over the data you sent. More than half the samples aren't like any paints I've ever seen. High silica just isn't typical of the materials artists use."

Candrew was pleased to hear Todd confirming his own ideas about those fragments. He pulled one of the desk drawers half way out and parked his feet on it, slouching back in his chair. "No. In thinking about it, I'm sure they were chunks of plaster that flaked off the wall. Probably nothing to do with the painting."

"That makes sense. Now the other three bits are interesting. Your notes described two as being red, which was why they originally caught your attention."

"I was intrigued to know what produced such an intense hue. The color of the flakes was unusual, not like any mineral I'm familiar with."

"And the third flake was very pale yellow?"

"Yeah. Sort of lemony color."

"Okay. Let's start with that one. What stands out in the analyses is the high titanium. Nowadays, almost all the white paint artists use is titanium dioxide. But that wasn't available until around 1925. Your cover note said the date on the back of the painting was 1901, so it doesn't match." There was a pause, then Todd asked, "Have you got the compositions in front of you?"

Candrew fished around in his briefcase and tugged out the folder with Mark's data sheets and the copy of his e-mail to Todd. "Okay. Here they are."

"Look at the analysis of the third sample. As well as high titanium there's lots of zinc. Well, titanium dioxide by itself has a rather spongy texture. It's usually mixed with zinc oxide to give a nice buttery consistency that painters like. So, taken together, the titanium and zinc suggests a recent pigment."

Candrew digested this information. "What you're telling me, then, is that there's no way the painting could have been done in 1901. And clearly, it has to be a lot more recent."

"Exactly right. And there's supporting evidence from the two red flakes. If you look at the analytical data, you can see they're rich in cadmium and selenium."

Candrew ran his finger down the column of numbers and confirmed the high percentages.

"By itself, cadmium doesn't help us much, but using selenium with the sulfide to make cadmium reds wasn't common until 1910. The first reliable pigments weren't introduced until 1919 by Bayer—the German company that makes our aspirins. Again, that's well after the 1901 date on the painting."

Candrew was impressed by the amount of information Todd had put together in such a short time. "I really appreciate all the effort you've made in tracking this down."

"Happy to do it. I got really excited with your compositions. It was fascinating to have a real world problem, and since I had most of the reference books in my office, it wasn't a lot of work." There was a pause. "You don't by any chance have information on phlalo pigments, do you?"

"No. That analysis needs a different type of machine."

"Pity. They were introduced more recently and would let us pin down the timing. But I think we can be pretty sure the painting's not 1901. It's a lot more recent."

There was a moment's silence and Candrew heard Todd flipping pages. "One other thing. I looked up the artist's name you gave me: *Friedlandt*. I couldn't find any reference. Tried a few variations on the spelling, but nothing matched. I checked from 1850 to 1950, so it looks as though he never sold commercially.

Could he have been an amateur?"

Candrew laughed. "That would certainly fit with the quality of the work. Which only raises the question of why Markham Smyth would hang such a shoddy painting in his office. Especially now we know it's deliberately intended to deceive."

"Yeah. And why would anyone want to steal it?"

Candrew sat mulling over the new information. It was clear the art work wasn't produced in 1901, but some time later: twenty years, fifty years later? He wondered how long Markham had owned the painting. And there was still the question of why that particular piece was stolen from a home with dozens of superb, world-class works of art. Candrew could think of several reasons. An unknown painting would be easier to sell: it could be unloaded at a second-tier gallery, unlike major works that would be easily recognized. And there was always the chance, of course, that the thief had no understanding of quality and just made off with whatever was easiest. The other intriguing possibility—one that Candrew had considered earlier—was that the theft was a decoy by Kontorovich's murderer who'd come back to remove incriminating evidence. Again, he wondered what that could be.

The thing that puzzled Candrew most was the underlying question of why Markham himself kept the painting, even if few people would see it in his private study. Sentimental value, maybe, perhaps painted by a relative? Or possibly, a close friend? But it's a fake. Why would anyone paint a fake? It wasn't as though they were trying to cash in by passing it off as the work of some well-known artist: even the signature was fictitious. Whoever painted this work was trying to disguise the real situation, a situation Markham must be protecting. *Protecting?* Could the landscape have been painted over something else, something that needed safekeeping, something more valuable? It was slowly dawning on Candrew that the value of the painting didn't necessarily mean artistic value. What was so important about a possible original work that it had to be masked with a more recent over-painting—one carrying too old a date and a false artist's name? And why was the art work hidden in full view?

* * *

Candrew joined the other faculty lounge regulars for lunch, pulling his chair up to the table. Charlie Lister was sitting opposite, his eyebrows raised, questioning. "Well, what did you think of Red's show?"

"Predictable. Typical Red work." But he quickly added, "Hey, I don't mean that as a criticism, I like what he does. That combination of natural stone and iron banding has an elemental feel to it."

"Lots of people there?"

"Yeah. He drew a good crowd. I don't know how much he actually sold, though." Candrew grinned. "In spite of his high-pressure salesmanship."

"My guess is most folks are put off by the thought of hauling several tons of rock back home." He smiled.

Candrew took the menu from Rosita, the waitress, and flicked open his napkin.

"I hear Gary Frank retired," Arlan Dee said.

"None too soon, judging by what the students say. Every year he talked a little bit quieter and his writing got smaller and smaller. The students joked that when he got to the point where his notes on the board coalesced to a single dot, and he was standing there in silence, it would be time to retire him."

A typical barrage of lunchtime banter ensued with everyone contributing their two-cents worth.

"He's long past normal retirement age anyway. It'll be a good chance to bring in someone younger and more dynamic."

"Can't say 'younger,' that's age discrimination."

"How long's he been teaching anyway? It seems like forever."

"As far as I know, this'll be his thirty-eighth year."

"And I think it's the thirty-eighth anniversary for that beat-up old Chevy of his. I'm surprised the thing's still running."

Lubie put down his fork. "Funny how we keep track of anniversaries. Almost every day must be an anniversary for something."

"Yeah, spot on," said Arlan Dee. "Yesterday was my wedding anniversary—and this year I remembered."

"After last year's fiasco, I'm not surprised."

There was laughter all round.

"And today's an important day here in New Mexico."

"It is?"

"Sure. Back in 1930, Clyde Tombaugh found a new planet: Pluto. Made the announcement on March 13th. That was Lowell's birthday, and Lowell was the guy who'd funded the observatory in Flagstaff where he used the telescope to make the discovery."

"Too bad Pluto isn't a planet any more. Just a cosmic underdog."

"That's science. New data means new concepts, our ideas change."

There was a moment's silence, unusual at the lunch table, and they all pondered this scientific 'progress.'"

Then a voice volunteered, "And March 13th is also the anniversary of the date when the planet Uranus was discovered by Herschel. 1781, if I remember correctly."

Candrew was astonished by the arcane knowledge of his lunchtime colleagues.

The speaker continued. "I always thought he was a Brit, but I'm just reading his biography. Turns out he started as a German musician who played the oboe and he actually wrote twenty-six symphonies."

"And talking of Germans," Lubie took a more serious tone. "in my part of the world, eastern Europe, yesterday was an anniversary with a more sinister connotation." Lubie—Dr. Lubinski—was a history professor with a specialty in twentieth century Europe and had spent his early years in Poland.

"Really? What's so special about March 12th?" Arlan Dee asked.

"That was the day in 1938 when the German Wehrmacht troops marched into Austria, or "Österreich" as they called it. Hitler, he'd been born in Austria, moved the army in on the twelfth, and the next day, March 13th, announced what we now know as the Anschluss. The beginning of the end for the Jewish community." The group fell silent. "Ironic it's so close to Purim." It was clear from the mostly blank faces around the table that they didn't know what that was. Lubie explained. "It's when the Jews celebrate victory in exile. Not much to celebrate in Austria."

Candrew sat quietly dissecting one of the tomatoes in his salad. So, yesterday's murder of Paolo in the Smyth's house had occurred on an important Austrian date. Interesting. But Paolo was an Italian Catholic, not Jewish. Coincidence? Maybe, but he found that an unsatisfying thought.

Candrew climbed the stairs to the second floor of Kinblade Hall, a small gesture to burning off a few of the calories consumed at lunch. As he turned into the long hallway leading to his office, there was someone—a male, probably a student—bending down by his office door, leaving a small, green-wrapped package: another tape! As far as Candrew could make out, it was the same person he'd seen delivering the previous one. This time, he'd no intention of letting him get away. But the student had spotted him and ran to the elevator which was still open. He leapt in, the doors sliding shut behind him. Candrew started to run towards the young man, but changed his mind, turned and retraced his steps down the stairs. Sliding his hand along the handrail for balance, he took the steps three at a time, stumbled, but caught himself. He got to the ground floor as his quarry was peering out of the elevator door. When he saw Candrew, he quickly withdrew, the elevator doors closing abruptly.

Candrew stood panting and cursed under his breath. Up or down? Fifty-fifty chance. He picked the lower level, hoping he'd guessed right, and scurried down the stairs to the basement. Luck was with him. His target was just stepping out into the hallway, running for the back door, when Candrew reached the bottom stair. And then he got another lucky break. Judy was coming out of the lab door as the young man ran full tilt down the passageway, skillfully negotiating the stacks of used equipment, wooden boxes and old filing cabinets.

"Stop him," Candrew yelled to Judy.

The fugitive was fast and Judy seemed in no hurry. As he raced past her she casually stuck out one foot. He tripped, flailing his arms, trying to move his legs fast enough to catch up with the lurching upper body. And failed. He slammed into a large metal tank of liquid nitrogen, ricocheted to the opposite wall with a resounding thud and sprawled full length on the floor.

Stunned and bruised, he made no protest when Candrew and Judy hauled him to his feet and dragged him into the lab. Subdued, he sat on one of the armless plastic chairs, head down, catching his breath. Judy handed him a plastic cup of Gatorade.

Candrew was surprised: the student was Joe Bennington. Only a week before he'd given him advice on summer field camps and helped him organize a part time job with one of the department's professors.

"What the hell are you doing leaving tapes outside my office door?"

Joe took a nervous swig of the juice, still breathing heavily, but didn't reply.

"And why are you making so much effort to avoid getting caught?" Candrew took a more conciliatory tone. "Look, I know what's on the recordings, even if it's often a bit inscrutable. It's no secret. So why are you leaving then outside my office?"

"Well, I, like . . . I'm not the one who made them. Really. I've just left them by your door."

"So who did you get the tapes from? Who made the recordings?" There was a long silence while Joe studied his shoes, then rubbed his bruised arm. "Come on. I'm not a bat. I don't have to be kept in the dark," Candrew said.

"I'm not supposed to tell you. She made me promise."

"She?" Candrew repeated it with increased emphasis. "*She*?"

"Well, yes." He hesitated, examining his shoes again. "Zona Pharn."

Candrew was dumbfounded. "I, . . so, . . then it was Zona who recorded the messages and you just delivered them? She made them in Santa Fe?" Candrew sat staring, shaking his head. "Anyway, how do you know Zona?"

Now that the secret was out in the open, Joe seemed more inclined to talk. As Candrew and Judy listened in silence, he explained how he'd met Zona through his brother who'd been in high school with her, at least when she actually attended. She'd been mostly home-schooled, only going to the local high school for occasional semesters. With his brother, he'd been to the commune outside Las Trampas where she lived with a small group of other free spirits. Although quite a bit younger than Zona, he'd stayed friends even after his brother had joined the Marines. He'd continued to see her once in a while.

"And then she asked you to deliver the tapes?"

"Right. She knew I was at UNNM." There was a long pause, Joe still breathing heavily. "I don't have any idea what's on them. She stressed, like, it needed to be a secret, who they were coming from. I wasn't supposed to tell anyone."

Joe had little more to offer, drained the last of the Gatorade and they let him go.

Candrew went back up to his office, taking the elevator this time. The neatly wrapped green package containing the tape was still leaning against the wall beside his door.

Chapter 21

The tape was an antiquated 8-track, just like the previous two. But this time, Candrew could play it right away because Renata's aging tape player was sitting on top of one of his filing cabinets. He dropped the cassette in, pushed the button. For a while, the only sound was a scratchy hiss: the tapes were not high quality, very amateurish recordings. Eventually, the distinctive soft syllables of an Hispanic male voice began delivering the message, almost certainly the same voice as on the previous tapes.

Greetings. Don't be fooled, things aren't always what they seem. Even if it appeared to be the proper day. Black and white are close together and it's easy to make a mistake. But that might seem odd if you're an expert. There are tasks that must be completed. For some jobs, at some times, there isn't any choice. It's real important to peer into a darkness bred in the past. This is not the path I would have taken, but it had to be done. A pebble dropped in a pool forms ripples that move outward— through distance, through time. And if the pool is blood

. . .

Silence, only the hissing of the tape. Candrew waited a moment and was reaching to switch it off when the voice resumed.

I care about people, everyone. You have no idea how much I care. But I had to retreat to leave. What seemed to be premeditated, indiscriminate was a moment frozen in time when life abandoned him—dancing on the edge before death pushed him over. Spring had gone, Fall came.

Now Candrew knew Zona was the source of the messages, he assumed the tapes were giving him information, however cryptic, about events in Markham Smyth's home. If that were true, and with this last tape coming so soon after the piano explosion, it must be Paolo who was the "expert". And certainly, "black and white" would fit with piano keys. But "close together"? And "easy to make a mistake"—what did that mean? What was the mistake? Had Paolo committed some sort of blunder that got him killed? What mistake was serious enough to lead to murder? Failing to pay his drug dealer like the inspector thought? And it was Spring now, why had "Fall come".

March in northern New Mexico is a gamble. While there might be a foot of snow on the ground one week, it's just as likely to be sunny and balmy the next. But it's *always* windy. As Candrew hurried across campus after his morning class, gust-swirled dust spun in sprightly whirls and dissipated. And a bright candy-bar wrapper, dropped by a thoughtless student, fluttering with them, adding a splash of color. Overhead, fast-moving cumulus clouds scudded northeast, the bulbous and curvaceous tops crossed by the arrow-straight contrails of transcontinental air traffic.

Candrew, hair tousled by the wind, was glad to step inside

the atrium of the Student Union. He ran his hand through his thinning hair and pushed the button for the elevator, heading for the fifth floor and lunch in the faculty club. After tossing his jacket on the rack, he ambled over to the corner table. Candrew was earlier than usual and only two of the regulars were ensconced—and they were already arguing, even if just in a good-natured way. The issue dividing them was advertising in textbooks. Not surprisingly, Ted Devereaux from the business office was in favor, he was always in favor of anything that made money. "Why not? Everything else students are exposed to carries ads. I'm sure the students won't be complaining."

Lubie and two other faculty members strolled over and joined the group, settling into their chairs. Lubie immediately leapt into the fray. "They just need to make sure that the spelling's correct—no *lite* or *foto*".

The usual free-for-all ensued.

"And what will they advertise? Telescopes in the astronomy textbooks?"

"Or busts of Plato and Aristotle in the philosophy texts?"

"Unlikely. They'll push the usual teen-age things, you know, iPads, smart phones, and the like."

"Well, I for one can't go along with it. The last thing students need is more distractions." The plump, jovial physics professor glanced around as if canvassing support. "I don't want to tell them to study the graph on page fifty, and then have them drift away into fantasies about what the advertisers are pushing on page a fifty one."

"Hey, fantasies—good idea. If you pick a text with an alluring centerfold, you'll double the number of guys in your class."

"That'll keep our chairman happy."

"Yeah, but effective teaching and good student evaluations are just as important as numbers."

"If the chair wants an unbiased view he can always go to

rate-my-professor.com and see what the students are saying—and they're never shy about expressing opinions."

"Or worried about offending the teachers."

Candrew had heard of the web site, but never found time to check it. Now he wondered what the art students had said about Helen Kontorovich. And also wondered what students thought about him. He made a mental note to Google the site.

Lunch over, Candrew braced against the wind once more as he made his way across campus to the School of Art. That's where he'd arranged to meet Renata at one-thirty. He knew she'd have Helen's cousin, Susan Cromwell, with her, and they all gathered in the newly redecorated foyer that featured paintings with a variety of styles and subjects by New Mexican artists.

Renata introduced Susan. After last week's brief telephone conversation, she'd arranged to visit campus on her way home from a beauticians' meeting in Phoenix that she'd been attending for the last few days. She shook hands. Like Helen, Susan was tall and slim. But there, any family resemblance ended. Unlike her cousin, who had rich chestnut brown hair, Susan was a redhead, although that was probably not her natural color. Her heels were a bit too high; her skirt a bit too short; and her neckline a bit too low. Ebullient and talkative, Susan—or Suzie as she liked to be called— was a marked contrast to Helen who was usually reserved in social settings, especially those outside the arts.

"Sorry I couldn't make it to the funeral," Suzie said, sounding genuinely sorry. "But being a single mom with two kids, it's difficult to leave at real short notice."

While they were casually chatting, the director bustled out of his office, dropped a sheaf of papers onto the secretary's desk and strode over to join them. Dapper, as always, he wore a tweed jacket with his precisely folded bow tie: today the tie was yellow with muted purple squares and dots. Renata made the introductions and he was appropriately subdued.

"I'm so sorry your visit to our campus is for such a sad reason. I want you to know that Helen Kontorovich was one of the Art School's outstanding faculty members. She will be extremely difficult to replace." Always the bureaucrat, the director was already thinking in fiscal terms. "I'm pleased to be able to let you know that we plan to honor Helen's memory by setting up a memorial fund in her name. I'm sure her friends, past students, and professional colleagues will be happy to donate." He beamed at the thought. "I consider it most appropriate to use the funds to provide graduate student assistance."

"That's a nice gesture," Suzie said. "Students never have enough cash. I like what you're planning to do."

The director, having discharged his official duties, talked informally for a few minutes before getting the departmental secretary to take them up to Helen's office.

The office was basically neat, but intense scholarly activity had left scattered books, papers and trays of slides, as well as a pile of CD's and thumb-drives, stacked haphazardly beside the computer. The impression was more of a technical workplace than one in the arts, although there were several oil paintings and some drawings on the wall opposite the bookshelves.

Suzie looked aghast. "I've been thinking about this ever since you talked to me on the phone. It's overwhelming." Her gaze swept slowly around the office, taking in the stacked folders, books, manuscripts, photographs and piles of papers. The filing cabinets promised more of the same. "I just don't know how I'll get it all sorted out. I haven't the foggiest idea where to begin."

"Your best bet is to get one of the faculty to pull out everything that belongs to the department," Renata suggested. "Then you can decide if you want to keep the rest, donate it, or junk it."

"Yeah. I suppose that's right." Distractedly, she tugged down her short skirt. "You know, I hardly ever saw Helen. I don't think there'll be much of sentimental value. Not stuff I'd want to have as a keepsake."

While they stood contemplating the practical problems, it was the small oil painting hanging beside the bookshelf that caught Candrew's attention. The sensuously posed woman in the portrait, with long hair splayed across a sumptuous background, looked to him like a work by Klimt, although he'd have been the first to admit he was no expert. Of course, there's no way it could be an original, Candrew thought, peering at it, but it looks damn convincing. Perhaps she'd borrowed it from Markham's collection for detailed study? That didn't seem likely since it appeared to be a permanent fixture on the wall. He knew she was an expert on late eighteenth century Austrian art, so maybe she bought it years ago—but even then, a painting by Klimt would not have been cheap. As he stared at it, he remembered Professor LaBarre saying Helen was an excellent painter capable of carefully reproducing the style of other artists. This had to be a copy.

As he continued looking around the office, his gaze came to rest on a silver-framed photo of Helen standing beside a man with a shock of white hair. He was sure it was Andy Warhol. Candrew realized how little he really knew about her. Although it was now clear she'd done her Ph.D. at Yale, he had no idea where she'd been an undergraduate. However, that would be easy to check: the faculty handbook listed the universities where professors got their degrees.

Idly perusing the wall of bookcases, Suzie said, "She's got such a lot of books. I read a book once, by Danielle Iron."

"Steele."

"Yeah, you're right. It took such a long time. I don't know how people can read so many. Hey, I guess it's their job. They probably don't get to do anything else." She stood in silence for a moment, apparently evaluating the academic life. "But I'll bet you a shiny new nickel they wouldn't have the foggiest idea how to cut hair!"

Candrew agreed. He couldn't imagine Helen with a pair of scissors in hand.

Together they spent an hour sorting books that needed to be returned to the library and then Candrew left, leaving Suzie and Renata to continue boxing up some of the stacks of papers.

It was nearly seven-thirty when Candrew arrived at Helen's house on the south fringe of campus. Suzie and Renata had got there only fifteen minutes earlier and were struggling to haul in loaded cardboard boxes. He grabbed one of the larger cartons and followed them. They stacked the boxes in a small side room that looked as though it was intended as a guest bedroom, but rarely used.

"I'll be staying tomorrow," Suzie said, "so I can bring the rest of the stuff over then." She peered at the piles of boxes towering along one wall. "There's tons more stuff to take care of than I was prepared for."

They ambled through the rest of the house finding no surprises, just the expected magazines, CDs, art work and scattered clothes. Judging from the contents of the refrigerator, Helen survived on cheese and yoghurt.

"Look at these poor things." Suzie was bent over several pots of wilting house plants. "They all need a drink." She scurried off to the kitchen to get a container and some water.

Renata smiled. "Suzie and Helen are at opposite ends of the intellectual spectrum."

"And opposite ends of the personality spectrum," Candrew said.

The utility room beside the kitchen had a heavy door that presumably led to the garage. It was locked. Candrew hunted around trying to locate the key, but couldn't find it. "That's odd." Once more he scrutinized the shelves in the utility room. "I'm surprised she bothered to keep the inside garage door locked. The house itself was closed up." He stood tapping his teeth, thinking. "She was only leaving for a few days."

"And you know, she never thought she wasn't coming back," Suzie mused.

Candrew stood looking at the bolted door.

"Well, we've got to get in sometime," Renata said. "Perhaps we should try and force it?"

Smiling, but saying nothing, Candrew pulled out his billfold and slid out a credit card. He pushed the card into the gap between the door frame and the lock, flicking back the beveled shaft.

Renata raised both eyebrows. "Well, well, well. Where did you find out how to do that?"

"You learn a lot of useful skills in graduate school."

"I must have skipped class the day they covered that."

Candrew swung the door open. The pungent smell of paint thinner and solvents was unmistakable—this garage wasn't intended for a car, it was an art studio. The three of them stood surprised, and in silence, looking around at the substantial wooden easel in the center, the large lamp on a tripod and the shelves loaded with paints and brushes. A stack of canvases leaned against the left wall under the only window in the garage—studio—and the panes had been covered with a sheet of heavy drawing paper that was taped around the edges. A comfortable, well-used arm chair stood beside the end wall, a half-empty coffee cup by the leg and a piece of worn carpet in front. The rest of the floor was exposed concrete splotched with paint. Metal shelves along the side wall to the right were loaded with tubes of paint, Gesso, brushes crammed into glass jars, sketch pads and a huge staple gun. A roll of canvas was propped against the end.

Disorganized paintings were leaning against the garage door, looking as though they'd recently been moved, and piles of sketch pads and paint cans were littered in front of them. It seemed as though the police had done a very superficial search and decided there was nothing of significance. *I bet they were responsible for locking the studio door*, Candrew thought.

"Look at all these," Suzie said. She was staring at the left wall of the studio where a row of blown-up photographic reproductions were held in place with push pins. Candrew followed her glance and immediately recognized the one on the end as a print of a Klimt painting he'd just been looking at. It was then that Renata stumbled over the group of unfinished sketches on the floor. There were three of them, each a partially completed work, and all showing the same corner of what appeared to be a Schiele. The complete painting was another of the reproductions on the wall.

The canvas on the easel, was unfinished, but clearly showed a landscape with two symmetrical hills and a river meandering through lush vegetation. Although the painting, was vaguely familiar, triggering a buried memory, Candrew couldn't place it. He was certain he'd seen the original somewhere—and not too long ago. In one of the Santa Fe galleries, maybe? On the floor beside the easel was an open three-ring binder. Candrew picked it up and flipped through the pages, scanning the copious notes on the paintings. He glanced at the photos clipped to several of the pages. The binder gave exhaustive information on the works of art, including design, canvas type, framing and pigments.

To no one in particular, Candrew said, "It looks as though she was making a concerted effort to get the copies as much like the originals as possible; trying to show the brush strokes and other precise details; trying to get the texture and colors exactly right." *Trying to be a precise counterfeiter?* he thought to himself.

Candrew turned to the shelves, rummaged through the partly-used tubes of paint and selected a white, red, green and violet. At the end of the middle shelf was a wooden palette with dabs of colors, all dried out. "Suzie, can I borrow these?"

"Sure. I don't need them. Why you asking me?"

"Well, it's your house now. So is everything in it."

"Yeah, that's right, I guess." She smiled uncertainly. "Anyway, you're welcome to keep all those things."

Candrew found an empty brown paper bag and dropped in the palette and paint tubes. He planned to get the paints analyzed, and see if Todd could compare them with the pigments on Markham's missing painting. And that's when he realized, the painting on the easel was just like Markham's stolen landscape—the landscape painted to deceive.

One of the shelves had a row of photographs, and most of the people Candrew didn't recognize. The two at the end, however, were in silver frames and showed Helen with a tall, elegant man—Phillipe LaBarre. In both photos he had his arm around her, and she was laughing. Further confirmation of their relationship, Candrew thought. At the end of the row of photographs stood several decorative metal cans with lids. He picked one up and opened it. The tarry aromatic odor was unmistakable—marijuana. Surprised, he opened the other cans and found they also had pot. But the ceramic jar in the middle had a white odorless powder he couldn't identify. Could Martinez be right about Helen using drugs, with Garcia being her dealer—a dealer who hadn't been paid?

To Candrew, Helen had been only a casual acquaintance and he'd hardly known her as a real person. Now, LaBarre's comments at the funeral, the paintings, and last night's view into her studio and private life were giving Helen substance, bringing her alive. Memories of a limp, bloody body sprawled across Markham's floor suddenly flooded in, taking him by surprise. He sucked in a sharp breath. What a waste.

As an academic himself, he knew she must have worked hard while an undergraduate and struggled against all the competition to get accepted by a first-class graduate school. And the years of creative research leading to the Ph.D. were only a prelude to detailed postgraduate work in her specialty. Finally, she'd gotten that coveted tenured university position. And then came the rewards: success, recognition, promotion—and death.

Chapter 22

Traffic flowing south into Santa Fe was light and the demands of driving—negotiating the road, watching other motorists, reading signs—took just enough of Candrew's attention to tie up the left side of his brain. That gave his creative right side unfettered freedom, and with free reign, speculations inevitably drifted back to the tapes from Zona Pharn.

Why would Zona, whom he hardly knew, be sending him puzzling bits of information, even if she did think of him as a "priest of the earth"? Why the need for secrecy? And why use old-fashioned tapes? Surely, a typed piece of paper would have been just as good? Plenty of questions; few answers. What seemed particularly odd was that she'd be giving information about events in the Smyths' household, while at the same time obscuring the message and trying to keep the source a secret. Zona had a central role in daily life at the Smyths' and might hear things that weren't common knowledge. Did she have information about the murders? But why did she want to tell him? Why not go to the police?

Candrew's rambling thoughts led back to their first meeting. He clearly remembered the chilly day of Kontorovich's murder when Zona had been scurrying across the snow-dappled hillside, burying something—or so he thought. But when he'd caught up with her in the garage, she'd claimed she was only putting fresh flowers on the dead dog's burial site. At the time, he'd accepted that explanation, but now, thinking back, he wasn't so sure. What would she want, or need, to hide? Something connected with Helen's murder? That would certainly explain the urgency. Documents? Clothing—blood-stained, perhaps? Identification? And, of course, the one thing the police had not been able to recover was the murder weapon. He wondered why he hadn't thought of it before—was Zona burying the gun?

All the police had learned from the ballistics experts was that the bullet that killed Helen Kontorovich had been fired from a pre-World War II German pistol. That triggered another memory: the lunchtime discussion about anniversaries, especially the German army annexing Austria: the Anschluss. So, Kontorovich's murder had been carried out with a Nazi weapon and Paolo had been murdered on a significant date in Austrian history, one involving the Nazis.

Candrew immediately realized that if these speculations were correct, they strengthened the case for a link between the two murders. Which was hardly surprising, since they both happened in the same house only days apart. But that connection was tenuous; there had to be something deeper. And where did the other odd events, like the incredible incident with the dead pet dog, fit in— if they fitted at all? And what was the significance of the stolen painting? Apart from the general layout of hills and river, he knew little about that piece of art, only that the date and the artist's name had been added solely to deceive. The artist's signature, Friedlandt, was certainly bogus, although it sounded German—or maybe Austrian? Helen had a partly-finished landscape on the easel in her studio, and was quite capable of producing a competent fake. But Markham's landscape had been on his wall for years, long before he knew her. The timing was all wrong; Helen couldn't have been involved.

The missing painting posed an ethical problem for Candrew. Should he tell Markham what he'd discovered from analysis of the pigments? That seemed only fair, since it was his painting. But maybe he already knew. It was like deciding to tell a woman her husband was having an affair. Markham may already know that artwork was not what it purported to be, after all, he'd kept the painting—a second rate one—hanging on the wall in his office. The fact that he was using it to cover his wall safe didn't seem sufficient reason.

As the highway crested the ridge and dropped down into Santa Fe, the low sun blazed, gilding hilltops, leaving lower slopes wrapped in indigo-blue shadows. Candrew swung off to the left, followed Paseo de Peralta and cut through to Hyde Park Road, heading for the Smyths' home. On his way to the airport in Albuquerque he was dropping off a preliminary copy of Renata's report on Markham's pre-Columbian pottery.

Gwen greeted him at the door. "Sorry about all the chaos. It'll be at least another day before they can fix the windows." She ushered Candrew in. "And Zona isn't here to help clean up the mess. Just vanished."

"Really? How long's she been missing?'

"Couple of days. At least that long since we last saw her. God knows where that girl's gone."

Candrew found this an interesting piece of information.

Markham came striding across the lounge, tossed the insurance policy he'd been reading on a chair and shook hands. Candrew gave him Renata's summary. "Thank her for me, will you? But tell her it's going to be a while before I'll get to it. Just too much going on." He nodded towards the flapping plastic sheets covering the window frames.

Gwen followed his glance. "It's like a damn yacht in here

with the sails luffing all the time. And way too cold." She headed off to the kitchen.

Traces of the acrid odor lingering from the explosion permeated the room, and gave it the smell of a cheap motel. "Police making any progress with Paolo's murder investigation?" Candrew asked.

"Not a lot. They're still interrogating people. The inspector's eager to talk to Zona, but she's disappeared."

"That's what Gwen said. Any idea where she's gone?"

"None at all. The police are treating her as a suspect, or at least a material witness. I got the impression they're about to issue a warrant for her arrest. When I talked to Liesl Sorenson, she couldn't remember Zona saying anything that would help." Markham ran the fingers of one hand through his thin hair and stood looking around the devastated room. "The police suspect the explosive was probably ammonium nitrate. Apparently, it's easy enough to get that stuff. They said it's widely used as a fertilizer. Still, someone needed to know what they were doing to wire up the detonator." He was silent for a few minutes, watching the plastic window coverings billow in the breeze.

"There any other suspects?" Candrew asked.

"Oh, yes. Martinez's prime suspect is Ronnie Garcia."

"Your handyman?"

"Yeah. He's certainly familiar with the house. And Martinez liked your estimate that Kontorovich's murderer wasn't very tall, since that fits nicely with Ronnie who's not much over five feet. On the night before the piano exploded, he could easily have snuck in. And he knows the alarm system." He paused, thinking back. "Both Gwen and Zona were out of the house. I was at Red Mulholland's opening, and Paolo and Carla were there as well."

"Has he had any experience with explosives?"

Markham shook his head. "Not that I'm aware of."

"And what about motive?"

"The inspector still thinks it's drugs, that he's a dealer. And didn't get paid."

The memory of Helen's marijuana stash flashed back into Candrew's mind. But marijuana? That seemed relatively innocuous. Hardly a reason for murder. Now, if the white powder he'd seen was cocaine or crystal meth that would be a different story, but he didn't have any real evidence. He made a mental note to tell the inspector and let the police analyze it. "So, they going to arrest him?"

"They would—if they could find him."

Candrew's eyebrows rose in a mute question.

"INS, or ICE, or one of those groups, has been checking up," Markham said. "He's an illegal immigrant. When Ronnie figured out he was a murder suspect, I guess he skipped back across the border. Which would certainly explain why I couldn't reach him over the weekend."

Gwen came back in with a silver tray of snacks and Candrew took some lemonade and a piece of cake. Markham poured himself a scotch. For the next half hour conversation centered around the explosion and Paolo's murder. Now that she'd had time to assimilate the stunning event, Gwen seemed devastated by his death. "It's overwhelming to have a close friend die in your home. You just feel helpless." She brushed away a tear. "Especially knowing Paolo was murdered." They sat in silence.

It was dusk when Candrew finally left and threaded his way through Santa Fe's twisting streets to join Interstate 25 on his drive south to Albuquerque. The sere hills were dotted with struggling junipers. Only where the Rio Grande provided moisture, was there a wide swath of green, an organic contrast with the sharp outline of the Sandia Mountains to the east. Broken clouds over the hills of the western horizon were lit from below by the last rays of the disappearing sun giving bright orange layers over the dark, grey-blue silhouettes. Traffic thinned as the last of the commuters from Santa Fe drove home to the Indian pueblos or the Duke City.

The first thing Candrew did after checking into the airport hotel was phone his colleague who'd given Joe Bennington a part time lab job. No one answered. Candrew then tried Mark Kernfeld and was luckier. "Look Mark, I'm sorry to be calling you at home, but Joe Bennington is in your igneous petrology class and I'm trying to find out who you have as the teaching assistant for the lab section."

"Hey, no problem. Michelle Ortiz TA's for me. She's doing a damn good job. Why do you need that information?"

"I'm trying to locate Joe in a hurry. Most times, students in lab sessions get to know each other pretty well. I was hoping your TA could tell me where he hangs out."

"Hold on a moment, I've got a university directory here somewhere."

Candrew stood impatiently looking around the hotel room, although sterile and generic it was comfortable enough.

He wrote down the number Mark dictated and dialed it immediately. Although Michelle answered on the second ring it was almost impossible to hear because of the pounding music in the background. "Let me hit the mute. Hold on," she yelled.

Candrew knew her well. She often came to the house to feed Chile and Pixel when he was out of town. Conscientious and personable, she was also an excellent graduate student. "I need to reach Joe Bennington in a hurry. Any idea where I can find him?"

"Well, he's, like, tied up on that copper ore project on Tuesday and Thursday mornings. I think he shares an apartment with a couple of guys over on the west side. I could try and track him down for you."

"Yeah. Would you do that? Tell him I need to see him in my office before ten on Friday. And stress it's critical, extremely urgent."

"Right. I'll be sure he gets the message."

The next morning, Candrew poured coffee, grabbed a

danish and a yogurt from the hotel's complimentary breakfast buffet and took the shuttle to the airport.

Not yet fully awake, he sat at the airline gate waiting to board, scanning the *USA Today* he'd brought from the hotel. His unfocused thoughts were pierced by the strident voice of an overweight man in a striped rugby shirt talking on his cell phone. " . . . Yeah. Yeah. So you think its par for the course, you think they'll punt?" He listened in silence. "I guess so. With the bases loaded it won't be a slam dunk. If you don't make them toe the line, they could throw us a curve and then you'll have to figure out how to get us off the hook. You'd better have somebody warming up in the bullpen." Another silence. "No. No. You can't just play defense or you'll never get to first base." Silence. "Well, I'll try not to strike out, but I'm already punching above my weight. When we get our ducks in a row, maybe we could take a different tack if we aren't in the pole position." He paused to listen to the announcement over the loudspeaker. "Look, my flight's been called. I just wanted to touch base with you before I left. Let me know if they want to get back in the game. The ball's in your court now." The man snapped shut the cover of his phone, grabbed his bag and hustled over to the walkway.

Intrigued by the half of the conversation he'd heard, Candrew realized it had been solely in sports clichés and he had no idea what business they were discussing. He understood why women, most with less interest in sports than men, could find the business world confusing.

Candrew had a window seat on the plane. He settled in and spent part of the flight to Philadelphia asleep, part of the time reviewing notes for his scheduled presentation to the investors and what time was left planning his questions for Clem Forleigh. After an on-time arrival, the airport taxi took him to one of the taller downtown buildings. He checked through the security barrier in the capacious lobby and the elevator whisked him swiftly to the twenty-first floor.

As the elevator doors parted smoothly and silently, he stepped into a plushly-appointed foyer. The polished granite floor reflected the company's logo etched into the thick glass panels. The chic receptionist, expensively perfumed and looking as though she modeled for *Vogue* in her spare time, raised a stylishly-coiffed head and coolly evaluated him. "Can I help you?"

"Yes. I've got an appointment with Gordon Marano."

She glanced at the calendar. "Professor Nor?" She had a way of peering down her nose as she spoke and managed to evoke the sense that *you're way out of your league here.* "He's expecting you."

Candrew was escorted to a spacious corner office with ultra-modern furnishings where Gordon greeted him cordially. "Hope you had a pleasant flight—if that's possible these days with all the damned security." He smiled, waved Candrew to the sofa and joined him in the adjacent chair. "Pity Brody himself couldn't have come with you. It's always good to have the principal on board at these presentations. He beamed at Candrew. "Although I'm sure you're on top of all the technical aspects."

Second best, but good enough, Candrew thought.

"I've put together a viable group of investors. They've got the interest and the resources to back Brody's proposed drilling project out there in New Mexico." He made it sound as though the forty-seventh state was located on the moon.

The half dozen potential investors sat around the conference room's enormous polished wood table as Candrew ran through his PowerPoint presentation explaining the geology with a series of simplified sketches and showing where the five proposed wildcat wells would be drilled. He concluded by asking if there were any questions. There were lots. Since these were investors, not geologists, most of the questions concerned money. Things like operating costs, potential profits, and the all-important return on investment.

The balding, heavy-set man in a striped gray suit leaned back in his chair. "What's the advantage of investing in New Mexico rather than going to the big petroleum provinces, you know, Alaska or the deep water Gulf of Mexico?"

"In either of those areas you'll be paying upwards of thirty million dollars a well," Candrew explained. "Chevron's just spent a hundred and twenty million dollars for a single well in the Gulf. And an offshore production platform will run a few billion dollars. In New Mexico the costs are much more reasonable."

"What's your environmental record like?" the lone woman in the group asked.

"No problems with the EPA—so far." Candrew grinned. "But the Sierra Club, that's a different matter." They all sniggered.

The man at the far end of the table had been jotting comments on his pad. Now he peered over his glasses. "Are you sure you can you compete with the big boys?"

"Certainly. They're lumbering beasts . . . " Candrew smiled, " . . . and we're fast, agile and respond quickly. And we can make money on oilfields that are far too small for a giant like ExxonMobil."

The barrage of questions continued for more than an hour and Candrew did his best to field their requests for information. Technical issues were straightforward, but for some financial details he had to refer them back to Brody McCullum, the president of the company.

After the formal meeting ended, Gordon Marano took Candrew back to his office. "I thought that went well, very well," he said. "Adrian, that's the guy with the thick glasses, is always difficult to read, but the others seemed satisfied with what they heard." Candrew was relieved to be told that. "And I thought you did a first rate job of explaining the project, both the risks and the rewards. You should ask old Brody for a bonus." He laughed and slapped Candrew on the shoulder. "You want some coffee?" When Candrew accepted, they sat at the desk for half an hour clearing up the few remaining issues.

Finally, Candrew left for his second appointment of the day.

The law offices of Starber, Whitney and Ray were five floors above those of the investment corporation and seemed to be higher in the pecking order as well. Appropriately, they were even more opulent with rich, finely-polished wood; glass and stainless steel doors; and oriental carpets covering much of the honed marble floor. A legal assistant had greeted Candrew at the elevator door and now she shepherded him past the two secretaries seated at burnished mahogany and glass desks, accompanying him down a passageway lined with lavishly-framed paintings and graphics. Clem Forleigh's office was at the end. With large plate-glass windows, it would have been flooded with light on a sunny day. Now, streaks of drizzle slid across the windows deforming the view of adjacent buildings, but the spacious office still retained a welcoming air.

Clem rose from his high-backed chair and came around the desk to shake hands. He was younger than Candrew expected, tall, medium build, athletic. His thinning hair was chestnut and he wore rimless glasses. But what stood out were the eyes: piercing. His direct look at Candrew was unsettling—not confrontational or arrogant, just confident. Clearly, a superior intellect lurked behind those intense blue eyes.

"How'd your meeting with the money-men go?" he asked, smiling.

"Just fine. About what I expected. They don't understand geology, but they sure know the financing." Candrew wondered how best to steer the conversation to eastern European art. "Anyway, I appreciate you taking time to meet with me."

"Not a problem. We can talk over lunch. I need to eat at some point and I can hardly bill my lunch break to a client—though I'm not averse to sending Waldhaven the bill for the meal." He guided Candrew back along the passage, asked the secretary to pull some files for him and they strolled over to the elevator.

When it arrived, Clem followed Candrew in and poked the ground-floor button with a well-manicured finger. The doors slid shut and a mellow bell chimed softly.

"So, you're the recipient of the Waldhaven Chair in Geology."

"Right. Benny Waldhaven's very generous and I appreciate that."

"He likes to support education," Clem said. "And Benny's been interested in rocks for years. He's amassed quite a collection. But then, he told me you'd been to see him in Denver, so you know what he's got."

"Yeah. Impressive, both mineralogically and aesthetically. I was particularly taken by the huge size of some of his specimens."

Clem nodded in agreement. "He probably told you that I handle most of his legal affairs, including the preparation of the papers for your endowed chair." He smiled. "When Benny called last Wednesday, he said you wanted to talk to me. So what can I do for you?" He tilted his head slightly to one side, turning the conversation over to Candrew.

Candrew was uncertain how to proceed. "As you know, in addition to his incredible mineral collection, Benny Waldhaven also has an outstanding art collection. While he was walking me through it, he mentioned that one of the paintings, a Schiele couple, is being claimed by an Austrian family. They're saying it was owned by their father and misappropriated by the Nazis during the war."

A fleeting smile flickered across Clem's face. "And why does that concern you?"

Before Candrew could answer, the elevator came to a stop at the fifth floor. Two impeccably-dressed, professional women stepped in. The slender blonde in a charcoal pantsuit, oblivious to Clem and Candrew, talked loudly about a pending real estate deal—all the way to the ground floor.

Chapter 23

The downtown sidewalks, shining and wet with rain, reflected distorted images of looming buildings as Candrew and Clem walked two blocks to the restaurant. The owner greeted Clem by name and escorted them to one of the few empty tables. "I often eat here," he said. "Not fancy, although the food's pretty good." He didn't bother to open a menu, just nudged one across the table to Candrew.

Wafting aromas made Candrew realize how hungry he was after his early, and marginally adequate, breakfast—danish and yogurt weren't very sustaining.

Lunch orders given, Candrew got back to the reason he needed to talk to Clem. "A friend in Santa Fe just inherited his father's art collection. It's mostly European with Austrian paintings particularly well represented. They're all from the beginning of the twentieth century, most acquired in the late thirties. I'm not sure he understands the potential provenance issues. Or the possible complications."

"You think some of the artwork might have been plundered from its rightful owners?" Clem didn't wait for a reply. "Heirs, for both sentimental and economic reasons, are getting more aggressive about recovering family art. And that includes sculpture, jewelry and books, not just paintings. There's a lot at stake. You've heard, I'm sure, that Klimt's portrait of Adele Bloch-Bauer recently sold for $135 million."

"Yes." *About the cost of a single ultradeep well in the Gulf of Mexico*, Candrew thought. "And I saw that an Egon Schiele landscape made over twenty million at auction in London."

"Absolutely. You must be aware that both of those paintings were repatriated Nazi loot." Clem stared quizzically at Candrew as if to be certain they were on the same wavelength. "There's increasing moral pressure for museums to return art stolen by the Third Reich that has found its way into their collections. And not just private museums, even some European national collections. Austria recently passed legislation requiring it to return art with a dubious provenance, but so far has been quite adept at stalling. Although, of course, it was finally forced to return the Bloch-Bauer portrait that the heirs then chose to sell."

Candrew sat quietly listening, sure he'd made contact with exactly the right person.

"Linz in Austria is a good example," Clem continued. "Ironically, the town was Hitler's birthplace and the setting for his planned übermuseum. Now the city's Lentos Museum has a Klimt portrait and a Nolde landscape and both are being pursued by heirs with restoration claims. The museum has rejected all these, saying there's no evidence for Nazi misappropriation. It's an interesting case because the doctor who owned the paintings shipped them out in 1938. The crates never arrived, but the Nolde finally turned up in a Salzburg gallery in 1953 and was sold to what later became the Lentos. So, a fifteen year gap in the provenance—lots of wiggle room for lawyers." He smiled.

Clem sipped his hot tea, then peered into the distance for a moment. "Private collections, like your friend's, pose different problems. The situation isn't simple; a legal quagmire. The overriding problem is to establish provenance and that presents major complications ranging from clear proof of title to statutes of limitation." He stared at Candrew with those intense blue eyes. "Can he establish legal title to the works?"

"You make a good point. I don't know, but doubt it." Candrew drank his soup, took another bite of the overgenerous sandwich, and adsorbed everything he was being told. Clearly, Nazi-looted art intrigued Clem and he was knowledgeable and eager to talk about it.

"Furthermore," Clem continued, "historical paths are often so convoluted it's impossible to trace the original owner. Deplorably, a large number were victims of the Holocaust." There was a long pause as he seemed to be considering how much more background information was warranted. "It's not uncommon for all ownership records to have been lost and, not surprisingly, those now in possession of the art works demand incontrovertible proof of previous history before they'll part with them. Many, many paintings have murky provenance from 1933 to around 1945, or even later. With large sums of money at stake, few dealers ask questions, and now innocent buyers could unwittingly acquire art looted by the Third Reich. I am sure Benny Waldhaven's painting will prove to be in that category." It was said with an air of finality, and in a tone of voice that might be used in summing up for a jury.

When Candrew described the paintings in Markham's collection, stressing their modern genre, Clem raised his hands and rocked his head to one side. "Your friend could always use the Elgin defense."

"What on earth is that?" It sounded as if it was a chess opening.

"The Nazis were interested in acquiring trophy art, like Renaissance and Dutch old masters. German expressionism was being destroyed. That, and the sort of modern works your friend

213

has—the Noldes, the Schieles, the Beckmanns—were classed as degenerate art by the Nazis and burnt, or very occasionally sold. Your friend saved this degenerate art from destruction. The situation is exactly like the marbles from the Parthenon that Lord Elgin shipped out of Greece to save them from destruction. The so-called Elgin Marbles are now in the British Museum, and there seems little chance they'll ever be returned. Hence the legal argument for an 'Elgin defense.'"

"So, even prestigious museums are having to justify keeping their dubious art works?"

"Absolutely. And it's not just the big museum collections that are under attack, it's also works in private collections. Like Liz Taylor's. She was sued by heirs demanding return of a van Gogh she's had since the early sixties, one that's now worth an estimated fifteen million. She bought it at Sotheby's in London, but heirs claim it was stolen from an ancestor by the Nazis in the nineteen thirties. The U.S. Supreme Court refused to hear the appeal, ending the case." Clem drained the last of his tea. "It's difficult to comprehend the scale of what was the largest theft of cultural items in history. In the six years after the war ended, roughly five million items were returned. But the *Art Loss Register* still lists 170,000 pieces of stolen, missing or looted art. Unless a family member with a cast-iron case chooses to claim a piece, not much is going to happen."

Candrew finished his coffee, they donned their coats and ventured back out into the cold, gray day, strolling the few blocks back to the office building.

On the ride up in the elevator, Candrew thought about Markham's stolen fake. "Markham, that's my friend in Santa Fe, has one painting that I'm sure is a forgery. It's a small landscape and nowhere near the quality of the rest of his own collection or the works inherited from his father."

"Forgery? That's a legal term and only applies if it's passed off as the real thing. Has he tried to sell it, representing it as genuine?"

214

"Not to my knowledge."

"Then no problem. Unless he wants to sue the dealer who sold it to him."

"I don't think so. As far as I know he's had it for years. It was stolen just a few days ago. Oddly, it was the only painting taken and the thieves left all the others."

"Really? How peculiar." Clem pursed his lips and stared at the mirrored wall of the elevator. "Your friend isn't Jewish, is he?"

"Not that I know of."

"I ask because the vast majority of artwork looted by the Nazis was owned by Jews. Although Jews in Austria had legal equality going back to 1867, within a month of the Anschluss, every one of their organizations was dissolved. That led to a complete loss of Jewish records and of continuity. The Nazis were as passionate about collecting art as they were of destroying the culture—and the lives—of its owners. With German efficiency they kept excellent records."

Back in his office, Clem gestured towards one of the arm chairs. "Give me a few minutes and I'll be with you."

He pulled his chair up to the glass-topped desk covered with neatly-arranged piles of papers, files and books. After retrieving his phone messages, he made a few short calls then fished around, found a note pad and jotted down some information.

For a moment Clem sat pensively staring across his office, before abruptly standing up. "There's someone I'd like you to meet. He's one of the other partners in the firm and may have some special insights into your friend's possibly-plundered art. I'll be right back." Leaving Candrew waiting in his office, he hustled down the passageway.

Candrew stood looking out the window at the dismal Philadelphia sky above and the stop-and-go traffic twenty-six stories below. He didn't wait long.

A tall, athletically-built, older man who appeared fit in spite of a receding hairline and thick glasses, followed Clem into the office. The face was vaguely familiar, although Candrew couldn't quite place it.

"I want you to meet Leland Smyth, Markham Smyth's brother."

Candrew was taken aback. Shocked, he stared, mouth open, not knowing what to say.

Leland Smyth showed a strong family resemblance, although he was slimmer and taller than his brother Markham, with a narrower face. Sandy-colored hair was thinning and receding. Cordial enough, he greeted Candrew with a certain reserve and Candrew felt he was being summed up, evaluated.

"So, you live in the topographic drama of Santa Fe?"

"Actually, north of it." Candrew sucked in a deep breath. "I'm on the faculty at the University of Northern New Mexico."

"Ah. A *yellowlander*." Leland smiled.

Candrew was surprised he knew the nickname for students from the university. He also wondered why Clem Forleigh had brought them together.

"I hear that you know my brother, Markham?" Leland paused and gave only a hint of a smile. "The family aesthete."

Candrew picked up on the hint of sarcasm. "I always assumed his artistic sensibilities were inherited from your father."

Leland ignored that. "Clem tells me you're interested in art that may have been plundered by the Nazis."

Candrew wasn't sure how to answer and became evasive. "Only in a general way. I don't have any specific pieces in mind."

Leland gave him a cold, perceptive stare.

Clem waved Leland to the chair beside a small table and they all sat down.

"Your father's collection has some outstanding works of art." Candrew felt he had little to lose. "Quite a few from pre-war Austria. But I don't think anyone has claimed they're Nazi loot.

And no one is suing for their return."

"Well, of course not. Nobody knows what he's got." Leland pursed his lips and stared off into the distance, then wagged his index finger at Candrew. "But wait 'til he tries to insure them, or the word gets around about what's hanging on his walls."

Candrew detected a note of bitterness. Jealousy?

Clem, saying nothing, leaned back quietly in his chair. Leland gestured, bringing him into the conversation. "My colleague here is fluent in German—I'm not—and he translated father's journals for me. So, he's well aware of all the background to the paintings that Markham inherited." Clem nodded in confirmation. "You, of course, are not."

Candrew sat in silence, wondering whether he was going to be told any of those arcane details.

Leland also seemed to be considering just how much he should disclose. He squirmed in his chair and finally said, "Our father was conscripted into the Germany army. With his background and experience he was soon assigned the job of hunting down works of art for Hermann Göring. The Reich Marshal's backing, of course, gave him essentially unlimited access to all the paintings that were being confiscated and stolen from museums and the Jews. In the late thirties he moved to Austria with Wehrmacht forces and was based in Vienna." He paused as if considering that event. "Vienna: what a city it must have been before the war. And I don't mean the fluffy waltzes of Strauss. I mean the intellectual forge of Wittengenstein, Freud, Mahler, Schöenberg and all the rest. And, of course, the painters. To think my father had a role in disassembling that."

"Don't be too hard on him," Clem said. "Given the opportunity, he chose to desert the Third Reich. And he took you two boys with him."

"But he didn't hesitate to abscond with a truck load of paintings. Very valuable paintings."

"True. But he saved them from the Nazis. . ." The Elgin

defense, Candrew thought. ". . . and as you well know, they were almost entirely degenerate art."

Candrew had heard that term for the first time at lunch, although he still didn't fully understand it. When he looked puzzled, Clem clarified. "The Fuhrer's phrase. Even though rejected twice by the Academy of Fine Arts in Vienna, Hitler set himself up as the ultimate art critic. And at the bottom of his list was modern art, which he hated and considered degenerate. Much was Jewish-owned and a lot of it destroyed, although some was auctioned to pay for neoclassical paintings that Hitler preferred."

Candrew turned to Leland. "So, your father, in fact, saved some art from destruction?"

"Possible, I suppose. It's a charitable view." He stared at Candrew without smiling. "The problem is the way the art works were acquired. A lot were simply stolen, removed for 'protective safekeeping'. Auctions were common, but with few buyers for degenerate art, prices were minimal. And it's widely known that collusion among auction houses and dealers often set values ridiculously low. At least works acquired in forced auctions are now recognized under German Law as *looted*. I like to think of our illustrious father picking up the apples when Hitler shook the tree. But trying to prove his role is like trying to nail a wave to the sand." He leaned back in his chair, arms folded, sullen, staring in silence. "And those are the paintings my cultured brother inherited."

"And all the art work went to Markham?" Candrew asked.

"Every piece of it. But then, he was always the favorite, always got what he wanted."

Before Candrew could frame a reply, Leland changed the subject. "I hear there's been two murders in my brother's home." He spoke softly with a trace of a smile. "Should I infer that they're related to the recent acquisition of all that Nazi-looted art?" he said, his tone supercilious.

"I have no idea," Candrew replied. "But one of the victims

was an Italian pianist who seems to have no connection to art stolen by the Nazis. Or, indeed, to any graphic arts."

"And the other one? Helen Kontorovich, she was in the art world."

Where the hell did he get that information? Candrew wondered. "That's right," he said. "Though as far as I know, Helen had no contact with Markham before she was asked to curate the collection."

"Well, you should be aware I did have some small role in that," Leland said. "When I found that my father had left all the paintings to Markham—'*the entire collection of my oil paintings, prints, watercolors and primitive art are bequeathed to my son Markham Smyth*'—I wanted a clearer idea of just what he was getting, and, of course, its value. One of the partners here at the law firm has enough money and artistic sensibility to collect high-end art. Moves in those circles. He suggested that I contact a professor at Yale." There was a pause.

"And did you?" Candrew asked.

"Yes. Very helpful, but the professor's now emeritus. He suggested an ex-student who he thought very highly of, Dr. Kontorovich. And she had the added advantage of already being in New Mexico." He frowned and peered at Candrew as if deciding how much to tell him. "The professor offered to call her."

"And this professor, would it be Phillipe LaBarre?"

Leland raised an eyebrow and gave a hint of a smile. "My, you're remarkably well-informed."

"He came to Helen Kontorovich's funeral," Candrew added by way of explanation.

"Bright woman. Sad she died so brutally," Clem said. "And seems to have been very close to LaBarre from what she implied."

"You knew her personally?" Candrew was surprised.

"Yes, I did. She collaborated with us as an expert witness for several restitution cases. First rate. Her detailed historical perspective on Austrian art works was absolutely invaluable."

Candrew glanced down at his briefcase, leaning against the chair leg. He'd been unsure what to do about the papers, but was now in no doubt. "I need to show you copies Helen made of some auction receipts she'd found hidden in the paintings,"

As he bent down to get the papers from his briefcase, Clem pulled a folder off one of the piles on his desk and handed it to him. "These?"

Candrew flipped through the pages he'd been given: faxed copies of everything he'd brought with him. "She sent you these?"

"Absolutely." He smiled at Candrew's lack of understanding. "They were faxed only an hour or two before she was murdered. I'm sure the killer didn't want anyone to have this information. Although I have to confess that I don't know whether he realized they'd been sent."

Candrew tapped his teeth, perplexed. For a moment all three of them sat in silence.

For someone who rarely corresponded with his brother and never visited, Leland seemed to be surprisingly well-informed about events in Santa Fe. He'd even remarked on the fact that LaBarre had been staying with Markham and Gwen for a few days after the funeral.

"Did you know that one of Markham's paintings was stolen?" Candrew asked.

Leland gave another hint of a smile and said slowly and quietly, "Yes, so I heard." No additional comments were volunteered.

Candrew probed. "It didn't seem to be of the same quality as the rest of his collection."

"That's what I was told. Ironic. He's losing his paintings the same way our father acquired them—by theft. And with a background of murder."

There was an awkward silence and Candrew broke in to ask, "When did you last see your father's collection?"

"Long time ago. Father and I didn't get along and it's been a while since I visited the house. Anyway, I found it impossible to consider the paintings from a connoisseur's point of view. I saw art that was stolen, not only for what it was worth, but also as part of a deliberate attempt to destroy a culture, a people." There was an extended, somber silence. "I suppose the old man wasn't all bad, at least not from our point of view. He did sell a couple of the paintings to pay for Markham and me to go to college. Of course, when I chose not to become a doctor, he got mad. Didn't say much, just showed it in his behavior. Markham, of course, could do no wrong, got away with anything he wanted. I guess in personality he was more like my father." Leland appeared to have talked enough about his father and the art bequeathed to his brother. Candrew sensed that he felt at least part of the collection should have been his, that the family heritage should have been shared. He wondered whether his concern was more for monetary value than artistic merit. But he did appear sensitive to the Jewish losses.

Seeming to gloat over the Smyths' misfortunes, Leland said, "It's certainly been a very strange time for Markham and Gwen. From what I hear, even her dog was killed. Now, who'd do a weird thing like that?"

Chapter 24

On the departing flight back to New Mexico, Candrew's fellow passengers had fastened their seat belts, turned off their cell phones, and watched the flight attendants strap themselves in as the plane accelerated down the runway and climbed through scattered clouds. After minor turbulence, they emerged into a pale blue sky lit by the setting sun's orange disk. Candrew reclined his seat and settled back, thinking over the events of the day.

In many ways, the presentation of the proposed petroleum exploration program to the investors was a challenge similar to teaching freshmen: explaining science to a non-technical audience. As a consultant for McCullum Oil, Candrew kept at the forefront of activities in the oil patch. And the fees were not an insignificant part of his income. It was about time he spent some of that money—he needed a new car, and his dishwasher was producing strange noises. But he resented the time he'd have to spend making decisions on replacements.

Dragging his thoughts back to the day's events, Candrew realized that information had flowed in different directions before and after lunch. At the morning meeting, while making his presentation to the oil investors, he'd provided everything and long ago he'd found that when you're talking you're not learning. In the afternoon, it was his turn to do the listening—and he'd learned plenty from Clem and Leland. Ironically, the afternoon was much more like geology. That's when he'd tried to assess the missing pieces, fill the gaps in the data and infer the overall pattern so he could solve the puzzle.

Make that plural, he thought. There were lots of puzzles.

How did Leland know of the murders? It was possible, of course, he'd read about them in the *Santa Fe New Mexican*, maybe on-line. But the dead dog? Someone close to the Smyths must have provided him with that curious piece of information. And if news came from close in, did that suggest the killers were also close to home? He found it hard to believe that either Markham or Gwen would be involved in murder.

Then there was the puzzling issue of the bogus painting. Clem Forleigh had mentioned how chaotic post-war Europe had been. As the U.S. rushed headlong into the cold war with the Soviets, the standoff assumed more importance than the war with the Nazis—that one was over. Many ex-Nazis made deals with the CIA and were regarded as cold war intelligence assets. Any key bits of information Markham's father acquired could have been kept and used as bargaining chips, if he needed them. As far as Candrew knew, the father had only brought paintings with him. Their value was self-evident—but the counterfeit one was an anomaly. Did it have some role in this? He couldn't even say whether the painting had been brought to the States with the others and didn't know the precise date when it was actually painted. This was a crucial piece of information because it would help establish whether it came from Austria or was acquired later.

Leland's relationship with his brother was obviously strained. He seemed antagonistic and almost every comment was delivered with an air of sarcasm. As far as Candrew knew, Leland had never visited Markham in Santa Fe, yet he seemed quite familiar with the area. He even knew the university's nickname.

It had been a long, intense day and with the hum of the aircraft engines and the subdued lighting in the cabin, Candrew slid into a somnolent daze. But his subconscious was still working flat out, replaying Leland's comments about pre-war Vienna, about the philosophers, artists and composers. And the name that stood out was Schöenberg. Candrew jerked wide awake—it was the name that linked everything.

Best known as the composer credited with introducing twelve-tone compositions, Arnold Schöenberg was also an accomplished painter. Not only was he a pioneer of atonal music, he'd produced over two hundred images of himself as well as portraits of others, his works including landscapes and abstracts. Two self-portraits were in Markham's inherited collection, a collection that had been bought, stolen or coerced from Jews in Vienna. When Paolo performed in Santa Fe, he'd featured works by Schöenberg and also by Alban Berg, another Austrian composer. And he'd left anyone who would listen in no doubt about how he coveted the larger of the two Schöenberg paintings in Markham's collection. And Paolo had died on the date of the Anschluss, the date the Austrians surrendered their independence to the Germans.

Helen Kontorovich had spent her whole professional career studying central European art and was an expert in early twentieth century Austrian expressionism.

An underlying connection was emerging—Austria.

As Candrew pulled into the faculty parking lot the next morning, the day was brisk and clear with a waffled pattern of high, thin clouds. Not for the first time, he noted that his Jeep Cherokee sported an array of dents and scratches, most acquired on his many field trips to the back country. It compared badly with the late model cars driven by his colleagues. Maybe time to trade it in?

224

On the way up to his office in Kinblade Hall, he detoured to the departmental office to collect the previous day's mail. Maria was slotting manila folders into a file cabinet and greeted him with the news that Joe Bennington had been asking for him. "Said he'd be back around nine-thirty."

That was good to hear. Candrew had wondered whether he'd actually show up. But Joe seemed to be one of those students who have a respect for authority figures, unlike most undergraduates who rebel against them.

"And there's a package for you." Maria pointed to the bulky cardboard box in the corner.

His research supplies and equipment went directly to Judy in the lab and Candrew wasn't expecting anything. Intrigued, he bustled over and checked the sender's address: *The Peacock Beauty Nook*. He frowned, puzzled.

Candrew hauled the bulky box up to his office, dropped it on his desk, and slit the tape sealing it. Inside was a mauve sheet of paper with a peacock's feather as a letter-head. He glanced at the signature: Suzie.

"Hi there! Hope everything is going well with you . . ."

Candrew took the hand-written, mauve letter, half expecting it to be scented, and slumped into his padded chair.

". . . That nice policeman who was investigating Helen's passing sent me a whole bunch of stuff. He said they wouldn't need it any more and so I could keep it. I don't know what to do with it all, so I'm sending it on to you in case the people down there at the university want it. There are lots of papers and some notebooks. Xeroxes of paintings as well. There was some personal things

*like letters and I didn't know what to do with them
all. Even these letters had information about art
and paintings and things, and in the end I decided
to let you have them all and let you choose."*

The letter rambled on about how she'd liked the university
and how friendly everyone was. It ended by thanking him for his
help and told him she'd stay in touch.

Candrew was pulling out the crumpled newspaper that
Suzie had used to pack the box, impatient to see what she'd sent,
when there was a knock on the door, promptly at nine-thirty. In
response to his shouted invitation to "come in!" Joe hesitantly
pushed open the door.

"Hi Joe. Appreciate you coming at such short notice." Trying
to create a cooperative atmosphere, Candrew asked, "How're you
feeling after your fall?"

"Okay." His reply was defensive, guarded, as if he was
uncertain what this meeting was all about. "I got a big bruise. That's
all."

"No broken bones, then?" Candrew smiled reassuringly. "I
need to contact Zona Pharn and thought you might know where
she is."

"She, like, works for some real wealthy guy in Santa Fe."

"Yeah, I understand that, but she left his house a day or
two ago and hasn't been seen since. Any idea where she might have
gone? Maybe friends in town?"

Joe fidgeted, appeared uneasy, and folded his arms. "Look,
I don't think it's right to tell you anything I've heard. I already feel
really, really bad about letting you know she was the one sending
the tapes."

"Joe, this is serious. The issue is murder." Candrew let the
word hang in the air. "I know it's hard to believe Zona would do
anything like that, but the police are treating her as a major suspect.

This is not a game."

"Murder?" He seemed dubious. "What murder?"

Candrew told him about Paolo's death.

Looking shaken, Joe put his hand on the edge of the desk to steady himself. "I, . . I don't know where she's gone. Honestly." He stared out the window for a moment. Candrew allowed the silence to drag on. Finally, Joe volunteered, "Maybe you could see if she's up at the place near Las Trampas where she goes quite a lot of the time."

"What sort of place?"

"Well, it's kinda like a commune. I've only been there a few times. There's another couple and their kids living there. And Zona's rock-worker boyfriend."

"You know how to get there?" Candrew asked. "Can you give me directions? How about a phone number?"

"No phone number. Cell phones don't work back up in the mountains." Joe hesitated. "Getting there's a bit complicated." He paused again, glancing round the office. "I could try and draw you a map."

Candrew shoved Suzie's box to the side and rummaged through the piles on his desk, finally locating a legal pad. He pushed it toward Joe. In an uncertain, spidery hand, he sketched a route that led along a National Forest service road northwest from the Hispanic village of Las Trampas. "I'm drawing just the last part. The dirt track goes, like, west off the high road to Taos." He handed the rough sketch to Candrew. "You sure she's accused of murder?" Joe was obviously perplexed.

"No formal charges yet, just a suspect."

When Joe Bennington left, Candrew studied the map in detail for several minutes, making sure he understood all of Joe's directions. Then, folding it neatly, he slipped it into the pocket of his jacket hanging on the back of the door. From what little he knew of Zona, a commune in the hills fitted well, although he'd got the impression that she spent most of her time at the Smyth's house.

Candrew checked the morning's crop of e-mails. Faced with the usual spam and administrative minutiae that diluted the few significant messages, he systematically worked down the list, responding to the relevant and deleting the irrelevant with the enthusiasm he used for killing ants that invaded his kitchen. The stack of snail mail was mostly unsolicited catalogs, the sole exception being an internal university envelope from Mark Kernfeld's lab. In it was a memo from Mark with the computer printouts of the microprobe analytical data for the last paint chip. He worked his way down the list of concentrations for the various chemical elements. But even without deciphering the comments scrawled in the margins, this cursory inspection told him that the composition was essentially the same as for the other flakes of paint, the ones that were high in cadmium and selenium. Disappointed that there wasn't additional information, and that the new data didn't provide more insight, he was still no closer to understanding why this enigmatic painting was faked, or at least painted over. And why Markham kept it in his office.

For a moment Candrew sat thinking, but then dragged over Suzie's box and began ferreting through, eager to unpack the contents, dumping the crushed-up newspaper packing on the floor. He pulled out half a dozen black notebooks. A couple were blank, but most of the others had pencil sketches of paintings with comments on materials and pigments. One was an address book. Remembering his discovery of Phillipe LaBarre's phone number in Helen's cell phone, he flipped through to the "L"'s—not there. That in itself was interesting. On impulse, Candrew thumbed on to the "P"'s—there it was: *Phillipe*. Just a phone number, no address, no e-mail.

Half a dozen large envelopes had been packed flush with the sides of the box. Several contained prints of paintings, and a couple were legal documents. The next to last one he opened had only photographs, most of them showing an elderly woman. Helen's mother, Candrew wondered? But the last photo of a tall, grey-haired, distinguished-looking man was certainly not her father—it was Phillipe LaBarre. He flipped it over: nothing was written on the back.

In the corner, under the crumpled newspaper, was a stack of letters tied together with string. Candrew removed the pile and fumbled with the knot, but gave up and cut it with scissors. All the letters were addressed in the same handwriting and he pulled one off the top of the pile, looking for the signature on the last page: *Missing you terribly, life has an enormous gap without you here. Lots of love, P.*

"P"? The letterhead on the first page clarified that—*Phillipe LaBarre.*

He took several other letters at random and slid out a few pages from each, feeling guilty that he was prying into private affairs. Much of what he read was professional, with discussions of painters, museums and art openings. But he stumbled on a few very personal, very specific reminiscences. A letter dated eighteen months earlier recalled a weekend that Phillipe and Helen had spent together in a bed and breakfast—there was a lot of bed, but not much breakfast. Candrew felt like a voyeur—but read on anyway.

One letter in particular was very explicit. LaBarre described showering after a brisk afternoon walk and, as he put it, the hot water brought back the memory of her smooth, soapy body and the feel of thrusting into her warm wetness. Aroused, he had "committed adultery with his fist" using, he explained, Edward Abbey's phrase.

Candrew was left in no doubt about the seriousness of the affair between Helen and LaBarre, one that had probably started when she was a graduate student and had certainly continued until her death.

Chapter 25

A key chore for the director of the School of Art, and for most department heads, is handling public relations. Often this is within the university—where it's critical to compete for limited resources by convincing others that your students are better educated, your faculty are internationally-recognized, your needs are greater. But it's also important to liaise with alumni, and hopefully, those who have become successful and wealthy will remember their old department fondly and support it. All these reasons convinced the director to host an annual spring reception at his home, and that's where Candrew and Renata were headed.

On the drive over, Candrew told Renata about the letters Phillipe LaBarre had sent to Helen. "There's no doubt at all the relationship was far more than just professional. Oh, sure, there's lots in the letters about art and paintings, but tons of personal stuff as well—very intimate personal stuff."

"Which would explain why he came all the way out West for her funeral."

The early evening of winter was already darkening the sky, one half blanketed with clouds, the other speckled with stars.

Renata held Candrew's arm as they followed the sinuous line of solar lamps up the driveway from the parking area to the house where the bright windows spilled pools of light across the snow-patched lawn, intruding on the dark shadows under the aspens.

The art director had invited his usual eclectic mix of alumni, supporters of the department, and university administrators who needed their egos stroked. Dapper, with his precisely-knotted, trade-mark bow tie, he met Candrew and Renata just inside the doorway. Strategically placed, he made sure no potential supporter of "his" Art School went unrecognized and ungreeted. "Come on in. Glad you could both make it. Luckily the snow held off." He shook hands, gestured them toward the crowded room and turned to welcome the next guests with his well-polished sincerity.

Renata waved to several friends across the room and Candrew noticed Anna Meagher hovering on the edge of a large group. She broke away to greet them. "It's so good to see both of you again." She gave Candrew a peck on the cheek and hugged Renata. "You probably know more people here than I do." Anna nodded her head towards the crowded room. "But there's someone you really must meet." She led Candrew over to a man standing in rapt attention, examining Zuni fetishes arrayed along the shelf above the fireplace. "This is Marcel. He did all the marvelous interior decorating for our home." She beamed at Marcel. "So creative."

Marcel Stent had shoulder length hair, wire-rimmed circular glasses and an oversized, drooping moustache. He bounded up to Candrew enthusiastically. "I'm so pleased to meet you. Anna tells me you're a geologist. Natural materials are all the rage right now, the in thing. And you're the expert." Pumping Candrew's hand in both of his, he gushed on. "Polished rock is so gorgeous. And all natural crystals, astounding."

"I'm not sure I can tell you much about rocks," Candrew said. "I look at mine through a microscope."

"Well here's one you can see with no magnification at all."

Marcel laid his hand on the polished stone of the coffee table and stroked it. "Such beautiful colors."

Candrew glanced at the granite table top with its carefully selected silver bowl and small group of maquettes. He recalled Anna's home where every horizontal surface was cluttered with framed photos, trinkets and glass ornaments. And he smiled as he remembered Renata whispering in his ear that the design philosophy was "too much is not enough".

Cradling his glass in one hand, Candrew swirled the liquid sending the cubes of ice bumping and reeling as if they themselves were drunk from the enclosing scotch. With Renata, he strolled into the back room and joined a group that included Anna where, not surprisingly, the main topic was speculation on who killed Paolo.

"I was absolutely stunned when I heard," Anna said. "The news hit me in one foul swoop." After a drink, or two, she pummeled clichés in curious ways. Anna rocked her head from side to side as though still unable to believe the murder. "That's the trouble with the unexpected: it's so unpredictable."

The tall, elegantly-dressed woman beside her said, "It's been nearly a week since Paolo was murdered. I don't know how much progress the police have made." She tilted her head to one side, making it into a question. "They've got several suspects to work with—there's Carla, Gwen—and probably quite a few enraged husbands."

"Which is probably why they're taking so long. Like looking for a noodle in a haystack." Anna laughed.

It seemed as if news that Ronnie Garcia had been elevated to prime suspect was not common knowledge. Candrew said nothing, but wondered what the chance of catching him would be if he'd skipped back across the border into Mexico.

"And I heard Paolo's father was a notorious, and extremely radical, politician in Italy." The speaker was a short, dumpy man in a garish checked sport coat who Candrew didn't recognize. "Rumors are flying. Apparently, a few months ago *El Mondo* ran a long article that revealed strong Nazi connections and anti-Semitism during the war."

The speaker now had Candrew's unwavering attention. He stood, head forward, lips pursed, concentrating.

"D'you think it could have been intended as a high profile, revenge killing?" someone asked.

"Yeah, if he'd been run off the road or shot in Italy I could understand it. But in the Smyths' house? With a piano? That doesn't make any sense." He looked around the group as if touting support. "And settling a grudge after sixty years?"

"It just doesn't seem fair either," Anna said. "Just 'cause his father was associated with those jack-footed Nasties all that time ago hardly seems a reason to murder the son now."

Speculation seemed to have run its course and conversation drifted to other gossip.

Candrew and Renata separated and he strolled over to a group of professors from the humanities—Candrew, of course, was from the inhumanities. The crowd of academics, all with drinks in hand, were swapping their well-rehearsed anecdotes and speculating on the odd way Paolo had died.

"Dante's son, wasn't he called Paolo?"

"Yes, that is indeed correct," confirmed the pencil thin literature prof with a halo of white hair.

"That what made him one hell of a pianist?" someone joked.

There were groans at the witticism.

A tall, bespectacled prof began holding forth in a high-pitched voice. Wearing a tweed jacket with leather patches on the elbows that he displayed like a union card, he held his unlit pipe by the bowl using the stem to point out things that benefited from emphasis. For him, conversation was an opportunity to display the well-turned phrase rather than a means of communication, although now he was complaining that students were rather poorly educated. "I'm sure that if you were so bold as to question a student here in art history, they'd think the *Burghers of Calais* was a fast food franchise."

"That served French fries?" someone quipped.

"I doubt it. Most of our students wouldn't even know that the burg of Calais is in France." Before this lack of knowledge could be blamed on inadequate teaching by the faculty, he quickly added, "Students hope to get by with the absolute minimum effort. Goodness knows, they pay enough in tuition, yet they want the very least for their money. Strange consumers."

"Talk to someone in the economics department." The short woman with cropped hair gave a sly smile. "They'll have an economic model that fits. They always do."

"John Maynard Keynes is the only economist I respect."

"Really? And why's that?" she asked.

"In old age he said, 'My only regret in life is that I did not drink more champagne.'"

Candrew thought about that—then headed for the bar.

Renata was there topping up her white wine. "Sad that Helen won't be part of these parties anymore." She let her gaze wander across the mixed throng. "Pretty amazing what you found out about her relationship with LaBarre. And talking of Helen, I forgot to tell you I looked up her evaluations on that web site."

"Really? What do the students think of her?"

"Remember it's a biased sample, just the ones who want to bitch. If they're generally satisfied, or haven't any comments, they won't take the time to log on. The main complaint seemed to be too much memorization of names and dates. That and too much stylistic detail."

"What the hell did they expect in an art history class?" The question was rhetorical. "Anything about her as a person?"

"Not a lot. Overall they seemed to like her, maybe 'tolerate' is a better word. The only real complaints were that she missed class too often, had a grad student teach. So, she seemed to be out of town fairly frequently."

"Interesting. I wonder if that's because of her expert witness commitments?"

"Or maybe she was heading back to Yale and LaBarre."

"Highly likely if you ask me," Candrew said.

He left Renata talking to an old friend from her department and set out for the buffet in the dining room, but on impulse stopped to ponder a painting that consisted of a coarse-grained pattern of small rectangular black dots. It seemed to be a greatly expanded digital image, though Candrew wasn't sure whether the pixels formed an outline of a standing figure or not. But the message was clear—it was painted right across the canvas: *This year's resolution is to improve my resolution.* Candrew grinned.

The director was sauntering past with a couple of guests and stopped beside him. "Our department wit." He smiled condescendingly. "Though to be fair, he's done very well since he graduated. Shows in both New York and Scottsdale galleries and, of course, down in Santa Fe." He smiled at the implied success of one of his ex-students. "We're delighted to have a couple of his works in the department's permanent collection. And, talking of our collection, we're still hoping that maybe Markham Smyth will donate one or two pieces. Together, his collection and his father's are too much for the wall space he's got."

That hasn't stopped many of the world's top collectors from amassing huge numbers of art works, Candrew thought. But what he said was, "With two recent murders in his house, I'm sure he's distracted."

"Quite," said the director. "That's why he's not here tonight. I hear rumors that his brother wants a more equitable distribution of the father's collection. So he may not be able to keep everything."

Where did he get that information? Candrew wondered. Could he be Leland's contact?

The director's entourage moved away and Candrew continued his odyssey to the refreshments.

Peter Meagher and several acquaintances were standing around the table, chatting when a rotund professor Candrew recognized from the mathematics department strolled up. Peter was in an expansive mood. He turned to the professor. "Beer? You want to try a *Santa Fe Wheat*?"

The prof faked an exaggerated French accent. "Santa Fe Huit. Mais oui. Zat only come in ze eight pack, not ze six pack?"

Peter groaned, flipped off the cap and handed him the icy bottle. "You want one too?" he asked Candrew.

"Sure. Why not?" He parked his empty wine glass and Peter passed him an opened bottle.

"I was expecting to see Markham here," Peter said. "He's a good supporter of the department. Anna said both he and Gwen were invited, but I guess things have been very difficult for them."

"That's an understatement."

"And Zona. She was supposed to help out with the catering. There's no sign of her."

"Yeah. Did you hear she's gone missing? Just disappeared into thin air." Candrew poured beer into a fresh glass, watching as the foam rose almost to the rim. "The police wanted to question her yesterday. I think they're going to put out a warrant for her arrest."

"Really? Why would she take off? You think she had anything to do with the murder?" Peter leaned forward with both hands on the table obviously thinking over the significance of the question he'd just posed.

"That I don't know. She was definitely around at the time the piano exploded." There was a lull in the conversation and Candrew changed the subject. "Maybe they could have brought Liesl Sorenson out of retirement and pressed her into service for this evening."

"I don't think that would have been a good idea. Gwen told

Anna that she can't be relied on anymore. Getting very strange, a bit dippy."

The cold air was heavy with the aroma of piñon smoke and the night sky bereft of clouds and brightly stellated when Candrew and Renata left the party. As Candrew drove around the south side of campus, they talked over the events and people. "I was fascinated by the gossip that Paolo's father had Nazi ties," Candrew said. "Though I'm dubious about it being the reason for the murder, especially since the old man died quite a few years ago." For a moment, he concentrated on driving the poorly-lit street. "But now that Markham's inherited what are almost certainly Nazi-looted paintings, who knows?"

Renata laughed, which surprised Candrew, until she said, "I just loved Anna Meagher's summing up that it was only 'the pigeons coming home to roast'."

Renata brought up the issue of Zona's disappearance. "I'm intrigued to know why she's vanished. Going missing like that makes her look guilty. I wonder where she is."

"It's possible I might be able to solve that problem." Candrew told her about his morning meeting with Joe Bennington. "If the map he drew is any good, with a bit of luck, tomorrow I may have an answer."

Chapter 26

It was already mid-afternoon; time was passing. Driving the old forestry logging road had been frustratingly slow and Candrew worried that Joe's chart wasn't up to the task of guiding him through the maze of tracks to where he hoped to find Zona. This whole trip was a gamble. He'd followed Joe's heavy line where the map indicated a main trail and negotiated several branches, all unmarked. At each one, he'd stopped to consult the sketch map, hoping he was interpreting the directions correctly.

The fork immediately ahead posed a problem: both branches looked well-traveled and the map was ambiguous. Candrew picked the left one. For nearly half a mile, the Jeep Cherokee bounced along the rutted track, even though he wasn't driving much faster than a brisk walking pace. In low spots, the car slithered through pools of muddy water left from the melting snow. The corrugated track twisted around starkly white, branchless trunks of leafless aspens, sinister, like moving through the columns of a deserted cathedral. And the abandoned Forest Service road was gloomy now that the growing cloud bank had moved across the western sun.

Candrew felt isolated, alone. He missed Penny. While his

wife almost never came on geological trips with him, they'd explored much of northern New Mexico together and her death had left a huge void in his life. That morning, he'd driven to Las Trampas along the "high road" to Taos, a road that snaked through the mountains further east of the Rio Grande than the main highway. This back route, a favorite of theirs, was completed only forty years ago and now connected some of the oldest Hispanic villages, villages that must have been very isolated communities before the road. Anglo artists, lured by scenery and solitude, had recently moved into the area, and he recalled the chilly Fall day when Penny bought the landscape painting that now hung in his office.

On their trips along the high road they almost always ate at the *Rancho de Chimayó Restaraunte*. Inevitably, his mind drifted back to last week's lunch with Renata when they'd been surprised to see Gwen and Paolo together. At the time, it certainly appeared more than just a sociable meal, but now that he knew of their affair, it explained the secrecy. His initial reaction had been shock when Anna Meagher told him about their relationship and he found it disturbing that Paolo was no longer alive. Candrew couldn't believe Gwen had any role in his strange murder, even if it did happen in her own home. Was it possible, maybe, they'd had an argument, a lovers' quarrel? But leading to such a strange murder? That seemed too far-fetched. Gwen didn't appear to be the emotional type who'd respond with violence. Although clearly, someone who knew Paolo was prepared to resort to violence.

The narrowing track through the aspens, and the increasingly frequent potholes, pulled Candrew's rambling thoughts back to the present. He'd gone another quarter of a mile when the track ending abruptly in a substantial berm. Forced to reverse more than thirty yards, he finally got to an area wide enough to turn around. When he made it back to the junction, he didn't hesitate to try the alternative route. That wound through scrub and led into larger and denser pines. He hoped everything was going to be worth the effort—he had no guarantee Zona would be at the house when he got there, if he got there. After another mile of slow driving, he'd speeded up a bit to save time and turned too fast into a sharp bend with muddied puddles, sliding, losing control. He spun the steering wheel, overcorrected and fishtailed, but managed to complete the turn. And then was faced with a locked, five-barred metal gate. Braking hard, he skidded to a stop only a few feet short. The gate sported a *No Trespassing* sign, large and freshly-painted. Again, he studied Joe's map. A line drawn across the trail seemed to be in about the right location, but it wasn't labeled as a gate.

He'd dropped the map on the seat, wondering what to do next, when he heard a motor. Before he could look around, his head was slammed back against the head-rest, the recoil flinging him forward, only the seat belt stopped his face from hitting the steering wheel. The impact as his car was struck from behind, jolted the Jeep forward. Confused, he sat blinking, trying to figure out what happened. Then a burly man appeared at the passengers' side, and a taller, heavyset guy grabbed the driver's-side door handle. He peered in through the window, the wide visor of his black baseball cap shadowing his face.

"Out!"

The car doors were locked. Candrew glanced in the rear-view mirror: a huge black truck with jacked-up suspension was flush with his back fender. In front, a mere two-foot gap separated him from the steel bars of the gate. Obviously, he wasn't going anywhere. But the deciding factor was the large caliber pistol in the bulky guy's hand, a pistol aimed directly at him.

Candrew lowered the window, leaving the door locked. "Look, I . . . "

"Out."

Candrew obeyed. He was helped, if that was the right word, by the powerful pistol-wielder who grabbed him under the arm and hoisted him to his feet. Before he had any chance to explain, or even get a good look at the man, he was spun around and forced up against the car, pinned by a large hand splayed on his back. "What you doing here?" he growled. There was a distinct Hispanic cadence to the words.

Candrew had no opportunity to frame a convincing explanation before he heard a distant, shrill voice. His captor waited and the voice, that of a woman, got louder. "Leave him alone." There was a moment's quiet and then he could hear rustling footfalls in the leaves. "Let him go." The pressure pinning Candrew to the side of the car eased, but only fractionally.

"Eddy, I know him. He's not a narc. He's a professor." The force applied to Candrew's back didn't change. The muscular man was obviously unimpressed by academics. "He's Dr. Nor. He must have come all this way just to see me." This time the pressure eased and Candrew was able to stand. He straightened up, gasped for breath and glanced around. The two brawny Hispanic men, both in camouflaged hunting jackets with multiple flaps and pockets, stood scowling.

To the side, looking apologetic, was Zona Pharn. "I'm real sorry about how we greeted you. Wasn't very friendly, was it?" She stood smiling at Candrew, the silence broken only by the wind sighing in the pines. "The local police, they're always nosing around. Makes Eddy mad. Even though we don't do drugs, they seem to think we're running a meth lab up here. This is our very own land, private, and we know they haven't got a search warrant, but that never seems to stop them. Eddy thought you were police." She glanced over at her boyfriend who was standing hands in pockets, face blank. "He was hassling you a bit as a warning." As if speaking on his behalf, she added, "Sorry again. Lucky I was out feeding our chickens. Goodness knows what Eddy would've done if no one was around."

The thought of what could have happened with the gun flashed through Candrew's mind. It was pure luck Zona appeared when she did.

Candrew was here to find the errant Zona. And he'd succeeded. But obviously he was in no position to force her to return to Santa Fe. The only option was to play along, rely on persuasion and hope Eddy and his buddy wouldn't decide to use their weapons. Leaving the vehicles at the gate, he walked with the others down the rubbly dirt road, apprehensive about what he'd got himself into. A bit late now, but he realized he hadn't told anyone back at UNNM where he was going.

"It's so beautiful up here. Real close to nature." Zona rambled on. "In the mornings, when you go outside, you get to see the really amazing sky, awesome, like a great blue dome protecting us all. And you hear millions of birds singing. The pines smell wonderful. Out here, nature has something for each and every one of our senses."

The group followed the track out from under the tall pines into a grassy glade. In front of them an earthship house sat low, much of it underground. Chopped wood was piled to one side with a tall stack of flagstone beside it. A couple of smaller buildings nestled behind the main structure. Two large dogs bounded up, the black one growling, baring its teeth. "Jefe!" Eddy yelled at it, grabbed for the collar, but missed. The growling stopped, but fangs were still bared. The dogs slowly circled the group, sniffing Candrew's crotch, panting and showing teeth. He didn't dare move, stood his ground and kept his hands still. Apparently, he passed their inspection and they went loping away.

"Now that you're here, come see where we live." Candrew followed Zona down four broad stone steps into a spacious, beamed room with a packed earth floor. She watched him survey the space. "Our earth dwelling is between the soil and the sky. It communes with both." She paused to give him more time to look around and absorb the cosmic ambience. "We made it like a kiva. You know, the way the ancient Anasazi religious meeting places were half in the ground."

As she continued describing the way they'd built the house, Candrew studied the interior, impressed by the satisfying proportions and inviting feel. To one side, blazing logs in a stone fireplace radiated warmth.

"Eddy grew up right near here, knows the local area real well. He's a stonemason, you know, and built everything with local rock. It's all natural material so it blends with the land."

Candrew recalled Zona's visit to his office a couple of weeks earlier when she'd asked whether using explosives and moving large volumes of quarried rock upset the earth's equilibrium. Now he remembered it was about Eddy. He glanced over at him, sitting at a small side table with his friend, a beer can in one hand.

"Let me get you some tea. Or would you rather have a beer?" Zona asked.

"No. Tea's fine."

The small, but functional, kitchen area was off to the side of the octagonal main room and, while waiting for the water to boil, Zona quizzed Candrew, wanting to know how he'd found out where she was.

"The third tape, the last one I got, gave some hints." *Almost as if you wanted to be found*, Candrew thought to himself. "There was enough information for me to figure out what happened." Bit of an exaggeration: he still didn't have it all worked out. "And by then, I knew the tapes were coming from you."

"You did?" Her voice rose in surprise. She hesitated, as though she was going to deny it, but instead said, "How did you figure that out?" Candrew told her about Joe Bennington. She looked betrayed. "I see."

"If it makes you feel any better, he made a valiant attempt to avoid getting caught and ratting on you."

Zona shrugged her shoulders. "Whatever."

"Anyway, why are you hiding out? Why did you leave the Smyths without telling anyone where you were going?" Candrew knew she'd have to supply answers before there was any hope of getting her to go back. "The police are treating your behavior as very suspicious. It sort of makes you a prime suspect." He paused, waiting, but Zona said nothing. "The police already know you lied about where you were when Helen Kontorovich was shot. What do you know about that murder?"

"Nothing. Honestly." Her eyes welled up with tears. "I wasn't even in the house when she was . . . you know, killed. The police were, like, already there when I got back."

Candrew knew that was true. "You told the officer you were at *Friends of the Planet*, but you told me you really went to the rabbi for Liesl Sorenson."

"Yeah, that's right."

"When the police inspector checked your alibi and found it didn't hold up, it didn't change your role as a suspect, but it made them wonder why you thought it necessary to lie. What were you hiding?"

Zona stared at the floor, shying away from eye contact. "I work for Mr. and Mrs. Smyth, they pay me. I wasn't sure it was good for them to know I was out on an errand for Liesl."

"What sort of errand? And what time did you leave?"

"Well, like I said, nine o'clock. And I went to the rabbi and then bought some things from the hardware store." Zona didn't elaborate.

Candrew knew Liesl was Jewish. "Why are you protecting Liesl Sorenson?"

"But I'm not," she said, a little too quickly.

"Anyway, the Smyths only pay you half time."

"But they give me a nice place to live. And it's close to town. Mr. Smyth has been good to me." She peered straight at Candrew. "Even though he's so evil."

"Evil?" That description of Markham took him by surprise. "*Evil?*"

Zona's eyes filled with tears and she sobbed quietly, her shoulders heaving. Eddy, a little unsteady from the beers, lurched towards Candrew. Zona waved him away. "It's okay, honey." She turned back to Candrew. "Yes, evil!" She spat out the word with searing intensity. "He helped his father steal all those old world paintings. They weren't his by right. Liesl told me everything. They'd stolen them from the Jews in Austria and then sent those real owners to die in the concentration camps. *Evil.*"

Although Candrew was sure most of Markham's inherited collection was Nazi loot, Markham and Leland would have been too young to have had any role in acquiring it. But Zona's intense feelings about it were something new to him.

Candrew wondered if Zona had similar strong feelings about Paolo Magnelli. And what insights she might have about life in the Smyths' home? Paolo had no connection to graphic art. He leaned forward in his chair. "What do you know about Paolo's murder?"

Zona put her hand to her mouth, looked at the floor and spoke in a barely audible whisper. "I'm sure his death was an accident." She took a deep breath. "Nobody's perfect."

There was a low blowing sound in the kitchen that steadily rose in volume to a piercing screech. The kettle was boiling. Almost mechanically, she rose and shuffled over to the cooking area where she went through the motions of making tea. Candrew had followed.

"An accident?" Candrew's voice was high and squeaky. "How the hell can an exploding piano be an accident?"

Zona hesitated, looked down at the tea cups, then started to explain. "I'd been chatting with Liesl, Miss Sorenson, in her apartment. It got late and I was going down the steps, back to my room, when I saw someone moving over in the main house, like, in the shadows." She stopped for a moment, dunking the tea bags; her tongue moistened her lips. "Normally, I would have been real suspicious, especially since the lights were down low and all." She paused again, as if wondering whether she should be telling Candrew any of this. "Then I saw it was Mrs. Smyth. She had a flashlight and was, sort of, leaning over that big piano of theirs. There was a bag down on the floor beside her. It looked like she had some sort of tool in her hand. I couldn't see what she was messing with inside the piano. I watched for a minute, but it's her home. Then I went into my room, went to bed."

"Are you absolutely sure it was Gwen Smyth? Could it have been someone else? Ronnie Garcia maybe? He's about the same height as Mrs. Smyth. And he's familiar with the house and knows the alarm system."

"Why do you ask about him?"

"Because, like you, he's taken off. Disappeared."

"I don't know anything about that." She looked at Candrew and immediately avoided his eyes. Almost inaudibly, she said, "That explosion, I'm certain it wasn't meant for Mr. Magnelli. It was intended for the Evil."

"You mean Markham Smyth? You think Mrs. Smyth planned to kill her husband?"

"He deserved it." She wiped her eyes with the back of her hand. "He always played the piano first thing in the morning. It was, like, real unfortunate Mr. Magnelli needed to practice and came out, you know, early that day."

Words from the last tape came seeping into Candrew's mind: *Don't be fooled, things aren't always what they seem*, and then, later, *it's easy to make a mistake*. "Good God. You're telling me Paolo was killed in error? An accident?" His forehead creased, tapping his teeth he glared at her. "You can't be serious? Surely, that's not what happened?"

"Yes. Yes it was. But really, it's not as sad as people think." Zona was crying again, but recovered and dried her eyes on her sleeve. "Death's not an end. And it's not a beginning either. The atoms of being aren't destroyed, not at all, they're just getting rearranged. They could, like, become part of the ground under our feet, the sky over our heads. We make new connections with the cosmos. We have the chance to enter other dimensions."

She'd been talking fast, but quietly, and now paused, looking at Candrew to see if he was grasping what she was struggling to explain. He got the distinct impression this view was parroted from some book she'd read.

"Our bodies are made from the stuff of stars," she rambled on, "even older than the planets. For a while we're organized into a body we call *human* and then, Poof!, we're dis-organized back to star-stuff." Hesitating, she picked up her mug of tea, but didn't drink. "What's a life that lasted only 45 years on a planet that's lasted 45 hundred million years? Just a flash. Like a meteor vaporizing from thing to atoms. No time for significance. Mind ends; only matter moves on."

Candrew was amazed. "And you think all that justifies Paolo's death?"

"Maybe not. But it isn't the end." She looked off into the distance for a while, saying nothing. "You're so understanding. I wanted you to know the truth, what really happened. That's all."

They sat in silence staring at their cups of tea. Candrew was shaken. He'd started out thinking Zona might have information that could help the police. Now she appeared to be intimately involved in at least one of the murders. Possibly both.

Chapter 27

Zona poured Candrew a second cup of tea. Nervously, he watched the steam spiral upwards. He'd learned more from her than he expected and sat tapping his teeth, wondering what to do next. Although convinced Zona ought to go back to Santa Fe and tell the police everything she'd told him, he was sure she wouldn't agree to that—after all, she had bolted from the crime scene without explanation.

Apart from the hiss of burning logs, silence pervaded the room, a silence broken unexpectedly when one of the large wooden vigas gave a sharp crack as it compromised with the falling outside temperature. The charred remnant of a burnt log in the fire toppled into the glowing ashes, launching a constellation of flying embers.

"Hey Eddy, we need more wood," Zona shouted, her voice shrill. Ambling over, he gave Candrew a sidelong glance, then looked at Zona as if to imply: *Why can't this gringo do something to help?* Leisurely, he grabbed a couple of split pine logs from the stack beside the hearth and tossed them on the fire, his actions sluggish and deliberate, a quiet rebellion.

Eddy rejoined his friend at a small side table and popped

the tab on his fourth beer. Wearing jeans, checked shirt and heavy boots, Eddy was barrel-chested with a shock of black hair falling over a full face. He seemed suspicious, as if trying to figure out Candrew's real motive for coming. Whenever Candrew looked in their direction, they were watching him. Occasionally speaking with low voices in Spanish, they left Zona and Candrew to their own conversation. Eddy had the parts of his automatic laid on newspaper. As he concentrated on cleaning the metal pieces, his friend sauntered outside and returned a short while later, stamping snow off his boots, and they spoke inaudibly. Eddy stood up, stared out the window for a moment and turned to Zona. "It's coming down pretty good. Guess those weather forecaster hombres got it right this time."

She went up the steps to the door, stepped out onto the portál, then glanced back at Candrew. "Well, if it keeps snowing like this, you're going to have real trouble getting back to town. Looks as if we've got several inches on the ground already." She stepped back into the warmth, pulling the door shut against the rising wind and falling temperature. "It'll be dark before you could, you know, make it out to the main road. And driving forest service roads at night, in the snow—not a real smart idea." Her brows furrowed for a moment. "Looks like you'll just have to stay here for the night."

"Yeah. I suppose you're right." Candrew sat tapping his teeth, worried. "I'd wanted to get back to Santa Fe as soon as possible, but if it keeps snowing, I'm not going to have a choice." He felt uneasy about being stuck out in the national forest, miles from anywhere, especially with this scary, unpredictable bunch.

As late afternoon light faded to the darkness of evening, Zona appeared anxious. Bustling around, she compulsively picked up jackets, tidied heaps of magazines, and lit another incense stick. She came and stood beside Candrew at the fire. "You'll have to excuse me. I've got food I need to prepare for our dinner." She took a couple of hesitant steps, then paused and turned back to him.

Apparently struggling to resolve the matter of what she ought to do, she suddenly gave Candrew an appraising look. "First, I've got a surprise for you."

In this house, Candrew wasn't sure that was good news. *A surprise?*

Zona told him to go and stand over by the banquette, the one with the hand-quilted pillows, then leaned in through a curved archway built from cemented river cobbles and called to a back room. Silence dragged on for several moments before an older man with thinning, sandy hair emerged. Candrew recognized him instantly. He'd met him only two days before in Philadelphia—Leland Smyth!

Candrew was at a loss for words. "I . . . well . . ."

Leland seemed to revel in the impact of his unexpected appearance. "I can see you're surprised to find I've materialized in the Land of Enchantment, here in the land of *carpe mañana*."

"Yeah. Right. You're the last person I expected to find here." Astonished that Leland would be visiting this isolated community in the backwoods of northern New Mexico, Candrew wondered what brought him. But the real shock was yet to come.

Zona sidled up to Leland, held his hand and turned to Candrew. "I want you to meet my father."

Candrew stared at them, stunned. He felt like a puppet with all the strings slack, and sank down onto the cushions, speechless. When he did recover his voice, it quavered. "Your father?"

"That's right, my dad." She looked up at Leland. "Let's all go sit by the fire. We can talk." Zona led Leland by the hand and Candrew slumped into a padded chair in front of the blazing logs.

Leland, still grinning, explained. "It's not so complicated. Zona's mother and I lived together in a commune north of Taos back in the seventies."

Candrew wasn't sure what to say. "Did Markham know about that?"

"No way. He was far too busy in Houston, chasing the almighty buck, to worry about what his older brother was up to." He paused, smiling at Zona. "My father knew. And he wasn't averse to giving plenty of unwanted advice. He didn't approve at all. That's when we really started arguing." Leland stared into the fire for a moment, as if trying to decide how much more detail to provide. "Anyway, soon after Zona's mother died of an overdose, that commune was abandoned, but a core group of half-a-dozen hardy souls bought a few acres close to the national forest, off the high road to Taos. So here we are, a suburb of the historic village of Las Trampas." He rocked back in his chair and clasped his hands behind his head: smug.

"My dad tried to persuade me to move back east," Zona said. Candrew glanced at her and then at Leland, expecting some family resemblance. There was none he could see. Zona must take after her mother. "But I had to stay here where mother's spirit was strongest. I couldn't leave her behind, just desert her, could I?" She seemed distracted for a moment. "And, . . well, I thought maybe I'd better not tell anyone about Leland being my father."

Candrew had to agree with that.

"I'm going to cook dinner in a minute," Zona said. "I'll get you both some coffee while you wait. Or, if you want, there's some homemade wine. Then you can talk. Okay?"

They both opted for coffee.

Zona didn't drink coffee, but back in the storage area was a large can of ground beans and an old style percolator which was kept for her father's visits. Now she dumped in six scoops and brewed a pot.

Sipping his coffee, Leland evaluated Candrew with an uncompromising glare. "So, why this visit to the New Mexican outback?"

Candrew had exactly the same question for him, but saw no point in prevaricating and replied honestly and directly. "I'm here trying to persuade Zona to go back to Santa Fe and talk to the police about the murders in your brother's home." He pursed his lips, considering the best way to proceed. "You're an attorney. You know that a suspect, even a witness, in a murder investigation can't just take off—at least, and not get away with it. And if . . ."

"Since when have you been dispensing legal advice?" He interrupted Candrew and fixed him with a haughty look. "And what's my daughter being accused of? There's no evidence she had any role in Markham's twin murders. Just because she lives and works in the house doesn't automatically make her a homicide suspect."

"True. But you can't deny she's a witness: she admitted seeing Gwen tinkering with the piano the night before it exploded." He stared Leland down. "And she helped hide a murder weapon. At the very least, that makes her an accomplice."

Candrew was gambling: the police still hadn't found the weapon used to kill Helen Kontorovich. Since his first meeting with Zona, the day Helen died, he'd wondered what she was doing out on the snowy hillside. He was fairly sure—though not absolutely certain—that she was burying the gun from that first murder. Which would mean she was directly involved in at least one of the homicides.

"Where's your evidence?" Leland demanded.

"I think that's something for the police." Candrew saw no good reason to reveal what he knew. *Let him work things out for himself.*

Zona was placing stoneware plates on a table over by the large window. Candrew raised his voice to be sure she would hear. "And I'd say that sending tapes about the events in the Smyths' home is something that needs explaining."

"What are you talking about?" Leland seemed genuinely perplexed.

"Zona was sending me audio tapes with hints about what was going on."

"Really?" He turned to his daughter. "Is this true?"

She nodded, but said nothing.

"If you're so convinced that your daughter had no role in either of the murders in the home where she works," Candrew said, "then what's the problem in having her return to Santa Fe and help the police?"

Leland kept quiet, apparently evaluating the legal options. They both drank from their mugs of hot coffee. Outside, the snow was piling up.

A Power Bar, consumed while he was driving the back road to Las Trampas, had been Candrew's lunch. Now, gnawingly hungry, he was ready to eat whatever Zona was serving. But he didn't recognize the smell.

Eddy and his compadre wandered over to eat when Zona called them, and they all sat around the circular, heavy wood table. Hoping her boyfriend would be more sociable, Zona tried to integrate him into the group. "Eddy's real good with batteries and wiring and stuff," she told Candrew. "We live off the grid, completely. He set up both our windmills and all the solar panels. They generate every bit of electricity we need. He made it all work." She beamed at him, obviously impressed by his skills.

Smiling, Eddy seemed to appreciate her flattery. He hesitated. "Yeah, I like working with all that electrical stuff."

"And he hooked up our stereo, so we get wonderful music," Zona said.

A large tureen sat in the center of the table and now Zona swept off the lid with a flourish. "Hope you like rabbit." She didn't wait for a reply, but ladled an ample serving onto Candrew's plate. The meat had been inexpertly prepared and broken bones protruded from the pink flesh.

"I was out shooting real early this morning." It was the first unsolicited remark from Eddy. "Them rabbits is, like, hungry with that snow and all, not real cautious. I killed a bunch." Clearly, he was proud of his skill with a gun.

Zona glanced at him, looking unhappy. "I don't like to eat meat, but Eddy said the rabbits would die anyway, not survive the cold."

A likely story, Candrew thought, but he nodded and took a mouthful of the stew. As well as rabbit, it had carrots, tomatoes, green chiles and tofu. That was fine, but there was also celery, lots of it, and he hated celery. The flavor permeated the stew.

Leland put down his fork and turned to Candrew. "I'm amazed that there have been two murders in Markham's home. This is still the 'Wild West'." He smirked. "Justice without the benefit of lawyers."

"But who's dispensing justice?" Candrew asked.

"And for what?" Leland shook his head. "LaBarre, who you've met, knew Kontorovich very well and seems to be convinced she'd figured out too much about the source of the collection. And of course, Markham was intimately connected with its acquisition through our father." He paused. "Assuming, of course, Zona's right and the Italian pianist was killed by accident, that Markham was the real target."

"Well, LaBarre was certainly knowledgeable about Austrian art, and don't forget Paolo had connections to Austrian music, even if not to the graphic arts."

There was a moments silence and Candrew ate just enough of the stew to take the edge off his appetite, but with the intense celery flavor couldn't gag down any more. Diluting it with chunks of bread, or washing it down with coffee, didn't help.

"I hope you like it," Zona said. "We grow all our own vegetables, then we can be sure there's no chemicals. Everything's natural, organic."

Candrew nodded noncommittally.

Later that evening, Zona led Candrew down a poorly-lit passage to the back bedroom. "We share the house with another couple. They're out in Arizona visiting an astrologer, so you can have their room." She pulled aside the heavy drape that served as a door. "The room's got great feng shui. We moved the bed and made it line up north-south, much better than it used to be. You should be real comfortable and get a good night's sleep."

But an hour later Candrew was still awake. Not that the bed was uncomfortable—just that the room was chilly, he was still hungry, celery flavor clung to his palate, and he was worried. And the half dozen cups of coffee he'd drunk didn't help. He pulled the blankets up to his chin, lay on his back, stared at the roof beams, apprehensive.

It had been a strange day, full of surprises. Now, however, Candrew was struggling to get used to the idea that Zona was Leland's daughter. Which, of course, made Markham her uncle. Could he believe Zona's account of Paolo dying by accident? And how would she know about that? Only if she'd been closely involved, Candrew thought. If she's right, then Markham must have been the real target, since he usually played the piano early in the morning. But the target for whose murderous intentions? Gwen's? Could she have wanted him out of the way, but killed her lover by mistake? Too bizarre.

Mulling over the possibilities, he became certain that anyone blatant enough to try to kill Markham by wiring explosives into a piano, wouldn't hesitate to try again. Clearly, his life was still in danger. Candrew had to get a warning to him as soon as possible. And to the police. Once more, he cursed the cell phone company for not providing service up here in the mountains. Maybe reception would be better at night? Slipping out of bed, he padded quietly through the main room, now lit only by the dying fire that cast formless shadows across the walls. Quietly, he let himself out onto the portál. It was bitterly cold, the sky still sheathed with clouds, but no longer snowing. A dog barked in the distance and wind chimes tinkled. The dim portál light splashed a yellow rectangle across the snow, it looked as though more than a foot had accumulated. Candrew pulled out his cell phone, pushing buttons in desperation, somehow hoping that in the quiet of the night it could be persuaded to work—it couldn't. Nothing had changed: *out of range*.

Troubled, he crept back to bed and, still fully dressed, slipped between the cold sheets. He had to get to Santa Fe as soon as the damned weather would allow. Even with four-wheel drive, his Cherokee wouldn't handle a foot of snow. Maybe, if he followed Eddy's jacked-up truck they could make it out to the main road—assuming, of course, that the snow didn't get any deeper overnight and that Eddy would cooperate.

Peculiar guy, Eddy. Bright enough to work with electrical gear and explosives, he could also handle weapons. Candrew trembled from the memory of staring down the barrel of his pistol, and then there were the rabbits which . . . he tensed. Was that a footstep? Or his imagination? He ought to lock the bedroom door—but there wasn't a bedroom door, only the heavy blanket hanging across the doorway. He listened, heard nothing, let out the breath he'd been holding. This was a strange house. Candrew wasn't sure the people living in it had a grip on reality. Zona might be in touch with the cosmos, but the real world was a different matter. He lay awake, shivering, at the mercy of his hosts and the weather.

Drifting in and out of fitful sleep, his mind dragged in distorted images of bloodied torn flesh, smashed bones, mangled bodies. He could end up like Helen, or like Paolo—a shattered form under a white sheet. He still had no idea why either of them had been killed. A reserved academic with an Ivy-League lover, and an Italian extrovert who thrived on social interactions—what linked their violent deaths? And was either connected to the folks in this house way off the beaten track?

He remembered thinking that art in Austria was the link between Helen's paintings and Paolo's contemporary music. But LaBarre was also an expert in Austrian paintings. Where had he gone after leaving the Smyths' home? Now that Candrew knew of the involvement with Helen, he realized what a shattering impact her murder must have been for him.

Sleep remained elusive. Candrew lay tense, finding it hard to believe Zona was involved in a plot to commit murder. She seemed too gentle, docile, too caught up with nature. But at least one small question had been answered: he now understood where Leland got his information about everything that went on in Markham's home.

Chapter 28

Early next morning, the sky was a bland, pewter gray. Windless and still, the only sound was the occasional thump of snow masses cascading down through tree branches. Although no longer snowing, the storm had left a legacy of glistening white clumps draped over pine boughs that drooped under the heavy loads. A thermometer nailed to a tree trunk read seventeen degrees.

Eddy clambered into his diesel truck and a moment later it wheezed reluctantly, then roared to life. Unsmiling and clearly pissed-off at having to drive under these appalling conditions, he and his Hispanic buddy swept snow off the windshield and rear windows and left the engine running to warm up. Only because Zona demanded it had Eddy reluctantly agreed to drive ahead and make a snow-packed route. And driving in this weather was not something Candrew was eager to do either, but with four-wheel drive he should be able to follow the big truck out to the highway.

Candrew stood with snow covering his boots, shivering, checking out the Forest Service track that led back to the main road. After a hearty breakfast—granola and fruit—he was no longer hungry, but still tired. He stamped his feet to keep them warm and, turning, stared at the amorphous lump where his Jeep Cherokee was encased under its white blanket. Zona helped brush off the accumulated heavy, wet flakes of spring snow so that he could open the door and start it. Their exhaled breaths formed patches of mist in the frigid air, but these quickly dispersed in the low humidity.

Candrew was pleased to be leaving. He looked back down the driveway to the house. Under its covering of snow, with a wisp of smoke drifting up from the chimney, it looked cozy, inviting. But he knew better, and was happy to be getting out of this uncertain situation

The heavy F-350 Ford pickup led, making wide, packed snow tracks along the indistinct route through the pines. Candrew struggled to keep his wheels aligned in the compressed lanes. He wished Eddy would drive faster, even though the rational part of his mind knew that rushing was not only foolish, but impossible. Nervous, he gripped the steering wheel tightly, irritated by the glacial progress. Candrew glanced at his watch: almost eight-thirty. This could literally be a matter of life and death. There was no deadline, no appointment, just time ticking away and he had to alert the police. He wondered whether Paolo's killer had worked alone, or was there an accomplice? And would they make another attempt on Markham's life? The Cherokee edged slowly forward. He thought about Kontorovich's murder weapon: he needed to tell the police to dig the area beside the buried dog. But mostly, he thought about Markham and the potential threat.

It had been difficult for Candrew to convince Zona to come with him, but over breakfast she'd finally been persuaded. And her father had reluctantly agreed to let her go back to Santa Fe and cooperate with the police. Leland himself stayed behind at the house to work on a brief for pending litigation. Claiming he was far from distractions, he expected to accomplish a lot, but Candrew suspected the real reason was that he didn't want to confront his brother. Unwillingly, he'd promised not to tell Markham of Leland's presence in Las Trampas. Now, Zona held the car seat tightly and sat in silence as the car swung uncertainly through the frozen ruts.

Candrew was pleased with Zona's decision to return to Santa Fe. Even with the complications of the heavy snowfall, his trip had been worth the effort. And, as if to complement his increasingly buoyant mood, the sun came out. Driving through a meadow area on the forested slopes opened up a vista to the east where the Truchas peaks were capped with snowfields bright with reflected sunlight. And the view, with the nearby tree trunks, reminded him of one of Markham's newly-acquired landscapes, a Schiele, if he remembered correctly. However, the intense sunlight was a mixed blessing—the tree shadows striped the Forest Service road with dazzling light bands and dark purple shadows, the extreme contrast making driving a challenge; sunlight flickered through the trees; and ice crystals glinted.

Though difficult, Candrew was able to track Eddy, following him along the twisting route. The muddy puddles Candrew had slid through yesterday had frozen over, leaving a layer of ice under the carpet of snow. On one of the sharper bends, he tried to stay in the tracks made by the big Ford, steering to the left, but the car opted for independence, took its own path straight ahead on the ice and plowed into a snow drift jerking Candrew and Zona forward. And they were both startled when the sudden stop broke loose snow stacked on the car's roof and it slid down the windshield leaving them with no view out, entombed. The windscreen wipers struggled, finally nudging the snow to the edges, leaving an arc of clear glass. Candrew peered out.

Although shaken, neither of them was hurt. Candrew shoved the car into reverse, the tires spun and he couldn't back out. He was stuck, *goddamnit*, even with four-wheel drive. He checked the time.

Eddy's pickup slid to a stop twenty yards ahead. The two men trudged back. With Zona behind the wheel of Candrew's

Cherokee, the three of them pushed, but the car only rocked back a foot before the tires slipped. They stood, hands on hips, pondering the situation in silence. Candrew had left his gloves in the car and pushing the snowy vehicle had left his hands numb. Now he thrust them deep into his jacket pockets attempting to warm them. His right hand felt the cell phone. Pulling it out, he tried to call—still no reception. Time was passing. How long were they going to be stuck here, for Christ's sake? How long before he could get a warning to Santa Fe?

"There's a chain in the truck," Eddy said. "Could try and tow you guys out, I guess." The friend muttered something in Spanish and Eddy nodded his head. "*Sí. Bueno.*" He slogged back to the truck, reached into the king-cab and hauled out some rubber matting. Dragging it over to the Cherokee, he slid it in behind the rear wheels.

"Okay. One more try." Eddy told Zona to turn the steering wheel hard to the right and accelerate very gently. They all shoved enthusiastically, especially Candrew: he wanted out. The car slithered, suddenly lurched back and its tires gripped the ribbed matting. And then it shot out onto the packed-snow tracks. *Thank God*, Candrew thought. But the sun had disappeared behind an ominous bank of dark clouds the color of bruises. It was snowing again. And the wind was picking up, intensifying the cold, making it penetrate. Candrew hurried to the car, compulsively glancing at his watch.

For the next few miles it was difficult to see the huge Ford truck in the swirl of fat snowflakes. Progress was too slow for Candrew's urgency. Even with the heater at full blast, his feet were cold from the melting snow on his boots, and his hands only just starting to thaw. He blew on his fingers to warm them, but kept a close eye on the track. The snow-loaded pines arched over, making the route seem like a dismal tunnel curving off to an uncertain end. Only the lack of trees showing where the Forest Service road led. Candrew struggled to keep Eddy's truck in view as it punched through the snow, occasionally slewing sideways in the deeper drifts. But it kept moving forward.

As they lost altitude, the snow flurries eased and finally, though not soon enough for Candrew, they got to the paved road. Eddy pulled off to the side, jumped down from the truck and swaggered up to the Cherokee where Zona got out and hugged him. She whispered something quietly that Candrew didn't catch. "Now, remember to do it," Zona said sternly. "I need to rely on you. So don't forget." She kissed him, ruffled his hair and got back in the car.

"I always do what you want," he said. "You know that, *mi amore*."

Traffic on the road had worn away most of the snow leaving clear tire tracks. Eddy turned his truck north towards Peñasco and roared off.

Making up for lost time, Candrew drove rapidly south through Las Trampas and Truchas on his way into Santa Fe. As he came over a rise far too quickly, he was forced to break hard for an overloaded, lumbering pickup truck. Annoyed at having to slow down, Candrew cursed the driver under his breath and crept along, driving up close, much too close. Eventually, the road straightened enough for him to hit the accelerator, swing out and pass, bumping across the rutted snow on the far side of the road.

Candrew was still trying to assimilate the fact that Leland was Zona's father. "So, Markham Smyth's your uncle?"

"Yeah." Nothing further was offered.

"You know that when you went to work in his home?"

After a long pause, as if this was a topic she didn't want to revisit, Zona said, "No. A friend told me about the job. I went and talked to them and they hired me. I hadn't seen Markham before in my whole life." Another long pause. "It wasn't until much later that my father realized who I was working for. He told me it would be best if I didn't say anything." She shrugged her shoulders. "I just kept quiet—even though I'd had my suspicions for a while. I don't see it makes any difference."

"Liesl didn't figure it out?"

"No."

"What did she think about you taking her job?"

"Didn't mind. She's been real friendly, really nice to me." For a few minutes, Zona watched the snow-clad hills swish past. "Until, like, the last few weeks. Recently, things have been totally weird."

"In what way?" Candrew asked.

"Well, for a start, she's got real critical of Mr. Smyth. Started when Ronnie Garcia uncrated those paintings. I think Liesl's got Mr. Smyth mixed up with some German guy she keeps calling 'von' something or other. Almost seems to think, like, they're the same person. Maybe she's sick, I don't know. She's been going to sleep at all sorts of odd times. And she doesn't eat much."

Santa Fe had only a light dusting of snow and the roads were dry. Patches of snow still clung to the car's roof and fenders and the rest of the bodywork was splattered with mud. Candrew drove too quickly along the gravel road leading to the Smyths' home, glad there hadn't been any serious delays. Glancing at the clock on the dashboard, he braked hard and swung into Markham's dry, heated driveway.

The police were already there.

Markham was clearly astonished to see Zona standing beside Candrew when he swung open the heavy, wooden front door. He mumbled a greeting, ushered them into the spacious living room and took their coats. The room had been returned almost to normal. The plastic sheeting that covered the broken window was gone, and the shattered glass replaced. A faint chemical odor from the glazing materials lingered. But most of the furniture wasn't yet back in place, and without the grand piano there was ample space.

Although the living room was warm, the atmosphere was chilly. Police inspector Martinez sat in the center, rigidly upright on a dining chair, his black notebook open. He'd thought it important to interview Gwen and Markham alone. A young, uniformed police officer hovered at the far side of the room, over by the fireplace. Irritated, Martinez had quit his questioning to let Markham answer the door. Now, Markham gestured with an open hand towards his fugitive domestic help. "I think you've already met Miss Zona Pharn. And this is professor Nor, from the university."

The inspector wasted no time on social niceties. "Miss Pharn, I'm a police officer in charge of inquiries into several major crimes that were committed in this house. I'm sure you recall talking to me after the murder of Dr. Kontorovich. That's still under investigation. What I want to ask you about now is the death of the Italian pianist." He flipped open his black book. "A Mister Paolo Magnelli." Zona stood staring at her shoes, still damp with melted snow. "You want to tell me why you took off so abruptly after his murder? Why you left the scene of a major crime and didn't tell anyone where you were going?" He scrutinized the top of her bowed head. "So, what happened to change your mind, make you decide to come back?"

There was an extended silence and Zona eventually said, almost inaudibly, "I was scared. That's why I left."

"Scared?" Martinez rocked his head to one side. "Of what? Or is it who?"

Hesitantly, still quietly, she replied. "Scared about what would happen to the noosphere."

"The what?"

"The noosphere. It's sort of like a world-wide consciousness, you know, the creative force in the world. And what with Dr. Kontorovich and Mr. Magnelli—that's paintings and music—both killed, I was afraid there'd be some big disturbance. I wanted to get really far away from this house, what they call the epicenter." No one in the room moved or spoke while her novel viewpoint was absorbed. Candrew was surprised she hadn't mentioned this before. "And I was afraid I might be accused of killing that musician," Zona said. "That I'd get the blame."

"And why would you think that?"

Zona shrugged her shoulders, but didn't reply.

"Miss Pharn, you work in this house where there's been two murders. You lied to the police about where you were when Dr. Kontorovich was shot, and then you took off after the second murder without telling anyone where you were going." He fixed Zona with a direct, uncompromising stare. "I'd call that very suspicious behavior."

Chapter 29

Inspector Martinez stood in silence, letting the seriousness of his inquiries penetrate. His gaze swept around the group, then focused back on Zona. "And what about the stolen painting? You know anything about that?"

Candrew was surprised he'd raise this issue when two homicides were under investigation, almost as if Martinez suspected there might be a connection. The location and timing fit: perhaps the crimes were related. Candrew tried to work out the chain of events, but he was lacking too many pieces—and a chain with even one missing link is useless.

"No." Zona's answer was barely audible. "I don't know anything about that."

"Then I should tell you," the inspector continued, squinting slightly and peering at her, "that, in your absence and as part of our ongoing investigations, we searched the rooms in the guest quarters where you live."

Her head shot up. "You did?" Zona's eyes were wide, startled. "Why would you do a thing like that?"

"Well, for a start, we hoped to find something that might

give us an idea where you'd gone. While I considered you a likely suspect in the homicide, it was possible, of course, that you were another victim."

"Yeah. I see." She didn't sound convinced.

"But what we found was rather more interesting. At the back of the closet in your bedroom, carefully wrapped and hidden behind coats, was the oil painting stolen from Mr. Smyth's office." He paused to let the implications of this register. "Can you explain how it got there?"

Tears welled up in Zona's eyes. She snuffled, said nothing, but didn't deny she'd put it there.

"Obviously, you're involved in at least one crime committed in Mr. and Mrs. Smyths' home." Martinez hunted through the fat folder leaning against the leg of his chair and produced a photographic print. It was a shot of the wall in Markham's office enlarged to accentuate the painting. He handed it to Zona. She glanced at it through teary eyes and nodded. Markham took the print, gave it a superficial glance and passed it on to Candrew.

Candrew had only been in Markham's office a couple of times and didn't remember the painting well. But now the image, although a bit grainy, stirred memories. A tantalizing recollection was crystallizing in his mind—not of the painting ripped from the office wall, but of the incomplete sketch in Helen Kontorovich's studio. This opened up a whole new perspective. There were already more questions than answers and this puzzling addition aggravated the situation. He sat tapping his teeth, evaluating the new insight and studying the photo.

No one moved in the hushed room. Candrew glanced around: Martinez was scribbling in his black book; Markham was alert, watching him; Gwen sat, hands in lap, head down; and Zona, crestfallen, studied the floor tiles. The room was warm and the inspector resumed his questions in a monotone. Candrew's eyelids, heavy from lack of sleep and the taxing drive back to Santa Fe, were drooping. And then, out of the corner of his eye, he sensed a slight movement in the passageway. There seemed to be someone standing—lurking—there. Before he could get his eyes wide open and focused, he heard Zona's voice.

"Yeah. I'm real sorry. I took the painting out of Mr. Smyth's office."

"You're sorry?" The inspector's tone was sarcastic. "Why would you steal the painting? What did you intend to do with it?"

"Well, I . . . because . . . I thought I might be able to sell it and, like, make some money. I planned . . ."

"That's a lie! All lies."

Zona was interrupted by a short woman, dressed in black, who emerged from the side hallway, the person Candrew had just glimpsed. It was Liesl Sorenson. "Officer, that's not true." Unsmiling, she looked around the room.

Martinez recovered quickly from Liesl's unexpected appearance. "Why do you say that? You got evidence?" For a moment he studied Liesl who stood rigidly, hands hanging at her sides, staring back at him. "How can you be so sure it wasn't Miss Pharn who stole the painting?"

"Because *I'm* the one who pulled it off the wall. That's why. It wasn't her." Liesl looked around the group again. The group stared back in shocked silence. "And *I'm* the one who talked her into concealing it."

Candrew was amazed by this, especially coming from a woman Markham had treated so well over the years. He was still holding the photo of the stolen painting and glanced at it again, thinking about Helen's studio. Why was she working on a copy? As an accomplished artist, she could easily produce a work of the caliber of the stolen painting. But with her finely honed art appreciation, she must have had a damn good reason to reproduce a poorly-executed picture.

Candrew seemed to be watching this bizarre turn of events

from outside himself. When he finally spoke, it was as if someone else was doing a voice-over. He heard himself saying, "I think you should know, inspector, that the painting Zona had hidden in her apartment was not what it appeared to be. The date is certainly wrong."

"Really? And how would you know that?"

"I had samples of the paint from Markham's art work analyzed. The chemical composition showed that some of the pigments weren't available in 1901, so it's got to be more recent." He paused to see if the inspector was interested in all this. He was. "And it's signed *Friedlandt*, but there's no record of any painter with that name." Candrew wondered how much speculation he should disclose. "Kontorovich was an accomplished artist. She could convincingly copy other works, and in the studio at her home there's a preliminary sketch of the stolen painting." He turned to Liesl. "Did you know the painting was faked, deliberately intended to mislead?"

"Well I can tell you it wasn't Helen Kontorovich's doing. The painting's been hanging in the office as long as I've worked for the Smyths. That meddling art woman, she was smart—too smart for her own good. She knew it wasn't a real work of art, that it was something much more than that. I'm sure Mr. Smyth was planning to have her take it down. Then they'd replace it with one of the new paintings from the father's collection. Or as you've just said, with a copy she'd made. That had to be stopped—the painting's too important. And I'll tell you something else . . . ." She paused in mid-sentence.

The police inspector waited, but Liesl volunteered nothing further. "So what's so important about this faked painting that you would want to steal it?"

A trace of a smile crossed Liesl's face. "Well, I . . ."

Markham broke in. "Perhaps I should explain." Hesitating, he chose his words carefully, if somewhat reluctantly. "My father commissioned this painting in Vienna early in the Second World War. He supplied the canvas. On that canvas were the names of the Jewish and Austrian gallery owners who collaborated with the Nazis in running sham auctions with rigged, low prices. There were several dozen names of those responsible for stealing Jewish-owned art as well as many other details of Nazi art theft in Austria." He pushed back his thin hair and paused before continuing. "It was a sort of insurance. He had no idea what would happen when he got to America, how he'd be treated. This was information he could bargain with."

"Half the truth!" Liesl, stabbing the air with her finger, pointed at Markham. "He's not telling you that the artist who did the painting was a Jew. And he's not telling you that his father had that Jew shipped off to a concentration camp. He removed him as a witness by sending him to die. Satanic family. And he . . ," pointing again at Markham, " . . . is the evil residue: the sins of the father handed down." Candrew recalled Zona's tirade when she expressed the same sentiments using almost the same words. Liesl glared at her long-time employer. "Markham Smyth deserves the same fate." She spat out the words with malice. "*He should die.*"

That phrase resonated in Candrew's mind: he should die. Liesl's words, and her attitudes, echoed Zona's. Candrew had always assumed that Liesl had been content working in the Smyth's house, but clearly he was wrong. When he glanced across the room, Markham obviously wasn't prepared for Liesl's outburst, and was shocked and surprised. If he was the intended victim for the explosion, then Liesl had both motive and plenty of opportunity—but did she have the means?

The inspector had been writing rapidly in his black book, but stopped and looked up. "This is all very interesting, but you're making serious allegations. Are they anything more than speculation? What actual evidence have you got?"

Liesl glowered at him. "You've got the painting. Go X-ray it.

It's under the top layer."

Beauty is only skin deep: the words from the eight-track tape floated into Candrew's mind.

"But why would *you* take the painting?" Markham demanded, then stood in silence, stung by the accusations, chest heaving as he breathed deeply, eyes blinking. He pulled himself together. "How did you know all this?"

"You've got yourself to blame." A smile flickered across Liesl's face. "A few years ago you left the office safe wide open, contents scattered across your desk, then left the house. I admit, curiosity got the better of me. I couldn't resist the temptation to see what you considered so important—and secret—that it needed to be kept locked up. That's when I saw the documents changing your family's German name of *von Lauerfeld* to *Smyth*. There were lots of foreign papers as well, but they seemed to be in German so I couldn't read them." She stared at Markham, then glanced around the group. "Included in the stack of papers was the X-ray image of the painting, showing all the devil names." She hesitated, breathed deeply, then said very slowly, "It's something I will never forget."

Markham scowled at Liesl, seething in silence. Candrew wondered if he knew about Helen making a copy of the painting. He turned to inspector Martinez. "It's my understanding that you never found the murder weapon used in the Kontorovich shooting." His voice rose at the end of the sentence, making it a question.

"Right. That's correct." The inspector didn't move his body, but swung his head around to question Liesl. "And do you have any information that would help us locate it?"

"No." She spoke without hesitation and without elaboration.

"The FBI guys who do ballistics were sure the bullet that killed Dr. Kontorovich was fired from a Walther pistol. They suspected a Model 7. Although that gun was made in Germany, it was used mainly in Austria between the wars. Both you . . ." he nodded to Liesl, " . . and you . . " he nodded toward Markham, " . . have Austrian connections." He glared at the pair of them. "Coincidence?"

Neither replied.

Candrew thought that illuminating. He'd reached the same conclusion on his own—but for Helen and Paolo.

"I might be able to help with the gun," Candrew said. He explained to the inspector his suspicion that Zona had buried the weapon beside Gwen's pet dog in the yard.

Up to this point Gwen had been sitting quietly, contributing nothing, but the reference to her deceased and much-loved dog prompted action. "You're suggesting that whoever did the murders killed my dog?" Obviously disturbed by the memories that welled up, she was on the verge of crying.

No one answered her.

Inspector Martinez called the police officer over and told him to go out to the police cruiser and radio for a crime scene investigation unit.

"So many bad things have happened—two terrible murders and a break-in," Gwen said. "And all this nasty business started right after my sweet dog was . . . executed."

Liesl looked her up and down, not with sympathy, but with hostility. "Yeah, that damned dog. Pampered pet. It ate more in a day than ten Auschwitz prisoners got in a month—if they lived that long." She looked at Gwen with undisguised hatred. "And it got more respect." The beach sign from her teenage years in New York was seared into her memory: *No dogs, No Jews.*

Two police technicians arrived promptly and Candrew showed them where the dog was buried. Gwen insisted on being there and stood beside Candrew, pulling on her gloves and watching the lanky young technician as he started digging. Carefully the two men shoveled away the dirt, frequently documenting their progress with digital photos. Loose sandy soil made up the top eight or nine inches, but below that the earth was packed hard, showing no sign it had been disturbed. Gwen and Candrew watched in silence.

"It's unbelievable that my poor dog can't even be left alone to lie in peace." Gwen peered at the man with the shovel. "This whole thing with the pistol is creepy."

Candrew nodded in agreement. And at that moment, the spade hit something which produced a metallic ring. He'd been certain the gun would be retrieved and smirked, feeling vindicated. The stocky partner bent over and picked up the object, knocking off the loose dirt. But the feeling of accomplishment quickly evaporated when the technician tossed him the chunk of rock. Candrew caught it: *pink and gray pegmatitic granite, almost certainly eroded off the Sangre de Cristo mountains. Irrelevant.*

Eventually, the whole area around the wooden box containing the dog's remains was cleared. No weapon. The taller of the two technicians leaned on his shovel. "I'm sorry, but I'm going to have to take a peek inside this box."

Resigned, Gwen nodded, brushed away a tear, said nothing.

Copper wire, still bright and shiny, looped around the dog's coffin and the young man snipped the strands with wire cutters. Tactfully, he raised the lid on the side away from Gwen and reached in with his latex-gloved hands. Candrew, waiting, watched his breath fogging in the frigid air. After several minutes the technician stood up. "There's no gun here."

His buddy stared into the hole they'd dug. "Okay, we'd better use the metal detector, sweep the whole damned area." He headed back to their police van to fetch the equipment.

"We probably should have done this first," the technician said, "but you seemed certain you knew where the weapon was buried."

"Yeah. Sorry about that. I was pretty sure it was here."

The detector turned up no traces of metal and with the

loose soil replaced and tamped down around the dog's coffin they hurried back to the warmth of the house.

Inspector Martinez listened to their account and said to Candrew, "I hope you do a better job of teaching than you do of criminal investigation." He gave a wry smile: any smile was a rarity for him.

Candrew ignored the jibe. "Only trying to help."

Martinez pursed his lips, thinking over this new piece of information. "Sort of lets Miss Pharn off the hook. At least as far as the gun's concerned."

Could someone else have dug it up after it was buried? Candrew wondered. *And if they did, where is it now?*

Chapter 30

"Ammonium nitrate." Inspector Martinez stood with his back to the window, the bright sky making him a mere silhouette. He flipped open a manila folder. "The forensic experts with the Alcohol, Tobacco and Firearms group are pretty certain it was the explosive that blew apart the piano and killed Mr. Magnelli."

"Wasn't that used in the Oklahoma City bombing?" Markham asked.

"Sure was. Real easy to get hold of. Lots of it around. Farmers spread it for fertilizer, and it's a common explosive in quarries and construction sites."

Candrew knew little about explosives. The topic last came up when Zona had been asking about Eddy's job and wanting to know if large detonations could change the Earth's equilibrium. Now Candrew realized that working in stone quarries, Eddy would be familiar with explosives, and have access to ammonium nitrate. Slowly, Candrew sensed where this was leading him, what his subconscious had been toiling away at and was now clarifying— Eddy could have been the source of the explosive for the piano, and it wouldn't have taken much. But Eddy's only involvement with the Smyths would have been through Zona. Did this mean she orchestrated the murder and had been a powerful enough influence to persuade Eddy to help? Was that the connection? Candrew wondered if he'd underrated her. Maybe she was more ingenious, more cunning, more careful than he'd thought. He remembered her story of Gwen "fooling around in the piano" the night before the murder. And what about her claim that the explosion that killed Paolo was an accident, and he wasn't the real target? Could he believe that? She'd already lied about stealing Markham's painting.

Candrew studied Zona, sitting head down, hands around knees, staring at the flagstone floor. He glanced across at Liesl. Blank-faced, she was watching Zona.

Now was the time for explanations. Candrew turned to Martinez. "I think Miss Pharn may have information that bears on the murder." She didn't move. "Zona, you need to tell the inspector everything you told me." He spoke rather sharply.

There was a long, drawn-out silence. "You have something I should know?" Martinez demanded.

Candrew prompted again. "What about Gwen Smyth?"

"Oh, yeah. Yes, I saw her." It was as though Zona sensed a loophole, an escape. "It was past ten in the evening. She was fussing with something in the piano."

"No I wasn't, you lying bitch!" Gwen glared at Zona. "I was watching a movie with Paolo and Markham, oh yes, and Carla. So I've got three witnesses. Well, two now." There was dead silence in the room. Candrew was surprised at Gwen's vehemence. "And you need a suspect?" She turned to Martinez, "How about Carla? She knew Paolo was fooling around, having affairs, and she was mad as hell. No problem with a motive."

There was another silence before the inspector said, "Well, right now she's under a physician's care, heavily sedated. I'll question her later."

Martinez sighed, shook his head, and turned back to Zona.

"Look Ms. Pharn, it's time you told us the whole story, the truth. Lying's only going to make things worse for you. Now, think carefully, explain exactly what happened."

Zona kept her eyes on the floor. "Well . . . we . . . I put some explosives in the piano. We sort of had to open the lid and put them down under all those wires."

There was a long pause before Martinez lost patience, irritated by her reluctance to tell everything she knew. "That's all? Nothing more? Are you lying now?"

Zona said nothing.

"How about the detonator?" When Zona looked blank, Martinez said, "What made it explode?"

"Oh, that. Yeah, there was a trigger thing. It was, like, set to go off when one of the piano keys was pressed."

"Where'd you get the explosive?"

"Like you said earlier, that monium stuff is real common. I didn't have any trouble buying just a little bit."

"How much did you get?"

She squirmed, then showed him her fist to indicate the size. Martinez looked skeptical.

"And who wired it in?"

"We made . . . I made . . ."

"Don't play games with me, young woman." Martinez interrupted before she could elaborate the obvious lie. "Who's the 'we'? Who worked with you to wire up the explosive?" He glared at Zona, waiting for an answer. None came. "Frankly, I don't believe you've got the faintest idea how to connect up a detonator. So, who did it? Who are you covering for?"

Zona became petulant. "I don't have to answer that." She pursed her lips as if to emphasize her intent to remain silent.

Candrew had strong suspicions, but no firm evidence. Now seemed an appropriate moment to probe. "Your close friend Eddy, he's had experience with explosives and he's good with electrical wiring. Did he install it for you?"

Zona remained tight-lipped. When she finally spoke, it was to say, "I'm not going to answer."

Martinez knew she was within her rights, but had confidence in police procedure. "We can easily follow up on this."

"She's covering up for Eddy Chavez," Candrew said. "He's driving a black Ford F-350 King Cab. License was 'NSF' something. Sorry, I don't remember the numbers."

"Don't worry, we'll track him down." Turning back to Zona, the inspector shot her an acid look. "There is, of course, the larger question of why you would want to turn a piano into a lethal weapon."

Again, no answer.

Candrew felt obliged to fill a few more gaps. "Explain for the inspector why you're sure Paolo Magnelli's death was an accident?"

"Accident? What do mean, *an accident*?" Inspector Martinez's voice rose and he showed as much surprise as the others in the room. "How the hell can a piano explode by accident?"

Candrew gave Zona a knowing look and nodded his head slowly, encouraging her to repeat what she'd told him yesterday.

Hesitantly, she started talking in a flat, even voice. "They planned to kill Mr. Smyth, the rigged piano was intended for him. He usually played early in the morning. That day, Mr. Magnelli was, like, the first to come, he got blown up. It was a mistake." She burst into tears.

Gwen had been sitting attentively in the leather, wing-backed chair. Now, stunned, she leapt up. "You mean someone was trying to kill my husband? Why on earth would they want to do that?" She took a step toward Markham, but hesitated. "And Paolo? The world robbed of his enormous talent by a mistake? Shit. How could a tragedy like that happen?" Her cheeks streaked with tears, Gwen was visibly shaking.

Liesl was not. She stood unemotional, straight-faced. "I

don't have any pity, even if it was a mistake. It's hard to feel sorry for that son of an anti-Semitic, Nazi sympathizer. Especially one who's a Catholic with as much concern for mercy as his wartime Pope." She glanced at Gwen who looked away. "How many 'accidents' do you think occurred in the Nazi death camps? Or in the roundups that preceded them. I have no remorse. This world's a tough place to live—and to die."

There was silence after Liesl's outburst. No one had anything to say. Martinez scrutinized her, his hand with the black notebook hanging loosely at his side. "Ms. Sorenson, you seem to think that the murder of the Italian pianist was justified and a few minutes ago you told us Mr. Smyth should die. You've also confessed to an art theft. With that record, you're going to have to come down to the police station and provide a formal, signed statement." He glanced at the police officer standing off to the side and then to Zona. "Same for you. We'll need your written version as well." He turned back to Liesl. "And we'll be getting a judge to issue a search warrant for your apartment."

"Won't be necessary. Go search all you want." Liesl glared at the inspector. But then she softened her attitude. "Before you do, there's a few items I'd like to get from my room and share with you. They may help you understand things, may help your investigation. Would that be okay?"

The inspector hesitated, then called over the young officer and told him to go with her to her upstairs apartment, but to watch her carefully.

While Liesl was gone—with her police escort—Martinez worked through his notes checking where each person was on the evening before the piano exploded. This was not easy because the window of opportunity was large. Explosives could have been rigged in the Steinway anytime after it had last been used, and that seemed to have been about mid-morning. With the fatal explosion a little before seven the next morning, it left roughly twenty-one hours.

Enthralled, Candrew concentrated on Martinez's systematic questioning. Just like science. Start with the available facts and develop an idea—an hypothesis. Then get more facts. If these support the initial concept, fine. If they don't, rethink, redefine and develop new ideas. Keep it up until the truth has been nailed. Which was exactly what the inspector was doing. But Candrew's subconscious was tugging to get his attention: *the full story is a second story*. The words ran through his mind—the words from Zona's third tape—and, of course, Liesl lived above the garage on the second floor, *the second story*. She was being implicated.

Martinez turned back to the group. "Okay. Let's move on. I've got more questions for all of you about Mr. Magnelli's murder—or maybe it was an attempted murder of Mr. Smyth."

"There's one person you don't seem to have considered," Candrew said.

Martinez peered at him, irritated. "Really? And who's that?"

"Phillipe LaBarre."

Candrew was thinking of his close association with Helen. And since he'd spent time at the Smyths' house he would have become familiar with the daily routine, so he'd know Markham played the piano early every morning.

"Where did he get the explosive? And when did he rig it?" the inspector demanded. He shook his head, unconvinced. "What about motive? Why would a well-respected professor from an ivy-league university want to kill an Italian pianist he'd only met a couple of days earlier? There's no motive I can see."

Candrew thought fast. "But if you can believe Zona, the real target wasn't Paolo, it was Markham Smyth."

"Same question," Martinez snapped. "What's the motive?"

Candrew was stumped. He had no plausible answer. He felt Eddy had to be involved, but that would implicate Zona—and

Leland? Turning to Martinez, he pursed his lips, thinking as he spoke. "Well, you've already established that there was no one in the house on Friday evening. Zona, of course, had a key, so entry wasn't a problem. She could have let Eddy in, and LaBarre."

"All speculation. No facts," Martinez snapped.

"And Phillipe wasn't even here on Friday evening," Markham said. "He left in the morning and told me he was flying to New York that day."

A young police officer was hovering in the doorway. Martinez waved him over and took the phone he was holding. The inspector turned his back on the group and shuffled over to the far corner of the room, talking quietly.

Gwen got up and came and sat beside Candrew. "You know, everything you said about LaBarre also applies to Markham's brother Leland—Zona for access; Eddy for explosives expertise. But the difference is, Leland had a motive since his father's collection of major art works went to Markham."

"True," Candrew said, "But he also has an alibi. Clem Forleigh told me he was representing a client in court the week before the explosion and for a couple of days afterward."

Candrew sat with his hands on his knees, looking down. "Revenge. The more I think about it, I'm sure that was LaBarre's motive."

"Revenge? For what?"

"Well, you probably know Phillipe LaBarre and Helen had a very close, intimate relationship—their correspondence makes that clear. So, Helen's murder would have come as quite a shock, a major blow to Phillipe. I'm sure he suspected Markham was involved. And from talking to Leland he'd become convinced that Markham had a major role in Helen's murder. Probably because Markham thought she'd found out too much about the history of the collection."

"I see why you're thinking 'revenge.'"

"If we can believe Zona, and I think we can in this case, then the exploding piano was intended for Markham. It could have been exactly as I said—Zona lent Eddy the house key and he and LaBarre snuck in and rigged the piano."

Chapter 31

In less than ten minutes the young officer escorted Liesl back into the room. She carried her sole possession from childhood: the leather valise, now faded and cracked with age. Slowly and with care, Liesl slid the latch and eased out the musty photographs of her parents. It was the one with her mother that she showed the inspector.

"See that?" She pointed at the fading, foxed image of her tall, elegantly-dressed mother standing in the drawing room of their opulent home. Oil paintings hung on each side of the fireplace. "That painting, the portrait on the left, is a Klimt." She stared at the group. "The thief hung it right there." Jabbing the air with her forefinger, she pointed at the art work Markham recently inherited from his father—and was now hanging on his wall. Everyone turned to look.

Candrew only glanced at the painting before turning his attention back to Liesl. She was wearing her usual black skirt and sweater. Over them hung a loose three-quarter length woolen jacket, also black. When she came back into the living room, he'd noticed that the right-hand pocket was weighted down by something heavy.

Now, captivated, he watched her slowly slide her hand into the pocket and, with everyone else distracted by the painting and the photograph, surreptitiously withdraw a shiny metallic object.

Candrew immediately realized what it was—a pistol: was she going to dispense her own justice? Yelling a warning to the others, he hauled himself up out of the chair, and flung himself at Liesl. She was further away than he realized. He caught his foot on the edge of the Navajo rug, tripped, and stumbled towards her. Fumbling with the gun, she got it tangled in her jacket and fired inexpertly.

A searing jolt of pain shot across Candrew's thigh and up through his whole body. Momentum carried him forward, but his right leg crumpled and he sprawled, falling full length along the rug. His head hit the flagstone floor with a dull thud, leaving him senseless. As the blackness subsided, it was replaced by a misty, unfocused grayness. Dazed, he shook himself and grabbed his leg, the trousers already darkening with blood.

Both Gwen and Martinez raced towards him, but Liesl spun round, facing them. "Back!" she ordered and raised the weapon. "Stay right where you are."

"For God's sake, he's bleeding. He needs help." Gwen pleaded with her.

Liesl leveled the gun at Markham. "This won't take a minute."

The shock of the bullet's impact and the concussion had left Candrew bewildered. The room was slowly swinging back and forth. He tried to kneel, to pull himself up, but was too weak and too dizzy.

Liesl stood at the far end of the Navajo rug, her back to him, the gun still aimed at Markham. "Like the prisoners at Auschwitz, Mauthausen and the rest of the camps, you know death is coming. You'll feel what it was like to be part of the Shoah, the Final Solution." For a moment, she stood without moving, letting the impact of her threat simmer. "Now *your* death will be inevitable. And soon." Her eyes narrowed.

Markham raised one hand as if to ward off the shot, or perhaps in supplication.

"At least you're not emaciated, starving. You're not tortured; you're not ill."

The words pierced the swirling mist of Candrew's mind. It cleared marginally, enough for him to sense the critical situation. Shaken and throbbing with pain, he summoned what strength remained, willing his hands to obey his brain. Silently, he slid them under the end of the Navajo rug, grabbing tightly. He was reacting by instinct: deep down, he knew what he had to do.

Candrew had landed in an awkward position, but his leg muscles, strengthened by years of field work, were strong enough to raise him—teeth clenched, lips parted—into a kneeling position. There was a desperation about this and, disoriented, he stumbled back. It seemed as if everything was happening in slow motion. He'd lost all sense of passing time. A lulling warmth was seeping through him bringing a pervading darkness. As if this was his last hold on reality, he kept a tight grip on the rug. His leaden body collapsed back, jerking the rug.

Not prepared to have the ground pulled out from under her, Liesl toppled. Falling, she squeezed the trigger. Already off balance when the pistol fired, she crashed down losing control of the gun. It skittered across the polished stone floor. The bullet hit the plate glass window just below center, shattering it and leaving a web of fractures radiating from the central hole. An icy blast of outside air blew acrid smoke from the pistol across the room.

At the sound of the shot, everyone dived for cover. Except Markham. Now there was dead silence as the ringing concussion of the gunshot echoed and faded. Markham, the blood drained from his ashen face, stood unmoving, rooted to the spot, breathing fast and shallow.

"Jesus Christ!" Martinez dragged himself up off the floor. The accompanying police officer grabbed the sprawling Liesl, hauled her up, and pinned her hands behind her. He eased his revolver out of its holster. She stood, sullen and defiant.

Martinez retrieved the gun, careful to pick it up by sliding his pen through the trigger guard. He inspected the snub-nosed weapon, its hard rubber hand grip imprinted with a large oval symbol: a script *W* and an interlocking *C—Carl Walther*. "Looks exactly like the type of weapon described in the FBI's ballistics report. The bullet that killed Dr. Kontorovich was fired from a Walther Model 7." He glanced down at the pistol he was holding. "Just like this one."

Liesl, arms still held behind her, stood glaring at Martinez. "Yeah, I know what you're thinking," she spat out the words, "and you're right. That's the actual gun used to kill the snooping art woman. Prying bitch." There was a long pause. Liesl kept her arrogant demeanor. "And I was the one who pulled the trigger."

Chapter 32

Efficient paramedics promptly answered the 911 call. Quickly appraising the situation, they inserted a drip in the back of Candrew's hand and wheeled him, barely conscious, out to the ambulance. With lights flashing, it pulled out of the driveway heading into town and the hospital emergency room, on the way passing police cars speeding up Hyde Park Road with sirens wailing.

After the police drove away with their murder suspect, and Zona had gone to her old room to collect some belongings, the house was suddenly deserted and quiet, almost an anticlimax. Alone in their living room, the Smyths stood in silence, dazed and shocked. Gwen was still shaking from the near murder of her husband, even though their relationship had deteriorated long ago. Markham just stared blankly into space.

"I hope Candrew isn't badly hurt." She looked down, biting her lower lip. "I keep hearing that awful thud of his head hitting the floor. And he lost so much blood."

"I'm pretty sure the wound wasn't life-threatening. He'll be fine."

"Well, I hope you're right. I couldn't stand another death in our home."

Markham ran both hands over his balding head. Deflated, he grunted and collapsed into the overstuffed armchair. "Even when you've known someone for years, you still don't really know them, know what makes them tick."

"You mean Liesl and Zona?"

"Right. Who'd have thought Liesl—a classic white-haired, little old lady—was capable of premeditated murder?"

"Yeah. It's hard to come to grips with aspects of that pair I'd never dreamed of," Gwen said. "I can understand her hating you, or at least your father, but why would she kill Helen Kontorovich?"

"I guess Liesl thought Helen was collaborating with me to remove every bit of evidence documenting provenance, you know, getting rid of all the information about where the paintings came from. Liesl was determined that none of the evidence for Nazi looting would be destroyed."

He glanced around the room with the blood-stained rug and the glass splinters. "That would also explain why she took the painting out of my office and hid it. The one with the list of contacts painted over."

Markham pulled himself up out of the armchair. "You want a drink?"

"You bet. Better make it a big one."

Markham went to the bar at the end of the living room while Gwen stood staring at the chaos. As Markham shuffled back with their glasses, she suddenly noticed the pool of blood on the stone floor and the blood stain on the antique Navajo rug, the dark, irregular patch contrasting with the starkly geometric triangles and the blue and ochre bands. "How could anyone survive losing that much blood?" She stood, fretting. "I'll get Zona to take the rug to the cleaners and . . ." She stopped short, turning to Markham. "I guess Zona won't be part of our household anymore."

Markham said nothing, just handed her the drink.

Gwen took a generous gulp, stood, and pulled her wool jacket tight, shivering. With frigid air pouring in through the shattered window, the living room was cooling rapidly. Gwen's gaze came to rest on the hole in the splintered glass. "Shit. Here we go again," she complained in a loud, pained voice. "Good God. I hope we didn't throw out that roll of polyethylene." Hands on hips, she stared at the glass shards. "I can see we're in for another week of that damned plastic sheet flapping in the wind."

The ambulance, lights still flashing, swept in off St. Michael's Drive, making a sharp right turn into the covered portál of Emergency reception at Christus St. Vincent Hospital. The medics wheeled Candrew in and he joined the other half dozen sick and wounded, all waiting more or less patiently. The lone exception was a disheveled man with a bloody rag around his arm, drunk and noisy even this late on Sunday morning, probably a victim from Saturday night.

Eventually, a young doctor, hands deep in the pockets of his white coat, hustled up to Candrew on the gurney. He listened as the paramedics explained what they'd learned about the shooting and described the medications they'd administered.

"A gunshot wound? Know what that means?" the doctor asked.

"Sure do. You'll have to report it to the cops." He grinned at being one step ahead of the doc. "But don't waste your time. This one was shot right in front of inspector Martinez. They know exactly who the perp was. She's already been arrested."

"She? His wife take a potshot at him?"

"Not his wife. Some old woman. No idea who she is."

More concerned about possible concussion than the flesh wound in Candrew's thigh, the doctor sent him for X-rays before having the gash stitched. Candrew was scheduled to stay in the hospital overnight for observation.

It was late afternoon as Candrew slowly eased back into consciousness. Unmoving, he lay trying to figure out where he was and what had happened, although potent drugs made that a challenge. His thoughts cleared a little. He recalled the police inspector; Liesl and the gun; the threat on Markham's life—and the gunshot. *He had to get help . . . he had to get help . . . he had to . . .* Sleep washed over him.

When he woke again, the last rays of the setting sun splashed light high on the wall above the television. Candrew was fully awake before he realized he was in the hospital and figured out the sequence of events that had brought him there.

"How you doing?" The cheerful nurses' aide came around the bed carrying a small tray with pills in white containers. Dutifully he followed instructions, swallowing them with a gulp of water. "You seem to be in good shape. But you're going to feel a whole lot perkier when those anesthetics wear off." She smiled knowingly. "There's visitors here to see you," she said in her bright, chirping voice. Then turning towards the door she called, "Come on in. He's awake."

Renata tentatively peered around the door, then sidled in, followed by Judy. Both talked at once, asking him how he felt. Renata pulled up a chair and sat beside the bed, still holding a large bunch of blue irises and daffodils. "So, how's our hero?" She looked concerned, but tried to sound positive.

Although he said, "Fine," his head was throbbing and the room shimmered a little. "What's this about a hero?" he asked.

"Well, you're the hero," Judy said. "You saved Markham's life. Or at least that's the way Gwen described it when she called and told Renata and me you'd been rushed off to the emergency room."

"To be perfectly honest, I can't remember much of what happened."

"The way I understand it, you foiled Liesl's attempt to shoot Markham and got a bullet in the leg for your trouble." In a hazy sort of way, it all seemed vaguely familiar. Candrew ran his hand over his bandaged thigh. "And you banged your head when you fell, which is why they're keeping you in for observation—the doc's worried about concussion."

"Apparently, they've fixed the other end of your body," Renata said. "Stitched up the tear in your thigh with no problems, although the surgeon said you'll probably have a bit of a scar. That'll be the only long term effect." She arranged the flowers in a vase on the window sill and went into the bathroom for water.

"I expect you'd like us to feed Chile and Pixel," Judy said, pragmatic as always. "We'll need to get your front door key."

"It's with the car keys in my jacket pocket." He paused, thinking, and added, "There's dog food in the utility room and cat food in the kitchen cupboard."

Renata came back with a plastic container of water. The daffodils were already releasing their heady perfume to the room. "Liesl Sorenson's been arrested and will probably be charged with murder. And they're going to charge Zona as well, as an accessary, I guess."

"I hadn't heard. But then, you're my first visitors." Candrew wasn't surprised. "What about LaBarre? And Eddy?"

"They're trying to track them down. The police don't think Eddy'll be hard to find. His truck's pretty conspicuous and they've got a good description as well as the license plate number. I don't know about LaBarre."

After half an hour of rambling conversation, only part of which he later remembered, Renata and Judy got ready to leave. "I'm going to stay over in Santa Fe, so I'll drop by early in the morning," Renata said. "See how you're doing."

"Oh, I'll be fine."

She smiled at the macho bravado. "Even if you're discharged tomorrow, you won't be in any shape to drive. We'll just leave your car at the Smyths' and I'll take you home." Renata said it in a firm voice that brooked no dissent.

After Renata and Judy left, Candrew felt a little better, although he wasn't sure whether it was a genuine lack of concussion or the cocktail of drugs that had eased his headache. But the wave of sedatives swept over him and he dozed fitfully all night, only being awakened by the nurse so she could take his blood pressure and give him more sleeping pills.

Chapter 33

Next morning Candrew woke with a view of bright, clear sky and feathery clouds over shadowed mountains. He felt much better—and hungry. Faced with typical hospital fare, he wolfed down a few mouthfuls of scrambled eggs, then lost his appetite and picked at the rest. As he sat up in bed, draining the last of the orange juice, he realized how all the disparate events of the last few weeks had come together. Now he understood the links and the probabilities.

Finally, he could grasp what drove Liesl's hatred, all the things that went into the mix—her loss of family, loss of country, Nazi looting, Markham's inheritance. And it was Liesl's seething fury that drove events culminating in the violence of Helen's murder, and he was sure that had led to LaBarre's attempt to kill Markham in retribution.

A bang on the hospital room door jolting him out of his reverie. "Come in!" Candrew shouted.

The loud knock had been delivered with authority and Leland Smyth strode in. "Sorry to disturb you, professor." He came over to the side of the bed. "How're you feeling?"

"I'm doing okay," Candrew mumbled, surprised Leland had driven all the way to Santa Fe to visit him in hospital.

"Now a good time to talk?"

Candrew smiled, glancing at the plastic tubing connecting him to the drip. "Sure. I'm not planning on going anywhere." With the bulky bandages on his upper leg, he adjusted his position in a fruitless attempt to get comfortable. "I appreciate you taking the time to come visit me." He hesitated. "Particularly when you must be worried sick about Zona."

"Yeah. I'll be going to see her at noon." Leland nodded, thinking. "I knew the way she felt about my brother, she'd often told me that, but I'd no idea just how much malicious influence Liesl was wielding. Sweet girl, although easily swayed, and that witch Liesl cast a spell over her."

"Very much my impression," Candrew said.

"Zona's my main reason for being here in Santa Fe, of course. She hasn't been formally charged with anything yet, but she's obviously a suspect as an accessory in that pianist's murder." He pulled the chair toward the foot of the bed and sat so Candrew could see him more easily. "She'll need help with litigation. Luckily, an old friend from law school practices with a firm down in Albuquerque. He's agreed to represent her. "And, of course, I'll contribute in any way I can."

An efficient, bustling nurse interrupted them. Short and dumpy with crinkly black hair, her name tag said *Sharon*. Leland stopped talking while Sharon straightened Candrew's bed, collected the remains of breakfast and, most important, supervised his pill taking. She also delivered the message that Markham was coming to see him after lunch. Then she added, "The police wanted to know if you're well enough to answer some questions. I told then you were." She tilted her head to one side, making it into a query.

Candrew said, "Fine," and Sharon left.

Leland had got up and was standing in front of the window,

hands behind his back. "You were right about so many things. But very wrong in one important way." He paused, glancing off into the distance, as if considering how best to phrase what he needed to explain. "You have to understand one crucial point. I don't covet my brother's art collection—I'm referring to the pieces from Father. My goal wasn't to get the paintings and then cash in on them. No, I want them returned. I want to get them back to their rightful, legal owners." Leland, still standing, breathed deeply, betraying the strong emotional content of what he was saying. "I know it won't be easy. I've been working with Clem Forleigh, but I can't do anything without title to the artwork. Father's will is watertight: it wouldn't be possible to force my brother to give everything back. And he doesn't seem to have any interest at all in restitution."

"But many of the rightful owners aren't alive any more," Candrew said. "They either perished in the Holocaust or died of old age."

"True. Quite true. However, there are legal heirs and they should get the inheritance that's rightfully due to them."

"Can't heirs sue to recover their art?" Candrew remembered what Clem had told him.

"Yes, they can," Leland said. "Unfortunately, it's a tortuous and drawn-out process. It isn't likely to succeed, even when the work is in a major art museum with a provenance that's pretty well documented. There aren't any records for the works my father acquired because the Nazis considered them degenerate art. And much of that was intended for destruction. So, no trail of ownership. Things that might have established ownership—like Liesl's photographs—are rare, difficult to find. A lot was lost."

Leland came over from the window and sat by the bed. "Helen Kontorovich had a key role in all this," he said. "She'd occasionally testified as an expert witness for Clem's firm, working with Phillipe LaBarre, but both times she was deposed, the litigation got settled out of court. I doubt Markham even knew she was involved."

"Why do you think Liesl killed her?"

"I don't have a ready answer for that. In the last few years, Liesl's got pretty unstable and could have had her own inscrutable reasons." He pursed his lips, thinking. "My guess is, she'd convinced herself that Helen was working with Markham to remove all evidence the paintings were Nazi loot, stolen from the Jews. I'm sure she watched Helen prying out the hidden auction receipts. The last thing she wanted was to lose details that could implicate our father and by association Markham. More than anything else, she wanted revenge. When she saw one of her parents' paintings hanging in Markham's home, it was more than she could take. The last straw. It pushed her over the edge. She wanted justice at any price, and as you saw, she thought of death as the appropriate punishment."

"Well, it's clear from the fact she shot Helen—and what she said when she heard about the attempt on your brother's life—that she doesn't regret either event."

There was an extended silence with both men lost in thought.

Candrew took a long drink. "When Liesl was told that Paolo's murder was really intended for Markham, she seemed to think that was the way it should have been."

Leland nodded. "And I was stunned to hear Phillipe was involved, although I can't say I knew him well. I only met him on the few occasions he appeared as an expert witness for our firm, often working with Helen, and it was obvious that their relationship was far more than just professional."

"So, you think he convinced himself your brother was behind her murder?"

"Yeah, I'm absolutely certain," Leland. "Phillipe must have thought Helen had found incriminating evidence that Markham didn't want her to have. Remember, Helen had faxed copies of all the auction receipts to Clem, as well as the identifying markings from the backs of the canvases. When I talked to the police inspector, he said LaBarre may have told us he was leaving on a Friday flight, but after the police checked they found he didn't fly out of Albuquerque until Saturday morning. And, of course, they don't know exactly where he was until then. But that gap covers the time when the piano was rigged with explosive. They now know he took an early morning American Airlines flight to Houston and then a connecting Air France flight to Paris. So, he's out of the country—and out of their jurisdiction."

"That certainly suggests he's guilty."

There was a long pause as they both thought about the twin murders.

"I never understood why Zona was sending me those tapes," Candrew said. "Can you throw any light on that?"

"Maybe," Leland said. "Zona was very confused. She never understood her role in life. On one hand she treated Liesl like a mother and followed her dictates, while on the other, she realized that a lot of things she was doing weren't right. Neglected when her own mother was alive, Zona then lost her early. Liesl was the substitute she depended on."

"But Liesl became dependent on Zona—codependency works both ways. Remember, Liesl was also abandoned as a child and probably craved companionship, stability, friendship."

"Yeah, she needed Zona, but on her own terms. Zona was almost like a teenager—rebelling, but needing to stay within the boundaries. The tapes you asked about were an attempt to compromise—to give out information about the crimes while not actually going against Liesl's dictates. See, she never gave you the facts. You had to work out the message for yourself. That absolved her."

Candrew nodded. He thought he understood. "In spite of everything, I feel sorry for Liesl," he said. "What did she have to lose?"

"Nothing, I guess. Everything had already been taken

from her." Leland looked compassionate. "She's lived her whole life knowing that her parents, her home, her childhood were lost. Everything was insubstantial. There was only revenge. It didn't matter to her now. She'd lived her life in exile. The Nazis stole a culture, not just paintings."

Candrew knew that from her earliest memories, Liesl was aware she'd never see her family again and was alone, adrift in a warring world.

"She talked to Zona a lot, especially in the last year or so," Leland said. "Many years ago when she'd desperately needed a job, the Smyth's home was a nice place to work. As she aged, resentment built—Zona told me that—and at the arrival of the paintings she freaked out."

Leland glanced at his watch. He had no desire to see his brother and got up to leave.

"One last question. Any thoughts about Gwen's dog?" Candrew asked. "That was such a weird incident. You think Liesl had any role?"

"Not *think*, I *know*. Liesl planned it. And one more time, Zona was persuaded to act as the accomplice, although it was done with very mixed emotions. It's another example of Liesl's powerful influence over her. Zona shipped the dog's remains to the Smyths from Española on her way up to the commune. *No dogs, no Jews.* Liesl's's mantra."

When Leland left, Candrew slumped back onto his pillows thinking about the evil of seventy years ago still rippling down the years, still precipitating more evil. Liesl's words resonated in his mind: *"Hitler was Austrian-born and claimed he learned anti-Semitism from the Austrians. Pah! He learnt it from the Devil."*

Nazis and Jews; predator and prey; good and evil. As Solzhenitsyn said, *"the line between good and evil is in the center of every human heart."* Today is the spring equinox, Candrew thought—equal day and night, equal light and dark.

* * THE END * *

Glossary

This murder mystery is set in the southwest where some of the words are of Spanish origin and may be unfamiliar or pronounced differently. So, here's a very short Glossary:

Arroyo: a natural stream channel. Typically dry most of the year, except for flash floods.

Banco: a solid bench built as part of a wall. Usually made from adobe.

Chile: the usual New Mexican spelling for "chili".

Duke City: Albuquerque (named for the Spanish "Duke of Albuquerque").

Latillas: (pronounced with the Hispanic 'y' for the 'll') Juniper or alder branches installed between vigas on ceilings.

Portál: quite different from a portal, this is a covered porch that has a beamed roof over an outside patio and usually runs along the side of a house.

Vigas: beams made from debarked tree trunks that are exposed in a ceiling where they hold up the roof.

5773671R00167

Made in the USA
San Bernardino, CA
19 November 2013